MOONGLOW

MOONGLOW

Katherine Sutcliffe
Maggie Shayne
Angie Ray
Lindsay Longford

BERKLEY BOOKS, NEW YORK

MOONGLOW

A Berkley Book / published by arrangement with
the authors

PRINTING HISTORY
Berkley edition / October 1998

The Penguin Putnam Inc. World Wide Web site address is
http://www.penguinputnam.com

ISBN: 0-425-16571-X

BERKLEY®
Berkley Books are published by The Berkley Publishing Group,
a member of Penguin Putnam Inc.,
200 Madison Avenue, New York, New York 10016.
BERKLEY and the "B" design
are trademarks belonging to Berkley Publishing Corporation.

PRINTED IN THE UNITED STATES OF AMERICA

10 9 8 7 6 5 4 3 2 1

MUSKETEER BY MOONLIGHT

Maggie Shayne

One

It was Halloween, and she was a prisoner in her own office. Hell, what made her think she could get the goods on an organized crime boss, anyway? She was getting a swollen head. Believing her own press. M. C. Hammer, big-city private eye. Right. The truth was that she couldn't remember a time when she'd felt more like plain old Mary Catherine Hammersmith, small-town girl.

She paced the office, pausing to glance through the smeared window at the street below. No colors down there. It was as if Newark had gone black-and-white and shades of gray—as dismal as the sky above it. The wind blew bits of paper and clouds of dirt over the pavement. The dark sedan was still parked out there. If M. C. tried to leave, its driver would follow. If she went to the safe deposit box where she'd stashed the tape, he'd get her when she came out. If she went home . . . she shivered. The thought of that dark stairway up to her lonely apartment was not appealing. They could grab her there just as easily. She wasn't even sure it was safe to get into her car. One twist of the key might make a hell of a noise and litter the streets with bits of a certain lady detective she'd grown kind of fond of.

Hell.

The phone rang. She snatched it up. "M. C. Hammer Investigations."

"Ms. Hammer?"

"This is her secretary." She said it automatically. Made her sound bigger than she was. Besides, the woman on the other end could be anyone. One of the bad guys, maybe.

"I need to speak to Ms. Hammer," the woman said. "I'm in trouble; I need help."

"Join the club."

"Excuse me?"

She calmed her voice. "Sorry. Ms. Hammer's out of town indefinitely. Look, try Ace Investigations over on Fourth and Main. They're good—they'll help you out."

The caller rung off without saying good-bye. M. C. felt bad. They always called, and they always needed help. Up to now, she'd been pretty good at providing it. She'd earned a reputation in the city. They called her a tough cookie, the working woman's hero, that sort of thing.

Right about now, she thought she could use a hero of her own. But she'd been too busy playing hero to bother looking for one. She'd never expected to face a situation she couldn't handle. She was facing one now, one she'd stumbled into unintentionally. She was only supposed to get the goods on Guido de Rocci's illicit affairs, so his wife could get a decent divorce settlement out of him. Instead she'd wound up with a tape of a phone call ordering a gangland hit, one that left no doubt who was in charge. Guido himself. And stupidly, she'd told the wife. Sylvia de Rocci went soft, and ratted her out to Guido. Seemed she got all mushy inside to learn her hubby wasn't cheating on her after all. No, he was just running the mob and killing people. What a sweetheart. So now Syl and Guido were a pair of happy lovebirds, and Mary Catherine was a sitting duck with a half dozen hit men standing between her and the tape.

She could call the cops—but her phone was probably bugged, and she'd be dead before they ever got here. Besides, everyone knew the mob had a few cops in its pocket. How could she be sure the cops who showed up wouldn't be on de Rocci's payroll?

She wandered to the window again. A bus pulled up at the stop, right in front of the entrance to Sal's Bar downstairs. People got off. People got on. An idea took form.

The slug in the sedan was watching *her* front entrance, and her car. But no one could see what she did inside the office. She could take the stairs down to her own front door, but instead of going out, slip through that side door that led from the entry hall into Sal's place. Maybe slide out the bar's entrance instead of her own private one, and onto the next bus before anyone was the wiser.

"Sounds like a plan to me," she muttered. She did a quick scan of the closet. It often came in handy to have a change of clothes or two at the office. Quickly, she shed the skirt and heels she'd worn this morning and replaced them with jeans and sneakers. A leather jacket instead of the tailored blazer. A baseball cap to hide the telltale riot of dark curls she fondly referred to as a black rat's nest. A pair of John Lennonish sunglasses.

Glancing in the mirror, she thought she could pass for a guy. A scrawny guy, but a guy. The purse would give her away though. She emptied it, filling her pockets with the essentials, including her .38 special. Great. This was it then. There would be another bus shortly. They were in and out at this stop all day. Usually drove her nuts. Not today, though.

She took her time, moved slowly into the hall, saw no one, took the inside stairs down to the landing, and tapped on the door that led into the bar. No one ever used it, and it was locked as usual. But Sal opened it in a second, and she sauntered in like she belonged there as he gaped at her. When Sal gaped his double chin turned triple.

"Is that you, Mary Ca—"

She stomped on his foot and he shut up. "I'm not here," she told him. "You never saw me. I mean it, Sal."

Sal's silver eyebrows bunched up and he wiped his hands on his bulging white apron. "You in trouble, kid?"

"You could call it that."

"What can I do?"

"Gimme a stiff drink, and pretend you don't know me from Adam."

He shook his head, but nodded toward a vacant stool and reached for a shot glass. As he poured, he muttered, "One good man is all you need."

"So you keep telling me." She took the stool and then the drink, sipped it as she eyed the patrons in search of goons.

"If you had yourself a husband you wouldn't be in this mess."

"How do you figure that?" No goons in sight. She turned back to Sal, downed the whiskey, and set the glass on the hardwood.

"You'd be home takin' care of him, instead of out playing cop-for-hire."

"Woman's place is in the kitchen, right, Sal?"

"Worked for a hundred years, kid."

"Well, not for me. I've never needed a man around cluttering things up, and I don't plan to start now. Never met one worth the trouble anyway." She heard the squeal of air brakes and twisted her head. "That's my bus. Gotta go."

"Where to?"

She worked up a grin for him, though her heart was in her throat. "I could tell you, Sal, but then I'd have to kill you. Later." And she hopped off the stool and hurried to the bar's front entrance. The bus blocked her from the view of the goon across the street, and she joined a handful of

others waiting to climb aboard. But she didn't breathe
again until she was in her seat, and headed out of town.

The bus was headed to Hoboken, but since she didn't
know a soul there, she got off at the terminal and caught
one heading in the other direction. There was really only
one place for her to go now. Her parents' place in Prince-
ton was out of the question. First place those thugs would
check. Nope, there was little choice. She had to go to Aunt
Kate's house of horrors. That's what she'd called it as a
kid. A gothic mausoleum way out in the sticks. They'd
never track her there. Aunt Kate was an outcast, black
sheep of the family. Mostly because she refused to go
Christian, and kept up the traditions of the best-forgotten
branch of the Hammersmith clan. Witchcraft, to put a
name to it. She had an old spell book that had been in the
family for more generations than anyone could count.
Mary Catherine had seen it once. Dusty and faded, with a
padded cloth cover that was threadbare with age.
    Briefly she wondered if one of Aunt Kate's spells could
help her out of this mess. But then she chased the silly
thought away. All that she needed was time and clear
thinking. A way to get to that tape, and get it safely to the
cops without getting her head blown off. She wouldn't be
safe until she did. Even if she turned it over to Guido, he'd
figure she knew too much to risk letting her live. She knew
the way thugs like him thought.
    Aunt Kate's then. She shivered at the thought. It was
All Hallows eve, and she'd be spending it in that spook-
house sideshow. She shook away the chill that danced up
her nape, and tried to relax on the long bus ride to Craven
Falls in upstate New York.

"Hello, Aunt Kate."
    Kate Hammersmith stood inside the arched, stained
glass door and blinked slowly. She wore a long black dress

with shiny moons and stars all over it. Homemade. Probably sewn together with spiderwebs, Mary Catherine thought glumly. Her hair was long and still dark, cut to frame her face. It made her look far younger than she was. She wore a necklace with a hunk of quartz on the end that must have weighed five pounds, minimum. "You could poke your eye out with that thing," Mary Catherine observed, just for something to say.

"You sound like your mother. What are you doing here, M. C.?"

"Aren't you even going to invite me in?"

Kate lifted one brow, then stepped aside and let Mary Catherine in. The place hadn't changed much. Muted lighting, nothing glaring or bright. Antique furniture. M. C. was no expert on guessing what period this stuff was from, but everything seemed to have clawed feet and satin. The place reeked of incense and the hot waxy aroma of recently snuffed candles.

"Well?" Kate asked, leaning back and crossing her arms over her chest.

M. C. licked her lips. "Well. I need a place to stay for a few days."

Kate's eyes narrowed and she suddenly looked way less irritated at the unannounced visit. "Are you in some kind of danger?"

"Nothing I can't handle. I just need to hang out until things cool down."

"Left in a hurry, did you?" Kate eyed her when she lifted her brows. "No luggage," she explained.

M. C. shrugged. "You look like you were on your way out. I didn't mean to mess up your . . . er . . . plans." It was Halloween. Probably crazy Kate's biggest night of the year.

Kate tilted her head. "Samhain is important, dear, but not as important as your safety. I'll stay—"

"No way, Aunt Kate. I'm fine. Honest. Not a soul in

the world knows I'm here. You go on. I'll curl up on the couch and watch some TV. Maybe thumb through that old book of yours and look for spells to turn bad guys into toads. You, uh . . . still have it, don't you?" As she said it her gaze strayed to the table in the corner where the dusty tome lay open.

Kate touched her shoulder, drawing her gaze back again. "The grimoire is not a toy, Mary Catherine. The spells are powerful, particularly tonight. An amateur could cause a complete disaster by making some simple mistake—particularly if she were a neophyte with as much Pagan blood in her as you have."

A little tingle danced up Mary Catherine's spine, but she only smiled at her aunt. "I was just kidding. Don't have a cow, okay?"

Kate studied her, her eyes probing, then shook her head, making her dangling earrings—all six pairs—jangle like bells. "If you want a spell of protection, darling, just ask. I'll take care of it for you."

"You know I don't believe in that stuff," M. C. said, her gaze straying to the book again.

Aunt Kate sighed. "You're sure you'll be okay alone?"

"Sure. You go on. I'll be fine. Really."

Looking worried, Aunt Kate nodded and turned toward the door.

"Hey," M. C. called. "Aren't you forgetting your broom?"

Kate glared, but when M. C. sent her a wink, she smiled instead, waved good night, and left her alone.

M. C. wandered the living room, flicked on the TV, searched the channels. An old black-and-white version of *The Three Musketeers* was playing, and she watched that for a while, but her gaze kept straying back to the dusty book on the table. Surely it wouldn't hurt to just peek?

No. She'd promised Aunt Kate.

Glancing back at the screen, she shook her head in dis-

gust. How could any man hope to hold his own in a fight
with those silly ruffles hanging from his sleeves? And
those hats! For crying out loud, were they supposed to look
heroic with puffy plumes jutting out of their hats? She
decided the Musketeers must have all been gay, and further
judged she'd far rather have her .38 in hand during a crisis
than one of those fragile-looking swords that seemed like
they'd break in a strong wind.

Despite the ridiculousness of the film, though, she felt
her heart twist a little when D'Artagnan leapt between his
lady fair and the evil villain, vowing to protect her with
his life.

Too bad heroes like that weren't around these days. She
wouldn't even mind the stupid hat.

The book called to her again, and this time Mary Catherine got up and wandered over to it. She reached out to
touch it, drew her hand away, then reached out again and
gently flipped some pages. And she paused when she read,
"Spell of Protection." The thing looked pretty simple.
You were supposed to be in a spot where the light of the
moon fell on you, during its first quarter. Light a white
candle. Envision the protection in whatever way worked
for you—a bubble of white light or a strong stone wall
around your body were given as examples. Then, keeping
that thought in mind, you just repeated the invocation written on the page.

Hmm.

Mary Catherine glanced sideways at the tall window,
and saw a thin beam of moonlight peeking between the
heavy velvet curtains. Hmm. She meandered over there
and opened the curtains, and sure enough the moonlight
flooded the room. It wasn't a quarter moon. But wouldn't
a full moon be even better?

If you believed in any of this nonsense to begin with,
which she did not.

She casually walked back to the table, where the moonlight spilled brightly over her and the book. Two candles sat there, one on either side of her aunt's precious old grimoire. One was pink and one was red. No white ones in sight. But a candle was a candle, right? And a long wooden match was laid there just begging to be lit. What the hell.

She struck the match and lit it, touching its flame to both candles because, hey, two candles were better than one.

She grinned. This was kind of a fun way to spend Halloween.

Okay, next steps: envision protection, and say the chant. She tried to imagine a bubble of white light surrounding her, and then tried picturing a bulletproof wall. But her mind kept straying back to that scene in the movie, where the Musketeer had vowed to protect his lady with his life. Cornball bunch of crap.

She read the words on the page, and heard the clock singing backup to her chant by striking midnight.

Without warning, something exploded and a ball of smoke enveloped her. Coughing, she waved it away, and suddenly she had the distinct feeling that she wasn't alone in the room anymore.

Two

Alexandre sat up and rubbed his head, eyes closed tightly. He wasn't certain what had happened. He'd been in the midst of a minor skirmish, setting to rights an insult to the king of France, when he'd heard a lady calling to him from afar. Fair damsels in need of aid were nothing new to Alexandre. He was sworn to protect the king, of course, but there were plenty of Musketeers available to the king at all times. Alexandre often got sidetracked protecting ladies in distress. He didn't mind the task at all, especially considering the delicious ways the fair maids often expressed their gratitude. He must have been clubbed on the head while distracted by the odd cadence of this particular lady's voice.

At any rate, he heard nothing of his enemies now, and imagined they'd fled, as his opponents often did before he'd finished with them. Clutching his rapier in one hand and righting his chapeau with the other, he got to his feet and peered through the odd smoke that surrounded him.

And then he went still and blinked in shock. He was no longer in the Provençal village where he'd faced off against the three ruffians only moments ago. He was inside a château, and staring into the very wide and frightened eyes of a beautiful—if oddly dressed—young woman.

He gave his head a shake and looked again. She was still there. Frightened as if she were looking at a ghost. Her eyes gleamed like dark sapphires in the moonlight, and her hair was a delightful mass of raven curls he imagined would feel like silk twined round his fingers. Never mind the odd clothing, or the odd feeling in his head. A beautiful woman like this one certainly took precedence over such trivial worries.

"*Bonjour, mademoiselle,*" he whispered, quickly removing his chapeau with a flourish and bowing deeply. Sheathing his sword, he gripped her small hand and drew it to his lips. Ah, warm salty skin, and a telltale tremble. She liked him already.

The hand in his jerked away fast. "Who the hell are you?" the fair lady demanded. "Wha-what are you doing here?"

He straightened, smoothed the luxurious plume, and then replaced his hat. "So it is English you prefer," he said. " 'Tis well I speak it fluently. I am Alexandre, one of the king's finest Musketeers, my lady."

"Get real," she said. "You are not."

"But I am." He took a step closer. She backed up, and it surprised him. "Do not fear me, pretty one. I am . . . a bit disoriented, but believe me, I have only come to help you."

"He-help me?"

"*Oui, ma petite.* I heard you calling out for help—a protector, a hero I believe you cried for." He rubbed his perfectly pointed beard with his fingers. "It is a bit of a blur, but I do recall that much."

She shook her head back and forth slowly, taking another step away from him. "This is crazy. This is nuts. You can't be here; this can't be happening."

He shrugged, smiling to himself, quite familiar with the

power of his presence on females. "Many a lady has been overwhelmed by my charm, little one. Do not be concerned. It is not a dream, *ma belle*. I truly am here. At your disposal." He let his gaze stray lower, to her lips, which looked full and tempting, and added, "Anything you need, pretty one, I assure you, I can provide." As he said it he moved closer.

The lady whipped a tiny weapon, which vaguely resembled a black powder pistol, from somewhere beneath the clothing she wore, and pointed it at him. "Don't you come one step closer, mister."

Amused, he reached out to snatch the toy from her hands. "What is this silly thing?" He gazed down the barrel, fingers grazing the trigger. The lady lunged forward, knocking the rounded end upward, away from his nose, just as the small device exploded in his hands. He felt his chapeau sail from his head and heard the looking glass behind him shatter. Alexandre dropped the weapon to the floor. "*Mon Dieu!*"

"You nearly shot yourself, you idiot!" she shouted. "Or did you?" Gripping his shoulders, she scanned his face, hands running up and down his arms in a most familiar fashion.

His fear faded quickly, and his notorious smile returned. "Ah, do not fear for me, lady. I am unharmed. But . . . eh . . . you may examine me further, if it would reassure you." He took advantage of her closeness to clasp her waist and pull her tight to him.

She drew back and punched him in the jaw so hard that Alexandre staggered backward and wound up landing on his derriere. But he never stopped smiling at her. "So," he said, rubbing his jaw, "you are shy, *non*?" He retrieved his hat from the floor, frowning at the neat round hole in the front of it.

"I'm the farthest thing from shy, Al. Touch me again, and you'll wish I were."

He was quite confused by her reluctance. Never had any lady sought to withhold her favors from him. They tended to swoon at a mere glance. But he'd already noticed this one's strangeness. Perhaps her mind was unbalanced. Pity. She was truly magnificent. He shook his head, sighing in disappointment but resigned to defeat. His first. Perhaps she'd come around yet, but for the moment he sensed it might be best to stop trying. "Very well, *ma chérie*. I will not touch you again. Until you request it, at least." He got suavely to his feet, smoothing one hand over the long, wavy locks he wore and brushing at his breeches.

"Don't hold your breath."

"Nonetheless, never let it be said that Alexandre failed to come to the aid of a lady in need."

"What I need is to know who does your hair. Captain Hook?"

"Why were you calling for help?" he asked, ignoring her puzzling question.

She looked at the floor, shook her head. "This is unreal."

"I can see you are greatly distressed. Has some rogue insulted your honor, then? Shall I call him out, teach him a lesson he will not soon forget?"

She closed her eyes and he noticed how thick and dark her lashes were, resting upon her fair cheeks. "You're the one who's gonna be distressed. I think I—I think I messed up."

"It is understandable, *chérie*. You are only a woman, after all."

Her head came up, eyes narrow. "Watch it, Al."

"I am only saying that whatever is wrong, I can make it right. So, tell me now, what has befallen you?"

"It's what's befallen you we have to worry about," she said.

He frowned at her. "I do not understand."

"Do they have witches where you come from, Al?"

He lifted his brows. "*Oui*, but they are not a problem. If they get out of hand, we simply hang them." Then he frowned. "You are not a witch, are you, lady?"

"No. Not . . . exactly. But . . . well, maybe you'd better sit down."

"If you wish it." He tucked his damaged hat under his arm and walked to the settee, but he didn't sit until she did. "Now," he said, "tell Alexandre what troubles you . . . but first, *ma chérie*, tell me your name."

She blinked. "Oh. It's Mary Catherine Hammersmith. But I go by M. C. Hammer. It's . . . sort of a joke."

"My lady Hammer," he repeated, lowering his head respectfully. "Now, why are you so troubled, eh?"

She looked decidedly sheepish. "I got into trouble. I needed help. And I found this . . . old book . . . with a . . . an incantation. . . ."

"A witch's spell?"

She nodded. "Right . . . a spell for protection. And I said the words out loud . . . and I must have messed it up, because the next thing I knew, you were here."

He smiled slowly, and lifted a hand to gently pat her head. "Poor Lady Hammer . . . you truly believe that you have brought me here by witchery?"

"Oh, I'm pretty sure of it."

"What makes you so sure, little one? Perhaps I simply heard your lovely voice asking for protection, and followed the sound to find you here."

"Well, that wouldn't have been possible, Al. See, you . . . you sort of . . . traveled . . . through time."

He studied her face. Poor, disturbed beauty. Surely he could find a way to pull her from her delusions! He must. She was entirely too beautiful to be a lunatic.

"You don't believe me, do you? This is the future, Al. The year is 1998."

"Oh, sweet Lady Hammer. Sssh." He ran his hand

through her hair. "You will be all right. I will find help for you, I vow it."

She closed her eyes, poor little thing. "I can prove it," she said.

"Oh?" He so wanted to help her get well. He wasn't certain, but he didn't think it would be quite chivalrous to seduce a lunatic. So until he cured her . . .

"See that little box over there?" she asked, pointing.

He followed her gaze and nodded. She picked up a smaller item, thumbed a button, and the box came to life all on its own. "*Sacre bleu!*" he shouted, leaping to his feet as tiny Musketeers, his own comrades, battled their enemies, all the while held captive inside the box! He drew his sword and lashed out at the thing, but its face was impenetrable.

The poor S.O.B. was still swinging his sword at the television set when the front door burst open and Aunt Kate appeared. Mary Catherine sank a little deeper into the sofa cushions at the glare her aunt sent her. She just stood there, looking from Al to M. C. and back again. Then, hands going to her hips, she shouted, "Mary Catherine Hammersmith, *what* did you *do*?"

Three

Poor Al. He'd just sat there looking stunned as Aunt Kate explained what happened to him. He hadn't believed it at first, of course. But by the time they'd shown him the electric lights, the microwave, and Aunt Kate's smoke-belching Buick, he'd pretty much accepted the truth.

Now, Kate paced while Mary Catherine sat beside Al on the settee. She felt like a kid called into the principal's office. "You should have listened to me," Kate muttered. She went to the book, glancing down at it. "Is this the spell you used?"

Getting up, Mary Catherine went closer and peered over her aunt's shoulder at the book. "Yeah, that's it."

"This spell specifically calls for the moon's first quarter. I can't believe you'd use it during a full moon! And on All Hallows eve, of all nights!"

M. C. shrugged. "I didn't exactly expect it to work."

"Work? You quadrupled its potency!" She glared. M. C. looked at the floor. "And what about the white candle? I don't see one here." Kate looked at the candles on the table. "Red and pink? You used these, didn't you?"

M. C. nodded. "Is that bad?"

Kate eyed Al, then M. C. again. "Red is for passion. Pink brings true love. Honestly, Mary Catherine, what were you thinking?"

Again M. C. shrugged. "Mostly about *The Three Musketeers*," she muttered. "It was on TV."

Kate frowned. "Well, that explains it. You wanted protection. You got yourself a protector—in exactly the form you were envisioning." She rolled her eyes, shook her head. "Goddess preserve us from neophyte witches."

"I am not a witch," M. C. said flatly.

"I think Alexandre would disagree with you there."

Al looked up at the mention of his name. He'd been sitting, pretty much ignoring them. But now he seemed to straighten his spine as he got to his feet and came forward. "Can this . . . this spell be reversed?"

Aunt Kate looked at the book again, drumming her painted fingernails on the page. "I think so. It will take some research, but . . ."

"Well, that's just great," M. C. muttered. "Meanwhile, I'm right back where I started, with the biggest criminal in seven states out to do me in."

Kate blinked. Al gaped at her. M. C. realized she hadn't told either of them just how much trouble she was in. Nor had she intended to. She wasn't a whiner, and she certainly didn't want to drag either of them into this mess. "Forget I said that. It's nothing I can't handle. Go on, Aunt Kate. Figure a way to send Al back where he belongs."

Kate tilted her head. "I can't do that, M. C. The only one who can reverse your spell is you. I can help, but—"

"*Non!*"

At his declaration, Kate and M. C. both turned toward Al in surprise. "Whaddya mean, no? You have to go back," M. C. said.

He stared straight into her eyes, and his were very dark, very deep. If it weren't for the long, crimp-curled hair, pointy beard, and stupid hat, she thought, the guy might actually be attractive.

"I am a Musketeer," he said, still holding her with his penetrating stare. "You brought me here to help you, Lady Hammer, and help you I shall."

Lowering her eyes, she shook her head. "It's not like there's much you could do, Al."

When she looked up again, he wore a knowing smile. "You know very little about what I can do, pretty one. Besides, no Musketeer would leave a lady in this situation. This criminal . . . he means to murder you, *non*?" She shrugged, and Al shook his head. "I will stay," he said firmly. "And when I've dispatched the villain, only then will I allow you to send me back . . . if you can."

Sighing heavily, M. C. lifted her chin. "What do you plan to do, Al? Challenge him to a sword fight? Look, I know you think you're some kind of superman, and maybe you are, in your own time. But you wouldn't stand a chance against this guy. He has weapons you haven't even imagined. Machine guns, and a dozen goons to do his bidding. You couldn't begin to—"

"Enough!" Al spun around, putting his back to her, arms crossed at his chest.

"Now you've gone and insulted him," Aunt Kate scolded. "I swear, M. C., didn't your mother teach you a thing about tact?"

M. C. threw her hands in the air. "I'm just trying to keep him alive, for crying out loud!" He didn't face her. He tapped his foot on the floor, waiting, she figured. She cleared her throat, moved closer, put her hand on his shoulder. "I apologize, Al. I didn't mean to insult you or question your . . . abilities. I just . . . well, hell, I dragged you here by mistake, and I feel bad enough about that already. If you go and get killed, I'll never be able to live with myself."

"And if I return, leaving you behind, never to know

whether this . . . this goon person succeeds in taking your life . . . I would not be able to live with myself, *chérie*."

She nodded. "I guess I can understand that."

Slowly he turned to face her again. "It is a question of honor, lady. I cannot leave you to face a killer alone. It is that simple."

M. C. tore her gaze from his and sought assistance in Aunt Kate. Kate sighed, shaking her head. "You won't be very successful in sending him back if he doesn't want to go. Besides, there are consequences to working magic on people against their will, Mary Catherine. It just isn't done."

Lowering her head in defeat, M. C. surrendered. "Okay. You can stay. But"—she looked him over again, head to toe—"but we're going to have to give you a makeover. I mean, the boots are cool, but the rest of this getup . . ." Kate elbowed her, and she realized she was on the verge of insulting him yet again. She cleared her throat. "It would be better if we dressed you in clothing more typical of what people wear in this day and age."

He rubbed his pointed beard thoughtfully. "I see. Yes, it is obvious people dress . . . quite differently today." This with a disapproving glance at her jeans and T-shirt.

M. C. looked at him with raised eyebrows. Then she reached up and removed his hat, eyeing the elegant, wavy locks underneath. "We'll have to start by chopping off this hair."

His smile was slow and almost . . . sexy. "No need." He reached up and removed the offending hair. "Frankly, my lady, I find the wig as offensive as you obviously do. I wear it only when I must."

"Sort of like me with panty hose," she said, grinning. Underneath, his own hair was dark, pulled behind his head and tied there with a thong. She wondered how long it was, and impulsively reached around his head to tug the thong away. Then, without thinking, ran her fingers through his hair to shake it loose. But her hands froze in mid-motion as his eyes, darkening, met hers.

"Maybe we should still cut it," Aunt Kate suggested.

Unable to look away, M. C. shook her head. "No. No, I think it's . . . it's fine." Why was her voice all hoarse?

"At last, something about me you like," he said softly.

Remembering herself, she drew her hands away from his hair. "You . . . um . . . you should shave."

His dark brows drew closer. "Men of this time do not wear beards?"

She averted her eyes. "Some do."

She didn't look up, but she could hear the smile in his voice. "But you would prefer to see me without mine?"

"I really don't care one way or the other. It was just a suggestion." She peered up to see him studying her. He was entirely too convinced of his own appeal.

"Come, Alexandre," Aunt Kate said. "I'll show you to the bathroom and explain how everything works. M. C., while we're up there, you run next door and ask Mrs. Johnson to loan us something for our guest to wear. He looks to be about Mr. Johnson's size."

Al started up the stairs. M. C. headed for the door. But before she left, she saw her aunt gazing worriedly at the red and pink candles on the table, a perplexed frown between her brows. She shook herself, though, and hurried up the stairs.

M. C. got the clothes, along with a curious glance from Mrs. Johnson, delivered them to her aunt, and then waited. She spent her time checking the cable listings, thinking she might be able to give Al a few lessons on life in the nineties by letting him watch television tonight and explaining things as they went along. She figured she'd best get him a gun, too, and teach him to use it. She really didn't see how the man was going to be any help to her at all. In fact, worse than that, he was an added burden. Now she had to worry about keeping him alive as well as protecting her own skin. Hell, things had gone from bad to worse, and they showed no signs of improving soon.

Aunt Kate cleared her throat, and M. C. turned, then jumped off the couch as if someone had goosed her.

Al stood at the foot of the stairs. The faded jeans fit him like a surgical glove, and the T-shirt strained to contain him. The guy was built like Stallone. Broad chest. Big shoulders. Biceps to die for.

Even when she could finally drag her eyes away from his body, she still couldn't catch her breath. His hair gleamed, neatly pulled back again. The beard was gone, and underneath it he looked like . . . like . . . he belonged on the big screen. A leading man to make the actresses' pulse rates go up.

He smiled then, and M. C.'s stomach convulsed. The man was absolutely, drop dead gorgeous.

"Oh, dear," Aunt Kate murmured.

He sent her a puzzled glance, but focused on M. C. again, moving forward. "Will I blend in now, do you think?"

"Not in this lifetime," she muttered, suddenly conscious of the fact that she hadn't run a comb through her tangles in hours. He looked worried. She bit her lip. "You look great, Al. You really do." He looked better than great. He looked like a Grade A hunk with a French accent. He looked like a *Playgirl* cover in search of a home. Her throat went dry.

His smile got bigger. "Good. It feels strange . . . but comfortable. Far more so than the dress of my day. Although I see nowhere to fasten my sword."

She looked across the room to where he'd left his weapon standing upright in a corner. The ornate handguard glittered and she wondered if it was real gold. "Men don't carry swords these days. I thought I'd teach you to use a gun."

He frowned. "If you're referring to that volatile toy you

pointed at me earlier, I think not. A sword and my own wit are all I need."

"But the men we're up against will have guns, Al. And—"

"You can carry all the . . . *guns* . . . you need, my lady Hammer. For me, my rapier will be sufficient."

She clenched her jaw. "You're very stubborn, you know that?"

He only smiled.

"It's autumn," Aunt Kate commented. "We'll get him a longish coat to wear, and no one will notice the sword at all. It's not a big deal."

"It will be a big deal if he gets a forty-four-caliber hole blown through that magnificent chest of hi—" She cut herself off, bit her lip.

Al moved forward until they were standing very close to each other, nose to . . . magnificent chest. "Something else about me that meets with your approval, *non*?"

"I'm only saying I would like to keep you in one piece, you arrogant, feather-hatted, Don Juan wanna-be."

"Ah. All the same, I am glad you find my . . . chest to be . . . *magnifique,* Lady Hammer. And I promise . . . I will remain in one piece, for you."

She swallowed hard, and told herself she was not the sort of woman who would respond to such outrageous, ego-based flirting. So why were her knees so weak?

"You can't keep calling me Lady Hammer, either," she said.

"What shall I call you then?" He touched her chin with a forefinger, lifting her head slightly so he could search her eyes. "Sorceress? Enchantress? *La Belle Femme?*"

"M. C. will be fine," she rasped.

"It does not suit you. I will call you Mary Catherine, as your aunt does. A lady as beautiful as you are deserves a name equally so."

Her throat was dry.

"Did the women of your time really fall for these lines, Al? I know perfectly well that I look like hell."

His fingertips brushed a curl from her cheek. "If this is what hell looks like, my lady, then I shall resolve to sin far more often."

Her cheeks heated. She couldn't believe it. She was blushing!

Beyond him, Aunt Kate sighed heavily, snatched up the pink and red candles, and tossed them into the garbage pail.

Four

M. C. settled onto the settee beside Al—not too close, of course—and thumbed the remote. The set came to life, and Al shot it one startled glance before regaining his calm and eyeing her instead.

"So, now you will tell me the secret of the little box with the tiny Musketeers trapped inside, *non*?"

She closed her eyes and prayed for patience. "There are no tiny people inside it, Al. It's just pretend." He cocked one eyebrow at her. "Make-believe," she said. He still frowned. "It's just moving pictures of people in costumes. Like a play."

The frown vanished. Wonder replaced it, and he stared again at the set. "But the players . . . they are so small."

"That's only a picture of the players. They aren't really there. See . . ." She sought an explanation he could understand, but found none. Then she glanced up when her aunt came in from another room, carrying her Polaroid with her.

She handed it to M. C. "Maybe this will help."

"Perfect. Sit still, Al." She pointed the camera at him and pressed the button. He jumped to his feet when the flash went off, then rubbed his eyes. "Sorry about that," she said. She took the photo the camera spit into her hand and watched it, waiting. In a few moments the image came clear. Al, looking like some lonely woman's fantasy come to life. Every inch the modern-day hunk. He didn't look a thing like a Musketeer now in his jeans and T-shirt. He could fool anyone—until he opened his mouth.

But what an attractive mouth it was.

Stop that!

She lifted her gaze from the photo, only to encounter the real thing, staring at her curiously. "Here," she said. "See? This is called a camera, and it takes pictures of people. Look."

He took the photo from her hand, then blinked down at it. "This . . . this amazes me."

"It's a photograph," she told him. "A similar kind of machine takes moving pictures of actors, and then the pictures are sent into the television set for our entertainment. Understand?"

Again he looked at the screen. Finally, he nodded, still staring. "And what sort of play is this?" he asked, pointing.

M. C. took the photo from him, tucked it into her back pocket, and then glanced toward the TV. "Oh, that's just a game. Two teams competing to see which wins. It's called football. Waste of time, really." The camera cut to a group of cheerleaders. Al gaped and nearly fell on the floor. M. C. snatched up the remote and changed the station. "Here's a movie. A story, you see? If we watch together, I can explain things to you as we go along, and maybe you'll understand the modern world better."

"What . . . what sort of . . . story?" he asked, his gaze riveted to the screen as the opening credits of *Casablanca* scrolled past.

M. C. sighed as she always did when Bogie was nearby.

"A love story. Sit down, Al. Relax. This is a terrific movie."

"A terrific *old* movie," Aunt Kate said, shaking her head. "Surely you don't expect him to learn about the modern world by watching this?"

"Sssh! It's starting." M. C. sat down again, thumbing the volume up a few notches.

Kate rolled her eyes. "He should be getting some rest. It's late and—"

"Aunt Kate, go on up to bed. Al and I will be fine."

Kate eyed her. "*Star Trek* is showing on channel 12." She said it without much hope in her voice. M. C. ignored her. "*Indiana Jones* is on 26 . . . or maybe the late news would be—"

M. C. sent her aunt a quelling glare.

"I found the . . . er . . . ball of foot game to be interesting," Al suggested.

M. C. looked at him with raised brows, then turned to her aunt. "He's becoming a nineties guy already." She got to her feet, pointing at Al with a decisive forefinger. "You are going to sit here and watch *Casablanca*. And you," she said, turning to Aunt Kate, "are going up to bed before you fall asleep on your feet."

Kate put her hands on her hips. "And what are you going to do, young lady?"

M. C. smiled. "Make popcorn. What else?"

She sauntered into the kitchen to do just that, and when she returned, Al was alone, riveted to the TV screen, Aunt Kate having finally surrendered and gone to bed.

Al dug into the popcorn with delight, and M. C. explained the film as it went along. The cars, the guns, the airplanes, the war. But when it ended, Al turned to her in confusion.

"He let her go," he said, shaking his head.

M. C. sniffed and rubbed at her eyes. "I know. It's a beautiful story, isn't it?"

"Beautiful?" He searched her face. "But you are crying! I thought you said this was not real! Make-believe, *non*?"

"Of course it's make-believe." She averted her face, rubbing the tears from her lashes briskly.

"Then . . . why do you cry?"

"Because it's so sad!"

"And yet you love it all the same? Though it makes you cry to see it?"

She nodded. Al frowned. "You are a foolish woman, Mary Catherine. And that . . . that story is foolish as well. He should not have let her go."

M. C. tilted her head and studied Al's face. "Well, I'll be . . . You were as moved by the film as I was, weren't you?"

"*Non!*" he said. "I told you, it was foolish. He loved her. He should have taken her away with him and let the war be damned."

He said it with such passion that she found herself staring at him in surprise. "You feel pretty strongly about it, hmm?"

Al nodded hard, then met her eyes. "Nothing is more important than love, lady. Not war, nor peace, nor marriage. Nothing."

Lowering her gaze, she said, "You sound as if you've been in love yourself."

Al shook his head slowly, but his gaze remained riveted to her face. "I have known many women, *ma belle*, but I have not loved. Some of them . . . claimed to love me, but it was my position, my sword, not me. The romantic image of the Musketeer. One day, I will find a woman who will love the man, rather than the colors he wears and the rapier he wields."

"I'll bet you will," she said softly.

He nodded, more gently this time. "And when I do, *chérie*, I will not let her go the way your foolish Rick of

the magic box did. I will fight for her. I will die for her.
I will even . . . even surrender my sword for her.''

She blinked, amazed at the way her heart tripped at his
words.

"You think I am foolish," he said, lowering his eyes.

"I think," she said, "that this woman . . . will thank her
lucky stars."

He smiled, and handed her the television guide her aunt
had been perusing earlier. "Another play," he said.

"Aren't you tired?"

Staring deeply into her eyes, he said, "I am more awake
than I have ever been, *ma petite*."

She felt her cheeks heating, so she averted her face,
burying her nose in the magazine, flipping pages. She
didn't think she'd ever met a more hopeless romantic in
her life. Who'd have guessed the French flirt was really
such a softy? "Oh, here's one. This time you'll get to see
what I do for a living as well as learn about life in the
nineties." He frowned as she set the book down and turned
to channel 8, where *V.I. Warshawski* was about to begin.

Alexandre was amazed at the strength and independence
of the woman on the screen, and slowly realized that Mary
Catherine was like her. He had no idea how to deal with
such a woman. And yet, as the film progressed he understood better the kind of danger she must be facing.

When it ended, he turned to M. C. "Like the woman,
you feel you have no need of a man to protect you, *non*?"

"Right," she said. And she said it firmly.

"Yet, you must have been afraid. For you sought help
from the book of magic."

She shrugged her small shoulders. "I . . . was only playing around. I didn't expect it to really work . . . certainly
didn't expect a Musketeer to show up."

She smiled, and as it had before, her smile touched him

on some very deep level. Made his stomach clench tight like a fist.

"I think you were afraid. Are you still, Mary Catherine?"

She lowered her lids to hide her eyes, and he knew she was. But thought herself too strong to admit it.

"Tell me about this trouble you are in," he said.

Nodding again, she began. And when she had told him all of it, he found himself amazed at her cleverness in having eluded her pursuers for as long as she had. At disguising herself and escaping even as they watched her every move. She was truly an unusual woman. Unlike any he'd known.

"You do not have to go back," he suggested. "You could go far away, leave this . . . this evidence behind."

"I can't do that," she said. "Guido de Rocci is a killer, Al. If I don't put him away, he's just going to hurt someone else. I can't let that happen."

He stared at her for a very long moment. "Finally, something about you I understand," he said softly.

"Do you?"

He nodded. "It is . . . a matter of honor, is it not?"

She stared at him thoughtfully for a long moment. "Yeah," she said. "I guess it is."

"Then I shall help you to retrieve this evidence."

She blinked as if surprised. "But how? I told you, they're watching the bank. Oh, they might let me get in and grab the tape, but there's no way I'll get out of there once I have it."

"*Oui*, they are watching. But they are watching for you, Lady Hammer. Not me."

Her brows bunched together, creasing her forehead. "Not . . . you?"

"I shall go into this . . . this bank, and retrieve the tape for you. It is simple, *non*?"

Her frown eased. "It *sounds* simple." Then she caught

her lower lip in her teeth, shaking her head slowly. "So
why do I have the feeling it won't be?"

"You worry for nothing, *ma chérie*. I am a Musketeer.
This is only a small task, and barely worthy of my skills."

She thought for a long moment, even got to her feet and
paced the floor. But finally she turned to him and nodded.
"All right, we'll try it. But you have to understand, Al,
it's going to be dangerous."

"I am not unfamiliar with danger, Mary Catherine."

She searched his face. But he got the feeling she didn't
quite believe him. "You'd better get some sleep. Tomorrow's going to be a big day, and you'll need to be on your
toes."

He frowned at the unusual turn of phrase. "A wise suggestion," he finally said.

"Come on, I'll take you to the bedroom." She reached
for his hand, quite without thought, he was certain. But
when his closed around hers, he felt the shudder that
worked through her. And more. The warmth of that small
hand nestled within his larger one. The pull of a longing
that seemed to well from somewhere deep inside him. The
tingle of an attraction more powerful than any he'd known.
And he realized then what she wanted.

"There is one thing I must tell you, lady, before I rest."

She tugged her hand gently, but he only drew it to his
lips and kissed its silken flesh before finally releasing her.
"Go . . . go ahead," she said, but her voice trembled just
as her hand had when his lips had caressed it.

He sighed. "I am a Musketeer, and as of this moment,
my mission is to protect you, and to see to it that your
pursuers are dealt with. This is my task, Mary Catherine,
and until it is done, it is where all my attention must lie."

She tilted her head to one side. "I'm not sure what
you're getting at."

He nodded. "I am being unclear. What I am saying is

that as long as I am your protector, I cannot make love to you."

She blinked twice, and then her eyes opened wide. "Wh-what?"

"I am sorry, *ma chérie*. It is a part of my personal code of conduct, you see. I cannot be distracted, even for a moment. Not until you are safe, and my task complete."

She gaped for a moment. Then snapped her jaw shut. "Of all the nerve! I swear, Al, I've never met a more conceited, cocksure, arrogant—"

He surged to his feet, and in one smooth motion swept her into his arms, dipped her backward, and bent over her to kiss her mouth, because he knew how badly she wanted him to. She went stiff in his arms, but as he worked her lips with his, her body melted, and her mouth relaxed, and he made love to her with his tongue until she trembled all over.

Then he straightened, careful not to release her until he was sure she wouldn't fall. Her eyes were wide and glassy, her breaths quick and short. "Do not be angry with me, pretty one. I, too, find it difficult to wait. But for now, you must go to your chamber alone, and I will rest here . . . and dream of the time when my job is done and I can give you what we both desire."

Her faced flushed, still panting, she clenched her fists and glared at him. "The only thing I *desire,* Al, is to get this tape to the police, Guido de Rocci behind bars, and you back in your own time and out of my life for good. Understand?"

He smiled very gently. "*Oui, ma petite.* I understand, *perfectly.*"

She made a growling sound like that of a lion about to spring, then whirled and stomped away from him and up the stairs to her room. Alone, and angry at him for denying her. He lowered his head, shaking it slowly. Poor *petite.* It frustrated him as well. And for the first time, Alexandre was tempted to forgo honor, deny his own code, and give in to the rapture he would find in her arms.

But no. He was a Musketeer.

He laid his rapier beside the settee within easy reach, and curled onto the cushions for a night he was certain would provide little rest.

Five

She didn't sleep well. Her rest consisted of punching her pillow, and wishing it were Al's gorgeous face—that and wondering why the hell she'd reacted to his kiss the way she had.

He was arrogant, all too sure of himself, lecherous, and infuriating.

But he kissed like he'd been born to it.

And she reacted like a woman too long without a man. That was all there was to it, she decided. It wasn't him, it was her own unplanned celibacy that had her hormones raging when he touched her. She'd never been good at choosing men. Every time she got involved, the guy turned out to be a loser, and so she'd decided to avoid the opposite sex entirely. That had been over a year ago. She guessed her body had its own opinion on the subject.

So maybe she should try again. But not with Al. Absolutely not with Al.

Why not?

Hell. He was too sure of himself, too old-fashioned, probably to the point of being chauvinistic, and he was going back where he came from just as soon as all of this was over.

And that, she realized, was the heart of the matter. He was going back, and there was no sense in her forming some sick attachment to him in the meantime. No sense at all.

All morning M. C. and Aunt Kate helped Al practice the role he was about to play. They talked him through it over and over again. Waiting for his turn in line, what he'd say to the teller at the window, how they'd take him into another room where he'd insert his key into the box and the banker would insert hers. He'd memorized everything from the box number to the fact that he must address the teller as Mr. or Ms. rather than "my lady," or "*ma chérie.*"

M. C. believed she'd thought of everything.

Before noon, he seemed ready. Aunt Kate had run into town to buy him a dark-colored trench coat that reached to mid-shin, since he was so damned insistent on wearing his sword. She'd also had a copy of the safe deposit box key made. M. C. thought it best, just in case, and she put the extra key in her jeans pocket where she could get at it in a hurry if she needed to. Despite Al's protests, they'd managed to talk him into wearing the Kevlar vest that M. C. had practically lived in for the past few days. And in spite of his objections, Mary Catherine was going to be waiting right outside the bank to back him up if all hell broke loose.

Her stomach was churning when all was finally ready and she got into Aunt Kate's car to drive back to Newark. She was forgetting something. She was sure of it.

Al, on the other hand, was far less concerned about the job at hand than he was about their mode of transportation. He eyed the car warily before getting in, then took his passenger seat looking a bit pale.

"It's perfectly safe, Al," M. C. assured him. "Put your seat belt on." When he frowned at her, she demonstrated by fastening her own. Lips tight, he pulled the belt around him, and snapped it.

"Good," she said, and then turned the key.

The motor came to life, and M. C. shifted into gear and pulled onto the street. Al's hand gripped her knee, and for once, she was certain it *wasn't* a come-on. His knuckles were white, and the pressure pretty intense. She closed her hand over his. "Easy, Al. There's nothing to this, I promise."

He met her eyes and seemed unsure. "We are traveling very quickly, are we not?"

She glanced at the speedometer. "I'm going thirty. We're practically crawling."

Another car approached, and Al looked up fast, eyes widening. "Watch out, lady!"

His shout startled her so much that she jammed the brakes and came to an abrupt stop in the middle of the quiet street. The other car passed, its driver sending her an odd look. M. C. shook her head, glancing in the mirror and thanking her stars that no one was behind her. She'd have been rear-ended for sure.

Sighing, she turned to Al. "Look, Al, I've been driving for over a decade now. Will you relax? Please?"

He closed his eyes slowly. "Forgive me," he said. "You must think me very cowardly."

She shook her head slowly. "I think you're only about half as nervous as I'd be in your shoes. Listen, Al, this is going to get worse. Once we hit the highway we'll be going a lot faster, and there are going to be lots of other cars on the road with us. Are you going to be okay with this?"

He licked his lips, nodding slowly. "It is just so new and strange to me."

"I know. You'll get used to it, I promise. Look, do you trust me?"

He stared into her eyes for a long moment. "Oddly

enough, Mary Catherine, I do. It is good, *non*? Since I am placing my life in your hands?''

She smiled. ''I'm an excellent driver.''

The blast of a horn made Al jump out of his skin and whirl around. M. C. glanced back to see a car behind them. She let off the brake, pressed on the accelerator, and got moving.

By early afternoon, they were back in Newark, and she thought it was a good thing Al had been given several hours to get used to traveling by car before facing the city traffic. What a mess. At any rate, he'd calmed down a lot. Enough so that he was now asking questions about how the car worked, and whether he could try driving it himself. The very thought had her almost as nervous as he'd been when he'd first got into the thing.

She parked a block away from the bank. Her hat and sunglasses were firmly back in place now, and she wore her leather jacket like a shield. ''That's the bank, over there,'' she said. ''You won't have to cross any streets. That's a lesson in itself around here. I'll stay here, where I can keep an eye on you in case anything goes wrong. Okay?''

''Yes, fine. I know what to do.'' He glanced around, his nervousness gone, every bit the protector now. ''Do you see any of your enemies about?''

She dragged her eyes from Al and looked around. Then she nodded. ''That dark sedan with the tinted glass, right across from the bank. That's one of Guido's goons inside it.''

Al spotted the car and nodded. ''Perhaps you should await me elsewhere,'' he suggested. ''You'll be alone, unprotected while I retrieve the tape.''

''Not quite unprotected,'' she said, and she took out her gun, then gave the cylinder a spin. ''He comes near me, he'll wish he hadn't.''

"I still don't like leaving your side, Mary Catherine, with one of them so close."

"He doesn't know this car, and he can't possibly recognize me from there. Go on, Al. Get the tape. It's the only way to end this thing."

Sighing heavily, he nodded. "I will be as fast as possible, my lady." He fiddled with the door handle for a minute, finally made it work, and started to get out without undoing the seat belt. It tugged him back down, and M. C. reached over to release it for him. Impulsively, she touched his shoulder. "Be careful, Al."

"Do not worry," he said, then he smiled at her and got out, striding purposefully toward the bank in his long dark coat, looking this way and that all the way there. Inconspicuous, he definitely was not. At least his sword didn't show.

His sword. It was at that precise moment that M. C. realized what it was she'd forgotten. This bank had been robbed six times in the past two years. As a result it had been equipped with metal detectors at the entrances and airportlike X-ray machines. "Oh, hell!" She had to stop him. But she'd never get inside with her gun. Quickly she pulled it from her jeans and jammed it under the front seat.

She jumped out of the car and ran toward the bank to stop Al, but he was already heading through the entrance. By the time she got to the door, a security guard was guiding Al to the X-ray machine and asking him to walk through it. She shoved the door open, lunged inside, saw the X-ray guy's eyes bug out as he looked at the screen, and then saw three security guards pull their weapons and head for Al, even as he reached for his sword.

"Al, no!" she shouted. Too late. In a flash the weapon was in his hand, whipping to and fro like lightning. The guards' guns sailed from their hands as if they'd sprouted wings. The bank's alarm shrieked like a banshee, and Al smiled, his eyes gleaming as he held the guards at bay. He was *enjoying this*, she realized in disbelief.

He backed past her toward the door, glanced her way briefly, and inclined his head. Then he was gone, out the door with the guards in hot pursuit. Already she could hear approaching sirens. She looked outside to see the dark sedan pulling slowly away from the bank. No doubt Guido's goon had a record and didn't want to be caught within a mile of a bank robbery. She looked up and down the street for Al, and caught sight of him as he leapt nimbly from the sidewalk to the hood of a parked car, swung his sword in an elegant arc to fend off his pursuers, and then leapt off the other side. She should go after him, she thought; she should help him.

But he'd all but told her to go after the tape. And she could always bail him out of jail—or the loony bin, where he'd more likely end up—later.

Poor Al. She hoped the cops didn't shoot first and ask questions later. She knew she'd better hurry. He'd never survive without her.

Quickly she went up to a frightened teller. "I know this is a bad time," she said, "but this is truly an emergency. My life is in danger unless I get into my safe deposit box right this minute."

"I'm sorry," the woman said. "But in the middle of all this, I can't possibly—"

"Please. I'm not kidding you, I could be killed if you don't help me."

The woman searched M. C.'s face, frowning. Then nodded. "All right. But . . . be discreet. I could lose my job for this."

"Thank you."

Within a few minutes, M. C. had the tape. Getting out of the bank with the cops there questioning people proved to be another challenge. But she found herself pausing to eavesdrop as she overheard the guards who had returned from the chase, telling their story to the police.

"The man was insane," one said. "Some kind of acrobat or something."

"Look what he did to my uniform!" said another, fingering the neat slash across the front of his shirt. "He coulda killed me."

"No way," a third commented. "He was too good. If he'd wanted to kill you, you'd be dead."

"Man, I never saw anything like it. He ducked into an alley, and we thought we had him cornered. But then he jumped onto a Dumpster and did a backflip right over the fence. And he wasn't even winded!"

Poor Al. Out there, being pursued like a fox by hounds, in an unfamiliar city. But she shook her head in wonder at the way he'd handled himself. She almost wished she could have seen it.

She tucked the tape into her pocket and sidled over toward the group of customers who'd already been interviewed. Briefly she thought about handing the tape to one of the cops on the scene, but it was too risky. If he were honest, he'd insist on taking her with him to the station, and that would leave Al alone on the run. If he were less than honest . . . She knew full well that there were several cops on Guido de Rocci's payroll, and it would be just her luck to pick one of them.

No, she wasn't handing this evidence over to anyone other than the top guy. The D.A. himself. But first, she had to find and rescue her self-appointed bodyguard before he got himself killed.

A cop gave the group of customers the okay to leave, and she slipped out with them. Then she ducked her head and pulled her cap lower as the dark sedan passed slowly by. Circling the block like a damned hungry shark. She couldn't walk around searching for Al. Not yet. She had to get to the car. She'd drive around looking for him. It would be safer that way. At least she could make a run for it if they recognized her.

The guy in the sedan passed her, and did a double take. Oh, hell. He was picking up a car phone now. She walked faster. She was nearly to her aunt's beat-up Buick when a second dark car pulled to a stop at the corner just beyond it. A man got out. Suit, sunglasses. Damn.

She ran for the car as the thug came toward her on the sidewalk, his hand reaching inside his tailored Italian jacket. She thought of her own gun, tucked under the front seat of the car. Hell. Almost there. She grabbed the door handle.

A hand gripped her arm, spun her around, and she stood face-to-face with Guido de Rocci himself. The barrel of a handgun jammed into her belly, and she held her breath.

"The tape," he rasped. "Hand it over, or die."

"I gave it to the cops already, de Rocci. And I hope they fry your ass."

"You're a liar," he said. "Hand it over."

She met his shaded eyes and simply shook her head. "Shoot me and those cops will be all over you like ugly on an ape, pal. From the feel of it, I'd say there's no silencer on that piece of yours."

"Oh, I'm not going to shoot you, Miss Hammer. Not here, at least." He tugged her away from the Buick, just as the other car came to a halt in the street beside it. And she knew if they got her into that vehicle it would be all over. She closed her eyes and prayed for a miracle.

Six

The miracle she was praying for appeared. Guido de Rocci stood on the sidewalk, facing the street, holding her pressed up against her aunt's Buick, his gun jabbing into her belly. His goons in their dark sedan had pulled to a stop in the street beside the Buick.

When de Rocci suddenly stiffened, she didn't know why. Until she looked downward. Al crouched comfortably on the sidewalk behind the man, and the tip of his sword nestled at the base of Guido's spine.

"Unhand the lady," Al said softly. And his eyes glittered.

He was smart, her Musketeer. The guys in the car couldn't even see him down there. The oversized Buick blocked him from their view.

Guido didn't move.

"Release her, man, or I'll run you through!" Al put a little more pressure on the sword, and Guido flinched.

"Okay, okay." He let his grip on M. C. go, but still kept the gun in her belly.

"Now tell your men to drive away." Again Al shoved the sword.

Guido grunted, and his jaw went tight. But he nodded to his goons. "Take one more turn around the block."

The dark sedan moved slowly away. But M. C. still didn't relax. Tough to relax with the barrel of a .44 in your gut.

"Very good, sir," Al said, and he got to his feet as soon as the other car was out of sight. "Now, put your gun down, and perhaps I shall let you live."

"You're some kind of lunatic. I can blow the broad away with no more than a twitch of my finger, pal, so put your blade down or she's history."

"If you shoot her, the soldiers from the bank will come running," Al said.

"Soldiers? What the hell are you, nuts?"

At that precise moment, one of the cops leaving the bank stepped out, glanced their way, and pointed right at Al. Several others followed as he came running, shouting that he'd spotted the suspect. The commotion took Al's attention away from Guido for the briefest instant, and Guido whirled on him, gun raised.

With barely a sideways glance, Al flicked his sword, almost carelessly, and the gun flew from de Rocci's hand and skittered across the sidewalk. Then Al backhanded the mob boss, and sent Guido sprawling.

The creep reached for his gun, even as M. C. was yanking the car door open and snatching up her own. She aimed it at his head. "Lie still, you slug. Al, get in. Quick!"

The cops ran closer, reaching for their weapons now. Al dove into the car, clambered into the passenger seat, and pulled M. C. in behind him. She slammed the door, turned the key, and laid rubber, cutting into traffic and drawing a half dozen horn blasts and hand gestures on the way.

Moments later, she heard the sirens. Hell, she was being chased by half the cops in Newark, and probably half the mob hit men as well. Traffic was bad. Almost at a standstill up ahead. She glanced at Al. He stared back, looking wor-

ried. And then she smiled and jerked the wheel. She laid
on the horn as the car bumped over the curb and onto the
sidewalk. People scattered like autumn leaves in front of
a strong wind. She took out a few parking meters, but
figured it was them or the pedestrians. She swung left, the
wrong way down a one-way street, but the fastest route
away from the city. By the time she emerged on a side
road, she'd lost them. Lost them!

"Hot damn, I'm good," she said, and slowed the car
down to keep from attracting notice, turning onto less and
less traveled streets until she was completely away from
the city.

Al didn't answer. She looked his way, and saw how pale
he was. Looked as if he might lose his lunch, too. "You
okay, Al?"

He swallowed hard, and nodded. "Of course," he said.
"The question is, are you?" The dazed expression left his
eyes, and they filled instead with concern as he scanned
her face. "Did that brute harm you, Mary Catherine?"

"No. But he would have." She drew a deep breath and
prepared to eat crow. "You were . . . pretty incredible back
there, Al. I didn't think you'd stand a chance against de
Rocci and his gun-toting goons. I mean, with nothing but
that sword. But you . . ." She shook her head and sighed.
"You saved my butt, Al. I owe you one."

He looked away, almost as if he were embarrassed by
her praise. "It is what I came here to do," he said. "And
what I have spent most of my life doing. You should not
be so surprised."

She nodded. "My mistake. I suppose a guy who fights
for a living learns a few things along the way."

"You suppose correctly."

She reached over to touch his shoulder. "I'm sorry I
doubted you."

He said nothing. Insulted at her surprise, she figured.

"Look, Al, I've never known a man like you, okay? I

mean, most guys . . . hell, they aren't tough like you. They haven't needed to be. The world's too modern. They don't need to hunt for food or cut wood for fires or learn to fight. They've got grocery stores and fuel oil and sophisticated weapons. Just aim and shoot your way out of trouble. Simple. Barely any skill to it. A trained monkey could do it.''

He finally looked at her. And he was smiling when he did, which relieved her a little bit. He'd saved her life, after all. Insulting him was the last thing she'd meant to do.

"It works to my advantage, their softness."

"Does it?"

He nodded. "That man seemed to think that because he had his pistol in hand, he had nothing to fear. He did not expect me to resist."

"I guess you taught him a thing or two," she said, and she couldn't help smiling back. "I wish I could have seen his face when you flicked that sword of yours and sent his gun sailing. I'll bet he looked like an air-starved trout."

Al frowned and tilted his head. "His mouth was open. And his eyes did seem to bulge a bit."

Mary Catherine laughed out loud, tipping her head back. "You're something, Al. You really are."

Al nodded, but his expression turned serious. "It will not be so easy next time," he said.

M. C. felt her smile die. "You're right. He's not going to underestimate you again." But then she brightened and patted her pocket. "But we're halfway home, Al. I got the tape."

Al sent her an approving glance. "I knew you would. What must we do next, to bring this de Rocci to justice?"

Mary Catherine licked her lips in thought. "We have to get the tape to the district attorney. I don't trust anyone else. I want to personally put it into his hands. But it won't be easy."

"Nothing worthwhile ever is."

"You got that right." She took another turn, picking up speed. "We're going to have to ditch the car, Al. De Rocci's seen it, and by now the cops have the plate number. Then we'll find a place to lay low, call the D.A. and set up a meeting."

Al nodded. "A wise course of action," he said.

"By the time we get settled in, D.A. Hennesey will be out of his office for the night. I doubt his home phone is listed." He looked at her curiously, and she clarified. "We probably won't be able to reach him until tomorrow."

"Then our immediate concern is for a safe place to spend the night," he said, cutting right to the heart of the matter.

"Right. We'll head into the next town, leave the car at a diner, and call a cab to take us to a motel."

"A cab?"

"A . . . car for hire," she explained.

Al frowned, rubbing his chin. "Would the . . . er . . . police not be able to question the driver of this . . . cab, to find out where we'd gone?"

M. C. clapped a hand to her forehead. "You're right. Hell, how are we going to get anywhere without a car?"

Al looked at her as if she were sprouting a second head. "You were right before, Mary Catherine. The modern world has made things far too easy."

Al kept it to himself, but he'd been as amazed by Mary Catherine's strength as she had been by his ability. Any other woman he'd known would have been in tears, become paralyzed with fear, or simply fainted away, had she found herself in a similar situation. A lowlife manhandling her, a weapon pressed to her tender belly. But Mary Catherine had defied the dog, insulted him, refused to cower.

She was, quite simply, amazing.

He suggested she drive far from the city, into as rural

an area as the modern world had to offer. And instead of "ditching" her aunt's contraption, whatever that meant, he'd persuaded her to trust its care to a farmer. Indeed, he'd managed to talk the kind man into letting them rent a pair of horses for the night, leaving the car as a sort of collateral to ensure their return.

The man's eyes had widened when Al had offered him a handful of gold coins in exchange for the use of his horses. He'd examined them carefully, while M. C. had elbowed Alexandre in the rib cage.

When he looked her way, she whispered, "Those coins are probably worth a fortune, Al!"

"Nonsense. 'Tis a pittance."

"Not in this day and age. If you have any more, hold on to them, for heaven's sake."

He shrugged, quite befuddled. But the man pocketed the coins, grinning hugely, and was only too happy to comply when Alexandre asked him to keep the car in his barn overnight. To protect it from the elements, he said, though his true motive was to keep it from prying eyes.

He thought he'd done quite well, until the farmer led two graying, swaybacked mares from his barn, decked out in worn saddles and bridles whose straps were split with age.

"Are these the only two you have?" Alexandre asked, running a hand along one horse's neck and feeling the matted coat in dire need of grooming.

" 'Fraid so," the man said. "Take 'em or leave 'em."

"Er . . . Al?"

Alexandre shook his head at M. C., then addressed the man. "Perhaps I shall give you more coin upon our return. So that you can purchase some oats for these animals, and perhaps a brush."

The man frowned, unsure about whether he'd just been insulted, but unwilling to let the possibility of more gold slip by him. Finally he nodded. "That'd be real kind of you, mister."

Alexandre nodded. "Then I shall, provided you keep all of this to yourself. The lady and I do not wish to be disturbed tonight."

The farmer smiled widely, and winked. "Mum's the word."

"Al," M. C. said, and she tugged on his long coat this time. He turned to her. "We'll only be needing one horse," she told him. "Unless you want to see me fall on my butt."

Alexandre frowned. "You do not ride?"

"Never have. And won't start now if we have a choice."

"A choice, my lady, is one thing we do not have. I shall teach you. Fear not."

She tugged him aside, her voice low. "Al, I mean it. I don't want a horse all to myself. Can't I just ride with you?"

His heart tripped over itself. So it was his closeness she craved, even still, after all she'd been through today. He stroked her hair and fought the desire rising like a tide within him. "I'd like nothing better than to hold you close to me in the saddle, sweet one. But I've already explained why that cannot be. Not yet," he added, lest she think he did not return her ardor.

Her jaw dropped. She closed it. "Get over yourself, Al. I'm scared to ride one of these smelly beasts all by myself, and that's all there is to it!"

He smiled slightly and nodded. "Of course you are. You, a woman who stands face-to-face with an armed blackguard, and looks him in the eye without a trace of fear. Of course you're afraid of an old, plodding horse."

"But it's the truth! I am!"

He closed his eyes briefly, the exquisite agony of self-denial like a firestorm in his gut. "Soon," he whispered, leaning closer and looking into her eyes. "It will be soon, Mary Catherine. And worth every second of waiting. I promise."

He held her gaze with his, and saw a gleam of passion flit into her eyes. But she blinked, hiding it quickly, looking away. "You're an arrogant jackass."

He laughed softly. "Nonetheless, neither of these mares looks strong enough to carry us both. Much as the thought of holding you nestled between my thighs with your back pressed to my chest, and my arms tight around your waist, might tempt me. I am afraid we have no choice."

She pressed a hand to her belly, biting her lip, a little breathless, he thought.

He turned back to the man, nodded his thanks, and scooped Mary Catherine off her feet and into his arms. He deposited her gently into the saddle, held her waist until she seemed to get her balance. It surprised him when she changed position, moving one leg to the other side so she sat astride, rather than sidesaddle, but he made no comment as he then bent to adjust the stirrups for her. A second later, he swung easily onto his own mount.

Then he turned to her. "Hold to the pommel, lady, and hand the reins to me."

She gripped the pommel until her knuckles were white as Alexandre set his horse into motion at a slow, easy pace.

"Great," she muttered. "So I suppose I'm stuck here on this animal's back until we get to the nearest motel, right?"

"Quite wrong, dear lady. We will be far less likely to be discovered if we make camp in yonder woods. Very deep in them, I should think."

"But . . . but, Al, I'm hungry. We haven't eaten. And we don't have blankets or . . . or *anything*."

"We have all we need, Mary Catherine." He looked back at her, wondering how a woman could be so capable and yet so utterly helpless at the same time. "Have no fear. I am your Musketeer, Lady Hammer. I will feed you and keep you warm. On my sword, I will.''

He saw her pale, and then her throat moved as if she were trying to swallow and couldn't.

Seven

She had no idea what he was looking for as they plodded deeper and deeper into the state forest that bordered the farmer's property. But he was definitely looking for something. Scanning the trees, eyeing everything around them, until finally, he nodded and drew his horse to a halt.

"This will do nicely."

M. C. looked around. "What will do nicely?"

"This spot. To make camp." He dismounted and walked to her horse, clasped her waist in his big hands, and lifted her down. As soon as she put weight on her legs, she felt the burn and pull of muscles she didn't know she had. Her rear end hurt. Al saw her wince, and smiled. "No doubt it will be worse in the morn. If I could have spared you the riding, I would have."

She shook her head and limped toward a soft patch of ground to sit. Al led the horses away from her, to a stream she hadn't even noticed before, and let them drink. Then he took an ancient-looking length of rope from one of the saddles, slicing it neatly in half with a dagger he'd pulled from his boot. "I'll picket them nearby, where there's grass," he said, and led the horses farther along the stream's bank.

M. C. leaned back on her hands and wondered what she'd got herself into this time. She was stuck here, alone with Al in the middle of the forest, for the night. Al, who'd somehow wound up with the idea that she was burning up with lust for him. Not that he wasn't attractive. He was. Very. Okay, so he wasn't the kind of man she'd toss out of bed for eating crackers, but he wasn't her type, either.

She frowned, realizing how little sense that thought made. Her types—the types she'd usually ended up dating, way back when she'd still been dating at all—were losers. Oh, they always seemed okay at first. But then they'd reveal themselves. There was Mike, who'd kept hitting her up for money. Kevin, who'd been busted for dealing drugs after their second date. And Tom, who'd been married. The slug.

And there was Al. A guy who put honor above everything else, who could handle a sword like some kind of master, and who was so polite it was sickening. A guy who'd refused to leave her until he knew she was safe.

Definitely not her type. Al was no loser.

Problem was, he had to leave. But why was that so important, anyway? It wasn't like she was going to go and fall in love with him or anything. Why not enjoy the guy while he was here?

He appeared then from the trees, his arms loaded down with limbs and deadfall. Dropping the pile to the ground, he shrugged out of his coat and crouched beside it. His jeans pulled tight to his backside when he crouched like that. And the black T-shirt he wore clung. He had great arms. Hard. Nice.

M. C. got up, deciding to keep her thoughts in line by keeping busy with other things. "I'll help gather wood," she said.

"Nonsense, lady. Gathering wood for the fire is a man's job."

Aha. There it was. She'd known there had to be something wrong with him. No man could be as perfect as he was beginning to seem to her. He was a chauvinist.

"This is the twentieth century, Al. There are no men's jobs or women's work anymore. Women in this day and age can be police officers or firefighters or world leaders if they want to. And men cook and clean and change diapers."

He went still, his back to her, still crouching over the fire he'd begun to lay on a bare spot of ground. "I have offended you," he said softly. "I am sorry, Lady Hammer. Chivalry . . . is a part of being a man, in my time. It is difficult to understand how it can have become an insult in only a few centuries."

"Chivalry." She repeated the word.

Sighing deeply, Al resumed piling dried leaves and twigs, adding larger pieces of wood on top of them. "Yes. The men of my generation are not fools, Mary Catherine. It has never been a matter of believing a woman *incapable* of doing heavy work. Only a matter of believing she should not have to do it."

"I see."

He straightened, turning to come close to her, and then dropping to one knee in front of her. "I do not think you do. In my time, Mary Catherine, we cherished our women. Treated them as the precious, beloved creatures they are. The only hope for the continuation of our race, the mothers of our children." He took her hand in his, tracing its contours with the tip of a forefinger. "Look at this hand. Beautiful, delicate . . . capable, yes, but small and fragile." Then he turned their clasped hands over, so his was on top. "Mine, however, is large, hard, and callused. Rough work, unpleasant tasks . . . are beneath a creature as magical as a woman. She . . . you . . . should be adored, treasured—respected as the beautiful being you are. The mother of mankind. Not asked to bruise this lovely hand on something as far beneath you as gathering wood."

She couldn't breathe. His voice had gone soft and deep, and it touched nerve endings somewhere inside her that came to life all at once. Then he brought her hand to his lips, and kissed it gently. "A woman like you should be given anything she desires."

"A-and . . . what if what she desires is to help gather firewood?"

He lifted his head away from her hand, but it tingled where his mouth had touched. Holding her gaze pinned to his, he smiled slightly. "Then she should gather firewood."

"You . . . don't think I'm too weak for the job?"

"Weak?" His brows rose. "I've never known a woman with your strength, Mary Catherine. But even the most fragile female has the ability in her to capture a man's heart—to bear his children. Surely the latter task takes far more strength than to gather branches from the forest floor. More strength, perhaps, than that of any man."

"I imagine so."

"I'll start the fire," he told her. "If you wish to gather more wood, then do so. But if you'd rather rest from the ride, consider me your humble servant." He bowed his head.

For just a moment she had the craziest feeling that she was some kind of queen, and the grass underneath her a throne. Whoa, what a sensation! She had to concede he wasn't exactly a chauvinist. There was, she decided, a difference between chauvinism and chivalry.

Al rose and returned to his pile of kindling, pulling a flintstone from his pocket and crouching again.

Mary Catherine got up and went to crouch beside him, reaching into her own pocket. "You can put the stone away, Al. I have something better."

He eyed the lighter in her hand. "Another wonder of your modern world?"

"You're gonna love this," she said, and she flicked the

lighter. He smiled when a flame appeared. She touched it
to the dried leaves at the base of the pile and watched the
flames lick up at them, catch, and begin to spread to the
kindling.

"Wonderful," he said.

M. C. sat back on her heels as the fire took hold, and
she began to think that maybe being up here with him all
night wasn't such a terrible thing.

"So, did you mean all that stuff you said about women,
Al, or is that a line you use to charm them out of their
pantaloons?"

He laughed softly, shaking his head. "I meant it."

"You really believe a woman can do just about anything
a man can?"

"Some women," he said. "You, for example."

"That's good, because I want to ask you to do something for me. And it might not be the kind of request
you're used to getting from women."

He met her eyes, a reflection of the growing fire dancing
deep in his own. "Ask me anything, Mary Catherine."

She smiled at him. "Teach me how to use that sword
of yours."

His eyes opened wide, but then his lips curved, and he
shook his head slowly. "Why should that request surprise
me coming from you? If you wish to learn, Mary Catherine, I will teach you."

This night was looking better and better.

"But first," he said, "I will find us something to eat."
He added larger pieces of wood to the fire, then rose,
glancing around the woods. "I saw signs of deer nearby.
Also possum, and quail."

"Um, I'd rather go hungry than eat a possum, Al."

He bowed slightly. "Then I shall not bring one for your
dinner."

*　　*　　*

He didn't bring her a possum. He brought a wild turkey big enough to feed a dozen people. M. C. had busied herself gathering more firewood and making a neat stack of it. She'd checked on the horses twice, and was beginning to get bored and more than slightly worried about Al, though she knew she probably should have known better. Then he showed up with the turkey. He'd quite chivalrously taken care of the nastier parts of preparing wild game far away from camp, lest her delicate female stomach protest.

She was glad of it, too.

This bird he brought was ready for the oven. Or the campfire, in this case. It didn't look anything like what she was used to seeing in the grocery stores or on Thanksgiving tables. It was skinnier, longer, and not as smooth and shiny.

She was surprised when he began cutting it up with his dagger. It was stupid of her to have expected him to roast it whole, she mused; it would have taken half the night. Then he skewered hunks of meat, and using forked branches to hold them up, set them to cook over the fire.

Before long the tantalizing aroma had her stomach growling out loud. He pretended not to notice, but she knew he had to hear it. Then she wondered why she cared.

He turned the meat until it was done, then handed her a sizzling, perfectly browned breast portion. One bite and she was in heaven. "God, this is good," she mumbled, and ate some more.

Al seemed equally enamored of his own helping of turkey. But as M. C.'s stomach got full, her mind turned to other matters. "Al, how did you get this bird without a gun?"

He reached down to his boot and withdrew the dagger. Then replaced it, as if he had answered her question.

"But . . . you couldn't just sneak up on the bird and—"

He shook his head. "The dagger is perfectly balanced. An excellent throwing blade."

M. C. blinked. "You *threw* your knife at the turkey? And you hit him?"

Al tilted his head. "It would hardly be worthwhile to throw the dagger and miss him, Mary Catherine."

"Oh. Well, how practical." She finished her meat, licked her fingers, and got to her feet. "So will you show me how to use the sword now?"

"Of course." He got up as well, his rapier dangling from a belt at his waist. He wasn't wearing the coat now, so the sword was in plain sight. M. C. stepped forward and reached for it. Al dodged her, shaking his head. "*Non.* You must learn *before* I entrust you with the actual weapon."

M. C. frowned at him. "How am I supposed to learn without a sword?"

"I brought you a . . . a practice sword," he said, and nodded toward the large tree behind her. She saw a long, narrow stick—a branch with all its twigs and leaves stripped off—leaning against the massive trunk.

"You want me to use *that*?"

"For now," he told her. "Trust me, Mary Catherine. I have no desire to lose a hand or to see you lose an eye when you make a misstep. This will be safer."

"You sound like my mother. 'You could put an eye out, Mary Catherine.' "

"A wise woman, your mother. It would be a shame for harm to come to such beautiful eyes."

She averted her "*beautiful*" eyes now, turning to pick up her stick instead of letting him see her blush yet again.

"They're like rich brown velvet, you know," he went on.

"Or mud," she replied.

Al chuckled, and it did something wild to her insides. He had a sexy laugh—she'd give him that much. She gripped her stick and turned to face him. "So what do I do with it?"

Al lifted his sword, holding his opposite hand up in the air behind him. "*En garde,* my lady."

Eight

Wielding a sword was nowhere near as easy as Al made it look. M. C. discovered that while trying to mimic his graceful moves with her stick. To her credit, she only whacked him upside the head twice, but he had a bright red welt to show for it. Still, he'd kept his patience, and she thought she'd mastered a move or two by they time they finished.

"Now," Al said, gently closing his hand on the hilt of her branch and taking it from her. "Try it with a real sword."

She was breathless, and she had no doubt her face was bright red from exertion—while he stood there as relaxed as if he'd just been napping. No doubt about it, the guy was in great shape. She, on the other hand, definitely needed to do more aerobics. Or something.

He dropped the stick to the ground and pressed his gleaming sword into her hand. "Like this," he said, guiding her fingers around the grip, then covering them with his own. "Ready?"

She nodded. Al stepped away from her . . . a good three feet away, and that made her grin. "How can I fight without an opponent?"

He smiled back at her, and it made her heart skip. "For now, your opponent is going to have to be make believe, *ma belle*. Imagine Monsieur de Rocci standing before you."

M. C. narrowed her eyes. "That should help immensely. Can I castrate him?"

Al frowned. "You are more bloodthirsty than I realized."

"Only for de Rocci," she said, and she lifted the sword as he'd shown her. "It's heavier than the stick," she said, then she brought it down in a sweeping arc.

"*Bon*. Now thrust! Parry! Dodge! Block!" As he shouted commands, she obeyed, and she couldn't deny she felt incredibly powerful wielding the weapon—though not exactly graceful, nearly tripping over her feet once. Still, when she finished, he nodded in approval. "You are an excellent student, Mary Catherine. You learn quickly."

She nodded, smiling, breathless. "I only wish you were going to be around longer." Then she bit her lip. She hadn't thought about his leaving lately, but now the idea made her inexplicably sad. And not just because he wouldn't be around to give her lessons.

She actually *liked* the guy. Amazing.

"I wish it, too," he said softly.

"What was your life like before I stole you away from it, Al?" Her voice was softer than usual, she realized.

"Ah, my life before." Did he sound wistful? "It was a grand adventure, Mary Catherine. To be a Musketeer is every Frenchman's dream . . . or it is in my time. I am respected and admired, even envied, by everyone I meet."

A man of stature, she mused. Successful and in love with his work. "Did you have any family?"

He lowered his eyes. "I was my parents' only child. They died of a fever when I was still young, so I was reared by my uncle, who had served with the Musketeers before he finally married and settled down. He is gone now, too. I have no family. But then, a Musketeer is better off without one. My life is my work, you see.''

"And love?''

Shrugging his broad shoulders, Alexandre smiled. "When love comes, *it* will become my life. For true love alone, would I lay down my sword. Until that day comes I am happy to fight for right and the honor of the king. Each day brings a new challenge, a new adventure.''

"A new woman . . . ?''

His smile changed to one filled with mischief. "Sometimes. A warrior never knows which day will be his last, so he tends to make the most of his nights. But sex is not love, my Lady Hammer. Those moonlight trysts meant nothing, neither to me nor to the ladies involved. And I think you are wise enough to know this.''

She wondered if it would mean anything if *she* were "the lady involved." Then told herself it didn't matter. He stepped closer, brushing a damp tendril of hair from her face. "You are tired now, and it has grown late. We should rest.''

Her throat went dry. "All right.''

Al stoked the fire, then laid the saddles on the ground to use as pillows. He put them very close together, she noticed. Then he picked up his long coat. Stretching out on the ground, he pulled the coat over him, then held one side up and looked at her. "Come, Mary Catherine. You know you've nothing to fear.''

"I know,'' she said, maybe a tad defensively. "I'm not afraid.'' Or if she was, it wasn't for the reasons he was thinking. Lying so close to him all night long—and not touching him—was going to be a challenge. It wasn't Al she was worried about, it was herself. Did women come on to men in his time? What would he think of her if she—

What was she thinking? He was the one obsessed with sex, not her. And since he'd vowed not to touch her until his role as protector was fulfilled, she didn't have a thing to worry about.

Did she?

"Mary Catherine?"

His brows were arched as he lay there waiting for her, looking like a centerfold—except that he had his clothes on. M. C. sighed and went to him, slid underneath the coat, and laid her head on the saddle.

"Good night, my lady. Sleep well."

" 'Night, Al," she said, but she didn't think she was going to sleep.

She did. Must have, because when she woke up, her head was no longer pillowed by the saddle, but by something far warmer, soft and firm at the same time, and with a much nicer smell.

She opened her eyes to the brilliance of dawn, and realized what it was. Al's chest. And his arms were wrapped around her, one hand buried in her hair. One of her legs had decided to rest atop both of his, and her arms were twined around his waist.

He smelled good. God, he did, and he was so warm and hard underneath her. She lifted her head, wondering if she could slip away before he woke. But when she looked at his eyes, she found them open, staring into hers, a fire burning in their depths.

"*Mon Dieu,*" he whispered. "You are . . . so beautiful."

His lips were only inches from hers, and pulling her closer, like magnets. Drawing her. She didn't fight it. She let her mouth be tugged to his until their lips touched. And then Al's arms tightened around her, and he kissed her. His mouth pushed at hers until she opened to him, then his tongue slid inside to lick and caress. She'd never known her mouth could be such an erogenous zone. She'd never been kissed like this. Tenderness and passion at once. She wanted him. It hit her like a bullet between the eyes. She wanted to make love to this man. Here. Now.

She was practically on top of him now, and as he continued kissing her, she moved the rest of the way. Her legs straddled his, and she felt his arousal pressing hard between them. But then his hands came to her shoulders, and gently, he lifted her away.

"Never," he whispered, "has temptation been so difficult to resist."

"For me, either." She leaned forward to kiss him again, but he held her away.

"Yet resist I must." He closed his eyes, as if in pain. "But if desire can kill a man, I'll not live much longer."

"Al, don't . . ."

"We mustn't. It was my vow, long ago—the code by which I've lived. I am your protector until you are safe. And only that."

M. C. went stiff, staring down at him in disbelief. "You're kidding, aren't you?"

"If I make love to you now, Mary Catherine, my thoughts will be of nothing else for days to come. I will be distracted, even weakened by a desire this fierce, the memory of a pleasure sweeter than any I've known. *No* . . . I cannot."

M. C. rolled off him and got to her feet. "Fine. That's just fine with me, Al. I didn't want to anyway!"

"I have hurt you." He rose and came to stand behind her, his hands massaging her shoulders. "Make no mistake, *ma chérie,* were it not for my vow, for honor's sake, I—"

"Oh, to hell with you and your damned honor."

She pulled away, busied herself dousing the dwindling fire, scooping dirt over the coals.

"You do not mean that."

"Let's just get out of here, okay? Let's just find a phone, call the D.A., and set up the appointment."

He stood where he was. "This is as difficult for me as for you, Mary Catherine."

She ignored him, embarrassed, downright stung by his rejection. "We'll have to find a car. Can't use Aunt Kate's even if no one's found it by now. The cops have probably called her by now—they'd have traced the plate number and—"

Mary Catherine stopped talking and bit her lip. "Oh my God."

Al was beside her in a second, his hands gripping her shoulders again. "What it is?"

"The license plate. Oh, God, why didn't I think of this last night? Al, Guido saw that plate. He can probably track down the car's owner as easily as the police can!"

"Your aunt?" he asked, looking worried.

"She could be in danger. We have to call her, Al, tell her to get out of the house and lay low for a while." She looked into his eyes, shook her head as a ball of dread formed in the pit of her stomach. "And we'd better do it fast."

The woman was a bundle of contradictions. First she denied wanting him, a habit which had begun to make him doubt himself for the first time in recent memory. Then she'd made it all too clear that she *did* want him. And then she'd become angry, unable, or perhaps—as stubborn as she was—un*willing* to understand his reasons. But all of that had fallen by the wayside when she'd realized she might have inadvertently put her aunt in danger.

As they rode side by side, he watched her. The way her eyes took on such intensity when she was worried. The way the wind tossed her dark hair and the morning sun made it gleam.

He'd wanted many women, had most of them. But never had he felt anything like what he was feeling now. It wasn't just stronger, it was different. An entirely new

brand of desire he'd never felt before. And it left him with
the odd sense that everything he'd experienced before had
been only a faint foreshadowing of this . . . this new and
powerful feeling.

Would it fade once they'd given in to its demand and
made love together? That was the way it usually worked
for Alexandre. But he had a feeling it wouldn't be the same
this time. Nothing seemed the same this time.

When they finally arrived back at the farm, the farmer
greeted them with a smile and a wave from his front porch.
Mary Catherine was off her mount almost before it came
to a stop, and heading up the steps. "Please," she said
breathlessly, "I need to use your phone. I'll pay you for
the call, but—"

"Sure, sure. Come on inside. So how was your ride?
The horses look none the worse for wear."

Mary Catherine didn't answer, just hurried past him and
into the house. Alexandre watched as the farmer leaned
through the door and pointed, then turned to face him
again, grinning expectantly.

Alexandre dismounted and took another gold coin from
his pocket, handing it to the man.

"Thank you kindly," the older man said, smiling.

Al nodded and turned to remove the saddles.

"Oh, now, don't you bother with that."

"The animals are hot," Al said. "They need to be
rubbed down."

"And Tony will take care of it," the farmer insisted.
Then he cupped his hands and yelled, and a young man
emerged from the barn. As he hurried across the lawn toward the house, the farmer said, "See, I took them coins
you gave me yesterday into town this morning and had
'em appraised. When I found out what they were worth, I
figured I could afford to hire me a hand around here."

Alexandre frowned. Perhaps Mary Catherine had been
right about the coins' value.

Tony arrived, looked at the horses, then at the farmer. "These are the ones? When's the last time they were groomed, anyway?"

"Been a while," the farmer said, chuckling. "Tony here is real experienced with horses. He'll have 'em in tip-top shape in no time."

Alexandre saw the way the boy's hands were already moving over the animals' coats. It was obvious he not only knew about horses, but cared about them. At least one good thing had come of his visit here.

Then the bang of the door drew his gaze, and he saw Mary Catherine standing there, looking pale and wide-eyed.

"What is it, *chérie*? Did you reach your aunt with the telephone device?"

She nodded, closed her eyes. "Guido de Rocci answered the phone."

Alexandre shook his head, not certain he understood.

"He's there, at her house, Al," she went on. "He has her, and he won't let her go unless we give him the tape."

Nine

There was no time to find another car. M. C. backed Aunt Kate's car out of the farmer's dim, dusty barn without a thought about how many cops might spot it on the road. If she saw flashing lights behind her on the way, she would keep right on going.

"It will be all right," Al said softly, touching her shoulder, drawing her gaze.

She glanced his way as she drove, saw the concern in his eyes. But not for Aunt Kate. His worry was for her, and for what she might be feeling right now. "How can you be so sure of that?" M. C. asked. "For all we know Aunt Kate could already be—"

"No." Al said it firmly. "De Rocci isn't stupid. He wants to trade your aunt for this tape. He cannot do that unless he keeps her alive."

M. C. tried to keep her eyes on the road, tried to keep her speed to within ten miles an hour above the speed limit, though every instinct was to press the pedal to the floor. If she showed up with cops in tow, the whole thing could turn into a standoff, with her odd, eccentric aunt playing hostage. Aunt Kate would be in far less danger this way.

"What do you want to do when we get there?" Al asked softly.

She glanced at him again, surprised that he would ask. He was the expert in fighting here. But she was the expert on nineties goons like de Rocci. "I don't think we have a choice, Al. I'll have to give him the tape."

Al's lips pursed.

"What?" she asked. "You think it's the wrong decision, don't you?"

"I think . . . you're wrong about one thing. We *do* have a choice. And we have to make it carefully. Mary Catherine, do you really think de Rocci will let you or your aunt leave that house alive once he has the tape?"

M. C. sighed, grating her teeth. Al was right. He was so right. "No, he won't. He can't. We'd have him dead to rights on unlawful imprisonment, breaking and entering, maybe assault. And he has to know I can testify as to what I heard on that tape, even if the tape itself is long gone."

"Then we cannot turn it over."

"But Al, what else can we do? He's there, and you can bet he's not alone. He knows we're coming, and he'll be watching for us. How can we . . . ?"

"There's always a way, Mary Catherine. Trust me."

She looked into Al's eyes, and realized that she did trust him. She'd trust him with her life. When the hell had she decided to believe in him this much? But no matter, she had. And she nodded to tell him so.

"Good," he said. "And let us not forget, your aunt Kate is not *entirely* without resources of her own."

They left the car nearly a mile from the house, hidden behind a neighbor's hedges on a side road. Then they walked. And not on the narrow lanes of the suburban-leaning-toward-rural town of Craven Falls, either. They crossed back lawns and vacant lots, skirting the edges of trees and bushes and woodlots where they could. And soon the gothic white elephant was in sight. Flat roof, widow's walk in need of another coat of white paint, curlicues of wood trim everywhere. Tall, narrow windows, their curtains drawn tight like closed eyes, as if the house were sound asleep.

A parked car with two men inside sat opposite Aunt Kate's driveway. A shadowy form lurked just beyond the back door. From their position behind some trees in the back lawn, they could glimpse him when he moved.

"They'll have a man at the front door as well," Al said. "What we need is another way inside. But first"—he glanced toward the car out front—"we should eliminate some of the contenders."

"Even up the odds," M. C. said. "Gotcha. I can take care of the ones in the car, Al. All I need is a roll of duct tape, a length of garden hose, and a pair of shears." She glanced around. "I imagine I can find all of that in the toolshed."

Taking her arm, he started toward the shed, but she shook her head at him. "No. Look, try to get a look inside, make sure Aunt Kate's okay. I can handle this part alone."

He frowned. "I think we should stay together, lady. It would be safer."

"I'm a big girl, Al. And I'm worried about my aunt. Please, I'll feel so much better knowing you're close by, keeping an eye on her."

Closing his eyes, he nodded once. "All right. I know you're more than capable." Then he closed his hand on her outer arms and drew her close to him. "Be careful, *ma chérie*." And he kissed her, hard and fast.

She blinked, tried to catch her breath, gave her head a shake. "Don't let them hurt her, Al. I'm counting on you."

"You have my word as a Musketeer, Mary Catherine. No harm will come to your aunt."

As soon as he said it, she knew it was true. Amazing how much faith she'd come to have in him. She looked at his face, dark eyes blazing into hers, one last time, then crouched low and made a dash to the toolshed. She didn't pause, but yanked the door open and ducked inside. Then she peered back toward the house to see how Al was doing, and caught her breath.

He gave a hop, reaching overhead to catch hold of a tree limb. Then he swung back and forth, faster and faster, his body sailing higher into the air each time, and finally, on the biggest upswing yet, he just let go.

His momentum carried him higher, and he flipped in midair before catching hold of the edge of the flat, tar-coated roof. Carefully, he pulled himself up and crept toward the widow's walk at the center.

M. C. couldn't believe it. He could have broken his neck. Shivering, she glanced through the shed's dusty window toward the guys in the car, but they hadn't moved. Didn't seem as if they'd noticed a thing amiss.

She flicked the lighter to see in the darkness and foraged for the tools she needed. It didn't take long to find them. She let the lighter go out, pocketed the shears and the tape, and carried the length of hose in one hand. As an afterthought she pulled out her gun with the other. Just in case. Then she crept out of the shed and across the lawn, keeping low, using the hedges for cover. When she ran out of hedges, she dropped to the ground and crawled right up to the car, which the fools had left running. Hadn't anyone ever told them how dangerous that could be? She ripped off some tape with her teeth, stuck the hose into the exhaust pipe, and wrapped it up tight. Then she took the other end of the hose with her as she wriggled on her back underneath the car. Right under the driver's seat, she found the air vent, and she stuck the hose right there.

Then she shimmied out again and made her way to the backyard, all without once being seen.

She smiled to herself. She was good.

But Al was better.

When she looked up she saw a length of rope dangling from a hidden corner of the roof. He'd left her a way inside.

What a guy.

When she crept down the attic stairs, praying none would creak and give her away, she wished to heaven she knew where everyone was. She got to the second-floor hall and started down it on tiptoe, passing each closed bedroom door with her ears straining and her heart in her throat.

Then one opened just as she moved past, and she was pulled inside. A big hand covered her mouth, and the room was utterly dark. She struggled . . . but briefly. That wide chest behind her; that scent. She stilled, waiting. The hand left her mouth, and she whispered, "Al?"

"*Oui, ma chérie.* Who else?"

"Did you find them? Is my aunt all right?"

"She is fine. In the next bedroom. De Rocci is with her. As far as I can tell there are two others in the house, one at the front door, one at the back. It would be best if we could eliminate them at the same time."

"That way neither has time to warn the other."

"Or to warn de Rocci," Al said. "The men in the car?"

"They'll be sleeping by the time we get downstairs." She couldn't see his frown, but knew it was there, all the same. "I'll explain later. Trust me, Al, they're not going to be a problem."

"I do trust you," he said. "It is odd, being in battle with a woman at my side. But even more strange to feel so certain she is equal to the task. You are . . . you are a special woman, Mary Catherine."

"Glad you realize it," she said. "Now let's get this show on the road."

"I'll take the back door," he told her. And she had no doubt he'd already checked the two men out, and decided the guy by the back door was bigger, or meaner, or more dangerous. Not that she minded.

"Let's make it quick and quiet, okay?" She didn't wait for an answer. "Meet you at the bottom of the stairs." Then she ducked out the door and headed down.

Al came behind her, and he squeezed her hand at the base of the stairs before they turned in opposite directions. M. C. drew her gun and crept into the living room. It was dim, but not all that dark, despite the fact that the lights were all out and the curtains drawn tight. She could see the guy fairly well. He was looking outside, expecting visitors from there, not from within. She crept closer, lifting her gun. She was almost right behind him when she heard a dull thud, a low grunt from the back of the house, followed by what had to be a body slumping to the floor. The goon heard it too, and spun. But she clocked him with the pistol butt before he came to a stop, and he sank to the floor like a limp noodle. M. C. pocketed the gun, yanked out the duct tape, and used it to tie him up. A little more over the mouth. Perfect.

She headed back to the stairway and met Al at the bottom. "Done?" he asked.

"*Fini,*" she replied. He grinned at her and they took the stairs together. "Now what?"

"Now, I go back to the roof, and you to the door of your aunt's room."

"Ah, we enter from two directions."

Al nodded. "But take care. Do not stand directly in front of the door, Mary Catherine. I've no desire to lose you now."

She caught her breath. Silly thing for him to say. He'd be going back when this was over. Losing her was inevitable. She gave her head a shake to rid herself of that thought. "Don't worry. I've done this sort of thing once or twice."

He nodded, and headed up the attic stairs. She gave him

a minute to get into position, then strode up to her aunt's
bedroom door and, standing to one side of it, reached out
and knocked.

"What is it?" de Rocci growled.

"Mr. de Rocci? It's M. C. Hammer. I brought that tape
like you said."

She heard footsteps coming nearer, a voice cussing.
"What the hell—how did you—?" The door was flung
open. De Rocci stood there, gun in hand, looking up and
down the hall. "Where are my men?"

"They sent me up," she said. She hoped she sounded
convincing.

De Rocci eyed her, glancing beyond her nervously, and
finally gripped her arm, pulled her into the bedroom, and
closed the door behind her. She had a brief moment to
notice her aunt, tied to a chair in one corner, a gag over
her mouth. The poor thing was wide-eyed with fear. But
then all hell broke loose. De Rocci pointed his gun at
M. C., yanked her weapon from her waistband, and demanded, "Give me the tape!" Before she could react, the
window behind him shattered as Al swung through it like
some kind of superhero.

Al landed in a ready crouch, his sword appearing in his
hand so suddenly that she never saw him draw it. De Rocci
whirled and fired. Aunt Kate sent a fierce look at his gun
and muttered something from behind her gag. It was all
over in a heartbeat. The bullet slammed into Al like a
sledgehammer, knocking him to the floor. His sword skidded across the hardwood, bumping M. C.'s feet and stopping there, and before de Rocci could turn around, she had
that baby in her hand. But she hesitated, trying to remember what the hell to do with it. De Rocci's weapon was
aiming at her as her fist clenched on the cool hilt.

And Al yelled, as if through grated teeth, "Parry!
Dodge! Thrust!"

She sliced de Rocci's gun hand, and he dropped the

weapon, cursing furiously. He lunged forward to retrieve it, but she lashed his rear end with the flat side of the blade, and he went sprawling on his face.

Al grabbed the fallen gun and held it on de Rocci. "Enough," Al managed. "It is over."

"Al!" M. C. dropped to her knees where he was. He'd pulled himself into a sitting position. His shirt was soaked in blood. She reached for him.

"Not yet, *chérie*. Untie your aunt, and use the ropes to bind de Rocci tight. Do it now. Hurry."

She nodded, understanding his urgency. He was going to lose consciousness soon, and he wanted to know she was safe before he did. She rapidly untied her aunt's hands and feet. "Are you all right, Aunt Kate? Did he hurt you?"

Kate nodded yes, then shook her head no, then reached up to undo the gag while M. C. rushed across the room to truss Guido de Rocci up like a Christmas goose. When he started cussing at her, she pulled the duct tape and smacked a strip across his mouth. "You're going down, de Rocci," she told him. "For a long, long time!"

There was a thud behind her and she turned, her heart aching as she saw Al lying on the floor, limp and unconscious. She ran to him, fell to her knees again, and yanked the T-shirt up so she could see the damage.

"Don't panic, Mary Catherine. The bullet didn't hit his heart," her aunt said softly. "It was headed that way, but I managed to give it a nudge."

M. C. frowned when she saw Al's wounds but didn't avert her eyes. She tried to wipe the blood away to see the injury better. "What are you talking about? What nudge?"

"Don't forget who I am, Mary Catherine," Aunt Kate said. "I pushed the bullet upward. So it would only hit his shoulder, the fleshy part, if my aim was any good."

"Al doesn't have any 'fleshy parts.'" Dabbing more blood away, M. C. caught her breath. Her aunt was absolutely right. The bullet had gone into his shoulder. She pushed a cloth tight to the wound to stop the bleeding. ''I can't believe it,'' she muttered.

''How can you still doubt? M. C., you managed to conjure yourself a Musketeer, and you still don't believe in magic?''

M. C. stroked Al's face with one hand, pressing a cloth to the wound with the other. ''If there were really such a thing as magic . . . ,'' she whispered.

''What, Mary Catherine? Tell me.''

She closed her eyes. ''He'd stay.''

But he wouldn't stay. It was over now, and she was safe. And it would soon be time for Al to return to his own time. His own duties. His own life. M. C.'s eyes burned inexplicably, and her stomach churned, and her heart felt as if it was breaking just a little bit.

''Call the police, will you, Aunt Kate? And the D.A. And an ambulance for Al.''

Aunt Kate nodded, reaching for the phone. ''We won't need the ambulance though. A scratch like that we can tend right here.'' M. C. opened her mouth, but her aunt shook a finger. ''Don't you go doubting me again, young lady.''

Lowering her head, M. C. sighed. ''I won't.''

Ten

Between the two of them, Aunt Kate and M. C. managed to get Al into the bed. He came around while they were doing it, argued a bit, but finally resigned himself to submitting. He was outnumbered anyway. Sirens were screaming closer by the second, so at least de Rocci and his goon squad wouldn't be sitting around the house much longer.

M. C. rolled her eyes and shook her head a lot when Aunt Kate used one of her concoctions on Al's wound, but the stuff seemed to stop the bleeding almost immediately.

Frowning, she leaned over the jar and sniffed. "What's in that stuff, anyway?"

"Some healing herbs, disinfectant, and cobwebs, dear. Now run into the bathroom and bring me some gauze and tape."

"Cobwebs?" M. C. asked with a gasp.

Al, who'd been lying back on the pillows, sat up a little, eyes widening with alarm. "Cobwebs?" he echoed.

Aunt Kate sighed heavily. "Fine, I'll get the bandages myself." And with a huff she headed off to the bathroom.

M. C. sat down on the edge of the bed, and instinctively stroked Al's dark hair away from his forehead. "Are you really okay?"

His mischievous grin appeared to reassure her, though she could still see the pain reflected in his eyes. "I have been far more grievously wounded than this, and survived, Mary Catherine. But if you wish to sit there and worry for me, I won't object." With his uninjured arm, he reached up, ran his hand slowly over her cheek. "You are beautiful when you are worried."

She lowered her eyes. "You never give up, do you, Al?"

"Never. And now, *chérie,* you are no longer under my protection."

She met his gaze, let him see for once that she felt the same way he did. "Unfortunately, you're lying in bed with a hole in your shoulder at the moment."

"It is of little importance. I will not be using my *shoulder, ma petite.*" His fingertips danced over her temple, and she shivered.

Licking her lips, she noted, "We have an audience."

Then there were footsteps thundering up the stairs, and the bedroom door burst open. Uniformed officers lunged inside, weapons drawn.

"And more arriving all the time, *non*?"

"Afraid so," M. C. said. Then she turned to face the cops. "You can put those down. The bad guys are gift-wrapped and waiting for delivery." And she nodded toward de Rocci even as she was reaching into her pocket for the tape. "That one's the baddest of the bunch, and this tape will prove it."

Holstering his gun, the first officer stepped forward. Another came behind him. "You'd best run outside and check on the two in the car. I don't think the carbon monoxide has killed them yet, but . . ."

The second cop was gone before she could finish. The

first one reached for the tape, but M. C. pulled it back. "I'd just as soon put this in the D.A.'s hands myself, if it's all the same to you."

The two in the car were hauled away by ambulance, while the others were taken in the backs of police cars. D.A. Hennesey insisted M. C. come with him, but she shook her head.

"I'm not going anywhere until I make sure Al's okay."

The D.A., a short, balding man with wire rims that made him look more like an accountant than a crime fighter, nodded. "I understand that, Ms. Hammer, but this is necessary."

"No it isn't. You have the tape."

"And de Rocci has other men in his employ, if all you've told me is true. Once we get your statement on the record, he'll have no reason to send them after you."

"No reason but revenge, you mean."

The D.A.'s brows went up. "Well, yes, there is that."

"I'm not afraid of him." She glanced at Al, sitting up in the bed now and sipping some brew Aunt Kate had whipped up, while Kate sat in a chair beside him to make sure he took every drop.

"Go with Monsieur Hennesey, Mary Catherine," Al urged. "I want you safe."

She frowned.

"I will be fine," he promised.

"And I'll see to it he is," Aunt Kate said. "Go on, honey, get this over with. We have things to do, you know." This with a meaningful glance at Al.

Things to do. Right. They had to send Al back. Holding his gaze for a long moment, M. C. said, "Don't do anything without me, okay? I want to have a chance to say . . ." She couldn't say the last word. Good-bye. It was too final. Too sudden. She didn't want to say it now. Maybe . . . maybe not ever.

Al's eyes darkened as they held hers—almost as if he were reading her thoughts. "I will be here waiting when you return, little one. I promise you."

Nodding hard, blinking at the burning behind her eyes, M. C. turned to the D.A. "All right, let's get this over with."

It took forever, or at least it seemed like it did. By the time M. C. got out of the local police department where the D.A. took her statement, it was well after dark. Big, black clouds had rolled in so that not a single star was visible in the sky. Matched her mood, she thought. She figured by the time she got back, Aunt Kate would have everything ready for Al's return trip. She'd have found the right spell in that big book of hers, and she'd have gathered up whatever obscure herbs or glittery crystals or eye of newt they might need.

Pausing at the front door, M. C. took out the photo she'd snapped of Al that first night. She'd been carrying it with her ever since. She stared down at his face, traced his shape with her finger, and wasn't surprised when a tear-drop fell from her cheek to land upon his image.

Sniffling, she tucked the photo away, and opened the front door.

The first thing she saw when she walked inside were the candles. Two rows of tall, elegant taper candles formed a path across the floor. They alternated in color, pink and red. She'd never seen so many candles all lighted at once.

She figured it must be part of whatever ritual Aunt Kate had devised.

Then the scent wafted up to tickle her nostrils, and she glanced downward. Rose petals littered the floor like confetti between the two rows of candles.

Frowning, M. C. took off her shoes, shrugged out of her jacket, and stepped onto the silky-soft path. "Aunt Kate?" she called.

No answer. But the candle-and-rose-petal path led up the stairs. And as she followed it, she heard soft music.

Lord, but this must be one complicated spell! At the top of the stairs, the path continued down the hall, and turned, going right through the open door of the guest room. "Where is everybody?" M. C. asked. Still no answer.

She moved on, into the guest room.

Candles glowed from every surface. The entire bedroom floor and the bed itself were cushioned with the tender petals. And a vase stood beside the bed with a dozen deep red buds nodding from their long, slender stalks.

And then Al came out of the shadows and crossed the room toward her. He stopped right in front of her, drew his sword, dropped to one knee, and held the weapon balanced on his upturned palms. Head bowed, he lifted it. "My gift to you, my lady," he murmured. Then he laid it at her feet. Taking her hand in both of his, he pressed his lips to her palm. His kiss was warm, and wet, and it left her skin tingling.

And suddenly she understood. This was it, the grand seduction. The one she'd been waiting for, dreaming of, wanting, since she'd first met him. But the pleasure of her surprise was dampened by the knowledge that this was also his way of saying good-bye.

She shook that thought away as he rose, still clinging to her hand. They'd have this. They'd have this one night, to remember.

"Aunt Kate?" she asked softly.

"Out for the evening," he replied, his voice low, tender, almost a caress in itself.

"And all of this?" She waved a hand to encompass the room.

He cupped her face between his palms. "For you," he told her. "All this . . . and more, were it mine to give."

"You certainly do know how to treat a lady." It was

meant to sound flippant, light. But her voice trembled instead.

"No, *ma chérie*. I have never wished to treat any lady the way I wish to treat you. I swear it on my sword."

She blinked, her eyes burning again.

"Mary Catherine . . . ," he began.

"No," she said quickly. "Don't say any more. I hate crying, Al, and you're putting me damned close to it."

"But why?"

Why? Because she didn't want to let him go, dammit! He was the first man who'd ever made her feel this way, and she knew she'd never feel it for any other. Why, when the unthinkable had finally happened to her, did it have to be with a man who couldn't stay? How could she vow never to fall in love and then do just that, when she knew it was impossible?

Fall in love.

Oh, God, that was exactly what she'd done!

"Mary Catherine?" His eyes searched her face.

She blinked away her shock, shook her head, and slid her arms around his waist. "Shut up and kiss me already."

He smiled. Devilish, that smile of his. Then he pulled her close, and kissed her thoroughly. His mouth worked hers, his tongue probed and explored, and locked together, they stumbled toward the bed, and fell onto its nest of rose petals.

Al never stopped kissing her as he tugged and pulled at her clothes, removing them one by one. His mouth traveled. Over her jaw, down to her throat, and lower. He muttered in French as he mouthed her breasts, and then her belly, and then her thighs. Sweet, erotic endearments, nearly as arousing as his touch.

She struggled with his clothes, too, until he pulled her into his arms without a stitch between them, and proceeded to make love to her more sweetly than she'd ever imagined possible.

And when her climax mingled with his, and she whispered his name, she knew she loved him even more now than she had before.

What, oh what, was she ever going to do without him?

They lay twined together for a long time as the candles burned low, Al stroking her hair, her back, holding her close and tenderly in his arms. But finally, he sat up a bit, looked down at her almost adoringly, and whispered, "It is time, *chérie*."

"I know," she whispered, and she couldn't keep her feelings in check any longer. M. C. Hammer, tough-as-nails lady detective, began to cry.

"Mary Catherine! What is wrong?"

She sniffled, tried to stop the tears, but failed. The touch of his gentle fingers on her damp cheeks only made her cry even harder. "I—I'm sorry, Al. I just . . . I just wish you didn't have to go."

"Go? Go? But my love, I thought you understood!"

She blinked, staring up at him. "Understood . . . what?"

"I gave you my sword. Sweet Mary Catherine, with it goes my heart. I told you once that I would only give up my sword for the woman who would be my true love, did I not?"

Shaking her head slowly, she stared at him.

"I love you, Lady Hammer. And love is more important than anything else. More important than life or death . . . or time itself. I will die before I will leave you, my love . . . if . . ." He searched her face, then turned his gaze away.

"If?" she prompted.

"If you feel the same," he told her softly, not looking at her, almost as if he were afraid to look at her.

Her heart swelled until she thought it would burst, and she ran one hand through his satin hair. "Oh, I do," she whispered. "Al, I really, really do. I love you."

He turned to meet her eyes, his wide and brimming. "Ah, *ma chérie,* do you mean it?"

She nodded hard. "But Al, can you really stay? Are you sure you want to?"

"I would live upon the moon itself, if it meant I could be at your side, my love." He kissed her, long and lingeringly. Then holding her nestled against his chest, he continued. "I have no ties to the past that would require my return. Your Aunt Kate said the decision to stay or to go was mine. And you yourself told me my gold coins are worth a fortune, Mary Catherine, so I can make my way."

"Oh, I have a few ideas about how you can earn a living, Al. You're not without certain job skills, you know."

"No?"

She nibbled his chin. "You sure you won't mind having a witch in the family?" she asked him.

"If you can tolerate a Musketeer as a husband, then I can withstand a witch as an aunt," he whispered.

M. C. blinked. "H—husband?"

"*Oui.* If you will have me."

Her smile was slow, but straight from the heart. "You'd better believe I will. And Al, there's another partnership I have in mind for us. Besides marriage, I mean."

"Oh, is there?"

She nodded. "Umm-hmm. But . . . um . . . we can talk about that in the morning." She pressed closer to him, curled her arms around his strong shoulders, and pulled him to her for another kiss.

"Very late in the morning," he whispered, and he held her even tighter.

Epilogue

Alexandre held his wife close to his side as they stood outside the door of her office in Newark. She'd told him her wedding gift to him was waiting here, though to his way of thinking, she'd already given him the gift of a lifetime just by agreeing to be his.

He was slowly getting used to this modern world. Everything moved quickly, too quickly at times, but with Mary Catherine at his side, he could adapt to anything.

He loved her. Adored her, and knew he would never regret his decision to remain at her side. He'd searched for a woman like her all his life. One who would love him for the man he was, rather than the colors he wore or the sword he carried. He'd had to travel through time to find her, but find her he had. And he would never, never let her go.

She squeezed his waist and smiled up at him. "Here it is," she said, and there was laughter in her voice.

"Where?" Alexandre asked her, looking up and down the hallway in which they stood. He saw nothing but the office door.

"There," she said, pointing.

He looked to where she pointed, seeing only a strip of white across the glass panel of the door.

"Go on, peel it away."

Frowning, Al leaned forward, got hold of one edge of the sticky white paper—"tape"; he vowed to remember all these new words—and peeled it slowly away.

Underneath the stuff, he read the words newly painted upon the glass, and smiled, his heart filling until he thought it would burst.

TWO MUSKETEERS INVESTIGATIONS
ONE FOR ALL, AND ALL FOR ONE!

MIDNIGHT LOVER

Lindsay Longford

One

The dreams started that first day, the day she saw the house.

The day she met Rafe Jackson.

Charlotte's six A.M. call had woken her up. Charlotte, the Realtor who'd patiently and sympathetically ferried Meggie from house to sterile house, had fallen victim to a plate of bad Gulf shrimp and oysters. "I'm *so* sorry, swee-tie. God, I wish I could stop the room whirling around long enough to show you these last houses. I swear on a stack of Bibles you'll love them. But Rafe's going to fill in for me," Charlotte moaned, her voice going wobbly and pitiful.

"Rafe?"

"Rafer Jackson. My second cousin on my daddy's side."

"Oh." Meggie twisted the phone cord around her finger.

"You'll like him."

Charlotte had said the same thing about each house she'd shown Meggie and Meggie hadn't liked any of them. What were the odds she'd like this Rafe-cousin?

"I can wait until you're feeling better." But could she? She'd made up her mind and now she wanted things settled, not left in this holding pattern. Dismayed, she ran her finger along the slippery vinyl cord.

Meggie liked Charlotte Hobbes even though the Realtor kept steering Meggie to houses with no soul. Charlotte had an easygoing charm that didn't demand conversation, didn't intrude on Meggie's space. Charlotte walked her through the houses and amazed Meggie by being smart enough to step back and keep the sales pitch low-key. Despite her rat-a-tat speech, Charlotte was comfortable to be around.

Instinct told Meggie this unknown cousin wouldn't be.

She'd come to Saw Creek, Florida, on a flood tide of impulse and decision. Finally wrenching herself out of the rut she'd allowed herself to slip into, she'd reached the painful decision to move, to find a place where she could start her life over.

Influenced by her southern father's stories, she'd stuck her finger blindly on a map, leaving the choice to fate. Foolish, impulsive, reckless, yes, but she'd needed foolishness, recklessness. She'd needed change, and Fate had sent her to this small town.

Having cast her future to the winds of Fate, though, Meggie found she'd used up her store of emotional energy.

With Rafer Jackson, she would have to put up with questions, small talk, with the give-and-take of social interaction. Too hard to meet someone new, to establish one more casual relationship. Still, did she want to lose one, two more days waiting around in the hotel?

Torn, Meggie hesitated before she lied. "I can wait for you. I don't mind."

Another faint moan issued from the beige phone. "No, I wouldn't think of it, not after you've flown all the way here from Wisconsin. Really, hon, it's not a problem. Rafe and I go way back. He owes me." Underneath the stifled moan, Meggie heard a steeliness as Charlotte mumbled, "Big time. He'll do it. For me."

Meggie wasn't sure how she felt about being somebody's debt payoff, but clearly Charlotte had roped Rafer Jackson into filling in for her, and Meggie didn't have it in her to protest, not in the face of one more pathetic moan.

But the moment Rafe Jackson knocked at her hotel door and his cool dark eyes met hers, Meggie's hackles rose.

Maybe it was his barely perceptible nod, maybe nothing more than the way his glance skimmed over her, briefly, dismissively. Or maybe it was the scent of male and soap, a scent she hadn't even realized she missed until now.

She wasn't prepared for the pain that seared through her.

She swallowed, took a step forward, and stopped, grief washing through her like a tidal wave, drowning her even now, even after all these months.

Rafe Jackson's scent drifted to her as he pivoted on his heel, not waiting for her reply. "Ready, Ms. Blake?" His low, smoky voice wrapped around her like the webs of fog slipping past her hotel window, a dark, midnight voice reminding her of all the midnights lost.

When she didn't answer, Rafe Jackson turned and lifted one thick eyebrow. The flicker of resentment surfacing from the depths of his eyes told her he was about as thrilled to be escorting her on a round of house-hunting as she was to be stuck with him.

He studied her for a moment.

His look was astringent, stinging her out of that deeper emptiness.

With his right hand he jammed sunglasses over the bridge of his long, narrow nose. Keeping his left hand casually tucked inside the tailored pocket of his gray suit jacket, he stood there, watching her, his eyes hidden.

The humming silence pressed against her, a living weight, and for a moment she couldn't breathe.

"Changed your mind after all, Ms. Blake?" His husky

voice rasped against every nerve ending in her skin.

The instinct that had surfaced earlier rang alarm bells, and it took every ounce of poise she had not to turn tail and run.

She didn't.

Later, she would wonder why she hadn't.

"Ready, Mr. Jackson."

A little too carefully she shut the hotel door behind her and walked beside him to the elevator, her breath shuddering inside her.

Like her, he kept a distance between them. As he held the elevator door for her, though, the sleeve of his jacket brushed against her bare arm, leaving a shiver in its wake. Meggie crossed her arms in front of her, staring at the elevator buttons as he joined her in the silent drop to the first floor.

Her arm fizzed where his sleeve had trailed along it.

She didn't like her reaction.

That burning tingle felt like betrayal. Hers, her body's. She didn't know which, didn't care.

Neither of them spoke again until they stepped out from the revolving front door.

"My car." At the curb in front of them, he gestured with his right hand again toward a low-slung dark car gleaming with fog-damp.

"Of course," Meggie said through gritted teeth. "I might have known."

The sudden turn of his head acknowledged her acid tone. "You don't like my car?"

His indifferent politeness was as shocking as a bucket of ice water in her face. Oh, he was meticulously polite, exquisitely courteous, a real prince of a guy. And she wanted to—to—something.

But there was nothing in his words to make her react the way she did, and Meggie knew she would never be able to explain to Charlotte how Rafer Jackson, Charlotte's second cousin on her daddy's side, her cousin who *owed* her, could make her feel like a cat with its fur rubbed the wrong way.

For pete's sake, she couldn't explain it to herself, much less to someone else.

"If you don't like my car, Ms. Blake, all you have to do is say so. I can make other arrangements."

"The car's fine. It's small." Too small to spend four hours trapped in its tiny space with a man who made her skin hum and itch, who struck sparks from her like a flint.

"So it is." With a beep of a remote, he unlocked the car and held the passenger door open, waiting with that stillness that unnerved her. "Is that going to be a problem?"

Yes, she thought.

"No," she said and forced a smile, thinking she would never, ever ignore her instincts again. "Of course not. I was merely making an observation." She walked toward him. "Your car's small. Fast. Foreign." Expensive, like his suit, like his sunglasses that were useless on a day like this.

"That's three. Any other observations?" His hand cupped the glossy metal of the door as she slid in and tugged at her skirt.

"If I have any, I'll let you know."

"There's a comfort." He swung the door gently to and fro. "I admire a woman who's unafraid to express her opinions."

"Now there's a comfort for me." Meggie tipped her chin up and shot him a level stare. "An emancipated man."

He didn't even hesitate, his response silky smooth in that midnight voice that made every bone in her body ache. "Charlotte's influence, that's all. A sensitive, nineties man? Don't put too much stock in it."

"Thanks for the warning."

"Didn't want you to get the wrong impression."

"Oh, I don't think you have to worry. That I'll get the wrong impression. Believe me, I won't." She smiled until her teeth hurt. "I never do."

At her words, he shut the door with a quiet snick. The tiny movement of his mouth might have been a smile.

She wasn't sure.

But she wouldn't bet on it.

Meggie watched as he strolled in front of the car and around to the driver's side. It was going to be a very long morning.

The clamped-down energy beneath his chilly remoteness made her cranky, edgy. She'd been prepared for a too-talky salesman, not for this man who didn't want conversation and interaction any more that she did.

She should have been relieved.

She wasn't.

And she didn't know why.

All she knew was that the reined-in energy pulsing from Rafer Jackson pushed at her until she wanted to climb straight back into the numbness of her cocoon and stay there, safe.

Unlike Charlotte, who was a comfortable woman, Rafer Jackson wasn't a comfortable man.

Not a safe man.

Oh, yes, she should have listened to her instincts.

On the road out of town, she watched the scenery pass by them in shades of gray and tried to ignore the sound of his slacks rustling against the seat as he downshifted on a curve, his left hand resting out of sight on the bottom of the steering wheel, tried to ignore the way he wrapped his right hand around the steering wheel once he'd shifted, lightly, lightly, letting the wheel turn smoothly underneath the strength of his long fingers.

Mile after mile passed in silence.

A silence she would have enjoyed except that she

couldn't close her senses to the man beside her.

Eyes narrowed against the threads of fog floating by the windshield, Meggie frowned. He'd been brusque, but to be fair to him, she hadn't been Miss Congeniality herself, not with her edginess growing by the minute until her skin itched with the need to get out of his car and call it a day. She shifted in her seat, ready to tell him to turn around, she'd changed her mind after all. She wanted to go back to her hotel.

"Giving up, Ms. Blake?" The flick of his eyes in her direction telegraphed his awareness of her intent and, somehow, despite his courteous tone, mocked her.

Evidently he was as aware of her as she was of him. Unless he could read minds.

"Not at all," she returned, her manner equally courteous. She was annoyed with herself, but that hint of mockery and the knowing twitch at the corner of his mouth triggered a contrariness in her she'd never known she possessed. "You've been—very helpful." Mimicking him, her smile was all mock innocence. "Charlotte will be so pleased."

"Well, God knows I want Charlotte to be happy," he said grimly.

Meggie clamped her lips together and swore she wouldn't say another word, not one. She'd give a hundred dollars, though, to know what Charlotte was holding over Rafe Jackson's head.

In silence, the world outside wrapped in gray, she faced front, her thoughts returning in spite of herself to Jonah, Jonah who should be with her, *here*. Not in some cold, unending darkness where she couldn't touch him, couldn't feel the scratch of his beard against her face, couldn't hear the sound of his voice, couldn't—*Couldn't.*

She swallowed against the thickness that clamped her throat shut.

Jonah had gone into the belly of the beast and never come back.

Rafe swung the car to the far edge of the pavement as he took a corner sharply.

And then, ghostly, rising from the mist, the house suddenly appeared before her.

For miles there had been only empty road along the river where fog hung in blurry gray ribbons over dark water—and now, emerging from the same fog, this house . . .

Longing pierced her, sweet, unbearable.

Slowly moving strands of moss and vapor shrouded old oak trees. A FOR SALE sign leaned against the tall gate. Vines crawled over a rusting iron fence, drooped and sprawled in abandon on shaggy grass, shivered, twisted in the hazy light.

But the house—*the house*!

"Stop," she whispered to Rafe, leaning forward to see the house more clearly through the tangle of weeds and bushes. Frustrating her, fog obscured the outline of the house. "Please, stop the car."

"Why?"

"I want to see the house." Twisting in her seat, the seat belt cutting into her, she pointed to the house now behind them.

"That one isn't on Charlotte's list." But he slowed the Porsche to a crawl, U-turned, and shifted to park. The engine rumbled beneath them. "You don't want this house, Ms. Blake."

"Don't I?" She rubbed at the cool glass windshield. "And of course you'd know. I mean, you know me so well." She couldn't tear her gaze from the glimpse of soft white boards that flashed momentarily through the fog.

"Right." He glanced in her direction, looked away before adding, "But I know this house. It's too big. And the yard needs a hell of a lot of work before you could move in."

Meggie heard the underlying message loud and clear. This house, this house where shadows lay long across the lawn, where gray mist draped oak trees and an enormous magnolia, this wasn't a house for a single woman, not a house for a widow.

Not a house for her.

Charlotte had filled him in.

"I want to see it."

"You'd be wasting your time."

And mine, she heard. "That's for me to decide, isn't it?" With an effort, she kept her expression pleasant, her voice from rising.

"Your time, your dime." He tapped the steering wheel, revealing an irritation of his own in the rapid beat of his fingers against the leather.

"My point exactly."

Then, in a movement so fast she jumped, he touched her wrist where it rested on the instrument panel. Heat rose along her arm, focused her attention on him, on his words. "Look, Ms. Blake, the fact of the matter is that the house needs work too. Sure, it's structurally sound. In fact, a family lived here until eight months ago." He sighed, and Meggie thought she heard a desolation in the stillness as he hesitated before saying, "But it's a fixer-upper, a house for someone with time and inclination to work on it."

"Did you know the family?" Meggie asked, suddenly curious.

"Yeah." A mask dropped over his face, and she had the impression she was treading on quicksand.

Her curiosity increased. "And?" she encouraged.

"They planned to turn it into a bed-and-breakfast place for their golden years. Sweat equity." Shading his face with one hand, he added, "And you don't strike me as a woman who knows her way around a hammer and saw. Believe me, you don't want this house. Hell, it would cost a fortune to finish it up the way it should be."

"I can afford it," Meggie said stubbornly and moved her hand to the safety of her lap, away from the pulse-quickening heat of his touch.

"Right. I'm getting the picture, Ms. Blake." His right hand tapped the steering wheel again, his left hand was out of sight. "But you said you were in a hurry, that you wanted to move in immediately."

"I know." Meggie had told Charlotte exactly that. And she'd meant every word. She'd come to this west coast Florida town to exorcise her demons and to shape a life for herself, a life without the shadow that inhabited every corner of her other home, that Jonah-ghost who broke her heart with memories. "But I haven't found the right place. If a family recently lived here, there's no reason I couldn't move in. If I wanted to."

In the face of her silence, Rafe continued, measuring out his words slowly. "What you decide is none of my business."

"True. It isn't." She shot him a slightly hostile glance. "This house is for sale. I want to buy a house. Why can't I take a look at this one? What's the big deal here, Mr. Jackson?"

The slap of his hand on the dash made her jump. "No big deal. You want to see the house, go right ahead. No skin off my nose. But I sure as hell can't imagine why you'd want to get sidetracked with this old barn."

Neither could Meggie.

But the house was the first thing in a long time that had broken through the constant numbness, shocking her with the intensity of her interest.

Well, Rafer Jackson had, but that was different. This house made her feel something, and she hadn't cared about anything in so long, hadn't *wanted* anything with this kind of urgency.

The last wish she'd made, the last thing she'd wanted was Jonah, alive.

"The mice and raccoons have probably taken it over. Spiders. Snakes."

"I think you're pulling my leg, Mr. Jackson," Meggie said gently. "I mean, if those people lived here only a few months ago, how bad could the house be now? Even in Florida, a house isn't going to fall apart in eight months."

"Yeah." He cast a quick glance off to her left where that faint ray of sunlight touched the faded white walls. He sighed again. "But I'd bet a hundred bucks the roof leaks."

"I see. You're looking out for my best interests." Confused, Meggie turned to study his lean face. The house meant something to him she didn't understand. Tentatively, she said, "You want to keep me from making a mistake."

"Right. This house would be a mistake for you. Okay, it's settled. That's that." Obviously relieved, he reached for the gearshift, his knee bumping hers. "Charlotte wants you to see this place a few miles up the river."

"I know." The impulse of certainty she'd felt on first seeing the house was flowing away from her. Her sigh matched Rafe's. "It's the one with the pool. She said it's to die for."

"Yeah, that sounds like Charlotte all right, but I don't know. I'm not a Realtor. The place is new. Has a security system. I reckon Charlotte figured you'd like that." He took off his sunglasses and hung them from the banded collar of a shirt the pale gray of the fog outside. His eyes met hers, and she thought she saw a flare of pity in their dark depths. "The safety factor."

"I see," she said once more. Safety. She'd had security, safety, and it had vanished like an illusion. She'd faced the worst—what was left to terrify her? No, the highest-priced security system in the world couldn't do anything for her.

"She thought you might enjoy the pool." Rafe shrugged. "People. Parties. You know."

Meggie didn't. Not anymore.

"Hell." Awkwardness clipped his syllables. "Ms. Blake, Charlotte said the river place would be perfect for you. Like I said, what you want is none of my business."

"And yet you keep making it your business, don't you?"

"Yeah, reckon I do." He shoved his sunglasses back on. His fingers drummed against the console between them, stopped. "You seem like a nice woman—"

"Do I? How surprising." Meggie didn't want his sympathy.

"Surprised me, too. We haven't exactly—"

"Bonded?" she asked sweetly.

His bark of laughter startled her. "No, I don't reckon we've bonded. Shoot." He shrugged. "But I can't help thinking you'd be getting in over your head with this property. I'd hate to see that happen. This old joint is going to be more trouble than it's worth. I think you should listen to Charlotte. And that's what I'd tell my worst enemy."

Rafe was probably right. That's what she was paying Charlotte for. Guidance. Charlotte knew the market. Charlotte had trotted cheerfully at her side through house after boring house. Charlotte was a nice woman, a well-intentioned professional. If Meggie were smart, she'd listen to Charlotte.

To Rafe.

Her gaze drifted again to the house.

Rubbing the tightness at her temples, she shut her eyes and let that seductive sight vanish. "Still . . ."

"Ms. Blake, you'd be wasting your time and money here."

"Think so?" Opening her eyes to cool mist, Meggie blinked.

Impatience spiked through Rafe Jackson's voice. "Look

at that yard, Ms. Blake. You thinking of mowing it yourself? You'd need a riding lawn mower. A yard service.
Too much work here. You don't want this house.''

"I suppose not.'' But Meggie couldn't look away from
the glimpse of tall, shuttered windows glinting in the gray
light. "But there's something about this place—''

"God only knows what.''

She took a deep breath. His reluctance only intensified
this peculiar desire to see the house. She whirled to face
him, discretion and manners finally lost. "What difference
does it make to you if I want to waste my time here? I
don't understand why you're trying so hard to keep me
from even *looking* at this house, Mr. Jackson. Do you have
some personal reason for not letting me walk through this
place?''

The grooves beside his mouth deepened, but he didn't
speak.

Meggie steamed ahead. "Or is it me? An instant dislike
for Yankee transplants in general? Because you don't
know anything at all about me.''

"Yankees are fine, Ms. Blake. I even like some of them.
As for you, you nailed it. I don't know you well enough
to dislike you.'' He bared his teeth in an imitation of a
smile. "I'm willing to learn, though, if you insist. You
want to waltz through the damn house? Be my guest.''
The sudden jerk of his head away from the house sent his
sunglasses flying toward the dashboard.

Leaning forward to retrieve the glasses and return them,
Meggie watched helplessly, stunned, as the contorted twist
of his left hand scooped them up. Abruptly, as if remembering, he thrust the hand out of sight and grabbed the
glasses with his right hand. One-handed, he hooked his
glasses over his ears, concealing his expression once more.

But she saw the way his mouth tightened and knew better than to show him the pity she would have rejected in
his place.

After all, turning her own warning back on herself, it was none of her business.

But she wondered about Rafe Jackson, wondered what had happened to him and his scarred, cramped hand.

Before she could say anything, he leaned across her, his right arm sliding across her waist as he opened the car door. "You're right. I was out of line." The thin planes of his face were harsh in the sudden brightness of the overhead car light. He didn't look at her as he said, "The lock box code is right 4, left 7, right 9. Go see the house for yourself, Ms. Blake. I'll stay here, if you don't mind." All emotion stripped from his low voice, he retreated once more behind that careful and exasperating politeness.

One foot on the ground, Meggie hesitated, unexpectedly arrested by Rafe's untold story, by the complex emotions ruling him. "I know you didn't want to play baby-sitter, Mr. Jackson."

"No, I didn't. But I didn't have to act like a son of a bitch. It's not your fault. I'm sorry."

"I told Charlotte I could wait until she was well. Why did you let her sucker you into chauffeuring me around?"

"Charlotte's been a friend as well as relative, and at a time when she didn't have to be." He unclipped Meggie's seat belt. "And she's not an easy person to turn down. Sometimes I think she's part witch."

"Good witch or bad witch? Which?" Meggie felt the corners of her mouth lift in a genuine smile.

"Damned if I know sometimes. Go look at the house, Ms. Blake."

"All right." Filled with a sudden energy and sense of purpose she hadn't known for over a year, she pushed free of her seat belt and stepped out of Rafe Jackson's sleek car into a world made gauzy with mist.

Like long, elegant fingers beckoning her forward, moss swayed gently on the nearest oak. Shadows underneath the tree shifted and moved into deeper darkness, calling her to follow, to taste that cool dimness. To rest.

"Ms. Blake . . ."

Far away, Rafe Jackson's voice hissed in Meggie's ears, slid down to her toes, curling them in her narrow sandals. Cool and wet, wisps of fog brushed her ankles like the long-lost touch of a lover's mouth.

To the rear of the property, right of the house, she saw the outline of a hedge walling in what might be a formal garden. Fading into the mist, almost unreal, the house shimmered in front of her.

And in back of her, she sensed Rafe Jackson's presence, dark in his dark car.

She wound her hands around the bars of the gate. Like the fog caressing the curve of her neck, the metal was cool, rough against the tips of her fingers as she grasped the rounded bars. Solid, *real*.

Not recognizing the hunger that had seized her, she held on to that metal as if it were a lifeline.

Her fingers tightened on the bars.

This house was like the answer to a question she hadn't known she'd asked.

She was a fool.

Taking a deep breath, she turned her back on the siren call of the house and perhaps its garden, but with every step back to the car, she felt the pull of the house, of that barely seen garden. Her sandals kicking up whiffs of dust, she strode back to the car, opened the door, and climbed in.

Clipping the seat belt around her, she laughed at the sight of Rafe's frown, and the sound was too loud in the silence. "Guess what, Mr. Jackson? You just made Charlotte a sale."

"You didn't even go inside."

"Sad, but true. And this will be a good story for Charlotte to tell over coffee at her next office meeting, won't it? 'The Widow and the Wreck,' she can call it." Meggie raised her hands as he started to speak. "Mr. Jackson, let's go wrap up the paperwork. The house isn't really a wreck. And it's the house I want."

Need, a low voice whispered in her brain, and she remembered that touch of mist against her cheek. *Need.*

Without a word, he punched in Charlotte's phone number and handed the cell phone to Meggie.

In between moans, Charlotte tried to change Meggie's mind.

Meggie told Charlotte she would have been an excellent Jewish mother. With Rafe Jackson at her shoulder, a presence she couldn't ignore no matter how hard she tried, she told Charlotte not to worry, that everything would be all right.

She told Charlotte to *hurry,* please.

Meggie wanted to sleep in the house tonight.

Finally, abandoning worry, advice, and caveats, Charlotte hurried, arranging everything by phone, with Rafe filling in for her.

Later, in the bank, Rafe's shuttered gaze met Meggie's.

"Cash?" he said as they waited for verification of Meggie's very large personal check and a troop of lawyers and accountants.

"I told you. I can afford this house. And its upkeep." Meggie crossed one nyloned knee over the other. The slight movement of Rafe's head told her that behind his dark glasses his eyes followed the movement.

"So you did. Silly me," he said and looked away.

By late afternoon on a day that turned to rain and drizzle, the river house was Meggie's.

Rafe and his unsettling presence long gone, the house was all hers. Hers alone.

She'd come to Saw Creek to get on with her life, whatever that meant.

Here in this house she could fill the emptiness with—

with *something*. She would make her life whatever it was going to be. A life without Jonah. But a life, she reminded herself.

Her life now. Alone.

She would fill her life the way she would fill this house she'd bought so impulsively, so foolishly.

Her house.

Hers and whatever creatures had taken up residence in its nooks and crevices. But, contrary to Rafe's evaluation and Meggie's own pragmatic expectation, the roof didn't leak.

Meggie shot the flashlight upward to the darkness of twelve-foot ceilings. At least it didn't yet.

And, as she'd said, how bad could the house have gotten in eight months? Not too bad, she decided as she swung the flashlight through room after room. Its previous family having been in the midst of several remodeling projects, the house was fine. Structurally sound, old-fashioned in its floor plan, it welcomed her, wrapped her in a serene quiet that almost felt like happiness.

She finally returned to the living room, and, stooping in front of the enormous fireplace, unusual in a Florida house, she shone the flashlight up the chimney. Curious bright eyes glowed back at her. She slammed the grate and pulled it tight. "Don't worry," she muttered. "I'm not about to start a fire. But the deal is, you don't get to come down the chimney. Got it, guys?"

The chirp of a raccoon answered her. She hoped it meant they had a bargain. Knowing raccoons were con artists, though, she tipped over an empty bookcase and blocked the fireplace entrance. Soot puffed out and drifted against her hands.

Brushing off her hands against her jeans, she clambered into her new sleeping bag and stared into the darkness while her house creaked and chittered around her.

Under one tall window, her suitcases made bumpy shadows.

As she drifted in a twilight wakefulness, on the verge of sleeping and waking, the dreams began.

Two

Slippery, steamy dreams.

Hot dreams that made her skin flush and burn.

A hand, rough-textured and scratchy, caressed the sole of her foot, brushed a knuckle against the arch, and touched the inside of her knee, sliding smoothly, smoothly upward.

Rafe Jackson's hand had slipped that smoothly over the surface of the steering wheel.

The dream-hand moved over her thigh, upward in slow circles. Her belly quivered, trembled, and all that heat gathered like a storm in the October night, gathered and coiled her muscles into knots.

Wanting, needing, she whimpered.

From a far-off place, the sound of thunder rolled toward her, the sound as real as the touch of this unseen hand.

Dreaming, *surely she was dreaming,* but she felt as if she floated over her body like the ancient Allhallows eve celebrants, awake but dreaming, the whole world stretched underneath her. She saw the dark room, the window open to the night air, saw the dark shadows of the garden vines flattened to the movement of unseen feet. Through the window glinting in the dimness, she saw, too, a distant flash of lightning and smelled the sharp tang of ozone.

She saw herself twisting and turning to the beat of an unseen baton, the symphony of her need rising to a crescendo. Like that scent of ozone preceding a storm, she smelled the heat of her own arousal.

How could this not be real? she thought, dreamed. All this richness of feeling and touch? She wanted it to be real.

Drugged with sensation, she turned her face to the hand that molded her chin, slipped over her neck, skimmed the side of one breast. Her nipple rose, sunflower to that heat and touch.

Her skin bloomed with a veil of perspiration and she twisted fretfully, all her muscles contracting. Her breathing quickened.

A breath as warm as the October afternoon had been whispered against her mouth, a breath scented with coffee and brandy. With a long peal of thunder, the beat of a distant heart came to her, the sound of breathing close to her ear.

Meggie.

Not Jonah's ghostly voice.

Even in this dream-state that felt more real than anything in the last year, she knew the voice wasn't Jonah's. She wanted it to be. Anything else seemed disloyal to him, a betrayal of her memories.

But it wasn't Jonah's voice that whispered to her in a smoky voice that left shivers in its wake.

A finger feathered her navel, traced the line below, and her skin jumped like a compass needle, following the true north of that touch.

Meggie. A sigh, a whisper on her mouth, moistening her lips, opening them to an unseen mouth and tongue that shaped them as that imagined hand stroked against her again and again, pressing.

Not Jonah's hand, not Jonah's touch.

Circling in ever-narrowing circles, the phantom hand teased her, tormented her with delicious suspense. And then, at last, a knowing, relentless stroke where she ached the most.

Ah, Meggie, come to me.

At the sound of her name murmured in that low voice, her body convulsed. Jerked in the twisted confines of the sleeping bag.

Meggie opened her eyes. Her body trembled, prolonged, luxurious tremors moving through it.

Awake, she wanted to be dreaming again, wanted that sense of being held, being—loved. Hungered for the touch of another human against her.

Huddled in the sleeping bag, her body still thrumming in the aftermath of her private storm, she stared around her. A paper on the floor lifted in the wind from the window. Meggie watched it sail across the dim ocean of the floor. Her body had lifted in that final spasm in exactly that same light, free way, drifting. Comforted.

The scrap settled in a corner.

"Meggie, my girl, you've gone 'round the bend, you has." Her long-dead father's voice chuckled in her brain. "Sittin' in the dark watching trash whoopsie-do in the wind. You need to take a good look at yourself, punkin'. This ain't no way for a grown girl to *bee*-have." His southern drawl stretched out the syllables with a faint chuckle.

Meggie smiled. Her father and anyone else who knew her would have thought she was a candidate for a straitjacket this last week. "It's okay, pops," she murmured into the dark. "Really. I may not know what I'm doing, but I'm all right." Drawing up her knees, she rested her head on her folded arms. Peculiar, though, this sense of being outside herself, trapped in the grip of some compulsion. She'd never had that sensation before. Wild, unpredictable, these impulses were driving her like the paper in the wind.

"And you like this adventure, my girl, don't ya? You forgot, didn't ya? Forgot how it felt to be alive and eager for the morning. My will-o'-the-wisp Meggie. You never change. All this craziness." Her father's voice faded into silence.

Lightning flickered beyond the window.

Her damp skin dried in the cool of the breeze, but that inner heat and hunger lingered.

She hadn't dreamed of Jonah.

Jonah was no ghost in this house. Her midnight lover had been a phantom, someone her mind had created out of her body's need for life, for solace. Not a betrayal of the past, but, maybe, an awakening.

That, after all, was what she'd hoped for in coming to Saw Creek. A beginning. Moving onward in its own way, like a seed left in the cold darkness, her body had sent its own signal, telling her in a silent language of muscle and sensation that she was alive, *here*.

Pulling the sleeping bag over her shoulders, Meggie walked to the window. Definitely a dark and stormy night. A night for phantoms and ghosts. The wind whipped leaves over the tall grass, plucked the trailing vines and threw them like streamers in the darkness. Out toward the garden, she glimpsed a large vine-covered shape rising from the center. In the hazy light, she thought for a moment she saw it shift, turn toward her house.

Once, years ago, months ago in that other life, she would have been frightened. Now, though, she leaned forward, wiping at the dusty window of her house as she'd wiped the window of Rafe Jackson's car. Peering into the darkness, wondering, dreaming, she lost track of time as she watched the clouds move fitfully across the sky, turning it and her garden into a kaleidoscope of illusions.

The decision arriving on the heels of the thought, she

dropped the sleeping bag and pulled on jeans and a sweat-shirt against the night's chill. Tugging on socks and boots by flashlight, she started to laugh. The sound echoed under the high ceilings of the vast room.

"Megan Blake, what on earth are you thinking of? You'll catch your death of cold." That, of course, would have been her mother's refrain. She would have scolded, nagged.

And Jonah? What would he have thought? Her breath caught on a mix of sob and laughter. "You understand, don't you, Jonah?" she whispered into the silence and darkness. No answer in the silence, only a certainty grow-ing in the deepest recesses of her heart.

Sweet Jonah would have opened the door for her and cheered her on. "Go for it, babe," he would have rumbled in his bass voice. She missed his sweetness most of all.

"Hey, raccoon neighbors, the house is all yours for a while. No wild parties, okay?" she yelled up the chimney and then headed for the door.

A clot of soot hit the bottom of the fireplace. She hoped it was soot and not the raccoons' opinion of what she was doing.

Outside, the wind slapped her in the face with raw en-ergy. The grass was wet, sprinkling her jeans as she made her way to the hedged-in garden. Her flashlight threw a cold beam of white light in front of her. Annoyed with its artificial brightness, Meggie clicked it off.

Walking through the dark yard and grass, she didn't worry about snakes. She didn't worry about night crea-tures. With the wind pushing and buffeting her, she felt at one with the night, ruled by a mad whim to throw her clothes off and dance naked beneath the scudding clouds and moon.

She didn't.

She had that much sense left.

But she whirled in huge circles across the grass, laughing and stumbling and tripping and raising her face to the last drops of rain, her hair a mad tangle of curls and rain against her skin. Her midnight phantom had loosed something in her, and she felt alive, alive. Released.

Breathless and giddy, she collapsed onto the grass inside the hedge and lay face-up on the ground, watching the last of the clouds vanish as bright moonlight streamed around her. The large, shapeless mound she'd seen from her window was to her right. Covered with kudzu and coralvine, the mound shivered with the wind as if it breathed.

Blossoms trembled at the touch of the night wind, shimmered with raindrops.

"You're mine," she whispered and didn't know to whom or what she whispered.

Meggie, came the sigh of the wind.

She didn't know how long she lay on the wet grass looking up at the sky and back at that form looming over her, but lying there, her mind empty of everything except the wonder of the world around her, the wonder of life, she felt peace seep up through the ground and into her soul.

Eventually, ground-chilled and curious to see what the vines and weeds hid, she rose to her feet and walked over to the mound. Pulling at coarse stems and tough lengths, she snapped off dead, woody pieces of vegetation, dropping them on the ground. Whatever was underneath was large, strangely shaped. Squarish on the bottom and rising to a rounded top, it was taller than she. Ripping vines on one side, she decided that tomorrow her project would be to bring order out of chaos here in the garden, here with this vine-covered thing.

As she tore at one more girdle of kudzu, she felt something warm and supple under her palm. It moved, flexed.

A snake? Startled, she yanked her hand away, a flutter of fear raising the hairs on her arm. "What the heck?"

But her subconscious knew in that instant that what she

touched wasn't a snake. Her heart beating like a snare drum with something that wasn't fear, she stared at the gap between leaves and branches.

Through that gap, moonlight gilded the streak of marble shining through the cleared vines. Fascinated in the old sense of the word, Meggie leaned closer, studying that gleam that moved with the moonlight. Yanking and shredding leaves, she tore at the cloak of leaves. Minutes passed until, hot and sweaty with her frantic ripping, she stopped. The rest of the job would have to wait for morning and hedge clippers.

Leaning against the shape, she let her fingers trace the long, sloping curve she'd freed. Her fingers dipped into an indentation, like a muscle. Again, her palm shaped the warm marble, her fingers lingering on its smooth texture, and suddenly she understood. The indentation, the curve— her palm cupped a lean, muscled flank. A male flank.

"A statue? In my garden?"

Charmed, Meggie touched the gleaming stone. Marble, its surface nevertheless felt like sleek skin and pliable flesh, warm to her hand. The last cloud blew past, and with more light Meggie could now see that the shape was that of a person, the statue's base a clunky oblong. Pulling herself up onto the base, moonlight streaming around her and dazzling her eyes with its gold, she stripped vines and leaves in a frenzy.

She would see the rest of the statue if it took her all night.

Perspiration dripped into her eyes as she ripped and tore and pulled at vines. A taut, narrow waist appeared. Then, long, muscular legs with calves tight in frozen motion. A wide, muscular back curved forward, bent as if the figure half-stooped. The dip of spine and bunched muscles lured her hand, seduced it into lingering in a slow caress of marble skin, skin as warm as the flank she'd first touched. When she wrenched a loop of dead wood from the front

of the statue, she stopped, her hand resting on a chest
where an unseen heart beat against her fingers.

She knew the marble should be green with algae, moss.
It should be cold with the rain. Marble didn't beat with an
unseen heart.

Not possible.

But her hand lay over a pulse that throbbed with
warmth, with life.

She would swear that steady pulse was real.

Her hand dropped and step by step, Meggie backed
away from the golden male in front of her.

Half-stooping, he rose from the oblong grasp of rough
stone and rock, one hand trapped in an unfinished base,
his shoulder slanted to the side as he fought to free himself
from his stony prison. Naked, the form twisted in agony,
straining to pull itself up. Muscles tightened and struggled
in heartbreaking failure.

No Michelangelo's *David*, this statue was beyond beautiful. It was man made divine by effort and strength, glo-
riously male.

No leaf hid this statue's masculinity. Meggie stared at
thighs and groin where carefully sculpted muscles turned
marble into noble maleness, and her skin flushed with the
heat of her dream. In that instant, memories of her phantom lover blurred, blended with this creature of stone.

Marble hair hung to his shoulders and lifted in an unseen
wind. His head was turned away from her, and she was
relieved past comprehension.

In the golden moonlight and with the memory of that
warm marble beating to a hidden heart, she almost expected his eyes to turn and meet hers, almost saw a slow
turn of that splendid head toward her. Believed for one
impossible moment that it did move.

Her heart thudded with terror. With desire.

Even as she backed away, though, Meggie yearned to

move forward, to touch the statue again, to see its hidden eyes. To touch that marble skin.

Abruptly the moon vanished behind a bank of storm clouds, and rain poured from black skies, the statue vanishing with the moonlight.

Released, Meggie turned and ran, fear speeding her feet. Beneath the fear, though, some other emotion ran through her, sparkled in her blood.

Was she still asleep? Entangled in some dream where she dreamed herself awake and, dreaming, ran, her heart bursting with fear and that nameless emotion?

Relief of a sort in that thought.

"You'll wake up, Meggie," she crooned, reassuring herself that she hadn't gone moon-mad. She raced through blinding rain into the safety of her house and shivered against its solid wood. "This is a dream, Meggie. It has to be. It's part of that earlier dream. Tomorrow you'll barely remember this."

Wet and shaking, she threw her clothes onto the floor and climbed into her sleeping bag, zipping it up tight to her chin. She wanted to go to sleep. She wanted to wake up. She wanted her own reality back, after all.

Meggie finally closed her eyes, or at least she thought she did, and willed herself to wake up to normalcy and the chirping of her raccoons in a moonless dark.

She woke instead to loud knocking at her front door and a bright October sun beating through her windows. Groaning, stiff from her camp-out on the floor, she heard Rafe Jackson's voice and knew for sure she was awake.

"Ms. Blake? You there?"

"Give me a minute." She saw the sodden pile of jeans and socks. Maybe she'd been sleepwalking last night. "I'll be right there." She threw open one of her suitcases, knocking her cell phone to the floor. Damn the man. His enigmatic presence was the last thing she needed after her disturbed and disturbing night.

Even though Rafe was no longer pounding at her door, Meggie sensed him waiting on the other side, a force that would disrupt her day as her dreams had her night. She paused as a thought struck her. He could give her information about the statue in the garden.

When Megan swung the door wide open, Rafe didn't move. This woman with the mass of curls barely held by a brilliant green tieback scarf was unrecognizable as the prickly, fastidious woman he'd met yesterday.

"Yes, Mr. Jackson? Come to borrow a cup of sugar?" Velvet-brown eyes flashed at him.

"Nope. Charlotte was worried about you." He squinted. A thin line of mud decorated her cheek. Grass and leaves clung to her hair, and a long, red scratch ran down one gently curved thigh to a slim ankle and narrow foot. He saw all those details in the first glance. The department might have taken his badge and gun, but his brain worked. A cop's brain never quit noticing, cataloging, no matter what.

"Tell her I'm fine. Thanks." The door moved toward his face.

She hadn't lost the prickliness after all. He stuck his hand in the path of the heavy wood. "Hold on, Ms. Blake. I'm supposed to see if you need a ride into town."

"A ride?" She hesitated, her light brown eyebrows drawing together. Confusion stirred in her velvety eyes, eyes, he reflected, that were as soft as her skin.

He cleared his throat, uncomfortable with the direction of his thoughts. "Since you're stuck out here with only foot power to get you anywhere." He kept his right hand at the edge of the door, knowing he was challenging her in some indefinable way and not understanding why he felt the need to do so.

She glanced down to where his hand rested. Her lower lip moved as if she might say something.

He didn't flinch. He'd seen the softening in her face yesterday when he'd grabbed for his damned glasses with his useless left hand. He wouldn't make that mistake again. He preferred Ms. Blake's prickliness to her pity any day. Keeping his gaze fixed on her face, Rafe made his voice cool and disinterested. "So. Do you need a ride, Ms. Blake? Now, or later. Up to you. I live to serve."

Her smile changed the shape of her delicate cat face. "Yes, I've noticed."

He dipped his head as she hesitated. "Giving you a ride won't inconvenience me, Ms. Blake." He found he wanted to have her in his car again, to have her subtle female scent in his space, to watch the flash of quick intelligence in those soft eyes. Well. Rafe straightened. Life apparently still had the power to pitch him a curveball. In spite of himself, knowing he was a fool even as he moved, he stepped closer. "Even Charlotte couldn't force me to do a favor if I didn't want to, Megan," he said softly and watched her eyes widen with awareness before she caught herself. "I *want* to give you a lift into town."

"Really?" She threw him a teasing glance and dropped her hand from the door, motioning him in. "Yes, Mr. Jackson, since you've offered, I would love a ride. I need to do something about transportation until my stuff arrives." Her smile turned mischievous. "But I don't believe you're dying to play chauffeur." She tilted her head, observing him with her clear, soft eyes that saw more than he wanted her to. "And no matter what you insist, I believe you'd do almost anything for Charlotte."

"Right." He tucked both hands in his pockets. Ms. Blake had homed in on his Achilles' heel.

"Actually, I plan to rent a car. I could do that over the phone, but I'd like to stop at a hardware store and a grocery store." Standing still, she seemed to be in constant motion, a grubby hummingbird who tempted him in ways he hadn't foreseen and sure didn't want. One foot tapped;

her hands spun a conversation of their own. "Come on to the kitchen with me? I have a couple of questions for you, too. If you don't mind?" She walked away, her fanny swaying gently in front of him, the fabric of her denim shorts stretching and loosening with each barefooted step down the dust-covered hall carpet.

"Questions?" He coughed as she left a cloud of dust in her wake. "About what?"

Turning, she threw him a quick look over her shoulder, a tumble of honey-brown curls catching on her purple T-shirt. "The house." A guarded look came into her eyes. "The garden. That's all." Curls flying, she spun around and headed to the kitchen, her fanny doing that little rumba swing.

Ms. Blake could have no idea what a terrific walk she had, he thought sourly as he followed her into the living room. He had an inkling she'd hate to know exactly how provocative her tiny hip twitch was, that she'd probably cloister herself in a full body cast if she did. He tried not to watch.

He really tried. For five seconds, and then he surrendered to the mixed pleasure of observing Megan Blake's easy curves moving through the old hallway.

A mixed pleasure because, as tempting as she was, he had no intention of scratching this particular itch. He knew better. No sense in wanting something you couldn't have.

"Water?" She turned on the spigot and gestured to the stream of clear liquid. "Last night it was brown."

"Thanks. I'll pass."

"I would, too, but I'm absolutely parched." She cupped her hands together, stuck them into the rush of water, and drank. "Think I can get the electricity turned on today?"

"Sure." Rafe checked out the kitchen, the open refrigerator door. Spiderwebs laced the corners of the room, hung from window edges. He shouldn't have let her buy the house. He should have told her—But he hadn't. He'd kept his mouth shut.

Taking his hand out of his pocket, he gently touched the yellow wallpaper with its fruit basket design. Wallpaper from another time, another life. He'd always liked this kitchen.

Yesterday Charlotte had caught him off guard, unprepared to turn down her request that was, in truth, only a simple favor. Like a flamingo with its head under its wing, he'd been so engrossed in his own misery he'd let Meggie talk herself into this house. Twinges of conscience had forced him to call his cousin this morning and tell her he'd check on the Blake woman.

And, of course, last night there had been—those dreams. Vague, disorienting, they'd left him drained this morning. And lonely, a loneliness so deep he'd fled his apartment with relief.

"Mr. Jackson?"

"Rafe," he said absentmindedly, his thoughts lingering on last night. Weird. He shook his head and returned his attention to Megan Blake. Dripping from her pointed chin, water spotted her cotton T-shirt, left it clinging to the skin underneath. He wanted to touch those spots, see if the skin there was as soft as her mouth looked.

"Fine. Rafe it is." She waved her hand carelessly. "I suppose you might as well call me Meggie."

With the tip of his finger, he touched her chin. "Meggie." Her fine-grained skin was silky.

She blinked, stepped back, the pupils of her eyes dilating until she was all eyes.

"You're dripping."

She stared at him.

"The water faucet." He gestured to the sink.

"Oh." She blinked again and wiped her chin, looking down at the tips of her fingers as if bewildered by her action.

Rafe wanted to lift her chin and tell her it was only chemistry, nothing more. Chemistry was swell, sex was swell, but she wasn't going to have to worry about any of that, not with him, anyway. "Uh, Meggie." He wondered if she'd looked in the mirror this morning. "Did you want to change your clothes? Wash your face before we drive into town?"

"Wash my face?" She stooped to look at her face in the glass of the window. "Mud." Rubbing her cheek, she avoided his gaze. "I went for a walk in the rain last night."

"Fresh air's healthful," he said gravely, amused in spite of himself by her defensiveness. "I'm sure you slept better afterward."

She went peony-pink from her neck to the top of her forehead. The words came out in a half-strangled croak. "I slept great."

"Did you now?" he said, interested in her reaction. "What a surprise you are, Meggie. A campfire kind of girl in spite of your uptown look. I'm impressed. No electricity, a storm, and a sleeping bag? These made for a good night's sleep?" Through narrowed eyes, he watched her quick pull at her shorts, the way she half-turned from him to look through the window before hitting him with a blazing smile that turned his heart over.

"Absolutely. Never heard the storm until it was almost over." Limpid brown eyes met his.

"Good for you." He knew she was lying. Every instinct he still possessed red-flagged the too-steady way her gaze never wavered from his. Her attempt at earnest sincerity tickled him. He couldn't remember a time in the last months when anything had amused him, but Megan Blake had made him smile twice today already. "About that mud?" He pointed to her face.

"Oh, sure." She turned her back and bent over the sink, splashing water on her bright pink cheeks.

In spite of his determination to keep his distance from her, Meggie intrigued him. He'd give fifty dollars to know why she'd lied about sleeping well, though. Such an inconsequential lie. And little lies were always the most interesting. He shrugged. Hell, he wasn't about to share his secrets—why shouldn't she have hers?

Idly, watching her splash and fuss at the sink, Rafe wondered if Charlotte had been plotting again. He wouldn't put it past her to have made up the oyster-and-shrimp story. Not like him to have fallen so easily for Charlotte's tricks. He'd have to have a word with his sweet cuz.

Lifting the bottom of her T-shirt, Meggie dried her face. Her words were muffled and rushed. "Give me about ten minutes, okay?"

"Ah, clearly you're an optimist."

"Ha. I promise I won't take longer. I never do. Time me." As she buried her face in her T-shirt, a band of pale skin showed above the snap of her shorts, her belly button peeping above the loose waistband.

Heat shot straight to his groin. He could never have imagined how fast, how strong his reaction would be to nothing more than a brief glimpse of Meggie Blake's neatly knotted belly button. A small, delectable inny of a belly button. He wanted to dip his tongue there, lightly, gently, and taste that tiny bit of Megan Blake. Tugging at a too-tight tie, he swallowed.

He must have made a sound.

"What?" She looked up at him, her hands falling to her sides. The hem of her shirt dangled in damp, stretched-out wrinkles. Her chin lifted, dipped, and she bolted for the kitchen door, her words trailing after her. "I'll go change." A leaf dipsy-dooed from her hair, and she slapped the door open before he could hold it for her.

She'd seen the hunger in his face. He'd tried to mask it, but she'd glanced up so fast. . . . He stooped to pick up the leaf that had settled near the open refrigerator. He toyed with its rounded edge. Coralvine. Ms. Meggie had been wandering in the garden last night in the darkness and rain. Maybe she'd gone roaming in that brief spell when bright moonlight had waked him from his sultry dreams of her.

What had she done outside, in darkness and rain or moonlight?

He wanted to know.

He couldn't stay any longer in the house, and went outside to wait for her on the porch. Leaning against the porch railing, he watched Meggie's silhouette through the window. She moved quickly as she had in the kitchen, competently. Collecting a pile of clothes with a jeans leg hanging from it, she raced back to the kitchen, then swung back through the door into the living room, where she plucked brilliantly colored woman stuff from a suitcase.

He liked watching her as she danced like sunshine from room to room, finally bursting through the screen door. "That was fast."

"Told you I could do it." She held up her wrist, where a slim bracelet of silver dangled, a watch face embedded in its links. "See, eight minutes."

He half-expected her to stick out her tongue in the universal nah-nah, thumb-to-the-nose gesture. He couldn't get over the change in her since yesterday, a palpable hum of energy and excitement creating a magnetic field around her, and he couldn't take his eyes off her.

She'd slicked her hair back and tied it off her face with a wine-red scarf. Fringed ends fell forward onto her shoulder and tangled with her hair. "Don't underestimate a woman intent on power-shopping."

"I was wrong, a fool." He almost reached out to touch the temptation of her bright hair. The intensity of his need to let that silk coil around his finger threw him off guard. "I should have known better."

"Exactly," she said with a satisfied smirk. She was

down the porch steps and into the yard even as she spoke. "Besides, I'm a woman of my word." She threatened him with a waggle of the scarf in his direction and whirled toward his car. "Don't cross me."

"I wouldn't dream of it. You terrify me." And she did. He'd never spoken truer words. Meggie Blake was more dangerous to him than she could guess.

She sparkled and lured him with softness and a touch of vinegar under the sweetness. Around her, his loneliness and desolation lifted. She was dangerous because she reminded him of all he'd lost. She made him want his other life back, the one he couldn't have.

Three

Reaching to shut the car door for her, Rafe held his folded sunglasses in his hand. He waited for her to swing her legs inside, his eyes following the movement. Catching his scrutiny, Meggie slanted him a knowing glance. His self-mocking grimace was all appreciative male caught in the act. "Hey, it's a nice view. What can I say? Are you going to sic the p.c. squad on me?"

"I might." She gave him a small smile. "Or maybe not." Meggie liked the way his eyes gleamed with wickedness. She liked even more the fizz of her blood in her veins when his dark gaze moved slowly, reluctantly, over her, leaving a rush of female response behind. "What a glorious, beautiful, wonderful day," she said, lifting her arms to the brilliant blue of the sky. "I should have moved here sooner."

"Ah, a testimonial to Saw Creek's clean air and sunshine. Maybe you ought to think about finding a part-time job with the county tourist bureau? Make a little money even. Put all that enthusiasm to a good cause."

Nothing in his face betrayed his teasing. Meggie was impressed. The best poker face she'd ever seen, that was for sure. Whimsically she wondered if he'd paid for his Porsche with a couple of good hands of cards. "A part-time job? Why? Does Charlotte have to pay you part of her commission and you're scared I won't be able to cover it?"

"Good point. I'll talk to her about that. I should have thought about my cut before I agreed to show you the houses. House," he corrected. "And you didn't even step through the front door. The way I see it, now that you've brought the subject up, Charlotte should hand over the whole commission."

"Oh, tough man. Picking on a poor sick woman recovering from bad shrimp. No sympathy for your cousin? Obviously you've never had bad shrimp."

"Not that I know of. Besides, Charlotte is probably getting all the sympathy she needs from Arnie. And from herself. Charlotte enjoys her dramas." He grinned, and Meggie was stunned into momentary silence. The mega-watt brilliance of his smile transformed his somber face and left her breathless.

"Speaking of Charlotte, does she know anything about the family who owned the house?"

A crack of plastic snapped her head upright.

The stem of his sunglasses lay shattered in his open palm.

"Yes. Charlotte knew the family." Not looking at Meggie, he juggled the broken bits, then stuffed them into his pocket.

"Terrific. How about you?" Impatient with the adrenaline and excitement sparking through her, Meggie wanted to shake him into giving her information. "Did you know them well? The people who owned my house?"

"Yes." He swung the door shut on her next question and strode around to the driver's side and slid in.

Before he stuck the key in the ignition, she laid her hand on his arm, stopping him. "Tell me, anything, please. I love this house. I want to know everything about it."

"That was what you meant earlier? About having questions? I thought you were interested in knowing about Saw Creek. Where the dry cleaner and the bakery are. Maybe the library." The keys swung from his lean fingers, and Meggie had the sense that he was buying time, sorting out his thoughts. "But it was the house you had questions about, huh?"

"Who owned the house? I saw the name of the trust on the paperwork I signed, and, yes, I *know* I should have asked Charlotte who the people behind the trust are, but, heck, I didn't care, not yesterday. But today—"

"Buyer's remorse?" His finger traced the ridge of a key.

"Not for a second. But everything was happening so fast, and I was determined to sleep in my house last night, no matter what."

He wove the key back and forth between two fingers. "I noticed. You were a five-foot-two steamroller."

"Don't get nasty. It doesn't become you."

"I'm never nasty. Especially not when I'm gussied up in my second-best suit." Again came that unsettling impression that he was changing the subject.

"And a very nice suit it is, too." It really was. Meggie liked the dark blue pinstripe. The Italian cut saved it from being boring. But finger to her mouth, considering, she said regretfully, trying to keep her expression as blank as his had been, "Makes you look like a banker, though, the more I think about it." A slightly menacing banker. "A banker who wouldn't think twice before calling in a loan from the Borgias."

Like Rafe's car, his suit was expensive, the fabric emphasizing the width of his shoulders, the way they tapered to a narrow waist, where a thin black belt was threaded through pant loops.

Her teasing mood vanished as images from her dream

flashed through her in a wave of heat and awareness. She glanced away from him, back to the garden, tore her gaze away from it, too, as her fingers tingled. "Okay, enough with the compliments about your ensemble."

"Oh, that's what the comment about the Borgias was?" Rafe tipped his head. "They were the poisoners, right? Pretty dangerous fellows from what I remember."

"Well, it *is* a great suit. Even if you do look like a rascally banker. Charlotte pick it out for you?" Meggie couldn't resist a teeny jab of her own. She was more comfortable needling Rafe Jackson than dwelling on thoughts of her statue and the way it had seemed almost alive in her dream-fugue. "Charlotte has good taste, I'll say that. She pick out the one yesterday? The three-piece gray number?" She gave him a smile as sweet as sugar.

"Nope. Charlotte doesn't pick out my clothes. Nor does my nonexistent wife. I actually manage to pick out my own clothes and dress myself."

Meggie wanted to bite her tongue. She hadn't been thinking about his hand. "I didn't—"

"Meggie. Don't worry. You made a joke." His tone was even, undisturbed. "I got it. I didn't think you meant anything else. I don't go around looking for insults."

Veering back to her main point, embarrassment making her rush her words awkwardly, she said, "Tell me about the house, the people, okay? I'm dying for the details. Tell me anything—everything you can."

"You ask a lot of questions."

"I want a lot of answers." Meggie's cheeks hurt with the effort, but she smiled through her mortification. "Because this house is special to me. I know, I know," she said as she caught his skeptical expression. Dismay made her stilted, too formal. Her words sounded strained even to her own ears. Trying to ease the situation, she was rattling on like an idiot. "I bought it on impulse. I ignored advice. But from the minute I saw this place"—she surveyed the shell driveway, the creamy white paint—"I knew I was meant to live here."

"Been at the Ouija board, have you?"

"It's the right season, although funny, I'm not into crystals and New Age stuff. But this house"—she paused, not able to tell him about the garden and the statue in the gold moonlight—"feels like it's always been mine, that I was destined to find it. I won't blame you if you laugh—"

"I won't laugh."

"But I've never known such a sense of—*possession*," she concluded, realizing that *possession* was exactly the right word for her connection to the house. "It's mine in a way nothing in my life has ever been. It has a joyousness to it. The people who lived here must have been very much in love. Happy," she said wistfully. "Were they?"

Rafe's arm jerked against her wrist. The keys jangled in his hand. "Yes. They were."

Meggie glanced down. Her fingers still gripped the hard strength of his arm. His muscle was taut under her palm, warm.

Like the statue's lean, muscled flank.

Scalded, she yanked her hand away. "Sorry."

"Don't let it go to your head. I won't break. You're not that strong."

Relieved that he'd turned her carelessness into another joke, Meggie raised her hands palm out to him in apology, in explanation. Widowed at twenty-eight, she'd learned to be careful. Otherwise, uncomfortable situations happened. People in Saw Creek didn't know her the way her Wisconsin neighbors and friends did. Her ignorance of local customs could lead to misinterpretation. She intended to put down roots here. She wanted to fit in as much as she could. She didn't want to begin on the wrong foot with anyone, and especially not with this man.

Choosing her words carefully but stumbling over them,

Meggie said, "I just don't want you to misunderstand. To think—"

"To think what, Meggie? That you were hitting on me?" He put the keys into the ignition. "Don't worry about it. I know you weren't. My ego's not that big."

"I didn't even realize—" Floundering, no longer interested in the previous owners of her house, Meggie tried to explain the awkwardness of the last year and a half. "It's just that—"

"That you're not the very merry widow?"

"Yes," she whispered, her throat closing. "I was excited about the house. I wasn't thinking. You're a stranger. You could have thought—anything. A lot of things." Her hands circling in futility, she sought desperately for the words to make clear what she meant. "I'm out of the habit of being around people. I've always been clumsy in social situations, and I've never been good at small talk. Even before Jonah—" She shrugged, her fists dropping to her lap. "And afterward, well, I didn't want to talk to anybody. To socialize. I—didn't have any tolerance for the wear and tear of friendship, of crowds." She took a deep breath. "I haven't been a nice person to be around for a long time."

"Niceness, politeness, they can keep people at a distance. Seclusion can be a way of protecting yourself. From strangers. Even from friends."

Struck by what he'd said, she shifted to look at him. She *had* been protecting herself. But she hadn't been able to keep Rafe at a distance. *That* was the problem. She kept forgetting that Rafe wasn't a stranger. Not a friend. He was in some category she couldn't define.

The corded muscle under her hand had felt as familiar as if she'd touched him the same way some other time, some other place, as if she'd known him all her life.

He'd intruded on her space, her emotions, and her energy from the first minute she'd seen him, and she'd reacted like a porcupine, bristling every time she was near him. In his presence, she couldn't find the walls she'd been hiding behind.

A wizard in tailored suits and a shiny black Porsche, he'd cast a spell over her. Meggie folded her hands tightly together. Rafe made her impulsive. She needed to be more cautious in her new environment.

She wasn't a person who touched people casually and Rafe Jackson was a man who would not be casual about anything. Two days in his company had taught her that.

He was a man who would consume a woman who let him into her life.

She was as certain of that fact as she was of her own name. She had no idea how she knew it, but she did.

After a long pause thick with tension, Rafe said, "Easier not to be around people sometimes." He fired up the engine. His voice was harsh, with an edge to it she hadn't noticed before. "I can understand that." Studying her, he nodded once and rested his left hand on the bottom of the steering wheel, an offering. "Our situations are different, but I didn't want to be around anyone after I got shot. I didn't want to deal with questions, with other people's feelings."

"Shot?" She was proud of herself for being able to keep her voice matter-of-fact, matching his.

"On duty. Eight months ago in Tampa. March." His left hand twitched. "My partner was in front of me. I didn't see the man come out of the alley doorway. The alley was clear. Then it wasn't. And Paulie was bleeding out all over the trash and junk."

"Your partner?" Oh, please, Meggie prayed. Let his partner be okay. Alive, laughing somewhere in some honky-tonk.

Rafe shook his head. Cleared his throat. "I was too late."

"I see." Oh, she did, she did. Not his fault, undeserved, but guilt anyway.

Guilt had no conscience. Like worms in an apple, it nibbled away, destroying peace. She understood survivor guilt, all right. Jonah's illness had been quick and dirty, and she'd done everything she humanly could, but she'd been left with guilt's malicious chanting that drummed in her head until she couldn't sleep, that whispered of what-ifs and things undone, words unsaid.

Rafe was trying to help her. He was handing her a gift the price of which she couldn't begin to fathom. And, hearing him, she wanted to cover his damaged hand with hers and heal it, to heal the pain inside his guilt-haunted soul.

Because she understood.

Instead, she kept her hands folded and listened.

"For a long time I stayed away from everyone, including my friends. I didn't want them staring at my hand." He fiddled with the gear knob. "I didn't need their—concern."

Meggie heard the word he didn't say. *Pity.* Rafe Jackson wasn't a man who would accept concern. Intuition told her that he would hate fake cheerfulness and reassurances. Why wouldn't he? She felt the same way.

"I hid away from everyone."

"Except Charlotte."

He nodded. "Except Charlotte. She made daily trips to Tampa until I was out of the hospital, and then she nagged me until I moved back to Saw Creek two weeks ago."

"That's why you agreed to do a favor for her even though you didn't want to spend five minutes in a stranger's company."

"Yeah." He held up his hand. His laugh was harsh. "My badge of failure. A reminder that I screwed up big time. And Paulie paid the price. Permanently."

Meggie didn't tell him he hadn't messed up. Words were inadequate for the pain screaming inside him.

In plain sight now, the blue-gray pucker of his scar was ugly, the twisted contortion of his hand painful to see, but not repulsive. The way it looked wasn't the issue. She grasped that.

In spite of his suits and car, Rafe wouldn't care about the appearance of his hand. It was a wound that would go deeper than sinew and bone. It was a soul-deep wound because he believed he'd failed his friend. For a good man, and she was beginning to believe that was exactly what Rafe was, that kind of wound would destroy.

He hit the wheel with his ruined hand. "And since you're so—interested, here's the rest of it, Meggie Blake. That house was my partner's."

"But you were Tampa police officers? I don't understand."

"Paulie and his wife and three children lived here in Saw Creek. The Tampa P.D. didn't require us to live in the city limits. Saw Creek is a nice place to raise kids, and it was only a forty-minute commute, thirty in the Porsche. When I stayed over with them."

Meggie heard the break in his voice. "What happened to his wife and children?"

"Liddy took the children back home to Georgia where her folks live." Blocking the blaze of sunlight streaming into the car, Rafe flipped down the visor. "You wondered if the people who lived here were happy. Oh, God, yes, Meggie. They were so happy the house blazed with it. I walk in there and the happiness takes my breath away still. Any other questions?"

"No." Meggie's heart ached. Rafe had waited for her on the porch, not inside the house where warmth and happiness lingered in the very boards and paint. For her. For Rafe, though, the happiness permeating the house was unbearable.

Now was not the moment to ask him about her statue. She had her demons to exorcise, Rafe had his. No matter how much she yearned to, she couldn't help him. Finally seeing the glint of sunlight, she was doing all she could to leave the cold emptiness of the last year and a half behind her.

Rafe tucked his hand out of sight and shifted into drive, letting the wheel spin under the flattened palm of his good hand, his beautiful, elegant right hand. "And now you know."

"And now I know," she repeated like a promise.

He left the windows open and U-turned down her driveway and onto the main road, the car's engine accelerating in a burst of power.

Wind blasted in, tearing at her hair.

"Want the windows up?" A kind of test in the look he shot her way.

She untied her scarf, and strands of hair stung her cheeks, clung to her mouth. "Nope, I'm no girlie-girl."

"And here I was hoping you were." Subtle shades of meaning she didn't understand in his tone.

"You don't like girlie-girls." She knew she was right.

"Maybe I do."

"Nah." She turned her face to the wind, letting it fill her with its power, with its smell of earth and flowers. Not crisp and sharp like Wisconsin. Sultry and luxuriant, a scent that made her want to stretch and purr. She stuck her arm out the window, letting the wind buffet her, push her arm back. "I may not be a hammer-and-nail kind of girl, but you're positively not a blonde-on-the-arm kind of guy. Or a brunette either," she added in fairness to her blonde friends.

"Think not?"

"Know so." She laughed as water from a standing pool splashed up on her elbow. "Oh, you wouldn't have the teeniest bit of trouble finding a trophy doll, but you wouldn't enjoy the experience."

"Might be worth finding out, though?" That tiny muscle at the corner of his thin mouth lifted.

"You'd be bored to tears."

"You're real sure about this?"

"Absolutely. I know these things," she added primly, drawing her arm in.

"You're psychic?"

"Irish. Same difference. It counts, even if the Irish goes so far back I couldn't find it if my life depended on it. And I'm smart, too. That's another reason I know things. So there."

"Such modesty. Such humility." He laid his hand over his heart. "I'm speechless."

"In some other lifetime, maybe. Come on, fess up. You're not into trophy dates."

"You're right. Girlie-girls bore me. Besides, I like women, not girls. And I really, really like smart women, Meggie Blake. Especially when they have a sassy mouth." He tapped her mouth. "Just so *you* understand."

Meggie went hot pink, blood burning her cheeks. She was speechless. Rafe's comment was a warning, not a compliment, but a glow of pleasure rippled through her.

He slowed as they approached the main intersection. The big plate glass windows of downtown Saw Creek stores were painted with Halloween pumpkins and ghouls. Some stores had spidery cobwebs strung in the doorways. The wind rustled the brittle ends of tall corn shucks tied to posts and fastened to the sides of shop entrances.

For a second, Meggie was disoriented.

Palm trees and pumpkins were a culture shock. Corn shucks and pumpkins were midwestern, northern, out of place in Saw Creek's October heat and next to its palm trees. "You're not in Kansas anymore, Dorothy. Or Wisconsin, either," she muttered under her breath.

Rafe gave a dry chuckle. "Florida and the Midwest are totally different countries."

"Probably not."

"They have different languages."

"Oh, sure," she scoffed. "I don't have to translate *y'all*. It travels."

"Long as you don't use it when you're talking to one person." He lifted an eyebrow. "Or we'll have to pack up your bags and send you back to Wisconsin and your big-city ways."

Even though Madison was the state capital, it had its own kind of small-town pleasantness. Saw Creek didn't seem that different now that she looked around at the people and the shop windows. "Nice town."

"Most of the time." Rafe guided the car around a blue-haired senior on a three-wheeled bicycle. "No town is a Norman Rockwell cover candidate these days."

"You have to be wrong."

"I'm not," he said bleakly. "But Saw Creek's okay. Slow-paced. If that appeals to you."

"You're more the urban cowboy, right?"

"Yeah." He frowned.

"You miss Tampa."

"Yeah. I do."

Meggie let the subject drop. After eight months, he hadn't come to terms with the changes in his life. She could understand that, too. *Irrevocable* was a hard wall to smash into.

Rafe steered them slowly through the surprising traffic on the main street, where fat pumpkins were stacked on the sidewalk and pots of carnations made pyramids of bronze and white. That fast she decided. "I'm going to carve a pumpkin this year."

"Kids drive by and bust 'em."

"I don't care. That's part of Halloween. Being a tad wicked. I'll open my door and scream at them, be the neighborhood curmudgeon. I can do that. I've had enough practice." She saw a series of pumpkins sculpted into fang-toothed demons and painted with neon-bright colors. "Maybe I'll have three pumpkins. For balance."

"Ah, the artistic temperament rears its head. Should be interesting."

"Darned right it will be. I'll turn those pumpkins into goofy, snaggletoothed ghouls, stick 'em on my porch, and put out bowls of candy for your non–Norman Rockwell trick-or-treaters." She frowned. "Unless Saw Creek's given up trick-or-treating in favor of a sanitized Allhallows eve?" She hoped not. Halloween needed that icy edge of danger.

"Nope. But don't leave your candy bowl on the porch. You won't have anything left except the sugar-free chewing gum. The bowl'll be empty after the first goblin stops by."

"You're raining on my parade, you know."

"Warning you, that's all. As for rain, it keeps the monsters in. Cool and crisp brings them out. So, depending on the weather, Halloween can get a shade hairy, even in Saw Creek."

"Good." She nodded. "That's exactly what I want. Hairy. Spooky. But why are you trying to pop my Halloween balloon?"

"Because I know kids. I was even one myself. Can't trust the little devils farther than you can sneeze."

"You're a cynic, Jackson."

"You'll get no argument from me on that point."

"And how did you know I'd have chewing gum?"

He shook his head. "I'm—I *was* a damn good detective, Meggie Blake."

"I'll bet you were," she said gently, letting the moment rest between them before continuing as if he hadn't brought up his past, a past that still haunted him. "Anyway, no matter what your little devils do, *I'm* going to spray cobwebs all over my porch, too, I am," she decided as she surveyed the different types of cobwebs festooning storefronts.

"Gettin' into the season, huh? Goin' to get down and funky?"

"You bet. I might even wear a costume."

"After seeing you with those leaves in your hair this morning, I could give you a couple of ideas."

"What? A tree?"

"Nope." His smile was guileless. "I was thinking more along the lines of a wood nymph."

"Oh." Meggie couldn't think of a comeback, not with that sly look in his eyes, that look that made her remember pictures of barely clad nymphs cavorting through the woods followed by lascivious satyrs. And, remembering his subtle warning, she kept to herself the smart-alecky comment that finally occurred to her about a costume he could wear.

Rafe angled the car into a parking spot in front of a hardware store at a strip mall. "The rent-a-car office is over there." He pointed two doors over from the hardware store. "Only car agency in town. If you'd rather go somewhere else, I'll drive you down to Sarasota."

"I'm sure I can find what I want here." She opened the car door. "Oh, who do I see about the electricity and phone service?"

He motioned to a large redbrick building set back from a park. "City Hall."

"Thanks. See you later."

Leaning across the seat, Rafe held the door as she scooched out. "I'm not going anywhere. I'll wait until I'm sure you have a car."

Surprised, Meggie stooped to look inside the open window. "You're going to wait for me?"

The grooved lines between his eyebrows deepened as she contemplated him. "You thought I'd abandon you to the evils of wild Saw Creek? Some opinion you have of me.''

''I don't have a clue how long I'll be. Why on earth would you waste your day waiting around for me?'' She was uncomfortable. ''Charlotte wouldn't expect it. I sure don't. It's not necessary. Truly.''

''Hell, seems like the *po*-lite thing to do.'' He put a spin on the words, an exaggerated southern lilt. ''My mama raised me to be a gentleman.'' He touched the knuckles of her hand where it rested on the slit for the window. ''Don't worry about how I'll amuse myself. Why, land's sake, sugarplum, look around you,'' he drawled. ''All this excitement. I'm a big boy. Shoot, I can entertain myself.''

''I'm sure you can.'' His version of a good ol' boy entertained her. ''But pluck the straw out of your hair, country boy.''

''Case of the pot calling the kettle black, isn't it, Meggie? After all, *I* wasn't the one with leaves in my hair and mud on my face this morning, was I?'' He lifted the tips of her fingers from their resting spot on the car window, and she felt the warmth of his skin right down to her ittybittiest toe. ''I want to wait. Leave it at that, all right?'' Like silk over a cat's fur, his voice rubbed over her, electrifying her. A midnight voice.

She wanted to arch her back, let that smooth voice caress her. Instead she loosened her fingers from the window and tucked her hands inside her pockets. Her hand trembled. ''Fine. Your choice.''

''Yes, Meggie, it is. I'd do the same for anyone.''

Hands in pockets, Meggie rubbed her tingling fingertips against the slippery fabric of her slacks. ''You sure know how to make a girl feel special, Rafe Jackson.''

''You're not a girl, though, Meggie. Remember? You're a smart woman with a clever mouth.'' His gaze lingered on her mouth, almost, she thought, in spite of himself.

But it was the words, the words. Spoken in his rich,

husky voice, they beguiled her. For an instant she was lost in a place of darkness and touch and scent. A world where the only sound was of hearts beating, together.

"Hey, lady, look out. Please." After bumping her, a gray-haired, Rollerblading man with knee pads, elbow pads, and a helmet whizzed by. "Sorry," he threw over his shoulder, grabbing on to the nearest pole and shredding corn shuck leaves as he tried to align feet and shoulders.

Released from the spell, Meggie shuddered.

"Hey, I didn't hurt you, did I?" Latched onto the pole, the Rollerblader swayed clumsily. "Jeez, I hope not."

"No, I'm fine," Meggie returned slowly, her gaze never leaving Rafe's.

Behind her, the sound of wheels clunked, scraped against the sidewalk. "If you're sure." Slowly the skater moved forward, wheels stomping as he regained his balance.

A dull flush touched Rafe's angular cheekbones. "Go do your errands, Meggie. You can find me in Java Joe's." He withdrew into the dim interior of the car.

"Java Joe's. Okay." And Meggie whirled away, shaking, her breath thick and labored.

What in God's name was happening to her? Who was this Meggie who dreamed of unseen hands and a wicked mouth that burned her to ashes? Who was this Meggie whose pulse bumped and raced around Rafer Jackson?

Her hands were still shaking when she pushed open the door of the rental agency.

Frowning, Rafe rested his chin on the steering wheel. The burgundy flash of Meggie's slight self vanished behind the glass doors. He didn't want this heat, this *need,* searing him. A touch of Meggie's soft skin, and he'd wanted to haul her into the car and touch his tongue against that spot at the base of her throat where her blood beat a rapid song under silky skin.

He'd told her his mama had raised a gentleman.

But he didn't recognize the man whose blood thundered in his brain, his groin, with a primal beat.

The subconscious ruled a man in spite of layers of civilization and training, he knew. But what he experienced around Meggie Blake was outside his comprehension.

And altogether terrifying.

He'd never been a man to lose control. Not his style. Not at work. Not in private. Control over everything. His sex life. His work. His relationships.

Effortlessly, Meggie ripped the reins of his control from him.

And he couldn't stay away from her.

That was the most terrifying fact of all.

He wanted to keep his distance from this slim, honey-haired woman with the soft, hopeful eyes.

And he couldn't.

Rolling up the windows and locking the car, he walked to Joe's, head down, thinking.

What was he going to do about Meggie Blake? And all that hope shining from her eyes? It was the hope that would destroy him if he surrendered to the need boiling up in him. Because he'd given up hoping.

But Meggie hadn't.

Four

For the week before Halloween, Meggie worked like a dog.

She didn't see Rafe. He had waited for her until she'd rented her car and arranged for electricity. Then he'd left, his sleek Porsche vanishing into the afternoon blaze of sunlight. She didn't know if she'd see him again, didn't know if he'd call.

She wanted him to, though.

She was drawn to his pain, to his wry cynicism. Like her garden, he summoned some emotion from the deepest part of her psyche. Every nurturing instinct she possessed bent toward him.

But she could wait.

Because her garden bewitched her absolutely, leaving no energy, no time for anything except it and the statue at its center.

Loading her rental van with shovels, clippers, hoes, and various tools the helpful hardware man had assured her she'd need, she'd headed for the grocery store and then for home, the equipment and groceries rattling and swaying in the back of the van. She'd unpacked her groceries,

stuffed everything that could possibly require chilling into
the refrigerator. Its comforting hum assured her she'd have
ice and cold beer sometime later. The sight of her soda,
beer, lettuce, and tomatoes in the refrigerator cheered her
with its ordinariness.

She was claiming territory.

Filling a thermos with store-bought ice and tap water,
she changed into shorts and a cropped top and headed toward the yard, driven by a sense of urgency she couldn't
explain even to herself.

The urgency had nothing to do with her feelings about
Jonah, nothing to do with the reasons she'd come to Saw
Creek. Instead of walking like a zombie through her days
as she had for eighteen months, she had a purpose to her
days, a sense of direction so powerful that she couldn't *not*
work.

In some corner of her subconscious, a clock ticked toward an unknown deadline and kept her working until she
thought she'd literally drop where she stood.

She didn't collapse.

And she didn't quit.

When she returned from town that first day, she dug up
weedlike vines with poisonous yellow flowers. Sweating
and puffing in the center section of the hedges, she
chopped at the shrubs surrounding the statue so that she
could have easier access to it. The night before, she'd
scraped and cut herself on dead branches and thorns in her
frenzy to see what was underneath the armor of greenery.
Because of the vines and overgrowth she hadn't been able
to reach high enough to look into the statue's face.

Perspiration streaming down her back, she hacked away
at the biggest branches near the statue base. If she could
only see his face, she—She could what?

Vines had crept over it again, and the statue seemed held
prisoner under a web of lacy greenery. Some of the kudzu
had grown back. The late afternoon breeze coming in from

the west and the gulf shifted the vines, stirring them as if with the statue's breath. Struggling to pull one particularly stubborn strand, Meggie wrapped the tendrils around her arm for better leverage. "All right, you devil weed," she huffed. "Give it up. I'm not quitting." Wrenching and digging her booted heels in the spongy ground, she gave a ferocious yank. Bouncing back on her rear, she lay stunned for a second. The vine whipped loose, showering her with dirt and dried leaves. And probably spiders. Shuddering, she hauled herself to her feet and paused to catch her breath. She spat out grains of dirt and opened her thermos.

Pouring cold water over her head and neck, drenching her shirt, she stopped, suddenly puzzled, studying the statue.

Last night, surely the statue had been closer to the far wall of hedges and bushes, closer to the rock wall at the back of the yard, not quite so near the house as it now was.

Dizzy with heat and exertion, she thought for a moment that the statue had moved. In her memories, that one hand and arm had been completely trapped in the rough stone base. Today, even through the chain mail of vines, she thought that more of the forearm showed. And she'd remembered the statue's position as more crouched. Hadn't it been half-stooped, as though pulling itself free of that stone base? It was straighter than she remembered, the long, ropy muscles of the back stretching tall. How could she have made such a mistake?

Meggie shook her head, water drops spraying around her. She was tired and hot and last night she'd been wrapped up in the remnants of that peculiarly erotic dream. For pete's sake, no wonder she couldn't tell exactly what she'd seen, what imagined.

But moonlight had made the night so bright. Pensively

she looked up at the sky. Off to the east, the first faint
white of the moon shone on the horizon.

By Halloween the moon would be full, a harvest moon.
A moon as golden as the one in her dream.

Her dream. Meggie shivered and a delicious chill raised
goose bumps over her arms, tightened her nipples under
her damp shirt.

When she could no longer see in the deep tropical night,
the watery moonlight casting heavy shadows, she went inside and showered in water that gurgled brown before running clear and silvery over her.

Without furniture, TV, or a radio, the house was silent
in a way she'd hadn't known in a long time. A peaceful
silence where guilt and anger and sadness didn't chatter in
her brain. This house offered hope. Life *would* be good
again. This was a good place.

Kicking the refrigerator shut, she uncapped a beer and
lifted it in a toast to the silent house, to the past. "To you,
Jonah, for all your sweetness, for everything you were. I
loved you, and I know you loved me. I did the best I could,
Jonah. And I believe you knew that. And I'll always love
you, one way or the other, Jonah, but I need my life back.
I want to be alive again, to *feel*. I can't stay anymore in
this gray wasteland. I need to be *alive* again, and not feel
guilty that I am and you aren't. Oh, Jonah, forgive me.
Please." Her throat closed on the words.

No one answered.

Nothing broke the silence and stillness.

But as she stood there, her beer foaming onto the floor
and hot tears streaming down her face, peace settled over
her like a blessing.

"Thank you, Jonah," she whispered and wiped the tears
from her face. "Thank you."

Later, sitting with a plate of tomatoes and a beer on her
porch steps, she looked out toward the river road and the
gate she'd left open. Too tired to put one foot in front of

the other, she nevertheless dragged herself down to the tall gate and locked it. She wasn't afraid to be alone in her house, but she wasn't stupid either.

Rafe had told her even Saw Creek could have its hidden side. She believed him. He'd grown up here. He knew the town. She didn't.

With blistered hands, she forced the lock to turn, lowered the heavy metal bar, and tottered back to the house and her sleeping bag.

Tomorrow, she'd order a bed.

She poked the blister on her thumb. And buy garden gloves. And pumpkins. She didn't want to forget the pumpkins.

Pumpkins were crucial to the whole spirit of Allhallows eve, she thought drowsily as she squirmed in her sleeping bag, trying to find the most comfortable spot for her protesting muscles. She definitely needed pumpkins for her jack-o'-lanterns.

After all, Irishman Jack hadn't been able to go to heaven or hell after his deal with the devil. Ordered by the devil to go back where he came from, poor Jack had wandered the earth by the light of a lump of coal the devil had tossed his way. Sticking it into a turnip, Jack had wandered the earth ever since, a spirit doomed to find peace nowhere in heaven, hell, or earth.

Meggie yawned. Halloween wouldn't have the same blithe ghoulishness without jack-o'-lanterns.

With that cheerful plan, she closed her eyes. Dropping into sleep like a stone, she never thought about her dream, never expected it to come again.

In her sleep, she saw the statue turning toward her as she walked in the garden, and she yielded to the spell of that golden, beckoning arm gratefully, as if her subconscious had merely been waiting for her phantom to appear.

She couldn't see his face, but his rough voice whispered in her ear. *Meggie. I'm here. Remember? Do you like this,*

Meggie, beautiful Meggie, Meggie with your beautiful, hopeful eyes? The unseen hand moved over her mouth, brushing with a feather-light touch on her bottom lip, sliding gently inside to touch the inside corner of her mouth, and all the while his other hand teased her breast, tracing ever-narrowing circles around its aching tip.

Dry-mouthed and needing more than that light touch, she murmured, "Yes, oh, yes."

The warm lick of his tongue over the side of her neck and down to her nipple left an ice-hot trail of dampness, chilling, burning, as the night breeze drifted where his mouth and tongue had been.

She remembered that touch. Remembered that fire.

And wanted it again.

Here, Meggie? Does this please you, too? Her phantom lover pressed a narrow palm against her abdomen and trailed his fingers over her breasts, back and forth, and fire leapt from her skin, consuming her. His thumbs stroked against the midline of her belly, grazed lower, lingered with a teasing touch that grew firmer until her skin vibrated from head to toe.

Meggie knew she was dreaming, but she saw herself lying on the floor in her sleeping bag, moonlight and mist drifting over her in a golden glow, touching her, seeping through the membrane of her skin into her blood and bones, claiming her.

And everywhere the mist and golden light touched, she trembled. Spiraling tighter and higher, urged by that phantom touch, her body rushed toward a distant peak.

Meggie, the voice whispered against her belly, lips brushing like the breeze against skin that quivered in its passing. *Come into the garden. Let me come into you, sweet Meggie.*

Then, in that moment when she thought she could stand no more, his mouth took hers, and his hand moved down her body and covered her, stroked her in the rhythm of his tongue against hers and showed her that she could indeed stand more, wanted more.

Awake, she lay there with the final tremors of her arousal dying away. Tears streamed down her face.

Only a dream after all.

But she knew her phantom lover. Knew his voice.

Deep inside her the voice still vibrated, still whispered, and held her in thrall to its promise.

Outside her window the moon cast a golden glow, a wash of magic across her floor. Her feet and arms and breasts were golden, too, in that light as she stumbled to the window and looked toward the garden.

Nearer yet to the house, noticeably nearer now, the statue turned toward her window, its face hidden under the arc of one lifted arm and shoulder, the other arm, as before, partially trapped in stone.

Like her statue, Rafe was trapped, not in stone, but by self-forged shackles of guilt. In vain and endless battles, statue and man struggled against their chains.

Rafe had lost himself in that blood-drenched alley.

Her statue was lost in the wilderness of the garden.

Pulling on a T-shirt and panties, Meggie went outside and pushed through the hedges to the garden. The vines would return in the morning. But during the midnight hours, she touched her statue, pulled vines from his sleek body, left it naked and moonlight-gilded before she curled at his feet, and slept, dreamless and deeply.

Her last conscious thought was of Rafe.

She woke to mockingbirds and sunshine and to a statue covered again in fast-growing kudzu, its face hidden from her. Surely it wasn't possible for kudzu to grow quite that fast.

Dazed, Meggie looked at the trail of flattened grass that led toward the house. Dream or no dream, she was positive the statue was not in the same place it had been.

''Come on, Meggie, don't weird out here,'' she scolded

herself, her voice mingling with a blue jay's shriek. "This is planet Earth, Saw Creek, Florida, and not the Twilight Zone. So what else could have happened? Think, doofus."

Was it possible that the movement of the rapidly growing vines had the power to shift the heavy marble and stone? Or, more likely, had some mischievous group of Saw Creek teenagers crawled over her fence and moved the statue while she slept?

That thought made her uneasy in a way the other explanations, real or fanciful, had not. The idea that she had slept half-naked in her garden while strangers invaded her garden and played tricks on her made her skin crawl.

On her trip into town, she watched for Rafe. He might know if kids had played with the statue. Maybe it was the custom for Saw Creek kids to steal the statue and cart it to the middle of town as part of Halloween. Or part of the rivalry between the two high schools and their football teams.

Any of those explanations made far more sense than the one that argued against reason and said the statue had moved on its own.

Meggie bought several troubleshooting lights. She intended to leave them on during the night. Light would chase away intruders.

She didn't see Rafe.

She missed him, missed him as though she'd always known him, always had him at her side.

Her days were filled with backbreaking physical labor and that frightening sense of time running out. During the days, she thought of Rafe, her thoughts coming again and again back to him as if some golden thread spun from him to her, joining them. Meggie couldn't shake the notion that the three of them, statue, man, and woman, were linked, held captive together in some way she didn't understand.

Under a hot sun, she weeded and clipped and chopped and worked until she could no longer see even by the glare of the troubleshooter lights she'd hung from the branches of trees and connected to the house with extension cords.

Her nights were given over to her phantom.

She couldn't wait to go to sleep at night. She put on perfume and shaved her legs. Then, as if waiting for a lover, she folded herself into the secondhand brass bed she'd found and had delivered. She'd set it up herself in the bedroom that faced the garden.

She knew she was obsessed and no longer cared.

Not even on the third night, when she found gardenia petals strewn across her moonlit floor, their creamy thick petals turning brown with her touch, their rich, alluring scent filling her lungs with every breath, seducing her.

She scooped the fragrant petals up, scattered them on her bed, drifted them across her naked body, over her thighs and breasts, and went to sleep. And in her dream of a garden with roses and gardenias in luxuriant profusion, the shape of her golden statue moved ever closer, seeking her.

The day before Halloween she phoned Rafe.

She had wakened that morning to the wet imprint of footsteps on her porch and in the damp ground of her yard. Clumps of glossy leaves from a gardenia bush lay beside the footprints.

"I'm sorry, Rafe, so sorry, but I didn't know who else to call." She spoke into her shiny white new phone and tried to minimize her uneasiness. "The footprints go all around the house, as if someone had marched barefooted past each of my windows, looking in." She didn't tell him about the gardenia petals and leaves.

"Have you notified the police?" His voice plucked at her nerve endings, her nerves still thrumming in the aftermath of the dream.

"No. But—I will. Thanks. You're right. I should have." Snapped back to reality by his question, she wondered why she had called him. More logical, as he'd suggested, to think of calling the police.

But she hadn't. Rafe wasn't even a detective anymore, but her first and only thought had been to call him. She hadn't thought of the police, not once. Maybe because she hadn't been afraid, not really, not even at the sight of those narrow footprints deep under her living room window. "I don't know what I was thinking of. I shouldn't have bothered you."

"Hold on, Meggie. You didn't." The sound of a spoon clinking against a cup came to her through the airwaves. "I'm glad you called, in fact."

Pleasure curled through her, slow and sweet. Primitive humans would have attributed this miracle of hearing a distant voice to magic. Maybe, she decided, modern humans had lost the capacity for amazement, all miracles and magic explained, the curtain drawn back to reveal the technology and wires. But magical it was, she thought, true magic to be able to see a loved one again, to hear his voice anew, on a piece of tape years later. "I don't want to disturb you."

"Too late for that, Meggie." His laugh, sleep-rough, buzzed against her ear.

"I woke you up, didn't I? I didn't think." She hadn't. She'd simply picked up the phone and dialed the number he'd given her on that first day in town. "I shouldn't have called. Stupid of me." Flustered, she searched for a polite way to disconnect.

"No, it's okay. Really. Anyway, you've—been on my mind." The sound of his yawn traveled through time and space to her. "Sorry," he muttered and yawned again. "You didn't wake me up, but I dragged myself out of bed five minutes ago. Usually I've been awake for a couple of hours by this time, but I've been short of sleep this last week."

"Me too."

"You haven't been seen on Saw Creek's version of the party circuit, so what have you been doing all alone out there, Meggie Blake?"

Funny, she hadn't felt alone. "Working. Settling in. Stuff."

"Are you afraid? Is that why you can't sleep?" His voice lost its sleepiness.

"I sleep. After a fashion. I wake up a lot. In the night." She sighed. "But no, being alone doesn't scare me."

"You're not afraid. You haven't been out late partying. So why aren't you sleeping, Meggie?"

Her pulse beat with the steady tick of the analog clock she'd hung in the kitchen. "Crazy dreams. That's all."

"Yeah? Tell me about your dreams, Meggie."

"Stupid stuff. I've been working too hard in the garden, that's all."

"Damn." A dish clattered against the floor. "You want some help?"

"Charlotte gave me the name of a landscape designer. I may call." But not yet. Later, if then. She wasn't quite ready for intrusions in her garden, not ready to share that private space.

"Doing all that grunt work yourself, huh?"

"For the time being." Meggie heard the gush of an open tap and pictured him sloshing water over a sleep-creased face. Familiar, the sound of his voice in her ear, natural, the clink and clank of his morning routine in the background. She blinked. So familiar were the sounds and feelings of this moment that their conversation seemed merely a continuation of the dream.

At the other end of their connection, Rafe made a smacking sound of satisfaction. "All right. Jump-started by coffee, my brain's alive again. Any footprints in the yard before today?"

"No."

"Anything else out of the ordinary?"

Meggie couldn't help it. She laughed out loud. "I suppose that depends on how you define *out of the ordinary,* Rafe."

He paused and the connection fuzzed, grew clearer as he moved. "Kids around? Maybe a black-caped stranger with a blood-lust?"

"I guess the last one would qualify as out of the ordinary, but, no, I haven't seen anyone lurking in the vicinity."

"What is it, Meggie? You're holding something back."

She hesitated, wondering if she should go for broke. He'd think she was certifiable, but she knew for a fact that the statue had been moved. Not for a second did she doubt herself. She'd left a marker last night and it was a good foot and a half in back of the statue's location this morning.

In the moonlight, she believed the statue moved and breathed.

In the sunlight where no mysteries dwelled, she knew the only explanation had to be pranksters. Pranksters who'd left their dew-drenched footprints behind. "Some peculiar things have happened."

"What kind of—things, Meggie?" Patiently and doggedly, he pulled her back to the subject. "Since you're not calling the police, tell *me,* Meggie. Everything. I don't care whether the details are important or not. Let me decide. Got it?"

"I can see why you were a good detective, Rafe. You don't give up. If I had anything to confess, you'd have it out of me in a heartbeat."

Meggie had never thought of silence as having a palpable weight until now.

Finally he responded, "Yeah, I earned my paycheck."

Once again she'd spoken without thinking. "You miss your cop work and Paulie, don't you?" she said softly.

"Like a part of me was chopped off." He cleared his

throat. "But everybody's got stuff. This is mine. I'll survive. I'll find another job. I'm not in any danger of being thrown out on the streets."

"But you wish it had been you and not Paulie killed in the alley, don't you?" she asked quietly.

Silence, thick and pained.

"Yeah. All the time." Despair roughed the edges of his voice, turned it harsh. "But all things considered, most people would say I'm a damned lucky man."

Meggie knew he would never think of himself that way, not until he could forgive himself for not being God, for being merely human and unable to save his partner's life. After a moment, not finding the words she wanted, she offered, "Want to play detective and solve the mystery of my statue that dances in the moonlight?"

"What the hell?" Something heavy banged against a counter. "What are you talking about, Meggie? What statue?"

"The one in the garden."

"There's a statue in the garden?"

"Yep. And it moves. Or is moved. Take your pick," she said flippantly. "Depending on your tolerance for the mysterious, you can opt for monkeyshines or magic."

"I'll be there in fifteen minutes. Stay put." She heard the line go dead.

Amused, Meggie stayed put.

She was in the garden dragging heavy branches onto a pile of clippings when she heard the rumble of his car's engine. Her pulse skipped, raced, and finally settled. Scooping her sweat-damp hair back, she strolled through the path she'd made in the hedges.

"Hi," she said. Yanking off her mud-stained gloves, she stuffed them in her back pocket. "Thanks for coming."

Yawning, he levered himself out of the Porsche. "No problem. My place is up the road. Let's see this statue, Meggie." Faded denim shaped itself to his long legs. He'd tucked the pants legs into scuffed heavy-duty boots. "Show me the tracks first, though."

"Sure. Come on. Nice outfit, by the way." She waved her hand in the direction of his jeans and worn Florida State T-shirt. She tried unsuccessfully to ignore the white-frayed placket of his jeans. "Uh, Rafe, not that I'm criticizing, but who presses jeans these days?" She gestured to the knife-sharp creases in the worn denim.

"My cleaner." Following her, he yawned again, and Meggie thought she heard the crack of his jaw. He tucked his sunglasses into the neck of his shirt. "He's of the old school. Takes pride in his work."

"You send your jeans to the cleaner?"

"Yeah." He grinned. "I'm a self-sufficient, nineties guy. Hey, I can even cook you dinner. Just hand me the phone."

"That's pitiful," she groaned, smiling back. "Sounds more like a seventies polyester kind of guy. Can't cook, college T-shirt—"

"Not my shirt," he said virtuously. "My dad's." He ran his left hand over his rumpled hair, smoothing it back. Stopping, he leaned against the magnolia, arms crossed, and surveyed her. "So, Meggie, what's up?"

Meggie crossed her own arms to hide the response his gaze aroused in her. Another week in this semitropical paradise, and she'd become a sex-mad crazy woman. What with her dreams and the way her body responded like a sunflower to the sun of Rafe's glance. Even in the beginning he'd had this effect on her, and her dreams had made her hypersensitive. Disgruntled, she scowled at him.

"What'd I do?" he asked innocently, grinning.

"Nothing." She smoothed out her scowl. It wasn't his fault she wanted to stretch out and bask like a cat in the sunshine of his presence. The man had that effect on her, damn him.

"I was admiring your own outfit, Meggie. Nothin'

more. It's—interesting." He grinned again, his teeth flashing in the lean darkness of his face. He surveyed her bare legs as she shifted under his gaze. "Wouldn't long pants be better, though?" he asked with a quizzical lift of an eyebrow. "Safer, don't you think? Not that *I'm* complaining, either." He gave the length of her legs another slow perusal that sent a rush of blood buzzing under her dirt-smeared skin.

"Snakes and bugs aren't the problem, Rafe," she answered sweetly and forced herself to meet his eyes. "I dressed for the weather. It's a hot day."

"Sure is, Meggie." He grinned again and then straightened, leaving her to wonder exactly what that Cheshire cat smile meant.

She was pretty darn sure he wasn't talking about the weather. This easygoing, relaxed Rafe charmed her. She'd had glimpses of this Rafe even on that first day, but each time she was with him, the changes in him surprised her. This was the Rafe he might have been before the night in the alley. "You want to see the tracks, or not?" she said, smiling back at him.

"Yeah. That I do." His mood turned serious. "Look, Meggie, like I said, Saw Creek's got its underbelly like any town, but I don't think anything serious is going on. I damn well don't like the idea that somebody or several somebodies have been trampling through here, willy-nilly."

"Believe me, I don't either." She beckoned him forward as she led him toward the front of the house. "Willy-nilly or otherwise, I don't want uninvited visitors."

He was at her side in one quick stride. Throwing a glance back at the gate, he asked, "You leave the gate unlocked?"

"Certainly not at night."

He touched her shoulder briefly, one finger grazing her upper arm. "Sorry, Meggie. Checking, that's all. Old habit.'' He anchored both hands in his back pockets. ''I didn't mean to offend you. I know you'd be—careful.''

In light of her recent impulsive, careless behavior, Meggie almost laughed. He was giving her credit for being the woman she'd been when she'd arrived in Saw Creek, not for the woman transformed by this house, transformed by her obsession with the statue in the wilderness garden.

Turning the corner of the house, Meggie pointed under the living room window. ''The tracks circle around the house. You can see how deep they go into the dirt.''

''Yeah.'' He stooped, one knee dropping to the ground. Pulling out a folding plastic ruler, he laid it against one print. ''Big guy.'' He measured between the steps. ''With a good-sized stride to him.'' He placed his foot next to the print. ''Like mine.'' Clicking the ruler closed, he frowned. ''Real big for a kid. For a kid who'd play tricks on a newcomer. The older guys, football players, yeah, they'd be this heavy, this tall. Maybe six two, six three. But I can't see them running around the house without doing something else. I think you would have seen them. Or heard them.''

''I've been leaving lights on at night,'' Meggie confessed in a small voice. ''To scare off intruders.''

She hadn't been nervous until Rafe's frown.

He was taking the tracks far more seriously than she had.

''I'll talk to the chief. See if any other complaints like this have come in. He could step up the patrols in this area.'' Swiveling on his knee, he faced her. ''In the meantime, what's this about the statue moving? That does sound like a prank.''

Meggie led him to the garden, to the statue in the partially cleared center of the garden. ''This one. It's—been moved. During the night.''

''I'll be damned,'' Rafe said in a tight voice. ''I didn't know that was still here. I thought Paulie's wife sold it or

loaded it up with the rest of their belongings when she left.
I reckon I shouldn't be surprised, though.'' He rubbed his
face with his shaking left hand. "She swore she didn't
blame me for Paulie's death, but I knew she did. That must
be why she left the statue."

"What do you mean?" Intuition speared through her.
Meggie thought she finally understood the way her dreams
and Rafe had connected in her subconscious. "It's yours?"

"Yeah. Mine," he said, walking slowly around the
statue, reaching out to touch the statue's ruined hand with
his own. "From before."

Yearning to press her mouth against the twisted shape
of Rafe's hand, Meggie lifted it to her cheek.

Five

"You made this?" Meggie touched the statue, brushed her palm over Rafe's left hand where it rested on the statue. "You made this, didn't you?

"Yeah. My little hobby paid for a lot of my toys. The Porsche. Expensive clothes. Stuff." Rafe saw the shadow of himself in the deepening brown of Meggie's eyes, saw the claw of his hand and felt the acid of self-hatred rise in him again.

For a few minutes, looking at the tracks of Meggie's intruder, he'd forgotten. He'd been himself, enjoying the sunshine, savoring the look of Meggie in her ragged cut-offs and curving long legs.

He stuffed his hand in his pocket, out of sight.

"Don't," she whispered. "You don't have to hide, Rafe. Not with me."

"I don't know what you're talking about." He swung away, turned back to her, caught by the tightening grip of her slender fingers against his bare arm. "Let me go, Meggie." He jerked away and she grabbed him again.

"Listen to me, Rafe. Listen, for a minute. That's all I ask, okay?"

He rounded on her as she shook his arm. "I meant it, Meggie. Leave me alone." Legs apart, angry, he faced her, faced down this slight woman who held out hope to him like a shining ball. "Here's the real deal, Meggie. You can't fix everything. I can't be a cop. I can't make my statues. And I can't forget Paulie's face. Or Liddy's when I told her what had happened. You don't understand."

She tightened her grip on him. "I didn't say I did. I don't pretend I can peer inside your head." She jiggled his arm less vigorously. "But I want you to look at this statue." She nudged him toward it. "You sculpted this before Paulie was killed."

"So what?" he snarled, an anger he hadn't felt even when he'd looked down, overwhelmed, at Paulie's body. "Yeah, I did a lot of sculpting and carving. When both hands worked." He smiled, his lips stretching thinly across his dry mouth. "I don't sculpt anymore, Meggie."

"Look at it, Rafe." Standing on tiptoe, she reached up and nudged his chin with her palm, forcing his head to turn toward the statue. "Why did you chisel it with one hand trapped in the stone?"

Stunned, he looked. He'd forgotten. Stepping forward, he broke away from Meggie's soft hand. "I—ran out of time. I wanted them to have it for their wedding." Running his hands over the rough, chipped base, Rafe pushed against the figure. The statue didn't even wobble. "Paulie never let me finish it. He said he liked it better unfinished. Like our friendship. Damn." He sank to the ground, his head in his shaking hands. "Damn him. I was supposed to go into the alley first, not Paulie. But I was driving and he got out of the car first."

"Rafe." Meggie knelt in front of him and took his hand in hers, her touch warm and silky against the scar. "You couldn't foresee the future, could you?" She leaned forward, her breath sweet against him. "Look at the statue and think about the way you sculpted it. With the hand trapped and—twisted in the stone.'' Her thumb traced his scar gently.

Furious with her, he raised his head and stood up, leaving her kneeling before him. ''Cheap shot, Meggie, and your psychology's not worth a damn.'' He yanked his hand away. ''You think the cop shrinks didn't nail me with that one, too? That I was faking this?'' He held his contorted hand in front of her.

He'd given the department shrink the minimum number of meetings and kept his mouth shut. Kept the lid on his grief and anger. But this woman with her eyes speaking of hope was ripping off that locked-down lid as easily as a kid picking at a scab. He wanted to shock that hope, that concern, right out of her eyes, wanted to make her see how terrible his failure was.

''They suggested you were faking your injury?'' she whispered, her eyes huge in a face gone pale. ''Cruel.''

''Isn't that what you were hinting, too, Megan? That my subconscious was imitating the statue I made for Paulie? Hey, I took a couple of psychology classes. I know where you were heading.''

''I didn't mean that you were faking.''

''Sure sounded like that. What were you suggesting?''

Her gaze shifted away from him, and she stuttered, started again, her starts and stops triggering a hunch he was too angry to pin down. Finally she stammered, ''I only thought it was an odd coincidence—that you and the statue—''

''Drop it, Meggie,'' he said, so enraged he could scarcely get the words out. ''Don't you think I wondered that I might be a fraud as well as a failure? Don't you think I stayed awake for nights wondering about that pleasant idea, too?'' Like a bull stuck with a matador's picks, he shook his head. ''But for whatever comfort it gave me, the doctors made it perfectly clear that I might be a bastard who'd let his partner down, but at least I wasn't a fake.''

"You're not a failure."

"And you know, of course, because you were there. In the dark and the noise. And the blood." The minute the words flew out of his mouth, Rafe regretted them. She was only trying to help, and he was attacking her like she was at fault, when all the fault, all the blame was his. His alone.

But Meggie never flinched. He gave her full credit for taking the blast of his fury and not withering under it. "No, I wasn't there. But you were. In those seconds, Rafe, those seconds before you heard the shot, what were you thinking?"

Her words stopped him cold. He couldn't remember. Nobody had asked him about those seconds. The shrink wanted to pry into his feelings. The department review committee wanted a minute-by-minute account of his actions, of Paulie's.

"And then, Rafe, when you remember those seconds, and you will, believe me, think about what you could have done differently, what you could have changed. In those final seconds, Rafe, would *anything* have made a difference?"

He strode away from her, slapping at a low-hanging branch from a tree. "Thanks for the psychoanalysis, Megan. I'll send you a check for the going rate."

Behind him, she sighed, but didn't say anything else. He didn't blame her. His behavior to her was beneath contempt, and he needed to apologize, but he couldn't, not with this rage blinding him, and her question droning in his ears. Keeping his back to her, he stopped. "I'll talk to the chief. About your intruder. I won't forget."

"I know you won't." The words were soft, sure.

He wanted to tell her not to count on him, he wasn't a man she could depend on, but he stalked off, a red haze blurring everything in front of him.

*   *   *

As he walked away from her, his wide shoulders straight, his spine stiff, Meggie almost ran after him, to beg him to stay and not bear his load of misery by himself.

She let him walk away. He needed time alone, to think. She wasn't sure herself what she'd intended with her question about the similarity of the statue's conformation to Rafe's injury. The idea had surfaced and she'd pursued it, the elusive nature of her dreams prodding her to ask the question.

She believed Rafe's injury was inevitable.

She knew he couldn't have foreseen his accident.

It was strange, that's all. Rafe's hand, the statue's. Odd, that they were the same.

That night, in her dream, she almost glimpsed the face of the statue. And when she went to the garden in those golden midnight hours, the statue had moved, turned. She stripped away vines in a madness born of need and desire, in a frenzy to see his face.

Every time her hands slid over the marble skin, she thought of Rafe. Every time her fingertips brushed over the rough base and the statue's hands, she saw Rafe's hands. The lean, elegant one. The ruined one. His badge of failure.

She hurried. Time was running out.

Halloween day dawned with a gust of rain and chill wind. The nip in the air was welcome after the heat of the last weeks. The rain wasn't. Meggie took it personally. If the drizzle didn't stop by afternoon, her cobwebs would blow away and the candles in her pumpkins wouldn't stay lit.

When the rain gusted away in a whip of clouds, Meggie finally succeeded in clearing out the worst of the mess in the garden, discovering a stunted gardenia bush in a shaded corner of the garden. Although it was a spring-and-summer-blooming shrub, one fragile blossom nevertheless gleamed in the glossy leaves. Meggie trailed her wrist across the flower, careful not to bruise it.

She left it there, hidden.

Gathering the rest of the branches, she decided to make a fire with all the dead brush in her garden, a final exorcism, a cleansing. An Allhallows eve bonfire. She would offer an invitation to the spirits of the dead who walked this night and, caught between the lands of the living and the dead, returned home to warm themselves at their hearth fires. When the flames reached high, she would scrape away the last of the fast-growing vines from the statue's face.

She would see the face of her midnight lover.

In the early hours of the evening, the moon huge and orange in a cloudless sky, she handed out treats to tiny frogs and pirates and little warrior princesses. Later she opened her door to hulking, hunchbacked creatures from horror flicks. She saw a Saw Creek patrol car pass her house several times and knew Rafe had done what he'd promised.

When the last trick-or-treater had left, she started her fire, kneeling before it as she'd knelt before Rafe earlier today. The flames licked through the smallest branches, burst in a fine splendor skyward to the moon, full and golden.

Against the chill, she'd brought a blanket to sit on, worn wool slacks and a pullover sweater. She'd coiled the hose nearby in case she needed it to douse rogue fires.

Climbing on the pedestal of her statue, she scrubbed away at a leaf stain and pulled vines until the body and face were entirely revealed.

And then she knew. Whatever the reason, whether the hidden psyche revealing the heart's truth or magic and illusion, she understood her dreams at last.

Rafe's voice in her dreams. Rafe's face somehow imprinted on the marble, his tortured face so bleak that it

broke her heart. No *Picture of Dorian Gray* that revealed
the evil in a man's soul, Rafe's statue showed his inner
torment, a torment born after the creation of this statue
that looked down at her with desperate, living eyes.

Opening a bottle of golden wine, she sprinkled some of
it with a hiss and sizzle onto her fire, an offering, before
pouring a glass full and sipping the mellow wine. Laying
the glass carefully on the ground, she took a red apple from
a bowl at her side and peeled it, tossing the curling strips
onto the fire before eating.

That done, she took lingering sips of her wine. The com-
pelling urgency had vanished. Whatever had pushed her
had vanished, leaving her peaceful and sleepy as she drank
the mellow wine and ate her apple.

And she waited, eagerly, for midnight, doubting, dreaming in her moonlit garden where the leaping flames threw
sparks into the golden darkness. Hoping for a miracle in a
world where miracles were always explainable.

In his dream, Rafe moved his hand, touched softness, silky
skin. In his dream, he sculpted the shape of a sweetly
curved waist, the tender fullness of a breast. His hands,
moving together, drifted slowly over the gentle slope of a
slim spine, dipped and rose over the slight swell of a feminine buttock. There his hands lingered in the twin dimples
on either side of that narrow spine, circled underneath to
lift breasts that trembled as he took one dainty tip in his
mouth, dampening it with his tongue and lips.

Rafe sighed and turned in his bed, his fingers moving
against cotton sheets so smooth and soft a man might believe he was caressing a living being.

But the sheets were cool, cool in the night, while the
shape he touched was warm, moving to his every stroke
and touch. Slender fingers trailed over his stomach, his
mouth, traced the tendons of his neck, and he shuddered
under the power of those feminine hands.

And in his dream his palms glided against fragile ribs where the skin was so thin that he knew it was flesh he sculpted and not stone. And all around him, moonlight streamed, chasing shadows to the recesses of hedges and shrubs. "Ah," he murmured, sleeping but dazzled by the gold brass of the moonlight, "aren't you beautiful? Inside and out, so sweet. I need you, Meggie. You make me whole. Touch me, sweetheart, touch me again. Make me alive again."

Softly, sweetly, the touch came again, and he bolted awake, his heart pounding so hard he couldn't breathe. "Oh God," he groaned, shaken by the intensity of his dream. Twisted in sheets, he hunched over his knees, disturbed. Rubbing his contorted hand where illusive sensations of warmth and silkiness remained, he scowled at the harvest moon outside his window.

By the moonlight in his room, he saw the digital-green numbers of his clock, the outline of the chair and bureau in his rented apartment. Silence and that magical golden light, rich, pouring through his window, a light that must have induced his dream.

He looked down at his hand. In the dream it had moved, straightened and traced the woman's breast, thumbed a delicate nipple that pouched in a sweet blossoming.

Meggie's breast.

Dropping the wrinkled sheet on the bed, Rafe rose and strode to the window, his naked shape a shimmer in the mirror above the dresser. Down in the courtyard, a cat moved under a bush, pounced, disappeared. Some creature squeaked, scampered away with a rustle of leaves.

Nothing else moved under the cloudless moon, and he turned to look again at the clock.

Midnight.

For the last week he had wakened at the same time from the same dream. And it was always Meggie he dreamed about.

Meggie, who'd tried to tell him something this afternoon about that damned statue before he'd erupted in pain and anger, blasting her because she'd dared to ask him to think about those final seconds eight months ago.

Pivoting, he walked to the foot of his bed and pulled on jeans. Metal snicked on metal in the silence as he zipped them up. Without stopping, he snagged the shirt draped over the foot of his bed and buttoned it, methodically tucked the ends into his jeans. He didn't let himself think about what he was about to do.

He didn't dare.

Outside, moonlight glittered off the dark shine of his car. The engine throbbed under him as he accelerated, leaving the apartment complex behind.

Awake, he felt now as if he moved in a dream, this golden landscape the dream and not the reality. Awake, he moved toward the Meggie of his dreams, wanting her with a need so powerful he would have walked through fire and hell itself to go to her.

The fury and rage of the afternoon had burned out, and from the ashes of his anger and guilt had come this longing for Meggie. For her, for the woman who'd squared up to him and demanded that he *think,* demanded that he face the statue, face himself.

He coasted silently to a stop at the end of her driveway. The gate was locked, and he walked the length of the fence until he came to the end of it where a gap between her property and her neighbors opened into the back of Meggie's garden.

Curled up catlike in black on a blanket on the ground, she waited for him by firelight. "Hey, Meggie," he said and waited for her to invite him forward.

"You came." She stretched lazily, her arms reaching up like her fire to the golden moon.

"I had to." He took one step forward. She was everything he'd dreamed. More—everything he could ever want, this delicate woman with the strength of a warrior.

"I know."

"I was furious with you."

She nodded and waited, silent.

"And I thought about those final seconds." He sighed. "Aw, Meggie, you knew all along, didn't you?"

She nodded again, and he thought he saw the glint of a tear slide down her cheek. "They were the key, weren't they? What were you thinking of, Rafe? What went through your mind as you walked behind Paulie?"

"I was pissed off at him. I *always* went first, and this time he made a game out of hustling out of the car before I turned off the engine and unlatched my seat belt. I forgot, Meggie"—he held his hands out in remorse and regret— "I forgot that I was irritated with him. I was about to pull him back, I had my left hand on his shirt, and then everything blew up. That's what I didn't remember, Meggie. I forgot that in his last moments of life, I was so p.o.'d with Paulie I was ready to punch him out. That's what I couldn't forgive myself for."

She reached behind her and lifted a glass that sparkled with liquid moonlight. In an oddly formal gesture, she raised the glass higher. "Would you like some wine?" Her smile drew him forward.

"I would." Equally formal, he nodded and accepted the goblet. "Thank you."

"You're welcome." She dipped her chin, and her wild, curling hair shone with firelight and moonlight. "I'm glad you came back, Rafe. I hoped you would." She reached out a slim arm and drew him to her side.

"Did you, Meggie? After I performed my best version of a volcano? Why?" He cupped his twisted hand behind her neck, carefully threading his bent fingers through those springing tendrils. Kneeling before her, he said, "Tell me why, Meggie. I need to know."

"I dreamed of you, Rafe, and didn't know it was you.

I dreamed of a phantom lover and it was you, all along.''

He'd known she was dangerous to him.

He hadn't guessed that she was his salvation.

"I dreamed of you, too, Meggie. But I knew it was you. Every night in my dreams I touched you, inhaled the scent of you, stroked your beautiful body. . . .'' He ran the back of his shattered hand down the side of her neck and imagined his fingers curved against the sleek skin. "Ah, Meggie, I knew it was you I wanted. But I didn't guess how much I need you.''

"Do you?'' Her smile was wistful. "Need me? I'd like to believe that. I know you want me.''

"That's been pretty obvious, I reckon, huh?'' He edged closer to her, letting her feel how much he wanted her. With his free hand he cupped her to him, thigh to thigh, belly to belly, and knew in the most primitive place of his being that Meggie was the woman he'd been waiting for all his life. She was the unexplored territory of his future.

Meggie leaned into him, allowed her body to listen to the language of his. Her body had spoken to her in her dreams, told her how she felt about the man in her arms, her midnight lover. Her dreaming soul had its truth; her wide-awake self needed more. Maybe reassurance that the bond she sensed between them was real, that he experienced it, too, this moonlight magic between them.

But Meggie couldn't look at him as she asked her question, didn't want to see the rejection that might lurk in his dark eyes. "Rafe, will I be only a notch on your bedpost? Because that's not good enough for me.''

As he started to speak, she laid her fingers against his mouth, silencing him even as his lips closed over her fingertips and gently bit. Shivering, Meggie forged ahead. She valued herself, and she had to know if he valued her as well, if he understood what she was offering with her wine, her apple, her body. Her heart. "Oh, I'm not asking for commitment, for permanence, but I have to know I have some importance to you, that when you look back on this night"—she placed her hand lightly against his hard cheek—"you won't remember it as nothing more than a grown-up version of trick or treat."

She tilted her chin down, burying it in his neck. Everything in her was stilled, waiting.

The back of his hand raised her chin and he held her eyes with his, the intensity in their depths so powerful that she swayed against him. "My moonlight Meggie, you don't have a clue. I can't get you out of my mind, my soul. You complete me. If I'd never met you, I would have gone through my entire life color-blind, not knowing the colors of the rainbow. You're my rainbow, Meggie. You give me hope when I didn't believe in hope any longer. You made me laugh; you forced me out of my cave. Nobody else was ever that brave."

"Really? That's how you see me? As brave?" She smiled into his neck, entranced by his view of her as brave.

"Impulsive, brave, and sexy as hell." He tasted the tender spot under her chin, a nice spot, but the dip at the base of her neck tempted him lower. "Oh, yes. *Very* sexy."

"Fine words, Rafer Jackson. You're a silver-tongued devil, you are." Smiling, she raised her other arm and circled his neck, both arms wrapping him tightly to her. "But I never thought of myself as brave until I came to Saw Creek. I used to be impulsive. Curious, but I'd become Megan Blake, buttoned-up, suburban matron."

"I like the unbuttoned Meggie." He nuzzled the edge of her sweater lower with his chin, a rasp of skin over her collarbone. "I'm crazy for my dream-Meggie, who never wears any clothes."

"Shameless hussy, she is. No . . . yes," she gasped as he lifted the bottom of her shirt and closed his long fingers over her breast, teasing it with small tugs.

"Do you like this, too, sweet Meggie?" He took her

nipple in his teeth, scraping lightly, and it was the husky
voice of her dreams, her phantom lover in her arms for
real, and not a dream.

Meggie's back arched, and she lifted her face to the
golden moon. In back of Rafe, the statue turned, and his
eyes, Rafe's dark eyes, plunged her into a world of golden
heat and sensation.

She pressed her mouth to the corner of Rafe's ear and
he shuddered against her.

"Witchcraft, Meggie, all your feminine charm," he
muttered against her mouth before slanting his own across
hers and opening her to a kiss so hungry that she forgot
everything except the need to answer his hunger with her
own, surrendering to his power over her as he surrendered
to hers.

Rafe lowered her to the blanket. He reached underneath
her, sliding his hands beneath the waistband of her slacks.
As she lifted her hips, urged upward by the encouragement
of his stroke, he slipped the button at the side of her slacks
free and toggled the zipper down, his knuckles brushing
against the silk of her panties, sliding the silk against her
until she dug her heels into the blanket. Inching her slacks
over her hips, down her thighs and calves, he covered her
body with his, let his lips tell her how he treasured her.

"Here, lovely witch-Meggie? Let me love you here."
Trailing his fingers upward from her thighs, he moved his
palm over her, until everything inside her coiled and tightened, seeking release from that lovely pressure.

"Oh, yes," she murmured and lifted, encouraged his
exploration. "But turnabout's fair play."

"I've always been a believer in fair play, Meggie
mine," he said, turning until she sprawled across him, her
hair tangled in his mouth. "Play away." He flung his arms
to the side. His grin was devilish. Moonlight played over
the planes of his chest, burnished them with gold. "Meggie, you're a miracle, you are," he said and bucked as she

touched him intimately. "My very own miracle."

And the whole time, loving him, letting him love her, Meggie burned in golden moonlight, wondering that love should come to her a second time and in this way. Lost in each other, they never noticed the rain clouds building overhead until a crack of lightning made Rafe lift his head and look up.

"Darlin' Meggie, Mother Nature's decided we need a cold shower."

"Spoilsport," Meggie complained. Using his thigh as balance, she stood up on tiptoes and kissed him, hard, not ready to let this Allhallows eve end.

The fire sizzled as the first drops of rain spattered them. Lightning streaked across the sky, stitching a witchery of its own. One bolt rent the heavens and Rafe gathered her to him, grabbing clothes and wrapping her in the blanket. Naked, he loped across the garden, his bare feet leaving deep prints in the mud, prints like those that had circled her house. His left hand held the blanket over Meggie, sheltering her.

Under the wet blanket, Meggie shrieked as the hair on her arms rose and the world around them exploded in white light. Behind them she heard an enormous splintering sound, as if rock and stone erupted from the earth.

Racing to the house, tripping and laughing, she clung to Rafe's narrow waist. Inside, with lightning crackling in an endless blue-white sizzle around them, she turned to Rafe. "Well, some people say the earth moves for them, but this is a first for me. I'm *very* impressed, Rafe Jackson." She shook her head back and forth, splattering his naked chest with drops.

"Meggie." His voice was strangled.

"What?" She looked up at him through the curtain of her dripping hair.

"Look." He held his hand out to her.

Puzzled, she reached out and took his hand in hers, curling her fingers in his strong grip.

"Look at my hand, Meggie." He extended his shaking hand, stretched out his trembling fingers.

Along the back of his hand, his left hand, a fine, golden line traced the length of what had been his scar. Nothing remained of the gray-blue pucker. "Your hand," she whispered. "What happened?"

"I don't know, Meggie." Dazed, he lifted his hand, brushed back her hair. "I don't know." He pulled her to him fiercely. "Come here and love me, Meggie. Make another miracle for me." He backed her against the wall and entered her, swiftly, with one thrust that lifted her against him until she wrapped her legs around his waist and let him carry her upstairs, to her brass bedroom where the scent of gardenias and roses still clung to the sheets.

There in the bed where she'd dreamed of him, they made love again to the sound of lightning crackling around them and to the music of their hearts.

"Meggie, come live with me," he murmured before dawn into her ear. "And be my love."

"Poetic," she said. "I think I recognize that poem. I've always liked a man with poetry in his soul."

"You have my soul. You know that. And I'll write sonnets to your breasts if you want." He lifted the fall of her hair, brushed it across his mouth, across her neck. "What else, my lovely, beautiful Meggie, will it take to make you mine?" He nibbled her nose.

"I think that will do very nicely," Meggie said, settling herself very nicely over him. "For now."

Hours later, she added, "And maybe another Allhallows eve celebration next year?"

He laughed and swung her around in circles until they collapsed on the floor and tried to decide which they preferred: bed, boards, or blanket. Meggie opted for the blanket because, she said, the "ambience was simply spectacular." Rafe voted for a retest.

When they went to check the garden the next day, ashes still smoked from the fire. The wineglass lay overturned near the shards of the statue. One hand, upturned to the bright November sky, lay near the fire. Nothing else remained.

In the days that followed, Rafe went to Georgia to talk to Liddy, Meggie at his side. "She never blamed me, Meggie. She left the statue because she couldn't take it with her. She had no place for it. She said the statue belonged to the house, to the garden. I thought she left it because she couldn't stand the sight of it, a reminder of me, of how I'd let Paulie down."

Meggie stood on her tiptoes and pressed a kiss to the corner of Rafe's mouth. Lifting her arms, she encircled him, drew him close to her. "Of course she didn't blame you. Like me, she's a smart woman, too. She knew you better than you knew yourself." Meggie nibbled at his ear, slipped her hand under his shirt.

"Wicked, wicked Meggie," he said and ducked into the shadow of a tree in the courtyard of Liddy's apartment complex. "If it were darker—"

"It will be," she murmured into his ear, "by the time we get back to Saw Creek. And the garden's lovely in winter." She grinned as he snuggled her up close to him.

"And no mosquitoes." He snugged her closer to him, and she felt his smile against her mouth. "I have a lovely bottle of wine in the car. Does that give you ideas, Meggie-mine?"

"Only if you can light a fire."

"Oh, I reckon I can." His laugh shook her. "Given the right tinder. Think you could help me, Meggie? Think you could help me start that fire?"

She could. And did, during a long, moonless night in

which the sounds of the garden and its scents surrounded them.

Years later they would talk about that Allhallows eve. Meggie argued for magic, insisting that magic was just truth not yet explained. Rafe insisted that love had wrought the miracle, freeing him as lightning had freed Meggie's statue.

SHADES OF MOONLIGHT

Angie Ray

Prologue

March, 1819

Jack Merrick, Viscount Merrick, knew that tomorrow George Firth would try to kill him.

Sipping brandy, Jack watched his guests waltzing around the ballroom. His gaze lingered on the fussily dressed man dancing with Jane Cottingworth. Firth was paying little attention to her; his gaze searched about for some other face.

Jack knew Firth was looking for Caroline, but there was no sign of her in the ballroom.

She probably had an assignation in the garden, Jack thought.

A strange sense of detachment enveloped him. He could see the ballroom with its fluted columns, gilded mirrors, and bright, flickering candles; he could see the blur of couples turning around and around. He could hear the violins playing the cheerful waltz; he could hear the laughter and the chatter. He could smell the burning wax, the perfume, and the sweat.

But it was all muted. As though he were watching it

from a great distance. He felt oddly isolated, even though he was talking and laughing with the circle of people standing around him.

He took a fresh glass of brandy from a passing servant's tray. The bite of the alcohol gave him a moment of physical sensation, a momentary reassurance that he was really there. But the liquor's comforting warmth soon faded and he felt more distant than ever.

A sudden urgency to be away from the ballroom seized him. He went out the double doors into the hall. There were more people there, and the volume of laughter and chatter was even higher. He passed through the crowd and climbed the stairs two at a time up to the tower room. He closed the door and locked it, shutting out the noise from below.

Rubbing his pounding temples, he glanced around the room.

It had not changed. The only light was from the full moon shining through the window, but it was bright enough for him to see the armoire in one corner, the gun rack on the wall, a straight-backed chair, and the old oak table with a bottle of brandy resting upon it. He hadn't been up there in a long time. He didn't like the room—it carried too many memories.

He withdrew a leather case from the armoire. He opened it and stared down at the contents.

The two dueling pistols gleamed dully against the black velvet in the dim light.

Perhaps it hadn't been such a good idea to have a ball the night before a duel, he thought. Perhaps he'd made a mistake. But then again, what was one more mistake in a life full of mistakes?

Sitting down on the chair, he placed the case on the table. He took out a pistol and carefully cleaned it. He poured the powder in, his fingers fumbling on his task a little. The powder spilled on the floor.

He drank some more brandy.

The sound of the pistol shot took him by surprise. Instinctively, he tried to duck, but to no avail.

Pain burst through his skull; a warm liquid dripped down his face. He brushed his fingers against his temple and stared at them.

They were a bright, vivid scarlet.

Damn, he thought. *Damn, damn, damn, damn. . . .*

And then everything went black.

One

March, 1820

Mrs. Madeline Spencer had expected Merrick Hall to be big. She hadn't expected that all of the houses on the small street where she lived in Baltimore could have comfortably fit inside it.

"Oh, my," she whispered, staring out the carriage window at the house.

The light of the three-quarter moon revealed a multitude of leaded glass windows, innumerable chimneys, and an overgrowth of trees and shrubbery. Ivy shadowed the casements at the south end of the house; moonlight picked out the bare gray stone wall of a tower and the jagged edge of the damaged roof above it at the north end.

She had not expected the house to look so . . . eerie.

She only hoped it was warmer than it looked. Traveling across the Atlantic Ocean from Baltimore to Bristol to Somerset to visit the house she'd inherited from her father's distant relative, she'd often thought she would never be warm again. If the house had fireplaces in the bedrooms, she thought, shivering inside the cold, creaking carriage, she wouldn't care how spooky it looked.

The carriage stopped in front of the house, and Madeline hurried up damp, slippery marble stairs to where the housekeeper, Mrs. Hubbard, stood waiting in the open doorway, a branch of candles held aloft in her hand.

"Welcome to Merrick Hall, mum," Mrs. Hubbard said. Fiftyish, with big, heavy bones and dark circles under her eyes, the woman looked as though she hadn't slept in ages. "Shall I show you to your room?"

"Yes, please," Madeline replied, gazing about the hall. Unlike the exterior, it was perfectly proportioned, with tall doors on either side. But upon closer inspection, she could see, even in the dim candlelight, the smoke-darkened ceilings, the dullness of the unpolished wainscoting, and the water-stained drapes hanging at the windows.

"What's in there?" she asked as they passed a door.

"It's the library, mum. There's over a thousand books in there."

"Good heavens! Lord Merrick must have been a great reader."

"Oh, no, mum," Mrs. Hubbard said, her footsteps dragging as she climbed the stairs. "He never opened a book in his life. You may want to throw them out. A lot of them were damaged when one of the maids left a window open and the rain got to them."

"What a shame," Madeline murmured. "And what a waste of all those books."

The housekeeper shrugged as they reached the top of the stairs. "Your room is this way, mum," she said, holding the branch of candles higher and gesturing toward the long corridor on the left.

Madeline paused, glancing at a staircase to the right, barely visible in the candlelight. It was smaller than the one she'd just ascended, and the stairs curved upward, the top disappearing into the darkness. "What's up here?"

Mrs. Hubbard's mouth drew down at the corners.

"Nothing much. Just an old tower. I wouldn't go up there, mum, if I was you. The stairs are dangerous and the roof is caving in."

Madeline frowned as she followed the housekeeper down the gloomy, portrait-lined corridor. "How sad that the house should be so neglected."

"Things aren't what they should be, and that's the truth." Mrs. Hubbard turned a corner and stopped. "Here is your chamber—oh, what is that dog doing here?"

The dog, a basset hound with sad, dark eyes, was lying on the floor, blocking the door of a room. He rose on wobbly legs to stare warily at the two women.

"I'm sorry, mum," Mrs. Hubbard said. "I'll summon the footman at once to put him out. I don't know how he always manages to sneak up here."

"That's all right, Mrs. Hubbard." Madeline unbuttoned one of her gloves and took it off so she could bend down and scratch the hound behind his ears. His tail wagged slowly. "What's his name?" she asked.

"Gengis." The housekeeper gave a disapproving sniff and opened the door.

Madeline stepped inside, looking back at the dog. "Come on, Gengis," she said.

The dog sat down and whined.

"He won't go inside," Mrs. Hubbard said. "He only likes to lie outside the door. This is your chamber, mum."

Madeline gave the dog one final pat, then turned to look at the room. She couldn't prevent a small gasp.

The room was as big as her entire cottage in Baltimore. She stepped forward, and a damp, musty smell assaulted her nostrils. Her gaze lingered a moment on the enormous bed, with its twenty-foot-high canopy and heavy velvet curtains, before she glanced around at the dark wallpaper and furniture.

"What a magnificent room," Madeline said politely, even though she found it rather overwhelming. At least there was a lit fireplace, although it didn't seem to give off much heat.

Mrs. Hubbard's eyes darted nervously about. "Yes, mum."

"It appears it could use a good airing, however," Madeline said, wondering at the woman's distracted air. "Perhaps you could see to it tomorrow?"

"Yes, mum." Mrs. Hubbard edged toward the door.

Briskly, Madeline unbuttoned her other glove. "I can see there is much work to be done," she said. "We may need to hire additional servants. But the first thing I want to do is have that tower roof repaired. I'll hire some workmen tomorrow—"

"Oh no, mum, you mustn't!"

Madeline stopped unbuttoning her glove to stare at the housekeeper.

Mrs. Hubbard bit her lip and hastily curtsied. "Beggin' your pardon, mum."

Madeline studied the woman's pale face. "Why mustn't I?"

The housekeeper chewed on her lip a moment more, then blurted out, "Because of the ghost, mum. He wouldn't like it."

"The ghost?" Madeline, having begun to worry that there was something seriously wrong with the house, almost laughed in relief. But she restrained herself, not wanting to offend the housekeeper, who appeared in deadly earnest. "Who, may I ask, is this phantom?"

"The former master—Lord Merrick," Mrs. Hubbard said. She lowered her voice to a whisper as if afraid the ghost might overhear her. "He killed himself, mum. Up there in the tower room. When he lost his fortune in a card game."

Madeline's desire to laugh faded. "What a terrible waste," she said quietly.

Mrs. Hubbard nodded. "His friend Mr. Townsend, who

found the body, tried to pass it off as an accident, but everyone knew the truth. Now Lord Merrick haunts this house, waxing and waning with the moon.''

"He waxes and wanes with the moon? I've never heard of such a thing."

"The family has always been odd," Mrs. Hubbard said, as if that somehow explained everything.

"Have you actually seen him yourself?" Madeline inquired.

The housekeeper shook her head. "No, but many others have. He always appears a few days after the new moon, his image very faint. But as the days pass, he grows more and more solid, and we start hearing strange sounds, and sometimes I even smell gunpowder. Then, the day of the full moon, the brandy starts disappearing."

"Ah. I see." And Madeline did see. Very clearly. Mrs. Hubbard was obviously taking advantage of this ghost story to do a bit of tippling on the side. Madeline made a mental note to keep an eye on the liquor stores. "I still don't see why the ghost would object to my repairing the roof. Even phantoms must dislike getting rained upon."

"He doesn't like strangers in his house."

"You forget," Madeline said gently. "It is now *my* house. This ghost will just have to accustom himself to that."

"Yes, mum." The housekeeper appeared doubtful, but her attention was distracted by the young blond footman who stepped over Gengis's prone body to enter the room with Madeline's trunk. "Put that by the bed, Warde," Mrs. Hubbard directed.

The footman—a lanky lad who couldn't have been more than eighteen—blushed when Madeline smiled and thanked him. After he left, Mrs. Hubbard said, "I will send up a girl to help you unpack and undress."

"No thank you. I can take care of myself."

Mrs. Hubbard looked shocked. "Very well, mum. Shall I bring you a tray?"

"No, I'm not hungry. Thank you. That will be all for tonight."

Mrs. Hubbard left, closing the door behind her.

"Come along, you troublesome dog," Madeline heard her say.

Letting out a long sigh, Madeline untied the ribbons of her bonnet and removed it, then inspected the room more closely.

In addition to the bed, there was an elaborately carved wardrobe and a dressing table. Idly, she opened a drawer of the table. Inside was a shaving set and a silver snuff box. She closed the drawer and wandered over to the window, where she could see more water stains on the drapes and wallpaper.

The room was as dark and faded as the rest of Merrick Hall. The state of the whole house was appalling—and judging from what she'd seen of the village and surrounding fields on her way here, the rest of the estate would probably not be much better. It would take an enormous amount of work to set everything to rights.

The idea cheered her enormously.

Madeline smiled, thinking of her mother's and aunts' chagrin if they could see the house. They had talked her into coming to this place for a "rest."

"You need to get away from the shipping offices—you're wearing yourself out," her aunt Ginny had said.

"You're getting so thin and pale—you need a vacation," her aunt Doris had added.

"Since that house in England you inherited won't sell, why don't you go for a visit." Her mother had been relentless. "You could do some sight-seeing for a month or two. It would be good for you."

Madeline had finally given in to their pressure. Or at least she had appeared to do so. What they didn't know was that she had decided that it was time Spencer Shipping opened another office in England. Also, she really needed to find out exactly what was wrong with Merrick Hall and why it hadn't sold.

Now, with attending to the new office and repairing the house and estate, she would be busier than ever.

She pushed back the stained drapes and looked out the window. A pale light reflected off the spidery branches of the trees scratching against her window and the silvery shrubs in the garden below. She glanced up and saw the three-quarter moon up in the sky, making her think of Mrs. Hubbard's story about the ghost that waxed and waned.

Turning from the window and walking over to her trunk, Madeline wondered how serious the housekeeper's drinking problem was. She would not like to have to fire the woman, Madeline thought as she opened the trunk and took out a stack of shawls. But perhaps she was jumping to conclusions too quickly. Perhaps it was someone else who was stealing the brandy, and Mrs. Hubbard was only the victim of a cruel practical joke.

At least she'd discovered what was wrong with the house, she thought as she put the shawls on a shelf in the wardrobe. If the buyers weren't put off by the condition of the property or the fact that a man had killed himself here, then undoubtedly they were put off by the "ghost."

Well, she would soon take care of all that. Briskly, she removed her black wool dress from the trunk and shook out the wrinkles. Once the house was cleaned and repaired, she didn't doubt this phantom would take himself off. She would have to keep a sharp eye out for the ghost—likely it was one of the village boys playing a prank. She remembered when her small church in Baltimore had started having "visitations" every Saturday night. Many of the townspeople had been too frightened to go to church the next day. Of course, it had turned out only to be Danny

Dawber, dressed in his mother's bedsheets, trying to avoid the services.

Madeline refolded the dress and arranged it neatly on another shelf in the wardrobe. Being forced to learn pages of Bible verses as a punishment, Danny had soon reformed his ways. She might use a similar punishment when she caught Merrick Hall's "ghost". . . .

Creak. Creak. Cre-e-e-eak.

Madeline paused for a moment, listening. The noise sounded like footsteps walking across the floor.

With a shake of her head, she returned to her trunk. Old wood often creaked. Even in Baltimore, where there weren't any ghosts. It might be a good idea to roll up the carpets in all the rooms and check the floorboards. Some of them might need to be repaired or even replaced. It really was a shame that this house had been allowed to go to rack and ruin. . . .

Clank. Clank. Clank. Clank.

Madeline, lifting a hatbox from the trunk, grew still. The odd noise sounded remarkably like clanking chains. She shook her head. My, this house was making her quite fanciful. Doubtless, it was nothing but the rattle of tongs or the coal scuttle as someone built up a fire, the sound carrying through the chimney flues. Heaven knew, the house was cold enough to need every fire lit. She only wished that the feeble flames in this room's fireplace sent out more warmth. Shivering, she put the hatbox in the wardrobe and turned back toward her trunk. It was as cold as a tomb in here. . . .

"OoooooooooooooOOOOooooohhhh."

She stopped abruptly as the eerie moan echoed throughout the room. She glanced about but saw no one.

Her heart beat a little faster. She'd never heard such a noise. It had sounded unearthly, ominous, *ghostly*. . . .

She laughed. How foolish she was. Wind could often make strange sounds.

Still chuckling, she lifted a stack of petticoats from the trunk and turned.

She froze, the laughter fading on her lips.

Standing in front of the wardrobe, his figure hazy and half formed, a bright glow around him, stood a tall man with black hair, gaunt cheekbones, and angry gray eyes. Only it wasn't a man.

It was a ghost.

"Dammit, woman," it snarled. "Are you deaf?"

Two

Madeline's first instinct was to scream. But her great-grandfather had fought the British in the French and Indian Wars; her grandfather had fought the British in the War for Independence; and her father had fought the British in the War of 1812. She would be darned if she screamed at the sight of one measly aristocratic English ghost.

The blood of her ancestors stiffening her spine, she said with only a hint of a tremor in her voice, "No, I'm not deaf. May I help you, sir?"

For an instant, he appeared taken aback by her polite response. But then he frowned ferociously. "Yes, you may help me. You may leave my house at once. I cannot abide strangers."

"That is unfortunate," she said. "Because you are going to have to endure me—for as long as I choose to stay."

"You will leave at once. Or else . . ." The stark pallor of his skin intensified and the bones of his cheeks grew more prominent.

She gulped a little as his face took on the ghostly appearance of a skull, but she didn't back down. "Or else, what? You are a ghost. What can you do besides make a lot of silly noises?"

To her relief, his face returned to a more human aspect, his thick, straight brows drawn together. "I assure you, I can do much more than make noise."

"Such as what?" she demanded boldly—if a bit recklessly. "Can you make a knife fly through the air and stab me? Can you pick up a gun and shoot me through the heart? You look too flimsy to do either of those things."

Dark color rose in his pale cheeks. "It would be most unwise of you to make me demonstrate what I can do."

"Am I supposed to be frightened by that statement? I'm not likely to be scared off by the threats of a coward who took his own life."

Again he looked taken aback. "You do believe in plain speaking, don't you? What if I told you that I did *not* kill myself—that I was murdered. What if I told you that being murdered makes a body very, *very* ill-tempered. What if I told you that I have sometimes been known to take out my ill temper on inhabitants of this house who have annoyed me. And what if I told you that I have frightened those inhabitants so greatly that they've run screaming from Merrick Hall, never to return?"

"I would think those inhabitants were very poor-spirited," Madeline said calmly. Her initial fear had almost completely disappeared. Fairly certain by now that he wasn't going to do anything too terrible to her, she looked at him curiously. "You were murdered? But then why do people think you killed yourself?"

"Because I was found in the locked tower room, with a spent pistol in my hand. All the evidence pointed toward suicide."

"How peculiar," she said, more and more intrigued by his tale. "Who killed you?"

"I don't know. I didn't see him." Stroking his rather long jaw with his fingers, he stared into the distance. "George Firth, most likely. He's the one that spread that ridiculous rumor that I'd lost a fortune to him. I'd *won* a fortune from him, and he might have thought he could avoid paying. Also, I was to fight a duel with him the next day. He probably decided he didn't want to risk his neck." He stared at her menacingly. "I suggest you don't risk yours."

Madeline ignored his oblique threat, mulling over what he'd told her. The fact that he'd gambled and planned to fight a duel indicated that he was wasteful and hotheaded. Still, she could not help but feel some sympathy for him. Even more than gambling and dueling, she hated injustice.

"What if we made a bargain?" she asked. "If you let me stay, I will help you prove that George Firth murdered you."

"I don't care about proving he murdered me." The ghostly figure glided over to the window and stared out at the moonlit garden. "All I want is peace."

"You could prove your innocence. Mr. Firth would be punished and justice served. Surely that would give you peace. Then perhaps you wouldn't be so ill-tempered and you could do something with the rest of your life—er, existence—something besides playing foolish tricks on people."

Turning from the window, he gave her a long, narrowed stare. "You have an impertinent tongue."

For a moment, she thought she'd gone too far, that he was going to carry out his ghostly threat after all. But she returned his stare steadily, refusing to show any sign of fear.

He stroked his chin again, allowing his gaze to travel over her. "Very well, I accept your bargain." A sudden smile appeared on his mouth. "It will be rather pleasant having a woman in the house again."

Instinctively, Madeline stiffened at the gleam in his eyes. But before she could respond, he disappeared.

Three

Jack Merrick woke from his ghostly slumber at an ungodly hour—eleven in the morning. In death, as in life, he never rose before the hour of noon. He was about to close his eyes again and go back to sleep when a vague memory tickled what used to be his brain. Something was different about today. But what? Oh, yes—the Colonial had arrived last night. Mrs. Madeline Spencer. He had agreed to let her try to prove George Firth had killed him.

Jack groaned and rolled over in his bed. What on earth had possessed him? He didn't want her here. She was bound to be a nuisance and an annoyance. He should have made her leave immediately. In spite of her skepticism, he had no doubt he could have done so without too much difficulty.

But he hadn't. He wasn't precisely certain why not. Perhaps because there was some remnant of a gentleman left in him that wouldn't allow him to bully a woman. Perhaps because her lack of fear had caught him off guard. Or perhaps because her accusation that he was a coward had piqued him. . . .

The thought made him frown. He didn't care what some

strange woman thought of him. Especially not Mrs. Madeline Spencer. She was obviously a busybody, and she had a sharp tongue. He did not particularly care for that. He liked women who were soft and amenable, who spoke with honeyed phrases and who knew how to carry on a flirtation.

Still, in spite of her deficiencies in certain areas, she had managed to accomplish one thing—for the first time since his death he hadn't been bored.

Unable to go back to sleep, he rose from the bed and floated out into the corridor. Death had not been at all what he expected. As a child, he'd listened to tales of melodious harps and beautiful angels. When he'd grown older and succumbed to the temptations of sin, he'd been warned about unbearable heat and consuming flames.

But he'd never expected this . . . nothingness. This half life of mind-numbing boredom. None of his questions about the afterlife had been answered. He hadn't been transported to a cloud or a fiery pit. Everything was exactly the same.

Almost.

He held up his hand and stared at his transparent fingers as he floated down the corridor. It had been a shock to discover he was dead. But it had been almost a greater shock to find himself a ghost. He had never believed in ghosts.

Being a ghost was not very pleasant. The only amusement he had was to scare the servants. But that had soon palled. They were too superstitious, too easily frightened.

This woman now, this Madeline Spencer . . . she had not seemed frightened at all. And if the truth be told, that was the real reason he'd let her stay. It wasn't often that a woman didn't run screaming at the sight of him.

He'd been annoyed at first when he'd heard the servants gossiping about the ''Widow Spencer'' who'd inherited Merrick Hall. He'd expected some elderly woman with a fluttering handkerchief in one hand and a bottle of smelling salts in the other.

Madeline Spencer's youth and poise had come as a rather pleasant surprise.

Although she wasn't in his usual style, she was pretty enough, with her curly brown hair and tall, curvy figure. Her blue-gray gaze was a bit too direct, and she had an air of morality that he would have found tedious if he were still alive, but it might be amusing to see if he could break through that formidable composure of hers, to see if he could make her forget her puritanical ways.

Yes, definitely, she would provide him no end of amusement. . . .

He stopped in front of Madeline's room, looking down at Gengis, who rested by the door.

"Good morning, boy," Jack said. "Is Mrs. Spencer up yet?"

The dog's tail thumped against the carpet.

"Ah, she is? Splendid. I'll just go right in then."

But Madeline was not in her room. And after searching all the rooms, he discovered she was not in the house. He waited, growing more and more impatient as an hour passed, and then another.

Where the devil was she? Had she left after all? But no, her things were still in her bedchamber. Annoyance ate at him. How dare she leave without informing him of where she was going or when she would be back. Such conduct was inexcusable. She should be here entertaining him, not jaunting about God only knew where all day long.

In a black humor, he returned to the library and sat at the window, watching the road.

A few hours later, Madeline stepped down from the carriage and entered the house, feeling very pleased with herself. Running lightly up the stairs to her room, she thought of all she had accomplished that day—she had spoken to the port master about docking permission and procedures and arranged for the necessary paperwork to be sent to her. She had visited several warehouses and found one with offices attached that was just perfect for her needs.

She paused by the door to scratch behind Gengis's ears, then entered her room, untying the strings of her bonnet. She only needed to sign the lease and she would be in business. Then she could focus all her attention on the house and the estate and the ghost. . . .

Her fingers stilled on the ribbons of her bonnet.

The passage of time had made the events of the previous night seem completely unbelievable. Had a ghost—a ghost!—really appeared in her bedroom? And had she really stood there arguing and bargaining with him calmly and coolly as if she spoke to ghosts every day of the week? Perhaps it had all been a dream.

But in her heart, she knew it hadn't been. She remembered everything too clearly—his anger, his threats, the gleam in his eyes. . . .

Frowning, she looked down at her dress. She'd worn it to bed last night and hadn't changed this morning, but obviously she couldn't wear the same gown forever.

He's dead, she scolded herself. *He can have no interest in seeing you naked.*

But something about that smile of his last night had made her uneasy. It had made her aware of the lateness of the hour, and the petticoats she'd been holding in her arms. It had made her aware of the impropriety of having a man—even a ghostly one—in her bedroom.

Perhaps if he'd been more like Thaddeus, she wouldn't have been so uneasy. Dear Thad had had fair hair, warm hazel eyes, and he would never have done something so ungentlemanly as spy on a lady.

If she had to be visited by a ghost, why couldn't it have been her husband? Dear Thad. But he would never be a

ghost, she knew instinctively. Being a ghost implied a re-
belliousness, a stubbornness, a resistance against authority
that were completely contrary to Thad's sweet nature.

Her fingers touched the buttons at her throat and she
looked about warily.

"Are you here?" she asked the empty room.

There was no response.

She didn't trust him. With his long nose, thin sensuous
lips, and knowing gray eyes, he was the epitome of an
aristocratic English libertine.

Setting her shoulders, she marched over to the wardrobe,
withdrew a sheet, and placed it over her head so that it
enveloped her like a shroud. She then unbuttoned and removed her dress underneath its concealing folds.

She had just gotten the dress off when she heard a muffled choking noise. Unable to see because of the sheet, she
swung toward the sound. "I knew it!" she exclaimed. "I
knew I couldn't trust you!"

Her only response was a loud scream.

"A ghost!" a female voice shrieked. "A ghost!"

Startled, Madeline pulled the sheet off her head in time
to see the housemaid, Lizzy, running away down the corridor.

"Oh, dear!" Madeline murmured. She bent down to
pick up her dress and the sheet, now lying crumpled on
the floor.

"Is something wrong?" a new voice—a deep, male
one—inquired. "I heard screaming. . . . Oh, I beg your
pardon."

She looked up to see Merrick standing in the open doorway. He looked a trifle more solid and the glow around
him was less apparent in the daylight, but he still had the
same gleam in his eyes that had been there last night.

Gasping, she snatched her dress from the floor, clutched
it in front of her petticoat, and glared at him. "Turn
around," she snapped.

His gaze traveled over her in a leisurely fashion before, with a wicked grin, he complied. "My dear Mrs. Spencer, I saw your petticoats last night. What difference does it make if you're *in* them?"

She blushed—she couldn't help herself. She'd hoped he hadn't noticed the undergarments. Annoyed at herself, but more so at him, she pulled her black wool dress from the wardrobe and yanked it on. "I would appreciate it if you would knock before you enter my bedchamber."

"You must be joking." He glanced over his shoulder at her.

"No, I'm not." She frowned at him fiercely, and, grinning, he turned his face away again.

"I can't knock." He demonstrated the way his knuckles made no noise against the door.

"Then you can speak." Keeping a wary eye on his back, she buttoned her dress as quickly as she could. "You can say, 'May I come in?' "

"You expect me to beg admittance to my own room in my own house?"

"This is *not* your house," she reminded him. "And this is not your room. They are mine, and I must have some privacy. It is very disconcerting to wonder if someone is going to pop into your room without warning or to wonder if someone is spying on you." She finished buttoning her dress. "You may turn around now."

He did so, a wounded expression on his face. "Rest assured I would never stoop to such depravity. Is that why you wore your dress to bed last night, because you didn't trust me?"

"Yes—" The implication of his question registered and she turned white, then red. "You—! You *were* spying on me!"

"I wouldn't call it spying. Can I help it if a woman comes into my bedroom and climbs into bed with me?"

"You were sleeping in my bed!"

"No, my dear, *you* were sleeping in *my* bed."

"If you had any decency, you would have left!"

"Sorry to disappoint you."

She clenched her teeth. "This will not do at all. You must move to another room."

"I must?"

She glared at him. "If you won't, then I will. And you must give me your word of honor that you will not spy on me again."

"What a to-do over nothing." He leaned against the doorjamb, his arms folded across his chest. "Did I tell you that when I died I was taken on a brief tour of heaven and the other place? In hell, they were all wearing snowsuits. In heaven, however, everyone was naked."

"You're making that up. I don't believe you."

"Think about it, my dear. God sent you into this world naked. Why would the afterlife be different?"

Her lips pressed tightly together, she marched over to the wardrobe and started to pull out her clothes.

He sighed heavily. "How stubborn you are. Very well. I will allow you the use of this room for as long as you are here."

A stack of shawls in her arms, she stared at him suspiciously. "And you promise you won't spy on me?"

"If you insist." Straightening, he wandered into the room and inspected the items she'd laid out on her dressing table. "What a little puritan you are."

Madeline moved over in front of him, shielding her brush and comb and perfume bottles from view. "If by 'puritan' you mean I have morals, then you are right."

His deeply hooded eyes took on a pained look and he glided away from the dressing table. "If you say so. Now that we have cleared that up . . . where the devil have you been all day?"

"I have been attending to some very important business this morning," she said, putting her shawls back in the wardrobe. "I intend to open a shipping office in Bristol—"

"My God, don't tell me you're in trade." He looked down his nose at her. "I suppose I should have guessed."

She turned from the wardrobe to look at him with a very straight gaze. "I am certain it will shock a lazy, idle, useless, aristocratic ghost like you to learn that in the real world people must work to make an honest living. I am sorry that you will have to endure something so intolerable as a person in trade while I am here. I apologize for offending your tender sensibilities."

"Mrs. Spencer," he said solemnly. "Has anyone ever told you you have no respect for your betters?"

She straightened the stack of shawls. "Frequently. My aunt Doris's husband never misses an opportunity to tell us that his grandfather was a baronet. Uncle Wendell has often commented that I am not properly impressed."

"Hm. If titles do not impress you, I will have to find some other way."

Startled, she stared at him. Seeing the glint in his eye, she realized he was deliberately trying to provoke her. Her eyes narrowed in sudden suspicion. Was that what he had been doing all along? Had he only been teasing her about sleeping in the same bed?

Regathering her composure, she said in her most dignified manner, "I must ask you to leave now. I need to comb my hair."

"Why should I leave because of that? I've seen women comb their hair before."

"I'm certain you have. But I am not going to let you watch me comb mine. It would not be proper. Please go now. I don't want to look untidy when Mr. Townsend arrives."

That wiped the smile from Merrick's face. "Thomas Townsend is coming here?"

"Yes. I sent Warde, the footman, this morning with a

note asking him to call on me at four this afternoon so I
could question him about the murder.''

Merrick's brows drew together. ''You did that without
asking me?''

Surprised, she stared at him. ''I thought you would be
pleased. We did agree that I would help you prove Firth
killed you.''

''How will questioning Townsend help? Firth is the one
that needs to be questioned.

''He wasn't available.''

His voice was cold. ''So you invited Townsend instead.
I have no idea what is acceptable behavior in America, but
here, it is completely beyond the pale for a woman to
invite a man to her house.''

''*You* are lecturing me on proper behavior?'' Madeline
could barely believe the gall of him. ''Oh, this is ridiculous. I refuse to discuss the matter any further. Please go
away. Mr. Townsend will be here any moment and I'm
not ready.''

For a moment, she thought he would argue. But then,
with a frosty glare, he disappeared.

She blinked a little at his sudden disappearance, then
shrugged and hastily pulled the pins from her hair. She
was just fluffing up the curls on her forehead when she
heard a distant bell ring.

A few moments later she entered the library, where Mr.
Townsend was waiting.

His gentle expression reminded her a little of Thad.
With even features and light brown hair, he was a year or
two older than her own twenty-six years. But there were
a few bitter lines about his mouth that made her think his
life had not been all pleasant.

''Mrs. Spencer?'' he inquired with a smile. ''It's a pleasure to meet you.''

She smiled back. ''And you, Mr. Townsend.''

"Don't smile at him like that," a voice growled in her ear. "You'll give him the wrong idea."

Her smile froze. She looked sideways and saw Merrick lounging by a tall bookcase, his arms folded across his chest. Quickly she looked back at Townsend. He appeared to have seen and heard nothing. "Please be seated, Mr. Townsend, and I will ring for refreshments," she said. She moved over to the bellpull and hissed out of the corner of her mouth, "Go away."

"No," Merrick said coolly. "I want to be here when you question him. Besides, it isn't proper for you to receive a gentleman visitor without a chaperone."

She had to restrain herself from rolling her eyes. What was that saying about the devil preaching propriety? Turning back to Mr. Townsend, she smiled. "I hope you don't think it terribly forward of me to invite you here."

"Not at all," he said gallantly. "In fact, your note quite intrigued me. You said you wanted to discuss Jack's death?"

"Yes." She seated herself on the sofa across from him and tried to ignore the way Merrick was prowling about the room. "I wondered if you might tell me a little of what led up to that night so that I might better understand."

"Understand what?"

"Why he haunts this house."

Townsend laughed out loud. "You don't really believe that, do you, Mrs. Spencer?"

Madeline, aware that Merrick had stopped pacing and was waiting to hear her answer, chose her words with care. "No, but everyone else appears to do so, and if I am to sell this house, I must find a way to get rid of the ghost."

"You want to get rid of me?" Merrick asked in mock plaintive tones. "I'm hurt, Mrs. Spencer."

Madeline ignored the ghost's inane remark and concentrated on Townsend.

"I see." Townsend's brow furrowed for a moment before he nodded. "Ask away, Mrs. Spencer, and I will do my best to answer your questions."

Merrick sat down in a chair and crossed his legs, drawing Madeline's gaze to him once more. She forced herself to look away.

"Did you know Lord Merrick well?" she asked.

"Yes, I did," Townsend replied. "We went to school together. He was the best of good friends, someone you could always count on, a great gun. He could outgamble, outdrink, and out . . . er, flirt, any of us."

"Oh, could he?" she murmured with a disapproving frown in Merrick's direction.

He grinned without repentance. "Remind me to tell you sometime about how Tom and I wagered who could steal the most bottles of brandy from the headmaster and the most petticoats from his wife."

Townsend grinned also, making Madeline wonder if he was remembering the same thing. "Everyone liked him. Especially the ladies. He was rich, good-looking, and amusing. What more could a woman want?"

"What, indeed?" she muttered. Mrs. Hubbard came in with a tea tray. Madeline waited until the woman left before she said, "It sounds as though he had a very pleasurable life. Why would he kill himself?"

Townsend took the saucer she handed him and lifted the cup of tea. "He didn't. It was an accident. Oh, I know people have told you otherwise, but it's just not true. Jack would never kill himself. Why would he? He had everything."

"Did he?" Her gaze traveled to Merrick again. He was looking out the window, his back to her. At this distance, with sunlight shining through the wall of glass, his image was less solid, more wavering.

"Beg pardon, ma'am?"

"Never mind." She blinked the glare of the sunlight from her eyes. "Did you never wonder if perhaps it was not an accident or suicide—that perhaps someone murdered him?''

''I wouldn't think so.'' Townsend took a small sip of tea and quickly set his cup back on the saucer. ''Although I suppose anyone from the ball could have sneaked upstairs and shot him.''

''From the ball?'' She straightened in her seat. ''What do you mean?''

''There was a ball here that night.''

''But I thought Lord Merrick was supposed to be fighting a duel the next day.''

''He was.'' Townsend grinned. ''He sent out the invitations immediately after Firth challenged him. He even sent one to Firth. Everyone thought it a great joke. Firth had fought only one duel before—with a boy barely out of leading strings. He'd spent the whole day—and the evening too—before that duel practicing his marksmanship.''

''So Mr. Firth didn't come to the ball?''

''Oh, he came. He had to. Or he would have been a laughingstock. He was furious.''

''Furious enough to kill?''

Townsend's smile faded. ''You really think Jack was murdered? That might explain why the body was stolen— to cover up any evidence.''

''The body was stolen?'' She glanced at Merrick, but he was still looking out the window, and she couldn't see his expression.

''Yes, the day before the coroner was to inspect the corpse, it disappeared. There were all sorts of rumors. Some said the Old Ones had taken it.''

''The Old Ones?''

''The people who live in the hills. It's said they are descended from a strange race that has lived in this area for thousands of years. A few believe the Old Ones took the body for some pagan ritual. But most think graverobbers stole it—to sell to medical doctors for dissection.

Body-snatching is a thriving business here, you know."

Madeline shuddered. "No, I didn't know. The night he was killed . . . you were the one who found him, weren't you?"

"Yes. I heard the shot and went to check on it immediately. I found Gengis, Jack's dog, barking and scratching frantically at the door to the tower. It was barred from the inside. I went back downstairs and got several men to come help me break it down. Inside . . . inside we found him, the pistol in his hand and blood running down his face."

Nausea churned in Madeline's stomach. "By any chance, did you see where Mr. Firth was at the time of the shot?"

"No, I didn't." He frowned a little. "He wasn't with the men who helped me break down the door, though."

"I see." She rose to her feet. "Thank you, Mr. Townsend. You've been a great help."

"Glad to be of service," he said, taking her hand. He smiled down at her. "It's pleasant to have a new face in the district. Are you planning on staying long?"

"Only a month or so."

"Ah, that is a shame. But perhaps you will change your mind and decide to stay. I will do my share to convince you, I assure you."

She smiled at him. "That's very kind of you."

He gave a slight bow and left.

As soon as he'd left, Madeline turned to Merrick. "What do you think?"

He was watching her with a rather brooding gaze. "I think you had better watch out for Townsend. He is something of a rake."

She waved her hand impatiently. "Oh, for heaven's sake. What did you think of what he said about Mr. Firth?"

Merrick glanced down at his sleeve. "What is there to think?"

She sighed with exasperation. "It certainly appears he had the opportunity to slip upstairs and kill you—not to mention the motive." She looked at him. "Was it really necessary to have a ball to taunt Mr. Firth?"

He arched an eyebrow. "Of course it was necessary."

"Of course," she muttered. "Foolish question." In a louder voice she said, "What were you doing in the tower room if you were hosting a ball?"

"I'd grown bored. I went up to the tower to clean my pistols for the duel. I barred the door, not wanting to be disturbed."

"By some woman looking for you, I suppose."

He grinned, but didn't answer.

"But how could Mr. Firth have gotten in if the door was barred? And how could he have left and the bar still be in place?"

Merrick shrugged. "I have no idea."

She put her hands on her hips. "You are not helping much. Let's go upstairs and look at the tower room and see if we can figure out how he did it."

"No."

She frowned at the terse reply. "Why not?"

"I don't permit anyone in that room."

Annoyance filled Madeline. Was he deliberately being difficult? "Why not?" she asked again.

"I just don't."

Yes, he was definitely trying to be difficult, she thought in disgust. But perhaps this wasn't the time to press the issue. "Is there another way out of the tower room? Another door? A secret passage? A window?"

"There is a window, but it is four stories up and there isn't a convenient tree or vine to climb."

"Hm. How peculiar. Mr. Firth must have gotten in some way. And then stolen the body to prevent anyone from

seeing that you'd been murdered. Did you know your body
was stolen?''

He frowned. ''No, I did not.'' He shifted. ''We've spoken enough about this subject. Let's talk of something else.
Like when are you going to buy some new clothes?''

She drew back, bewildered by the change of subject.
''How can you talk about clothes at a time like this?''

''Well . . . I hate to tell you this, but it is very distracting
to try to think when there is a woman hovering around,
looking like a big, black crow.''

''A big, black—'' She stopped herself with an effort.
''I am in mourning for my husband,'' she said coldly.

''Hm. That's a shame. Black does nothing for you.''

''And you are an expert?''

''I hate to boast''—he put on what she supposed was
meant to be a modest expression—''but yes. Many ladies
came to me for sartorial advice.''

''I'll bet they did,'' she muttered.

His eyebrows arched. ''Why, Mrs. Spencer, whatever
do you mean?''

''I mean exactly what you think I mean. Your friend
was very clear about you. Gambling, drinking, and *wom-
anizing*. That was what he was going to say, wasn't it?''

He smiled. ''Probably.''

''Didn't you ever . . .'' She hesitated.

''Ever what?''

''Ever do anything worthwhile?''

His smile vanished. ''Like open a shipping office?'' he
sneered.

She didn't look away. ''No. Like take care of your
house and your estate and your tenants.''

For a moment he stood very still. Then his mouth curved
upward rather ruefully. ''I was never meant to be a country
squire. I much preferred gambling and drinking and making love.'' He stepped closer to her. ''You should try them
sometime.''

"No thank you." She sat down on the sofa and folded her hands primly in her lap. "Now, may we discuss your murder?"

He sighed. "You really are a little puritan. And a little bulldog, too."

"First I'm a crow, now I'm a bulldog. I really don't know what any woman saw in you. It couldn't have been your way with words."

He grinned. "What a sharp tongue you have! Maybe I should have called you a hedgehog. But I've always been rather partial to hedgehogs. Did I tell you I had one as a pet once? It liked being stroked—as long as I stroked it in the right direction—"

"Lord Merrick," she said sharply. "If you will not be serious, then I am going to make a list of things I need to do tomorrow."

"You are going to work? How dull you are."

In reply, she walked over to the desk and reseated herself. She took out a sheet of paper and licked the tip of a quill before dipping it in ink and beginning to write.

"First thing tomorrow, I'm going to the quay to speak to the port master again. I will have to get up at six o'clock—"

"Six? In the morning?" he asked in tones of revulsion.

She didn't bother to reply. "Then, I'm going to go into the village and—"

"And buy a new dress?" he asked hopefully.

"And hire workers to fix the tower roof, and drapers to measure the windows for new drapes, and gardeners to clear the underbrush away from the house—"

"They won't come."

She ignored him. "After that, I will return here and question Mr. Firth—"

"Firth! I thought you said he was not available!"

"He wasn't available today. But his message said he would be delighted to come tomorrow."

Merrick's brows drew together. "You really must quit this habit of yours of inviting men here."

"I am a respectable widow," she said. "There is nothing the least bit wrong with having a gentleman visit me for a short time to discuss some business." Rather fiercely, she dipped the quill in the ink again. "Perhaps it would be better if you stayed away. It would probably be upsetting for you to see the man you suspect of murdering you—"

"It won't bother me at all."

She laid down the pen. "Nonetheless, I think it would be better if you didn't come. It is rather difficult to question someone when there is a ghost hovering about and making rude remarks—"

"Are you saying you would *prefer* that I not come?"

She hesitated. Then she said bluntly, "Yes."

"I thought that might be the case."

She waited, but he said nothing more. "Well?" she asked impatiently.

"Well what?"

"Will you stay away?"

He smiled at her frowning face, a devilish sparkle in his gray eyes.

"No, I'm afraid not, Mrs. Spencer."

Four

Madeline was a little surprised by Mr. Firth's appearance when he was shown into the library the next afternoon. She had expected a more villainous sort—not this foppish gentleman. He was dressed all in dove-gray silk with frothing lace at his wrists and neck and a diamond pin stuck in his jabot. His hair was curled and there was rouge on his cheeks.

"I don't know if I can bear the stench of this fop's perfume," Merrick said disdainfully.

Madeline wasn't sure whether she could either. But she was still angry at the ghost for refusing her request to stay away, so she gave him an admonishing glare, then greeted Firth and invited him to sit down. To her dismay, the dandy seated himself next to her on the sofa.

Merrick's frown grew blacker. "This knave is not to be trusted, Mrs. Spencer. Send him packing."

Ignoring this advice—and the ghost—Madeline explained to Firth that she wanted to ask him about Merrick.

Firth's oily smile disappeared.

"There's not much I can tell you. Except that the man was a bounder and a wastrel. It was no surprise to me to hear that he had killed himself. I'm only surprised some-one else didn't do it first.''

Madeline edged a few inches away from him, trying not to inhale his rancid perfume. "You didn't like Lord Mer-rick?"

"No, I did not." Firth stretched his arm along the back of the sofa and leaned toward her. "He was an arrogant bastard—if you'll forgive me, Mrs. Spencer—and a blight on our community here."

"Not as much of a blight as your foul face," Merrick muttered.

Although Madeline was inclined to agree with the ghost for once, she smiled politely at Firth. "I understand that he owed you money and that he died the night before you were to fight a duel with him."

"Yes, that's true." Firth puffed out his lace-clad chest. "You've probably heard the rumors that he shot himself to avoid paying me. He cheated me out of my money, as well as the pleasure of shooting him myself."

"You were a better marksman than he was?"

Firth gave her a sharp glance. "Of course. In fact, I've often wondered if he didn't shoot himself because he was afraid to face me."

Merrick snorted. "Mrs. Spencer, I cannot endure the presence of this lying, beetle-brained fribble much longer. If you don't get rid of him soon, I will be forced to take action myself."

Madeline's gaze flickered uneasily to the ghost. She couldn't blame him for being disgusted, but she hadn't finished her questions. She looked back at Firth. "What did you do when you heard the pistol shot?" she asked.

"Nothing. That is, I didn't hear it. The musicians were playing a jig at the time, and the noise in the ballroom was quite loud. Then Townsend came in, looking deuced pale, asking for help to break down the tower door."

"Did you go?"

"No, why should I? Townsend was all dirty and disheveled from thrusting himself against the door." He rearranged the lace of his cuff so that it fell just so. "I wasn't about to destroy my toilette for the likes of Merrick. Townsend returned a short while later and told everyone there had been an 'accident'—but the truth soon came out, and everyone knew the coward had shot himself."

The venom in his voice shocked Madeline. "How can you be so sure it wasn't an accident—or even murder?"

"Murder?" Something flickered in his opaque brown eyes. "Who put that idea into your head?"

"He doesn't really sound like the kind of person who would kill himself—"

"You didn't know him. He was a liar, a cheat, and a scoundrel, and he was *exactly* the kind of coward who would kill himself. He deserved to die—"

"Not as much as you do for wearing that hideous coat."

Firth's mouth dropped open. "What did you say, Mrs. Spencer?"

Madeline straightened in her seat. Good heavens! Had Firth heard the ghost? "I, uh, said, I much admire you for wearing that fabulous coat." She cleared her throat. "Now, who were you dancing with the night of the—"

"You always did look like a damned caper-merchant, Firth," a deep voice interrupted her. "Do you call that a cravat?"

Firth tugged at his cravat and looked around uneasily. "I . . . I must go, Mrs. Spencer. I, er, have another appointment."

"But Mr. Firth!" Madeline exclaimed, following him as he took quick mincing steps out into the hall. "I have more questions."

"My appointment is urgent," Firth said, his eyes darting nervously about. He picked up his hat, gloves, and riding crop and headed for the door. "Perhaps some other time. . . ."

He stopped, staring at Gengis, who had been resting in front of the door. The dog rose to his feet and growled.

Firth glared at the dog.

"Quiet, Gengis," Madeline said automatically. She forced herself to smile at Firth. "Would it be possible for you to come again tomorrow? I promise I won't take much of your time—"

"I'm afraid that would be impossible." He minced toward the door. "I'm a very busy man—"

In his haste, Firth stepped on Gengis's tail. The dog yelped, then snapped at Firth, his teeth tearing a hole in the man's pantaloons.

"Damn hellhound!" Firth, his face turning red with fury, raised the riding crop over his head as if to hit the dog.

Shocked, Madeline grabbed his arm. "Mr. Firth, please! You stepped on his tail. It's only natural . . ."

Her voice faltered as Firth turned on her, an ugly snarl on his lips, the whip still raised. Hastily, she stepped back, but Firth came after her, a cruel light in his eyes.

Suddenly, he stopped, his gaze fastened on something behind her. The color drained from his face and his eyes bugged out from his head.

"Merrick!" he croaked.

Merrick grinned evilly. "Yes, it is I. I usually don't bother to appear to worms like you, but when you start threatening helpless women and animals, I have no choice. Since I 'cheated' you out of a duel, I suggest we have another one right now—being a ghost has not hurt my aim at all."

"I . . . I . . . I refuse to fight with any ghost!" Firth's teeth chattered with fright. "Especially one as despicable as you! Mrs. Spencer, forgive me, but I am leaving at once, before . . . before I'm tempted to do violence to this . . . this cad!"

He practically ran from the house, followed by Gengis's

excited barking and Merrick's scornful laughter.

Merrick turned to Madeline, a satisfied smile on his face. "He's gone."

"Is he insane?" She was trembling. "I think he was going to hit me!"

"Firth is the worst kind of coward—exactly the kind of man to commit murder and try to make it look like a suicide."

Madeline struggled to regain her composure. "Yes . . . yes, I suppose he is."

"You suppose?" Merrick said sharply. "What do you mean? Isn't it obvious he is the murderer?"

"Perhaps. Except . . . except he says he was dancing at the time of the shot."

"Obviously, he's lying."

"But why would he lie when it will be easy to prove it?"

"I doubt he expected anyone to check up on him."

"You may be right. But let's not forget there was a whole houseful of people. It could have been one of them. Did anyone else have a reason to want to kill you?"

"Probably. I annoyed several people during my life."

Madeline shook her head. How could he sound so careless? "We must find out if anyone saw him dancing at the time of the pistol shot." She thought for a moment. "Is he married? If so, his wife could probably tell us whether or not he was dancing."

"Yes, he's married."

Alerted by something in his tone, Madeline stared at him. "You know something about his wife?"

Merrick looked down at his sleeve. "Caroline and I were . . . friends."

Distaste soured Madeline's mouth. "You were sleeping with the man's wife?"

"Actually, I wasn't." He smiled crookedly. "But even if I was, you shouldn't look so disapproving, Mrs. Spencer.

It is very common here—expected even, as long as the parties involved are discreet. Only shopkeepers expect their wives to be faithful to them.''

"Mr. Firth is not a shopkeeper."

"No, he is an idiot. He never should have married Caroline. It was obvious she cared nothing for him."

"Was she the cause of your duel?"

"Certainly not. Our quarrel had to do with his taste in clothes."

She sighed in exasperation. "Are you never serious? This habit of facetiousness is very annoying."

He smiled. "More of your bluntness, Mrs. Spencer? I must tell you, you are unlikely to win any suitors with it."

"Since I am not interested in suitors, I don't care."

His brows lifted. "If you are not interested in marrying again, what are you interested in?"

"My shipping business mainly."

He rolled his eyes. "Oh, please. You are not going to lecture me on the virtues of work, are you? I don't know if my stomach can take it."

"I never lecture," she said primly. Hearing a bell ring, she walked out into the hall, glancing over her shoulder to speak to Merrick. "However, you should not dismiss something that you have never tried. I can only pity you for never knowing the satisfaction that comes from a morning of hard work. . . ."

She paused as a footman entered the hall, staggering under the weight of the packages he carried in his arms.

Distracted from her efforts to reform Merrick, Madeline smiled in delight. "Oh, Warde! Take those up to my room, if you please. Thank you."

Merrick's gaze turned sardonic. "Ah, I'm beginning to understand your satisfaction. Obviously you spent the morning working very hard buying out all the shops in Bristol."

"Oh no, I bought those in the village on the way back

from Bristol. I bought a jar of leeches and syrup of rhubarb from the apothecary's, ribbons and a very fine cheese from the village shop, and I ordered three new dresses from the mantua-maker's—''

"Ah, so you took my advice," he said, his gaze wandering over her black silk dress. "Wise decision."

Ignoring the interruption, she continued, "—and I bought candles from the candle maker—''

"Not those smelly tallow ones, I hope."

"—and ordered new wheels for the broken cart in the stables from the wheelwright—''

"What did you do? Buy something from every shop in the village?"

"Why, yes." She paused in her recitation of purchases. "That's exactly what I did."

"Very clever of you."

"Clever?"

"The villagers will worship you forever."

She lifted her brows. "It would appear it takes very little to win their loyalty then. In truth, I purchased the things because they seem to need the business. The people appear very poorly off. The children in the streets are in rags, the shopkeepers thin, and the shops and cottages in need of repair—''

"So you thought to play Lady Bountiful. How generous of you."

She frowned, her gaze searching his face. Was he really so uncaring as he seemed? The neglect in the village had been going on for much longer than the year since his death. Something had been seriously wrong here. But what?

She supposed it didn't really matter. The important thing was that she would set things aright—the village, the estate, the house . . . and Lord Merrick, too.

She frowned again, thinking of the response of the village carpenter when she'd asked about repairing the tower roof. In spite of his obvious poverty, the man had refused.

"What exactly did you do to the workers that were hired to repair the roof?"

"Nothing much. I just smiled at them. Like this."

He demonstrated the "smile"—an insane, demonic grin. Something that looked like blood poured down from a wound in his temple. Madeline shuddered. "Why are you being so stubborn? Why won't you let anyone in the tower?"

He scowled. "I don't want a bunch of rustics in there. The clatter they make is enough to drive a ghost insane. Not to mention their ceaseless chatter. 'Do you think the gentry mort was sitting here when he killed himself?' " he mimicked savagely. " 'Look—ain't that a spot o' blood?' It was unbearable, I assure you."

Shadows dimmed the usual sparkle in his eyes. She caught a glimpse of a pain so dark and so deep, it shook her to her core. "I . . . I'm sorry. I didn't think—" She bit her lip.

He turned his head slightly, and the shadows disappeared. There was only amusement in his eyes now, making her wonder if she had imagined the pain.

"Don't look so stricken," he said lightly. "It's not your fault."

Madeline bit back further words of sympathy. *Had* she imagined the pain? She didn't think so, but she couldn't be certain. In any case, he obviously didn't want her sympathy, so she only said, "The tower must be fixed."

"You truly are persistent." He eyed her speculatively. "What if we made a bargain?"

The silky tone of his voice made her forget about the fleeting expression she'd witnessed, and look at him warily. "Another bargain?"

"Yes. If I am to have to listen to hammers and saws making a racket all day long, I deserve something in return."

Foreboding filled her. "Such as?"

"I will promise not to scare the workers," he said, smiling provocatively, "if you will allow me to watch you comb your hair every morning and evening."

Her mouth fell open. "Why do you want to watch me comb my hair?"

He just smiled, not responding.

"Will I get to keep my clothes on?" she asked suspiciously.

"Of course," he said, as if he'd never thought otherwise. "Unless you *want* to take them off. I would not object."

"Very kind of you," she muttered. She considered for a moment. She supposed he was not asking for much. It was a trifle improper, true, but really, it would be no great thing to allow him to watch her combing her hair. She suspected the only reason he was asking was because she'd made such a fuss yesterday about him leaving while she did so. "What about the drapers and the gardeners?" she asked.

His eyes sparkled. "Ah. For a few additional concessions, I would be very glad to—"

"Never mind," she said hastily. "I accept your bargain."

He smiled brilliantly. "Excellent. I will see you tonight then."

He disappeared, leaving Madeline with an uneasy feeling that she'd just made a terrible mistake.

He watched her that night.

She sat at her dressing table, pulling the comb through her hair, while he lounged near the fireplace, his dark, unreadable gaze on her. When she finished, he nodded and disappeared without a word, leaving her strangely disappointed.

She wasn't sure why. Nothing had happened. Of course,

she hadn't *expected* anything to happen. What could happen with something so innocent as combing her hair? She had often combed her hair in front of Thaddeus. He had never paid much attention when she did. There was nothing especially fascinating about a woman combing her hair.

Although Merrick had certainly seemed to find it so. He hadn't looked away once. Her scalp had tingled as she combed, as if it were his fingers running through her hair instead of the teeth of the comb. . . .

Oddly restless, she prepared herself for bed and climbed under the covers, only to find that she was unable to relax enough to go to sleep.

She tossed and turned, trying to find a comfortable position on the feather mattress. If only it wasn't so cold here, she thought. In spite of the fire in the hearth, she was freezing.

Staring up at the canopy, she decided she wasn't working hard enough. At home, she had worked all day and even late into the evenings sometimes, so that when she went to bed she fell at once into an exhausted sleep. She hated lying awake in the dark, all alone, with nothing to do but think.

Why did he look at her like that? And why had he looked so sad earlier? What was he thinking, feeling?

She wished she understood him better.

She turned over and punched her pillow. He was a peculiar man. So proud and haughty. So smiling and charming one moment, so bitter and angry the next. She thought of everything Firth and Townsend had said about him. How had Merrick inspired such friendship in one man and such hatred in another?

But obviously the enmity between Merrick and Firth had something to with Mrs. Firth . . . Caroline, Merrick had called her. Had he been in love with her?

Madeline pushed the thought away. It was none of her

business if he had been. She was supposed to be helping him prove that Firth had killed him, not poking her nose into his love life. But she couldn't help but be curious about the woman who'd apparently caused so much trouble. . . .

Madeline sat up suddenly, remembering her earlier idea to ask Firth's wife about his whereabouts at the time of the murder.

It was an excellent idea.

First thing tomorrow, Madeline thought, lying back down, she would ask the woman to come over. And if she was lucky, she would discover the truth of the matter. And then, Merrick could finally find peace.

Do you think the gentry mort was sitting here when he killed himself? Look—ain't that a spot o' blood?

Remembering the look in his eyes when he'd talked about the workers, Madeline's heart ached. How terrible to have been killed in the prime of one's life. And then to be accused of killing oneself! It would make anyone bitter and angry, she supposed.

She wondered if Thaddeus had felt bitter to lose his life so young. She doubted it. He had never complained. Not even when he had reason to do so. She had no doubt that he was now enjoying his heavenly reward.

She looked at the empty pillow beside her. In the past two years, she had often imagined Thaddeus lying there, smiling at her. She tried to do so now.

But instead of Thaddeus's light brown hair and smiling hazel eyes, she saw dark hair and tormented gray eyes.

It was many hours before she fell asleep.

Five

Dusk was falling when the workmen left, and Madeline, excited by what she'd discovered up in the tower, hurried down the stairs to the library, hoping to find Merrick so she could tell him.

He wasn't there, however, and before she could seek him out elsewhere, the housekeeper came in with the news that Mrs. Firth had arrived and was waiting in the drawing room.

So was Merrick. Madeline paused in the doorway when she saw him. Gengis resting at his feet, he stood with his arm along the mantelpiece, his gaze fixed on Caroline.

And no wonder.

Caroline Firth was exquisite in every detail. Dressed in some gauzy creation, with jewels in her ears and at her throat, she perched on the sofa like a rare butterfly, her shining curls falling artfully onto her creamy shoulders. She had limpid, long-lashed eyes, a tiny nose, and a rosebud mouth that quivered with distress when Madeline asked her about Merrick.

"I loved him so much," she said, tears standing out on her lashes. She dabbed at them with a handkerchief pulled from her reticule. "And he loved me."

"He did?" Madeline said, casting a surreptitious glance toward Merrick. His gaze was still on Caroline, a small smile at the corner of his mouth. Puzzled by his expression, Madeline turned back to the other woman. "But you were married to Mr. Firth, weren't you?"

"It had been arranged by my family. And perhaps I could have been happy with him if I hadn't met Jack. When I met Jack, I fell in love with him immediately."

Merrick's smile widened, and Madeline, disliking his smug expression, raised her brows and made her voice skeptical. "Immediately?"

"Don't sound so disbelieving," he said, his eyes gleaming at her. "Some women found me irresistible."

Madeline gave a small snort. "I can't imagine why."

Mrs. Firth put her handkerchief away. "I think it was the way he had of looking at me with a half-smile on his face, as if he was thinking the most deliciously sinful thoughts. He could make me feel all shivery inside—if you know what I mean."

Madeline did indeed. Although he hadn't been smiling at all last night or this morning when he'd watched her comb her hair.

"He listened, too," Mrs. Firth continued. "I never got the impression he was thinking about his horses or his dogs or his crops when I was with him."

Madeline found it difficult to believe any man could think of such mundane subjects in this beautiful woman's presence. "Mrs. Firth, I wanted to ask you about the ball the night he died—you were there, weren't you?"

"Yes. It was terrible. I still haven't recovered from the shock."

"Did you hear the shot?"

"Of course. I ran inside immediately, but no one in the ballroom had heard it because of the music."

"Did you happen to notice where your husband was?"

"Yes, he was in the ballroom."

Madeline frowned. "Are you sure?"

"Yes, of course. Why?"

"Mrs. Firth, forgive me, but I've heard a rumor—that your husband killed Lord Merrick."

"George?" Mrs. Firth laughed. "He would never have the courage. Besides, he was definitely in the ballroom. I saw him dancing with that little slut, Jane Cottingworth. He could not have gotten back so quickly." She dabbed her eyes again. "I see I must confess the truth."

Madeline clasped her hands tightly. "What truth?"

"The truth is . . . *I* killed him!"

Madeline stared at her in amazement. "*You* killed him?"

Mrs. Firth looked up from her handkerchief, her lashes dewy with tears. "Yes. At the ball, he had asked me to run away with him, but I refused. An hour later, he was dead. I might as well have pulled the trigger myself!"

Madeline sat back. "But you didn't."

"Didn't what? Pull the trigger?" Her tears disappeared. "Of course not!"

"Forgive me, Mrs. Firth. I misunderstood—"

"You did indeed! How could you even suggest such a thing? I loved him! I loved him so much I ache with it every hour of every day! Oh, I never should have come here. I only came because George was raving something about a ghost and I thought my dear love had come back for me. Oh! oh! oh! You don't know what it's like to love someone so much and have to sacrifice your happiness for your honor. . . ." Sobbing, she ran from the room.

Madeline took a step after her. "Wait, Mrs. Firth, I did not mean—"

"Let her go," Merrick said. "Caroline always did like to make a dramatic exit."

Madeline frowned at him. "How can you speak so callously? The poor thing. She must have been very much in love with you."

He made a scoffing noise. "So much, in fact, that she tried to stab me with a letter opener."

Madeline's mouth fell open. "What?"

He shrugged. "She was becoming rather too . . . devoted to me. In view of her husband's antagonism, I thought it better that we not pursue a more intimate relationship. When I told her so the night of the ball, she grabbed the letter opener off the desk and tried to stab me."

"Good heavens," Madeline said faintly.

Merrick grinned. "Women often become desperate when I threaten to leave them."

"Do you think she might have been the one to kill you then? If she's telling the truth about her husband, it doesn't seem possible that he was the one who murdered you."

He was silent for a moment. "There's one little detail you've forgotten—the locked door. Unless she's added magic to her other tricks, I don't see how she could possibly have gotten into the tower."

"Oh!" Madeline suddenly remembered the discovery she'd made earlier. "I nearly forgot to tell you! I was in the tower today—"

His brows met in the middle of his forehead. "I told you not to go up there."

"I had to go up with the workmen to convince them that you really weren't there," she said only half truthfully. Although she'd needed to reassure the workmen, she'd been intending to examine the tower ever since he'd refused to do so himself. "It is fortunate I did go, because guess what I discovered?"

"I have no idea," he said, his voice bored.

"Guess," she insisted.

"A skeleton with a gun in its hand hidden in the wall?"

"No," she said. "I found a drainpipe!"

"A drainpipe," he repeated. "The Colonies do not have drainpipes? I always thought Americans were a backward people, but I hadn't realized they knew nothing of rudimentary plumbing—''

She tapped her foot impatiently. "Don't you see? It goes right by the tower window. The murderer must have climbed it to enter and escape the tower!''

"Ah, yes, I do see now. Caroline must have scaled the drainpipe, shot me, shimmied back down, and reentered the ballroom looking as fresh as a daisy.''

"Must you always be so sarcastic?" Madeline frowned. "Although you're right—she would have been filthy if she'd climbed the drainpipe. Do you think it's possible she was already in the tower room and somehow rigged the door so that the bar would fall into place after she left?''

Merrick sighed. "Mrs. Spencer, how should I know? Frankly, I think it's impossible to discover who the murderer is at this late date. This whole search has become quite tedious. Why don't you just forget about it.''

She stared at him. "Forget about it? When we've made such progress?''

"What progress?''

"Well . . ." Actually, he was right, she realized. Since she now had doubts that Firth was the one who'd killed him, she had actually moved backward. But stubbornly, she refused to give up. "I'm getting closer to the truth, I'm sure. I can sense it.''

"It will make little difference in the end. I will still be dead.''

"But won't it gladden your heart to know that people won't think you killed yourself?''

"Why should I care what people think?'' He turned slightly away. "You don't know much about death.''

"Not as much as you, obviously. But my life has not been untouched by death. I am a widow, after all.''

He looked at her. "Ah, yes. Tell me about this husband of yours.''

"Thaddeus was kind and gentle. And handsome. And good-natured—"

"A perfect paragon," Merrick commented mockingly.

"Yes, he was," she said, not acknowledging his mockery. "His father and he started the shipping business and it became very successful."

"Was he a ship's captain?"

"No, he didn't care much for the sea. He worked in the office. At first, the business was slow, but he had to spend a lot of time there. Unfortunately, he was not very good with numbers, so I started helping him. The business began to take off soon after that, and we were very busy all the time."

"How did he die?"

"His father took him sailing one day." She looked out the window. "A terrible storm came up and the boat sank. Both men were lost."

Merrick was quiet for a moment. "You never had children?"

She shook her head. "It was our greatest disappointment."

"How long ago did he die?"

"Two years," she said, looking down at her hands.

"And you still mourn him?"

"Yes." She tilted up her chin, waiting for him to make some sarcastic remark. "I suppose that seems foolish to you."

"No, not at all," he said quietly.

She stared at him in surprise. She hesitated a moment, then asked, "Did you ever love someone?"

"Yes," he said. "But she died also."

"Oh!" Madeline said involuntarily. "I'm sorry."

"You needn't be." His lips twisted. "I recovered. There are many ways to console oneself, after all."

Her momentary sympathy for him vanished. "With women?" she asked disapprovingly.

He raised his brows. "Surely even a little puritan like yourself must remember what it's like to be pleasured."

She gasped. "Lord Merrick, you forget yourself."

"Oh, come, Mrs. Spencer. What place does propriety have in our situation? Let us speak frankly to each other. Can you not admit that sometimes at night in your lonely bed, you toss and turn, unable to rest because you long to be held, to be touched, to feel that physical release, that rush of sensation, that mind-numbing pleasure?"

His words engendered a dark, forbidden heat deep within her. She tried to suppress it, but tendrils curled through her, spreading outward. "You mustn't say such things," she whispered.

"Why not? Why not, Mrs. Spencer?" He moved closer, staring at her with a dark intensity that made her blood race. "Would it be so terrible to admit that what I say is true?"

"I refuse to listen to this talk." She turned away, her heart pounding, her body awash with strange sensations. "Good night." She hurried from the room, her head held high, but once outside, she rubbed the gooseflesh covering her arms.

She paused by the stairs, listening for sounds of pursuit, but everything was quiet.

He must have realized he'd gone too far, she thought, ascending the stairs slowly.

Gengis lay on the floor outside her door. She bent down and hugged him, burying her face in his fur. Warm, smelling pungently of dog, he licked her cheek with a wet, rough tongue.

She chuckled rather shakily. "Behave yourself, sir." She rose to her feet and went inside her room, stopping when she smelled a faint, sulfurous odor.

She inhaled sharply. "What are you doing here?" she choked out. "Leave at once."

He rose from the chair by the fireplace slowly, his dark

gaze never leaving her. "Aren't you forgetting something?"

She stiffened. "I don't think so."

"You promised to let me watch you comb your hair," he reminded her.

"I don't want you to watch me tonight," she snapped.

"Too bad." He folded his arms across his chest and leaned against the bedpost. "An agreement is an agreement. I listened to those damn carpenters hammering and gossiping away all day—I deserve my reward."

She opened her mouth to argue. But then, glancing at his face, she closed it again. She had never seen him look so . . . implacable.

"Oh, very well," she said crossly. She never should have agreed to let him watch her comb her hair. She didn't like it. She didn't like the way he stood so still, the way his gaze never wavered. It made her feel . . . things. Things she'd never felt before. Things she didn't want to feel. Things that frightened her with their intensity. . . .

Impatiently she walked over to the dressing table and sat down. She yanked out her hairpins and jerked the comb through her hair.

"Not like that," he said quietly, moving to stand by the wall next to the dressing table where he could see her face. "Do it slowly."

"I'll comb my hair anyway I like," she retorted.

But in spite of herself, she began to comb more slowly under his gaze. It was difficult to comb through the curls and it took her a long time. Her hair crackled a little with static electricity and floated out and down over her shoulders.

She found herself staring into his eyes, unable to look away as she pulled the comb through the waves of her hair.

"Madeline," he said huskily, his eyes very dark. "Madeline . . . I will let you hire the drapers. And the gardeners. And anyone else you want. If you will just take off your dress."

The comb came to a halt in her hair. "No," she whispered.

"Madeline," he said. "You would still have your petticoat on. It would not be a big thing to let me see you in your petticoat. There's really not much difference between it and a dress, and I've already seen you in it. Besides, I'm a ghost. What could I do to you?"

She bit her lip. He was just a ghost—why was it sometimes hard to remember that? Maybe because his image kept growing more and more solid. She could see the neatly trimmed nails of his fingers now. And the shadow of a beard on his chin. And the rim of black around the gray of his irises. . . .

The look in those eyes made her tremble. She set the comb down on the dressing table and clasped her hands in her lap. Curiosity and dread fought within her. Curiosity to have a small taste of something she had never before experienced. Dread of unleashing something she might not be able to control.

"Madeline . . ."

Why had she never noticed before what a beautiful voice he had? It flowed over her like silk and velvet, an almost palpable thing. Her skin tingled with the vibration of it, her lips burned with the brush of it.

"Please, Madeline . . ."

As if under a spell, her hands rose to the neckline of her dress, and her fingers began to fumble with the buttons. The room grew almost unbearably silent and an eternity seemed to pass as she undid each one.

When she finally finished, she stood up and allowed the dress to fall in a pool at her feet. She glanced at him quickly, almost furtively.

The planes of his face had grown hard and angled, and his nostrils flared slightly. She caught a brief glimpse of a raw, intense hunger in his eyes before he stepped back and his expression was concealed by shadows.

Trembling, she sat down at the dressing table again and forced herself to look in the mirror instead of at him as she resumed combing her hair.

But looking in the mirror was a mistake. She saw herself as he must see her—with her hair wantonly hanging around her face, her petticoat cut low across her breasts. Every time she raised the comb, her breasts lifted, almost escaping the confines of the petticoat. Worst of all, her nipples thrust prominently against the tight, thin muslin.

"Madeline . . ." His voice sounded hoarse. "I can't touch you. I wish to God I could, but I can't. Will you . . . will you touch your breasts for me?"

She laid down the comb. What he suggested was shocking . . . but she wanted to. Dear God, how she wanted to. Her breasts ached with the need to be touched. . . .

Slowly, not looking away from him, she reached up and cupped her breasts and rubbed her thumbs across the nipples.

His eyes blazed. He stepped toward her, the dark purpose on his face making her gasp. Her hands grew still on her breasts.

Then he stopped. His hands clenched and unclenched into fists.

"Oh, God, Madeline." His voice lapped over her skin, husky, rough, tortured. "Oh, God, I'm sorry, Madeline."

He vanished.

She sat frozen, staring at the spot where he'd been. She couldn't quite believe he'd left. How could he do that to her? She wanted . . . She wanted . . .

Slowly, painfully, she undressed and climbed into bed. She felt tense; her skin was on fire. There was an ache deep in the pit of her stomach.

In the dark, alone, she touched her breasts again. They

tingled painfully. She turned her face into the pillow, the yearning inside her so intense she felt as though she were being torn apart.

Dear God, what was happening to her?

Six

After a nearly sleepless night, Madeline woke very early the next morning. Shaking off her lethargy, she dressed and quickly combed her hair, praying that Merrick would not appear.

He didn't, but instead of being glad, she was oddly disappointed. Restlessly, she walked over to the window and pulled back the drapes. The sun was shining, but the windowpane still felt cold when she leaned her forehead against the glass. Her thought from last night echoed in her head.

What was happening to her?

She had never felt such a dark, consuming fire when she was with Thad. With Thad, everything had always been safe and comfortable.

Last night, with Merrick, everything had seemed dangerous and disturbing.

She straightened from the window. Merrick was a *ghost*. She was a fool to worry about last night. Nothing had happened. Nothing *could* happen. No matter how much she wished it would. . . .

Blocking the scandalous thought from her mind, she

went downstairs to the library. She wouldn't think about last night anymore. She *wouldn't*. She'd been planning to go over the estate ledgers—she would do so now. Poring over columns of figures would divert her. At least, she hoped it would.

In fact, the ledgers turned out to be a fairly successful distraction.

A tidy bookkeeper herself, she was appalled by the state of Merrick Hall's ledgers—they revealed years of systematic neglect. But what surprised her the most were the entries from a period over two and a half years ago. Unlike the rest of the entries, these were written in a strong hand, the numbers complete and accurate. They showed expenditures for improvements to the property and a detailed accounting of all income and expenses.

Then, abruptly, after about six months, the entries stopped and thin, spidery ink strokes replaced the bold, clear writing. The improvements stopped, and the columns of figures never balanced.

What had happened? she wondered. Had Merrick taken an interest in the estate for a short while? Had he hired a steward and authorized the improvements? But if so, why had he suddenly abandoned his efforts after six months?

Her stomach growled, and she looked up a trifle bleary-eyed from the books. The clock on the mantel indicated that it was almost noon.

She went down to the kitchen and found Mrs. Hubbard there, eating scones at the well-scrubbed table.

Flustered, the housekeeper rose to her feet. "Beg your pardon, mum. Did you want something to eat? I can have a tray ready immediately—"

"That won't be necessary, Mrs. Hubbard," Madeline said. "If you don't mind, I'll just join you."

Mrs. Hubbard looked uneasy, but said, "If you wish, mum."

The housekeeper sat stiffly as Madeline took a scone

and spread strawberry preserves on it. Pretending not to notice the housekeeper's discomfort, Madeline spooned whipped cream onto the scone and took a bite.

"This is excellent, Mrs. Hubbard," Madeline said, hoping to put the woman at ease. "Did you make the jam yourself?"

"Aye, mum, that I did." The older woman relaxed a little. "I was cook here before I became the housekeeper."

"You've been here a long time then?"

"Oh, yes, mum. Since I was a girl. I was born not far from here."

Madeline poured herself a cup of tea from the small pot on the table. "Then perhaps you can tell me what happened here two and a half years ago. I was looking at the ledgers and it appeared as though Lord Merrick had hired a new steward and was making improvements to the estate."

"Oh, that was when his lordship inherited the house. He brought his wife with him."

Madeline's hand jerked. Tea dripped onto the wooden table. Quickly, she set down the pot and carefully wiped up the tea with her napkin. "His wife? He was married?"

"Yes, indeed. Lady Phoebe was a pretty young thing. Although she wasn't too happy to be living in the country. But his lordship insisted, on account of her having a bun in the oven."

Madeline's stomach flipped. "She was with child?"

"Aye, and none too happy about it. She was more interested in parties and enjoying herself than in being lady of the manor. She used to sit in the window seat for hours up in the tower, watching the road, hoping someone would come to relieve her boredom."

"But didn't Lord Merrick take her to parties?"

"Some. But there weren't that many in the area. And he was too busy poring over the ledgers and working on the estate to entertain her ladyship much."

Madeline was stunned. "*Lord Merrick* was the one who kept the estate records?"

Mrs. Hubbard nodded. "He was doing a fine job of it, too, until her ladyship died in childbirth. He took her death, and the babe's, very hard."

Madeline swallowed a lump in her throat. Why hadn't he told her? "How tragic," she whispered, forcing the words past the constriction.

"Yes, it was a difficult time," Mrs. Hubbard said. "He took off for London, and we didn't see hide nor hair of him for over a year. Then there was a big house party at Lord Buckleigh's down toward Cheddar and Mrs. Firth was a guest. Or Miss Brown, I should say, as that was her name at the time. All the gentlemen seemed bent on pursuing her, his lordship included. But then she married Mr. Firth, and Lord Merrick lost all his money, and . . . well, mum, you know what happened then."

"Yes, I do," Madeline murmured.

"It hasn't been easy living in a house with a ghost in it. But at least his lordship's year will be up in a few weeks, and he will be gone."

Madeline had been lost in her own thoughts, but at this, she returned her attention to Mrs. Hubbard. "His year will be up? What do you mean?"

"These kinds of ghosts—the ones that wax and wane with the moon—they only stay for a year. Then they go away."

"Go away where?" Fear coursed through Madeline. "And why? Why would someone be a ghost just for one year?"

Mrs. Hubbard shrugged. "I don't know. But I know it has something to do with the Old Ones."

"The Old Ones?" Madeline had to force herself to think calmly. "Oh yes, I remember Mr. Townsend's mentioning them. They live hereabouts, don't they?"

"Aye, that they do. They have their own heathenish

religion and never set foot in a proper church.'' Mrs. Hubbard lowered her voice to a whisper. '' 'Tis said his lordship's grandfather married one of them. Some say she was
a witch. Her sister, Old Mother Efa, is still alive.''

Madeline straightened. ''Could Mrs. Efa tell me more
about where he is going and why?''

''Perhaps.'' Mrs. Hubbard frowned. ''She keeps to herself mostly, but comes to the village shop once in a while.
She lives in a cavern in the gorge—if you go to the edge
of the down, you'll see a steep path that leads to it.''

''I will try her.'' Madeline drank the last of her tea and
stood up. ''Thank you for your help, Mrs. Hubbard.''

It was a long walk across the windy downs to Mrs. Efa's
cottage, and Madeline didn't arrive until late afternoon.
When the stooped old woman opened the door, she stared
at Madeline steadily for several moments. Madeline started
a little at seeing her eyes—the light gray irises encircled
by a ring of black were very similar to Merrick's.

Without a word, the woman let her in and closed the
door against the wind howling outside.

Relieved to be out of the cold wind, Madeline glanced
around the warm, cosy room. Sweet-scented herbs hung
from the ceiling and a pot of spicy-smelling stew simmered
on the hearth. She took off her cloak and smoothed her
windblown hair.

''I am the new owner of Merrick Hall,'' Madeline explained, seating herself at the table where the old woman
indicated. ''I've come to ask you about the ghost.''

''Ah.'' Mother Efa poured out two cups of amber liquid
and gave one to Madeline. ''You wish to know why he
waxes and wanes with the moon.''

Startled by the woman's perception, Madeline nodded
and gulped some of the liquid. It tasted of honey, wine,
and spices and had an oddly soothing effect.

Efa studied her a moment, then sat down at the table

with a bundle of herbs and spread them out. "Lord Merrick's grandfather killed my sister," she said, sorting the herbs with gnarled fingers.

"He did?" Madeline was shocked. "Why?"

"Because he was a selfish, greedy brute." She pinched the leaves off a sprig of parsley. "He hated us, and tried to keep her away from us. Even when she fell ill and we could have helped her, he refused to let her return. Because of his selfishness, she died." Mother Efa refilled Madeline's cup. "Why should I help the grandson of the man who caused my sister and me such grief?"

Madeline met her gaze steadily. "Because Lord Merrick is also your sister's grandson."

The woman was silent for a long time. Then she rose to her feet and went over to the fire to stir the stew in the pot. "Our people are always given a second chance."

Madeline blinked, wondering if she'd misunderstood. "A second chance?"

"A chance to change history."

Madeline frowned. "But how can he change history?"

"That is for him to figure out." The woman's hands moved deftly over the herbs. "But he must do so before the moon sets on the night of the twelfth full moon after his death."

"What if he fails?"

"If he fails . . ." The wind rattled the door and swooped down the chimney, making the fire flare for a moment. But Mrs. Efa did not look up from her task. "If he fails, then he is doomed to oblivion."

Oblivion. Madeline shuddered. It sounded so . . . empty. "And if he succeeds?"

"I do not know." Efa tied a group of herbs into a bundle. "No one has ever succeeded."

No one has ever succeeded? Madeline's head began to ache. Why did this all have to be so complicated and mysterious?

"Changing history is like going against the current of the river," Efa continued. "Few have the strength—of mind or body. It will not be easy."

"No, I don't suppose it will be—especially when he has so little time to figure out what to do." Madeline rubbed her temples. "It's a shame he didn't know sooner that he had only twelve months to change history."

Efa shook her head. "No, my dear, not twelve months. Twelve *moons*."

"Twelve moons?" Madeline repeated, her lips feeling stiff. "But there's a full moon tonight. Does that mean. . . ."

Efa nodded, her gray eyes calm but serious.

"Yes, my dear," she said solemnly. "His time will be up tonight."

Madeline left the cottage, her brain spinning. Tonight was Merrick's last chance—he must do something before the moon set or he was doomed to oblivion. But what exactly must he do?

Even if she could figure out the answer to that question, what would happen then? Would he remain a ghost? Or would he go to heaven? Would she never see him again? The thought made her heart ache. She had known him such a short while. But in some strange way, she felt connected to him, as though their fates were intertwined, as if unless she could somehow help him, she too would be doomed to oblivion. . . .

Shivering, she pulled her cloak closer against the buffeting wind and quickened her pace as she turned onto the path that led down a hill. She must hurry. There was so little time. . . .

In the distance, she saw two figures next to each other on horseback.

Who on earth would be crazy enough to go riding in this weather? she wondered rather absently as she hurried across the field. One was a woman, she could see. It looked like Mrs. Firth, but she couldn't make out the man's features since his back was to her.

The woman suddenly turned her horse and rode off. The man turned and cantered toward Madeline.

It was Mr. Townsend.

"Good day, Mrs. Spencer." He reined in his horse alongside her. "It's late for you to be out walking—it will be dark soon. May I escort you home?"

"It's not too much farther," she said. "Perhaps you should escort Mrs. Firth instead."

He looked at Madeline for a moment, then sighed and dismounted. Leading his horse, he fell in step beside her. "I assure you, Mrs. Spencer, there is nothing going on between Mrs. Firth and me. It's true I loved her once, but Jack's death changed all that."

"Why would his death change your feelings for Mrs. Firth?"

"Jack and I argued over her the night of his ball. I . . . I told him I wanted her to leave her husband and run away with me. Jack called me a fool and said some rather unflattering things about Caroline. I didn't believe him, of course, and challenged him to a duel. He told me to go to hell, and stormed off. I immediately proceeded to seek out Caroline and told her my plan, but she refused. She claimed to be in love with Jack." Townsend smiled rather ruefully. "He always did have a way with women. None of the rest of us ever had a chance when he was about."

"But Jack told her that night he wasn't interested in her."

Townsend's brows rose. "Did he? I never heard that. I only know that the accident happened a short while later. It was a terrible shock. The ironic thing is, Caroline came to me about a month later and begged me to take her away. But it was too late. I could hardly bear to look at her. I felt so guilty."

"Guilty? Why would you feel guilty?"

He opened his mouth to respond, then shut it again. He looked at her, his expression difficult to read. "I suppose because I had argued with him earlier. I thought perhaps his anger had made him careless with the pistols and that was what caused the accident." He glanced up at the rapidly darkening sky. "Come this way. There is a shortcut through the woods."

The trees sheltered them from the wind somewhat, although the branches overhead creaked and swayed. Following Townsend down a winding path, Madeline mulled over what he had told her. How sad that he'd fallen in love with a married woman. She wondered if Caroline's rejection was what had carved those bitter lines in his face. She hoped that he'd recovered by now. And that he'd gotten over his guilt. Knowing that Jack had been murdered would help. Clearly, there was nothing Townsend could have done to prevent that. . . .

They came out of the dark woods and Madeline saw the full moon rising over the roof of Merrick Hall. She gasped and quickened her pace. "Oh, we must hurry!" she said to Townsend, raising her voice to be heard over the wind.

"We must? Why?"

"I have discovered a way to help Lord Merrick's ghost."

"His ghost?" In the darkness, Townsend's voice sounded quizzical. "Don't tell me you are a believer after all."

"I know it sounds bizarre—but yes, I have seen his ghost." She peered at him, trying to see his reaction to her words. "And talked to him."

"Talked to him!" A beam of moonlight revealed an intent look on his face. "What did he say?"

"He believes he was murdered."

A branch fell onto the path and skidded across the dirt, startling Townsend's horse. The mare sidled nervously.

"Easy, girl." The horse calmed under Townsend's soothing touch and he looked back at Madeline, his eyes bright
in the moonlight. "I knew he didn't kill himself! He's not
the kind of man who would ever commit suicide."

She looked at him curiously. "You were very loyal to
him, weren't you?"

Townsend hesitated a moment, then nodded. "I tried to
be. I'm not sure I succeeded." He pushed aside the branch
of an overgrown bush so she could pass. "Tell me more
about Jack's ghost. Did he say who killed him?"

She shook her head. "No, he didn't see the murderer.
But I'm hoping to discover the truth tonight."

"Tonight! How?"

"Mrs. Efa said that he must change history before the
moon sets on the night of the twelfth moon after his death.
Which is tonight. So you see, we don't have much time."

Townsend's eyes narrowed thoughtfully. "Mrs. Efa?
Many people believe she is a witch."

"She seemed a kindly woman to me."

"I don't know if I believe what she told you, but I wish
you luck." He stopped by a wall with a small gate in it.
"Is there anything I can do to help?"

Madeline hesitated, then shook her head. "I don't think
so."

"I must be on my way then—you need only go through
this gate and through the garden to the house."

"Thank you, Mr. Townsend."

With a nod, he remounted and rode away. Madeline
watched him a moment. Something niggled at her brain.

But the thought refused to clarify itself. She opened the
gate and hurried through the garden, pushing the thought
to the back of her mind. She couldn't puzzle it out right
now. She must find Jack. He didn't have much time. . . .

"So you decided to come back at last," a harsh voice
said.

Madeline jumped and whirled around.

There, lounging against a tree, stood Merrick.

Her hand crept up to her throat. His dark hair fell over his forehead; his eyes, glinting silver in the moonlight, sent tremors racing down her spine. He looked so real, so touchable, she could hardly believe he wasn't alive. Only the faintest blurring around his broad shoulders and the almost imperceptible aura enveloping his elegant figure revealed that he was not a man, but a ghost.

Unbidden, a memory of his husky voice pleading with her to touch her breasts came to her . . . along with the look on his face when she did.

She trembled. She felt as though she stood naked before him, as if she had exposed the deepest, darkest corners of her soul. . . .

"I didn't know you could come outside," she said inanely.

"Now you do." He looked at her coldly, as if last night had never happened. "Where have you been?"

The soft quivering inside her grew still at his brusqueness. For a moment, she felt intense hurt. But then, with an effort, she controlled the emotions roiling through her. This was no time to act like a love-starved ninny. She must tell him what she had learned.

"I visited Mrs. Efa." She was proud of how steady her voice sounded. "She told me why all of this is happening. You are being given a chance to change history—"

"I already know about that."

"You do?" She gaped at him a little.

"Everyone around here has heard those ridiculous stories." He glanced up at the rising moon. "No one believes them."

Madeline's cloak flapped in the wind. She clutched it to hold it still, an odd uneasiness stealing through her. "You don't believe that you must change history?"

"If I were going to change history, I would make it that the pretty little serving girl I tried to get into bed when I was fourteen would have said yes the first time I asked her. It took me almost a year to get her to agree.''

"Fourteen! You—'' She paused, looking at his face. Although it was night, she could still see his expression in the bright moonlight. His eyes were no longer cold. Instead, they gleamed with . . . laughter? Satisfaction? Anticipation?

"No,'' she said quietly. "I won't let you do that.''

The gleam faded. "Do what?''

"Change the subject. You always try to change the subject whenever we start discussing anything to do with your murder. You can't do that anymore. Mrs. Efa said tonight is your last chance and I believe her. We must do something.''

A black frown carved deep lines into his brow, and all traces of laughter disappeared from his eyes. "What do you suggest?'' he asked, his voice cold again.

"I . . . I don't know. Perhaps if you stay out of the tower. Perhaps if we hide at the foot of the stairs and stop whoever tries to go up—''

"You really think the murderer will sneak into the house and try to kill me all over again? That's the stupidest thing I ever heard.''

She glared at him. "Do you have any better ideas?''

"Yes, I do. You must leave.''

"Leave! But why?''

"You little fool, you can't go around asking people questions about a murder. Sooner or later, someone is bound to get nervous.''

"Good. I hope they are. They might do something that will reveal the truth.''

He stared at her a moment, then turned away and looked at a silver-limned bush of rosemary. The wind whistled a haunting melody through the leafless trees, and dappled moonlight shone through the branches onto his averted face.

He turned back to her and said quietly, "I see I am going to have to be more blunt. I don't want you here. You've been a nuisance ever since you came. God deliver me from busybody women. I want you to leave."

She stepped back, feeling as though she'd been struck. She stared into his cold eyes for a long time. Something inside her, something tender and new and fragile, withered and shrank. "Fine." Her throat tightened, but she managed to say anyway, "If that's the way you feel, I'll leave immediately."

Clutching her skirts, she ran out of the garden. He watched her go, waiting until the cloak billowing out behind her disappeared from sight before he slowly followed.

Inside, however, he did not seek her out. Instead, he went into the library and crossed over to the brandy.

His hand did not pass through the bottle.

Lifting the decanter, he poured himself a glass and drank it.

The meddling little fool. Didn't she understand? He had to protect her. He couldn't allow her to be hurt.

He never should have allowed her to stay here. It had been his own weakness that permitted it. But there had been something about her that made him let her stay.

He'd never known a woman like her. If things had been different. . . .

But they weren't. He was dead. Or almost dead. He wasn't sure which. None of this made any sense. But if Madeline was correct, then after tonight it would all be over. He was glad.

He poured himself another brandy . . . and then another. The liquor was smooth against his tongue and throat, but it left a burning sensation behind.

He felt something soft and wet nuzzle his hand. Looking down, he saw Gengis licking his fingers. "Hello, old friend." Jack scratched behind the hound's ears. "You'd best enjoy this—it's the last time I'll be able to scratch

you in just this spot. After tonight I'll be in oblivion—or
hell.''

The dog whined softly.

"I know, I know. I've been a fool. It was your bad luck
to get stuck with such a damnable master.'' He cupped the
dog's jowls in his hand. "I want you to do something for
me, Gengis. I want you to watch after Madeline. She's a
strong woman—but not so strong as she thinks. You take
care of her, boy, you understand?''

Gengis gave a sharp bark.

Jack smiled crookedly. "I know. I wish I could too. But
I can't. It's impossible. You have to do it for me—''

The front door opened and slammed shut. Jack tensed,
then released the dog and drifted over to the window.

He saw the black-clad figure of Mrs. Spencer climbing
into the carriage. The door closed, there was a crack of a
whip, and the carriage set off down the road.

Jack watched it go. It grew smaller and smaller, then
turned a corner and was out of sight.

She was gone.

He swung away from the window and went back to the
brandy. He poured out some more, his hands shaking a
little. He drank. The brandy numbed him, it gave everything a glow. He heard music. . . .

Gengis whined.

"Sorry," Jack mumbled. "She left. She left us both.
Perhaps it's better this way.''

Following the sound of the music, he walked out into
the hall, shutting the door quickly before Gengis could
follow. He heard the dog yelp and scratch furiously at the
door, but he ignored the noise as he walked toward the
ballroom.

The doors opened and he blinked as he saw ghostly
figures dancing around. They grew more and more solid
until he didn't know whether what he saw was real or not.

It was like a dream where he knew everything that was going to happen but couldn't stop it.

Slowly, he looked around. He saw Firth dancing with Jane Cottingworth. For an instant, his gaze met Firth's. Firth's mouth twisted into a snarl of hatred.

Jack turned away. He took some brandy from a passing servant and drank it. The liquor ran soothingly down his throat and he looked around for Caroline Firth, wondering what poor fool she had on her string now. There was no sign of her.

His brain felt a little foggy. There was a distance between him and everyone else in the room. He felt like an invisible stranger at his own ball in his own home.

A compulsion to go up to the tower room came over him. He tried to ignore it, but the compulsion only grew stronger. Sweat broke out on his forehead. Catching sight of Townsend, Jack started toward him. The compulsion eased a fraction, and he could breathe again.

But before he could reach his friend, Townsend stepped out through the French doors.

Jack stopped. Doubtless Tom had some assignation in the garden. He would not appreciate being interrupted. Besides, after their argument over Caroline, Tom might never want to speak to him again.

Jack turned away, and the compulsion returned, stronger than ever. He felt it pulling at him. He tried to resist, but he couldn't. He found himself walking out of the ballroom and up the stairs.

He stopped in front of the door to the tower, sweat pouring down his face. He didn't want to go inside. He knew what would happen if he did. His stomach knotted. He tried to turn away, but as if compelled, he reached out and opened the door.

He went inside and locked the door.

The moon shone through the window, illuminating the armoire, the gun rack, the straight-backed chair, and the table with the brandy. He immediately went to the bottle, poured himself a glass, and drank it. The fiery liquid soothed the knot in his belly and the glow returned.

He took the case from the armoire and set it on the table. He opened the case and took out a pistol and polished it. He poured the powder in, his fingers fumbling on his task a little. The powder spilled on the floor.

He stared at the gun, strange, nightmarish images whirling through his brain. Firth glaring at him, hatred in his eyes; Townsend staring at Caroline with longing; Phoebe screaming on her deathbed and cursing him to eternal hell. . . .

But then, strangely, the pain of those memories faded, and he thought of Madeline. Sweet, stubborn Madeline. How beautiful she'd looked last night in her petticoat, combing her hair. How he'd longed to touch her, to hold her.

He could have done so tonight. In the garden, when she was standing there looking so hurt and angry, he could have reached out and touched her. And he had wanted to. God how he'd wanted to.

But he hadn't. He couldn't. She deserved someone who could make her happy. Someone better than him. A real man. Not a ghost of one. . . .

He lifted the pistol and pointed it at his temple.

Seven

"Stop!"

Barely able to believe what she was seeing, Madeline leaped from her hiding place behind the drapes and ran to his side. She grabbed his wrist.

She felt the hard bone and muscle resist her hold. But then, slowly, he lowered the pistol to the table.

"Madeline?" He blinked at her hazily. "What are you doing here? I saw you leave."

"You saw Lizzy leave, wearing my dress. *I* came up here and hid behind the drapes to try to save you from the murderer. I can't believe I was so blind." She began to shake and her voice came out in great gasps. "I thought I had figured it out, that Mr. Townsend had killed you. I remembered how Mr. Firth said that Townsend came to the ballroom all dirty, and I thought it must have been from climbing the drainpipe. I thought he was jealous of Mrs. Firth's attachment to you and killed you in a rage, only to feel guilty and remorseful afterward. But it was you all along, wasn't it? That's why Mr. Townsend felt guilty—he knew, didn't he? He knew that you'd shot yourself and he thought you'd done it because of your argument with him."

She dashed a hand across her wet eyes, her breath rasping in her lungs. "You lied to me. The signs were all there—the way you kept trying to avoid the subject, the way you tried to discourage me from asking questions. You killed yourself, didn't you? Didn't you?"

He stared down at the pistol.

"Why?" she asked. "Why?"

He raised his gaze to hers again, his eyes full of the heartrending sorrow she'd glimpsed once before. Only this time, he made no effort to hide it.

"I couldn't bear it anymore—I couldn't bear the emptiness after Phoebe and the baby died."

Her breath caught. His wife. And the baby. Oh, God. Oh, dear God.

She wanted to put her arms around him and hold him tightly, to try to ease his pain, but she couldn't. She *couldn't.*

"So you wasted your life," she said, forcing herself to sound cold. "Instead of facing your grief, you gambled and drank and whored."

A spark of anger entered his eyes. "And what of you?"

"Me?"

"Yes, you. Haven't you done the same thing, only with work? You've worked yourself to the bone to avoid your own grief, haven't you?"

She stared at him, her lungs unable to suck in air, his words spinning in her head.

He passed his hand in front of his eyes. "I'm sorry. I shouldn't have said that. Leave me. Let me kill myself. Forever this time."

"No." She took a deep shuddering breath. "No, you can't do that."

"Madeline . . ."

"No! How can you be so selfish? Can't you think of anyone but yourself? You are needed here. Your friend

needs you. The estate needs you." She clasped his hand.
"I need you."

"Madeline . . ." His face tortured, he slumped back in
the chair. "If only I'd met you a year ago, maybe things
would have been different. But it's too late now."

She tightened her grip on his hand. "It's not too late;
you can still change things—if you want to."

"And then what? I go to heaven instead of hell? I don't
deserve heaven. Go away, Madeline. Let me die in peace."

"So you're just going to give up?"

"Madeline . . ."

"No, don't say it." She let go of his hand and backed
away from him. "I don't want to hear any more of your
excuses. If you want to kill yourself, I'm not going to stop
you, you selfish coward."

Tears running down her face, she unlocked the door and
ran down the stairs.

He sat very still after she left, her words ringing in his
ears.

You selfish coward.

He'd never thought of himself as a coward. Nor of himself as selfish. The words stung. They weren't true.

Were they?

He thought of the other things she'd said—about Tom
and the estate. It was true he'd never thought about how
his death would affect them. He'd been too drunk to think
of much of anything. Was he really a coward?

He looked down at the pistol. It would be so easy. So
easy to end it all. The pain, the hurt, the confusion. And
the yearning. The yearning for what could never be.

All he had to do was pull the trigger.

Madeline was in her room, combing her hair fiercely, when
she heard the shot. She jerked in her seat, and the comb
slipped through her suddenly nerveless fingers. She half
rose to her feet, her heart beating with slow, painful

thumps against the wall of her chest. She felt as though she was being bruised from the inside out.

Oh, dear God, what had she done?

She had thought she was doing the right thing. She had thought she had to force him to see that he had to make the decision himself. She had thought that he would see that what he was doing was wrong.

She sank back into the chair, tears welling up in her eyes. It was all her fault. She should have stayed with him, held him, talked to him. But she hadn't believed he would really do it. How could he? How could he do such a thing when she loved him so much?

And she did love him. Burying her head in her arms, she began to sob. She loved him so much that she ached with it. And she hated him. She hated him for the horrible, selfish, cowardly thing he had done. . . .

"Madeline?"

She grew still. Slowly, unable to believe her ears, she lifted her head and turned.

Eight

He stood in the doorway, the aura around him glowing faintly.

"Jack?" she whispered.

He took a step toward her, then paused, looking at her face. "Madeline . . . what's wrong?"

"I heard the shot. I thought . . ."

"Oh, God. Madeline, I'm sorry. I threw the pistol against the wall and it discharged." He moved to her side, but didn't touch her. "Before I go, I have to tell you something. That night at the ball, I was drunk, I'd been feeling sorry for myself, and for a few minutes suicide seemed like the answer to all my problems. But I never intended to go through with it. The sound of the pistol was a shock. I even tried to duck, but it was too late."

His hand passed in front of his eyes. "This time . . . this time it didn't seem to matter. I was already dead. But then I realized that everything you said was true—I *was* a selfish coward. I don't know why I never saw it before. Suddenly, I knew I couldn't let you down. I couldn't take the coward's way out." He took her hands in his, and stared intently into her eyes. "It's only a few hours until the

moon sets, and then I'll be gone. But I couldn't leave without telling you . . . I love you, Madeline."

"Oh, Jack." Her eyes glistened with tears.

His hands tightened on hers. "Don't cry, Madeline. I
can't bear it."

"Oh, Jack," she said again, pulling her hands away
from his. But then she slid them around his neck, and
suddenly he was kissing her as if he would never let her
go.

Fire burned through her veins and lights spiraled behind
her eyes. For a moment, his arms held her so tightly
against him, she felt as though he were imprinting himself
upon her.

But then, with a deep shudder, he pushed her away and
stepped back. "Madeline, you may have saved me from
hell, but there can be no happy ending for us. I'm still a
ghost. And when the moon sets, I will be gone forever.
Leaving you is hard enough. Please don't make it harder."

Her lips and skin tingled, her body pulsed. "Jack," she
said in a low voice. "Don't push me away. I want you to
make love to me. I've only been half alive these last few
years. You were right—I've kept myself busy to avoid
feeling anything. I've spent all my time in small dark
rooms, hiding from my pain. But I need to know that I
can still feel. That I can still love. Please, Jack. Please
make love to me."

His eyes black as midnight, he took her into his arms
and covered her mouth with his, kissing her with a fierce
desire that made her feel weak at the knees. She made a
noise that was half sob, half laugh, and kissed him back
just as fiercely.

He lifted her and carried her to the bed, shedding clothes
along the way. Within a few minutes, they were both naked, and she sighed with pleasure at the feel of his skin
against hers.

His hands and lips explored her, tracing and caressing

every curve, every hollow, until she was quivering all over. Feverishly, she explored his body in return, the heat inside her growing and growing until she thought she would perish from the flames.

It was a relief when he finally moved over her and nudged her legs apart. He entered her, and she almost cried out at the pleasure of it. He began to move within her, and she pulled at his shoulders, urging him on.

"Wait just a little longer, Madeline." His voice soothed her, even as his hands playing with her breasts drove her wild. "Ah, you feel that? Go with it, Madeline. Let yourself go. . . ."

She closed her eyes and stars spun around in a dizzying circle. They spun faster and faster and faster until they exploded in a bright burst of blinding light.

For one small, short, infinite moment, everything in the universe was perfect.

She came down from the heights slowly. "Oh, Jack," she whispered, when she could finally speak. "I never knew . . . I never dreamed . . ."

His arms tightened around her.

"Neither did I, Madeline. Neither did I."

She woke up several hours later, curled up against Jack's side. Carefully, she eased away from him and looked down at his sleeping face.

It was still night, but a moonbeam illuminated him. She stared at him, noticing his tousled hair, his shadowed jaw, the protrusion of his Adam's apple, the strong bones at his collar, and the hair sprinkled across his chest. She could see his ribs, and the flat indentation of his navel, and the blades of his hipbones, the now flaccid manhood, the muscled thighs, squarish knees, and long slender feet.

She looked and studied, memorizing every detail, until the moonlight started to fade.

The moonlight was starting to fade. Dread stealing over

her, she rose from the bed and pulled on her crumpled petticoat. She crossed to the window and looked out.

The moon hung low in the sky far across the horizon.

She put her hands on the glass and leaned her forehead against it, watching the moon sink, unable to look at the bed and watch him fade away. Tears filled her eyes, and the moon became a white blur as it sank lower and lower, and finally disappeared.

The tears spilled over and ran down her cheeks. Her hands slid down the glass and she clenched her fists at her sides, trying to control the sobs building up in her throat. The sky grew lighter, but the darkness inside her kept building and expanding.

He must be in heaven now, she thought. She knew she should be happy for him. And she was. But, oh! How she wished he could have stayed.

The door opened behind her, and she heard the clank of the coal scuttle.

Lizzy, Madeline thought, wiping her cheeks. Come to kindle the fire.

She closed her eyes. *Good-bye, Jack. I'll never forget you—*

"AAAAAAAAAHHhhhhhhhhh!"

Madeline jumped at the piercing scream. Turning, she saw Gengis and Lizzy in the doorway. Lizzy was covering her mouth with one hand, while the other pointed at something.

Madeline followed the pointing finger to the bed.

"A man!" Lizzy screamed. "A man!" She turned and ran down the corridor.

Madeline barely noticed. She stared at the man lying there, blinking sleepily as the sunlight shone in his dark hair and gray eyes.

He turned and looked directly at her. A smile crooked his mouth. "You look as though you've seen a ghost."

"Jack!"

Without quite knowing how she got there, she was back in his arms, laughing and crying, and raining kisses on his face.

"Jack! Jack! What are you doing here? I thought you were gone—"

"Well, you were wrong, weren't you?" Turning her over so she was lying beneath him, he smiled down into her outraged face. "Be quiet, Madeline, and kiss me."

Presented with this offer, Madeline decided her questions could wait. Willingly, she complied.

Gengis, still standing in the doorway, perked his ears toward the couple and the strange sounds they were making. He watched them for a moment from big brown eyes. He made a sort of snuffling sound, like a deep sigh coming from the very depths of his canine soul. He wagged his tail once. Twice.

Then he nudged the door closed with his nose and sank down on the floor. Laying his head on his paws, he went back to sleep.

"I don't understand," Madeline said sometime later, when Jack finally allowed her to speak. "Why aren't you in heaven?"

He held her more tightly. "Perhaps I am."

"Jack, be serious." She wriggled against him.

"I am." He buried his face in her hair.

"Jack . . ."

He lifted his head and smiled down at her. "Apparently, when the Old Ones said 'a second chance,' they really meant it."

She ran her hands over his arms and chest, feeling the reassuring presence of hard bone and muscle, rough hair and smooth skin. "But you were dead. Where have you been all this time?"

"Right here. I never really went away at all. As with the moon, it only seemed that way."

Madeline shook her head, not really understanding. "I don't think we're going to be able to tell people that."

"No," he agreed, wrapping a strand of her hair around his fingers. "We'll have to tell them something else. Maybe the gunshot didn't really kill me. I was wounded, and wandered away in a delirium."

She looked at him doubtfully. "Will anyone believe that?"

"They will have to. Unless they want to admit they believe that superstitious nonsense about the Old Ones." He kissed her ear, and her cheek, and her lips.

"Oh, Jack," she said, sighing against his mouth. She kissed him back, and for a long time there was silence.

But then she pushed him away and looked up at him. "Jack, there's just one thing. . . ."

"What, my love?"

Her eyes were very serious. "I can't guarantee your happiness. I have to know that you won't turn a gun on yourself at the first sign of trouble."

"Madeline." His arms tightened around her. "I was a fool. A drunken, stupid fool. I've learned my lesson."

She relaxed against him. "I love you, Jack."

"And I love you, Madeline."

He started to kiss her again, but she stopped him once more. "Jack, there's one other thing I must ask you."

He sighed. "Yes, Madeline?"

"What about the shipping business?"

"I suppose I can get used to a wife in trade if I must," he said reluctantly. "Of course, there will be a price. . . ."

She stiffened a little. "A price?"

"You must let me watch you comb your hair every night. And that's not all. You also must. . . ." He bent down and whispered in her ear.

Her cheeks turned rosy red, and for a moment he thought she would refuse.

But then her arms slid up around his neck and she kissed him.

"If you insist, Jack. If you insist."

THE WOLF KEEPER

Katherine Sutcliffe

Prologue

1746

The sound of rain was everywhere—flowing in the gutter along the ancient tile roof, tapping the shingles, falling gently through the shifting tree branches like soft distant whispers. It spattered on the stone floor of the convent outside the priest's chamber, and the intermingling of water and wind against the windows sounded like souls crying in the night.

Father Francis Marriott dropped to his knees and genuflected before the carved replica of a crucified Christ on the wall. He clasped his trembling hands together beneath his chin and stared a long moment at the dancing candle flame before him. He tried to pray, but all the pat words and phrases he had murmured reverently throughout the years scattered in his mind like withered leaves. He bowed his head and closed his eyes. A mistake. The memories rose up within him, images he thought he had buried long ago, vague shapes and voices that called out from the past as frighteningly clear as the tinkling of the rain from the eaves. For a moment the walls of his cramped, cold chamber seemed to recede, and the circle of the candle to grow more brightly around his bowed head.

Then the sound . . .

The priest's blood warmed in his veins. It flushed his face and made his heart pound in his temples until even the wind and rain became insignificant compared to the thunder of the advancing coach and four.

"Let it pass," he whispered to his frail white hands. "For the love of God . . ."

Yet it came on, drumming, filling the black night with the slash and crack of whips and the careening grate of iron wheels on stone slabs. Above him, the miniature representation of Christ appeared to quake; the floor beneath him seemed to shift. The sounds magnified until the very walls pulsed in and out and he was pressing his skull between his hands and crying out, "Satan, get thee behind me! Satan, get thee behind me!" over and over.

Silence.

Father Marriott opened his eyes. The candle on the table near him dripped pale wax and sputtered in the quiet. The rain had stopped. The wind had ceased. He glanced about the room, feeling the chill rise up around him, a frigid vapor as palpable as the fear moistening his brow. He listened, heart hammering, blood rushing through his veins and throbbing behind his eyes as his body attuned to each sound and movement beyond his barricaded door.

At last it came, the slow, clumsy scrape and shuffle of Sister Elizabeth's feet on the flagstone. Father Marriott sat on his heels in the brightness of the flaring candle flame, detecting the whisper of her habit upon the floor and the narrow walls of the claustrophobic corridor. He remained unmoving, his thin fingers twisted in fear around the white clergy's collar at his throat as he stared at the door, waiting.

Then the rap of her fist on the heavy wood.

"Father Francis?" Elizabeth called. "Father . . ."

Slowly, slowly, he climbed unsteadily to his feet and moved toward the door, hesitating, reaching for the bolt with shaking hands, gripping the cold iron as if it could somehow save him from the reality of that dreaded moment.

"Yes?" he managed to call.

"Father, you have a visitor."

"Yes?"

"Christopher Guaire, Father. Earl Lycaon."

He closed his eyes and whispered, "Oh, God, why hast thou deserted me . . . ?"

"Father, the earl is in a great hurry."

"Then tell him to leave."

"He won't leave until he's spoken with you."

"Very well." He almost shouted. "I'll meet him in the office off the cloister."

He waited, listening with his brow pressed against the door as Elizabeth moved off down the corridor, then he pulled open the door and, with his cassock fluttering in the draft of frigid air swirling down the dim-lit causeway, made his way to the cloister, pausing only long enough to glance out at the distant black shape of the coach and the prancing, snorting horses silhouetted against the night.

Then on, through the oratory where a half dozen lit tapers danced in the darkness, illuminating the dais and altar cloths and the pale, glowing faces of the marble Virgins and saints and Christs that gaped at him with knowing, grim eyes. On, down one long corridor after another, and out a door to the cloister, whose bare flagstones were lit briefly—too briefly—by the flash of the moon overhead. Still, he hesitated as he reached the door of his office. He tried to breathe. And pray. The ability deserted him.

Finally, he entered his office, only to be brought up short at the sight of the tall, cape-clad man standing before the fireplace, his back to the priest. There was no mistaking that form. Few men stood as tall, as arrogantly powerful, and sinister, as Christopher Guaire, Earl Lycaon.

"Close the blasted door," Lycaon demanded. "And lock it."

Father Marriott complied, and moved to his desk.

Lycaon turned so his profile was lit by the intensely hot fire—so hot the priest felt sweat rise to his brow. Yet, Lycaon appeared cool, his pale skin showing not so much as a faint blush in the heat.

The priest sat down and did his best to breathe evenly despite the venomous influence filling the atmosphere. *He must not show fear.* Lycaon despised weakness as much as he craved it. Still, he felt crushed by an immense and overwhelming force, as he always did in Lycaon's presence. The very air crawled with some strange and ghastly influence that made him shake.

"My lord. I didn't expect you until later in the month."

Slowly, Lycaon turned his pale eyes on the priest.

Father Marriott sat back in his chair. "You'll be pleased to know that your donation last month will go to a worthy cause. We plan to refurbish the north cloister and dedicate it to your father's memory."

"How very kind of you," came the droll response. "I'm certain his eternity spent in hell will be far less agonizing knowing his name is attached to the same church that refused him his last rites."

"Why are you here, my lord?"

"I have a request. Come, come, you needn't look so startled, Father. You knew the time would eventually arise when I would require *something* from the fortune my family has donated to this establishment through the last generations. After all, if we cannot expect to die with a minute hope of going to heaven, we should at least demand some form of satisfaction while living."

"As you well know, my lord, this convent is exceedingly poor. I cannot think of anything we could possibly provide you."

As Lycaon moved away from the fireplace it seemed to Father Marriott that the light moved with him, as if drawn from the fire itself. The flames dwindled. The candles sputtered. Yet, a hazy red glow swirled around the earl's legs as he walked toward the desk. Father Marriott strove to rise. Impossible. A sense of total helplessness crushed him. He could scarcely breathe, and although he struggled to look away from Lycaon's eyes, the effort was futile. The green spheres trapped him, as did the shocking and disturbing handsomeness of his features. Lycaon was far too perfect, too beautiful to be human. Had he been born into a less cursed existence he would have known unequalled success in society.

"My son is in need of a companion," said Lycaon. "A governess, if you will. Since his mother died, he's fallen behind in his education and social skills."

Father Marriott's eyes widened briefly. "There are schools—"

"No one will accept him."

"You're an educated man, my lord. You could teach him yourself."

"He'll have nothing to do with me."

With a great effort, Father Marriott managed to look away. "I'm sorry. I'm certain your wife's death has had a terrible impact on the lad. But I cannot think of how I can help."

"There are women here who can teach him."

"Surely, my lord, you cannot expect me to allow him here—in this place of Christian goodness. The last time we allowed a member of your family to reside here these hallowed grounds became a place of mindless hell."

"My father came to you for help. Instead, you locked him away for seven years in the bowels of this place of 'Christian goodness.' I wonder what killed him in the end, his . . . affliction, his imprisonment, or the fact that, thanks to you, he believed God had abandoned him."

"What I did was for the good of this village, my lord. Surely you can understand that."

Lycaon remained silent, then said, "She'll come to Lycaon."

A chill of horror overcame the priest, and he began to tremble. "My God, Lycaon. Are you completely insane? Do you truly believe I should send one of these God-fearing women into that ... that ..."

"Devil's lair?" Lycaon asked softly, his lips curling in something less than a smile.

Outrage overcoming his fear, Father Marriott left his chair and leaned upon the desk. "You demand too much of me and this church."

"You *owe* me."

"There is no amount of money that will entice me into sacrificing one of my lambs."

"You don't want to see me angry. Do you, Father? You wouldn't like to see me take out my frustration on this place of God, or this village. Would you?"

"Fiend!" Father Marriott cried.

"Aye, I'm a fiend. A devil. I'm also the monster who financially supports this church and convent, not to mention this entire cursed, ungrateful village. I am, therefore, capable of destroying both, should I decide to do so."

"You wouldn't—"

"Are you willing to risk it? Just because my ancestors haven't ... killed anyone in two hundred years doesn't mean it couldn't happen ... if provoked. Perhaps my predecessors simply had more patience than I."

Father Marriott turned away. His legs felt as rigid as iron bars and his earlier resolution now seemed as impossible to grasp and hold as water. Stiffly moving across the room, he covered his eyes with his hands and did his best to maintain his reason. *Think. Think.* What was he to do? *What could he do?*

"Surely there's someone you can ... spare, Father.

Someone unfamiliar with my . . . reputation."

"Yes. Perhaps. Let me think. You've caught me off guard, of course. There *is* a young woman—a novice. Amelia McBain is her name. She's not been here long. Not really suited to the cloister, I'm afraid—has quite a hard time adjusting to the strict prescripts of the church. We suspect that her purpose for joining the convent was to escape her sisters' fate—all unhappy victims of arranged marriages to much older men. I've been meaning to write her father and discuss the situation—you know, suggest that he remove her. She means well, of course. She's spiritually dedicated, but . . . emotionally, intellectually I fear she is ill prepared to succumb to the rigors of a nunnery. She would likely satisfy your requirements. She's very good with children." Looking over his shoulder at Lycaon, Father Marriott asked, "Would you care to interview her?"

The mist lay thick under the overarching boughs of the trees that lined the long path from the convent to the Lycaon cemetery. The trees themselves looked ghostly, as did the scattering of tall, ancient grave markers dotting the enclosed plot. Father Marriott stood on the steps of the ancestral mausoleum, solemnly watching the approach of Amelia McBain's small form through the darkness. Her steps were quick and without digression. Occasionally the moon reflected from her face, but gave little evidence of her features—which were comely by any man's standards. Amelia McBain possessed a character and courage far exceeding her twenty years. Father Marriott suspected that she would have made some wealthy, tottering old man a companionable wife, but therein was her problem. She was far too spirited and intelligent to submit herself to such an unfulfilling existence.

Reaching the elaborate wrought iron gates, Amelia paused and appeared to search the plot of crowded weathered tombstones before calling, "Father? Are you there?"

"I'm here," he called, and lifted his hand.

She advanced, then stopped at the bottom step. Her hands clasped at her waist, her expression one of curiosity and concern, she regarded Father Marriott with a face radiant with naïveté and sweetness. She had enormous eyes and lips shaped like a cupid's bow—lips that seemed constantly curved in pleasure, even here, in this awful, unhallowed place.

"You wished to see me, Father?"

"Yes." He nodded. "You're probably wondering why I asked you to meet me here."

She glanced around. "I suppose I've done something wrong again. Perhaps I laughed too loudly following vespers? Or is it that I overslept this morning? I assure you, Father, it won't happen again."

"True, Sister Elizabeth voiced her displeasure over your recent frivolity, but that's not why you're here. What have you heard about this place?" He motioned to the building behind him.

"Nothing. As long as I've resided here no one has spoken of this cemetery except to say that we aren't allowed to speak of it or come near it."

"Do you consider that odd?"

"I find it very curious. Yes."

"Has anyone ever mentioned the name Lycaon to you?"

She remained silent for a long while, which caused Father Marriott concern. "Well?"

"I overheard whispers once. That some years ago a man named Lycaon resided in the northernmost wing. That he eventually died there of some terrible affliction."

"Did they say what that affliction was?"

"No." She shook her head.

Father Marriott wrung his hands and looked off in the dark.

"Is something wrong, Father? You look dreadfully pale. And you're trembling. Come; lean on my shoulder. I'll help you back to the—"

"No! God help me, I can't think what to do."

"Father, shall I bring Sister Elizabeth? Are you ill?"

"Desperately so! Ill of the mind. Ill of the heart. That I should bring you here is a disgrace so terrible I will no doubt suffer foul conscience for the rest of my days on this earth. I cannot do it! Go, girl. Get away from this place before it's too late. Don't look back and vow you'll never come here again."

In that moment the clouds obscured the moon and a rush of frigid wind embraced the cemetery. It rattled the few remaining leaves on the scattering of twisted elms; it laid low the unkempt tussocks clustered around the sinking tombstones.

Novice Amelia McBain did not retreat, but hurried up the steps to take the shaken priest's hand. "Whatever it is can't be so awful, Father. If it's in my power to help you, then I shall do so."

"Kind child, you know not what you offer!"

"Is it not our destiny to give of ourselves, Father, no matter what the reason, or the cost?"

He pulled away and in his haste stumbled back against the ornate door of the tomb. As if moved by some unseen power, it swung open, revealing burning sconces that cast a hazy yellow glow over a line of crypts. Great silver crosses adorned each coffin and as Father Marriott, his heart in his throat, stared down on the crypts, silvern shadows, cast from the suddenly erupting moon, filled the dreaded tomb with glimmering light.

Amelia stepped forward, her features fearless and calm as she regarded the words carved in the wall behind the crypts:

An t'Arm Breac Dearg

Below that a replica of a badge: An arm in mail rising out of a crown and holding a dagger.

"Stand back!" the priest cried, and grabbed her arm. "Leave this place quickly. Come, come, child. You mustn't dally. This tomb is a dreadful place of unrest and evil."

"But how can that be?" she asked. "When it's located so near this church?"

"I fear you'll learn the truth soon enough" was the response as Father Marriott struggled against the rising wind to close the tomb doors. When at last he looked at Amelia his countenance was rigid and his eyes like glass. He pointed to the horizon, little more than a reflection of moonlight on white-tipped waves. Yet, even as they stared across the bay of Loch Tuath, to the small island of Ulva, there came the intermittent glitter of lights from Lycaon Castle, which stood like a gray mountain overlooking the churning waters of the loch.

"You'll go there, my child, and attend the young Guaire. You'll learn him books and, God willing, the ways of God."

"To Lycaon Castle, Father?"

He looked away and covered his face with his hands.

"I've recently heard stories of Lycaon Castle," she said, then took a startled step back as Father Marriott turned his frightened eyes on her.

"What have you heard?" he demanded.

"That Earl Lycaon has sheltered Charles Edward Stuart since his defeat by Cumberland."

A moment passed before her words appeared to register with Father Marriott, then his countenance relaxed. "Yes." He nodded and grasped his hands together. "Yes. I've heard that rumor as well."

"Earl Lycaon must be very kind, with much compassion and care for those who support Charles. I understand there is a reward of thirty thousand pounds offered to any man who captures the young pretender.''

"Lycaon is more in need of prayers than money, child.''

"I would be honored to attend young Lycaon,'' she declared, smiling up at Father Marriott.

Father Marriott, his gaze yet fixed on the far-off shimmering lights, took a ragged breath, then swallowed. "Lycaon will send a boat for you tomorrow evening. Know that if you care to leave the island, you're free to do so. I trust you'll remember your prayers, child, and know that God walks with you always.''

Without speaking again, Amelia McBain moved down the path toward the convent. Father Marriott watched her disappear into the darkness before drawing back his shoulders and taking a shaky step away from the Lycaon tomb. A sudden chill stopped him short, and he spun around, frantically searching for some movement among the scattering of ancient grave markers.

At last, he gathered his courage and called, "My soul is doomed! Are you pleased, Lycaon?''

Nothing.

"Answer me. Will she do for your purposes, Lycaon?''

The wind moved, and a moment passed before the simple whispered response lit upon his ear like a cold breath:

"She'll do.''

One

Standing on the rocky shoal of Ulva Island, Amelia stared back across Loch Tuath, her eye following the towering spear of the far-off convent chapel that thrust like an arrow into the pewter sky. Around her the air hummed with the cries of seabirds: shags, guillemots, kittiwakes—all rushing to nest amid the sheer sides of cliffs before the sun dropped completely beyond the horizon. A chill ran through her, a melancholy that rushed upon her with vivid images of home—Ardersier on Loch Ness, where she spent her carefree days playing along tumbling burns and looking out for fabled creatures that purportedly gobbled up errant fishermen and little girls who would not eat their porridge.

Daylight waned, as did her patience. Where was Lycaon?

Taking up her bag, she moved along the footpath, walking rapidly over rocks and through shallow inlets of tide, watching as the few people inhabiting the minuscule village peered at her through the heavily barricaded windows of their houses—odd white staring houses that glittered in the failing sun like rows of teeth. No doubt the occupants questioned why a young woman in a novice's dress would be wandering their cobbled street, evidently lost, and more than apparently fed up with waiting for a nobleman who was to have had his man meet her at the dock hours ago.

What an odd little village it was! Fishnets draped from house eaves. Rusted anchors lay propped near doors, as did sheets of tattered sails that had been set aside for repair. She thought the houses unusual, their having been built so closely together, with hardly a space between them large enough for a man to move. And the people—stony faces, hard eyes, pressed lips. And where were the children?

At last, she happened on a bent old man whose face was partially obscured by a large hat. His skin looked like leather. His legs were twisted and he dragged one foot in the dirt as he walked with the help of a cane. He seemed in pain, and Amelia hurried to help him. She stopped short, however, as he raised the tip of his cane and pointed it at her.

"I know what y' want, girl. 'Tis out of the question. Y'll not find a solitary man in this village who will show y' the way to *his* castle. We'll not have yer soul on our conscience, no ma'am. If yer smart y'll go back to yer convent and stay there. That habit yer wearin' won't save y' from the likes of Lycaon—nor will yer prayers to the Almighty. If it's God y've come to preach to his lordship then y'd best save yer breath. 'Tis naught that's goin' to help him or his cursed soul. Now out of my way. The sun is about to set. No man or woman in his right mind will be caught out of their homes after dark."

He shoved Amelia aside and shuffled toward a little house where a woman stood in the open doorway. They spoke, then looked back at Amelia before entering the house and slamming the door behind them. Amelia watched somewhat idly as they appeared at the window and gazed at her with round eyes and stern expressions— then swung the shutters closed and bolted them fast.

Alone, her bag at her feet and the wind whipping at her habit skirt, Amelia turned her face up and allowed the cool kiss of impending rain to touch her cheeks and clear her mind of the sense of discomposure she had felt the moment she stepped off the little boat and onto Ulva's shore, and that the old man's odd rambling had only worsened. With her eyes closed, she murmured a short prayer and did her best to disregard the memory of Father Marriott's face as she'd bid him good-bye mere hours ago.

The gray daylight took on the purple hue of dusk as Amelia, bag in hand, followed the infrequently traveled road that meandered along the precarious cliffs overlooking Loch Tuath. Around the distant point of Gometra came the blustery dusk winds, curling the loch into specks of white foam that reflected the occasional splash of the blood red sun like sparkling rubies. Too soon the wind grew biting, pricking her cheeks like little needles and causing her eyes to water and her nose to grow numb. Below, the waters roared with a force that seemed to shake the ground on which she walked. Overhead, the clouds grew denser, darker, lower, forming misty images that crept through the occasional copses like long silver threads.

The limbs of the trees—mostly oak, with an occasional hazel crowded close—twisted together as if waging a war for sun and space. Amid their gnarled, knotty roots and wind-contorted trunks there was only blackness. Impenetrable. Cloistering. It yawned around her and sucked the air from her lungs. She became aware of struggling for each breath, of hearing it rush in and out of her chest and mouth and nose. It burned her throat and made her stomach queasy. Her head began to feel dizzy, so she searched out a stump near the road and sat down, tossing her bag on the ground.

A tree branch scraped her shoulder. A tangle of vines slid across her feet, feeling like an insect or an animal.

Leaping from the stump, she stomped her feet, stumbled back, and plowed into something that moved from the impact of her weight. She spun on her heels and blinked hard. The bulk swung back and forth, forcing Amelia to focus hard before the image began to take shape:

A great gray seal, hanging by a rope from a tree branch, its throat cut.

How long she stood there, frozen by some confused, paralytic disbelief, staring into the animal's round death-glazed eyes, she could only guess. But suddenly its stench overwhelmed her, and covering her nose and mouth, Amelia grabbed her bag and began running, her feet maneuvering the increasingly rutted road as if by magic . . . or divine intervention. At last, unable to gasp another solitary breath from the thick air, she slowed to a stop and, bending at the waist, waited for the shock and fear to pass and reason to ease the band around her chest.

There is absolutely nothing to be frightened of, she told herself. *It was only a seal. There are thousands of them in the waters around these islands.*

But how many do you find hanging from trees with their throats slashed, Amelia? she asked herself.

Still, the roaring in her ears continued until the realization struck her that the odd noise was not emanating from inside her head, but from up ahead—and growing louder like fast-approaching thunder. She stepped back nervously as suddenly a monstrous black form loomed before her, two fiery eyes winking down at her and the clattering and rattling of chains so intense she was forced to cover her ears with her hands.

"Whoa!" came a voice amid the cacophony.

Stones and dust bit into Amelia's face and hands as the coach and four snorting, laboring horses managed to stop mere feet in front of her. The fiery eyes became lanterns that cast a nimbus of light over Amelia as she stared up at the somber-faced driver, who continued to struggle to keep the high-strung horses under control.

The coach door slowly opened and a man stepped out. He was bent, with a white beard that reached his chest and silver hair that spilled down his back. Amelia thought he looked as old as Ulva's weather-eroded hills. Like the village folk, his expression looked oddly ... expressionless as he regarded her up and down without speaking. At last, he said, "Sister Amelia McBain?"

"Yes!" she cried, her relief as sharp as the sudden gust of frigid air that whipped around her. "I'm Sister Amelia. Are you—"

"Thomas Baird," he interrupted, his dour countenance melting into one of ... what?

Concern?

"Come along, Sister. Quickly! There will be rain before long. The road is treacherous when muddy."

He helped her with her bag and into the coach. It was plush burgundy silk and velvet, with fine brown leather seats that wrapped around her in a comforting fashion. As the driver cracked his whip and shouted to the horses, Thomas tossed a red and black plaid lap blanket over her knees. Only then did she realize how badly she had been trembling—not from cold but from fear. The image of the dead seal came rushing back, and she was forced to close her eyes briefly, to take a long steadying breath that managed to calm her a little, though not completely.

"My apologies for failing to meet you when you arrived," Thomas Baird said, but he did not offer an explanation for his tardiness. Instead, his features took on a guardedness as he noted her face in the illumination of the gaslight near her head. "You look ... frightened. Has something happened?"

"Yes. Something very odd. I was resting near the edge of the wood when I happened on ... there was a seal hanging by a rope from the tree. Its throat had been cut."

"Ah." He nodded, but offered no further comment, leaving the clatter of hooves and rumble of steel wheels over the rocky road surface to fill up the quiet space inside the coach.

Minutes passed before Amelia, her frustration mounting, said, "I thought to be met by Earl Lycaon himself, and perhaps his son."

"Lycaon rarely, if ever, ventures to the village."

"Perhaps that explains the villagers' behavior when I mentioned his name."

Thomas Baird looked into the dark outside the coach window. "Lycaon is a remote and very private man. Their ambivalence is understandable."

"They think him cursed. I hardly call that ambivalence."

She thought that Thomas Baird smiled, though she could not be certain. The gyrating light made reading his wizened, bearded features next to impossible. Still, there was a softening in his eyes as he turned them on her that had not been there before. His lids grew sleepy, as if weary, and for the first time since she'd climbed aboard the coach he appeared to study her with interest. The intensity of it made her uncomfortable. It reminded her of the first time she had stood before Father Marriott and prepared herself to justify her reasons for wanting to pledge her life to the convent. She'd been afraid that at any moment he would point out that her wit was too sharp, she was too opinionated for her own, or the convent's, good, her ideas were far too progressive.

"Will you tell me something about young Lycaon?" she asked. "I should like to be prepared before meeting him, I think. Is he a good boy? Is he bright?"

"He detests his father."

Amelia blinked.

"Young Robert blames his father for his mother's death. Celia died one year ago today."

"Was there an accident—"

"She killed herself," he confessed bitterly. "Stupid woman. She should have stopped thinking of her own unhappiness and thought of what her actions would do to the boy. He was left understandably devastated, and has never recovered fully."

The rain began, thumping against the roof and sides of the coach, causing the road to grow thick and slippery. Occasionally the coach wagged from side to side, coming perilously close to the cliff edge.

Upon their arrival at Lycaon Castle, Thomas showed Amelia to a suite of rooms that overlooked Loch Tuath and the waves that pommeled the cliff sides below the castle walls a hundred feet below. The chambers were a far cry from the austere bleakness of her cell back at the convent—cold stone walls and floors devoid of anything remotely comfortable, or comforting.

In truth, the vast quarters, with lush tapestries on the walls and colorful carpets on the floor, reminded her of the home in which she had grown up—her room overlooking Loch Ness and the surrounding hills. She made a mental note to write her parents and sisters and inform them of this unexpected turn of events. They would not be surprised, of course. Father Marriott had frequently penned her parents lengthy notes describing her lack of solemnity and reverence toward her responsibilities, going so far as to hint that her personality might not be right for the austerity of the church. Amelia had yet to understand why her devotion to God and her fellow man could not be carried out with gaiety and a light heart. How was she to brighten people's lives when forbidden to laugh or to sing out the praises of God and heaven? More often over the last weeks she had been commanded to lie prostrate before the high altar, saying nothing, but only lying prone with her face to the ground as she prayed for redemption for her irreverent behavior.

Her heart squeezed and she took a quick ragged breath, hoping to quell the rise of burning that would likely make her eyes tear and bring a lump to her throat. She did not like to think that Father Marriott was right. If she was not cut out for the nunnery, then what was left her besides returning home . . . and facing her sisters' fate?

The thought checked her abruptly, and she frowned, far too familiar with the choking hopelessness that closed around her throat.

A knock at the door interrupted her thoughts. She hurried to open it, finding Thomas Baird with a child at his side. His big gnarled fingers held the boy's slender ones with infinite gentleness as the lad suddenly turned and buried his face into Thomas's side.

"There, there," Thomas crooned. "Stand up, lad. Stand up. Sister Amelia has only come here to help."

"I don't want her help," he declared with much vehemence.

"Present yourself, Master Robert, and remember who you are. A young man of great dignity and circumstance. Good lad. Shoulders back and chin up. Wipe your nose."

Robert sniffed, then wiped his nose with his coat sleeve. Although he did not lift up his chin, he did peer at Amelia through the fringe of black, slightly curly hair falling over his brow.

Amelia smiled and stepped back into the well-lit room, remaining silent as Thomas escorted the young man across the threshold. Only then did the impact of the boy's appearance give her pause.

Robert stood tall for a boy his age, and was very slender. But it was the shocking beauty of his face that left her temporarily speechless. His eyes, green as emeralds, were shadowed by lashes as thick and black as the crown of luxurious hair that exaggerated the ivory color and smoothness of his young features. His nose was sharp, his cheeks without the plumpness of youth, but slightly concave. At last, Amelia found her voice. "How do you do, Master Robert. I'm so very pleased—"

"This was my mother's room," young master Robert announced in an accusatorial tone. Then, as if to add to her discomfiture, he pointed toward the window and said, "She flung herself from that very ledge. I saw her do it. She did it because she hated my father more than she loved me."

Thomas closed his big hand over the boy's shoulder. "Enough," he whispered.

"You'll regret having come here," Robert told her flatly, his pale lips turning under and his chin beginning to quiver. "If you're clever you'll go back to St. Mary's before it's too late—before he drives you to leap from that ledge as well. God won't help you here. Not here. You've come to hell, you see."

Startled, Amelia looked at Thomas, whose face twisted somewhat in despair. "Remember yer manners, lad," he scolded quietly, and gave Robert's hand a stern squeeze.

Jerking his hand away, Robert backed toward the door. "I don't care what either of you say. You'll never make me love him again. Never!"

He ran from the room, leaving Amelia to stare after him, her breath caught, her mouth fallen open in voiceless amazement. Then, quickly recovering herself, she started for the door, only to be brought up sharply as Thomas called, "No! Leave him alone. It won't do you any good to try and console him, poor boy. He is beside himself with despair and confusion. I fear your coming here will only add to his unhappiness and anger." He hurried to the door before looking back. "His lordship should not have brought you here. I was against it all along. But what is done is done. I suppose we must make the best of it."

"When will I meet Lycaon? Soon, I hope. I should like

to speak with him extensively concerning that poor unhappy and disillusioned child.''

"You'll not see him tonight. Perhaps tomorrow morning. Yes, perhaps then.''

"But—''

"Never unlock this door between midnight and dawn.
No matter what you *think* you hear; no matter *who* calls
out your name. *I* take care of the boy at night. No one
else. Do you understand me, lass?''

She nodded, but she did *not* understand. Not in the least.

Thomas slammed the door in her face, and somewhere
in the distance came the sound of weeping . . . or perhaps
it was simply the soughing of the wind and rain clawing
at the window where, according to young master Robert,
Lycaon's wife had leapt to her death.

The room was very bright when she opened her eyes. The
assault of sun spilling through the windows made her
groan and turn her face into the pillow. A moment passed
before she realized that she was not at St. Mary's. Nor had
she missed morning mass. Sister Elizabeth would not be
storming into her cell to demand that she spend the next
hours on her knees repenting for her flagrant laziness. She
stretched, allowing her feet to peek out from beneath the
blanket she had shivered under throughout the night.

"Good morning.''

She bolted upright, clutching the blanket to her chin.
The bleary form of a man reclined in a chair before her,
legs slightly spread, elbows resting comfortably on the
chair arms. He wore a black velvet coat on which was the
familiar badge of a mailed arm rising out of a crown and
holding a dagger. Wide white ruffles spilled from under
his sleeves and over his long-fingered, graceful hands. His
black breeches were tight, and highly polished black boots
reached to his knees. But it was his face that arrested her.
Like the boy's the night before, this countenance was one

of supreme beauty and masculinity. His eyes were like
green fires burning. His lips curled in a fashion that
brought an unfamiliar warmth to her cheeks.

"Lycaon?"

He nodded, and a wave of black hair spilled over his
brow. There was a slight tinge of gray at his temples,
which only added to his aristocratic mien.

"You're not at all what I expected," she confessed, sti-
fling a yawn.

"Neither are you," he replied.

"I visualized some short, bald man with a huge belly
and jowls like a hound—among other things."

"And I expected some plain, demure little sparrow with
eyes as dull as coal and a complexion as gray as slate. I
was wrong. Obviously. Your eyes sparkle like morning
dew and your cheeks glow with sunlight. And how do you
explain that?" He wagged one long finger at the red hair
that tumbled in riotous curls over her shoulders. "I thought
nuns were supposed to cut off their hair."

"Well, I'm not a nun yet, you see. I'm a novice. We
don't cut off our hair until we've taken our final vows."

"Then perhaps I should try to persuade you not to take
your final vows. It would be a dreadful shame to shear
something so incredibly beautiful."

She lowered her eyes and tucked the blanket more
closely to her body. A warmth sluiced through her, and
some feeling, not quite nervousness, centered in the pit of
her stomach. Doing her best not to smile at his outrageous
flirtation, Amelia curled her legs up under the blanket and
bit her lip.

Lycaon leaned forward, his elbows on his knees and his
fingers laced loosely together. "Would you mind explaining to me why you slept on the floor, Amelia, when there
is a bed there—a very comfortable bed as I recall—at your
disposal?"

"The bed is very nice, I'm sure, my lord." She

shrugged. "My only explanation is that I've grown accustomed to less than comfortable accommodations. At the convent we sleep only on a thin mattress, you see."

"When God asks that you give up all earthly comforts and possessions, he means decent beds as well? I hardly think that even the most dedicated and reverent apostle could function to his potential after sleeping on a slab of rock all night."

A giggle spilled from her and she drew the blanket up higher, to the bridge of her nose. Peering at Lycaon over the cover's edge, she said, " 'Tis a good thing Sister Elizabeth and Father Marriott aren't here. I fear you would be spending the next hours on your stomach before the high altar praying for redemption."

"Would you like me to leave so you can dress?" he asked.

"Yes, thank you."

He lingered still, his eyes as dark as forests, studying her face. At last, he slowly stood. The tail of his coat flowed over his thighs, the silk lining making a whispering sound that, strangely enough, sounded overwhelmingly masculine. He took several strides for the door before pausing. His back to her, he said, "What did you mean 'among other things'?"

She frowned.

He partially turned, offering her his profile, which looked taut, suddenly, his jaw rigid. "When you mentioned that I wasn't what you expected."

"Oh. That." She chastised herself for not choosing her words more carefully. "Just by the way the villagers described you I expected someone more . . . intimidating."

"I see. And how did my son describe me? Come, come, Amelia, you needn't squirm. I'm certain he was very frank about his feelings for me."

"My lord, I sense that he is most overwhelmed by the loss of his dear mother. I suspect that you both are."

"Then you suspect wrong," he replied. Removing a key from one of his pockets, he tossed it on the bed, and in a voice that was far less congenial said, "You failed to lock your door last night. I suggest—I demand that you do so from now on." Then, as gracefully as the wind, he quit the room.

"What in God's name were you thinking in bringing her here?" Thomas said. "What did you think to accomplish? There is absolutely nothing she can do to help the boy, Christopher. You know that. Why put her life in danger? Why risk revealing yourself this way?"

Christopher Guaire, Earl Lycaon, slid his arms into the sleeves of his morning coat, then adjusted the garment across his shoulders. Dragging the black velvet drapery from the mirror on the wall, he regarded his reflection, touching his fingertips to the dark hollows below his eyes, then to his dry lips. He focused on his hands, studied them closely in the glass, turning them one way and then the other before looking again into Thomas's eyes.

"I've applied to a dozen schools. None of them will take him because of my family's . . . reputation."

"Bah! What do they know, the bunch of hypocrites. If the truth be known they are all hiding a lot of skeletons in their dungeons. How can you condemn a child for the sins of his forefathers?"

Thomas paced, one hand cradling an open book as he searched the brittle, yellow pages. Turning from the mirror, Lycaon plucked the book from Thomas's hands and flung it across the room. "Can you not give up this asinine idea of finding some miracle cure for this damnable curse? For the last three hundred years we've suffered from it. It's ripped our lives and futures apart. Were there some recourse we would have found it. But we both know there is only one recourse—"

"Hush! I'll not stand here and listen to you discuss the annihilation of yourself and the boy—"

"It has to end!" he shouted, causing Thomas to step back. "Do you think I enjoy seeing the look of loathing on those villagers' faces? Not to mention my son's. Robert has every right to hate me. I killed his mother."

"Nay, you did not! You had nothing to do with her leaping from that window. You must cease blaming yourself for that."

"What choice did she have? She either ended her life, or she brought another cursed child into the world. Had I half the courage she had I would have followed her."

Leaving the room, Lycaon moved down the long unlighted gallery flanked with busts and portraits of his ancestors, doing his best to contain the anger swelling in his chest. Upon arriving at the library, he stopped short at discovering Amelia browsing through the multitude of books lining the shelves. Gone was the entrancing young woman with the flowing fiery hair he had watched sleep in the early hours of morning. This mouse of a girl was colorless and pale, her movements restricted, her head in a perpetual bow, even as she perused the embossed titles. He took a deep breath and felt his earlier anger slide from him, and the realization occurred to him that she had had the same effect on his emotional turbulence as he'd watched her sleep.

"Good morning—again," he said.

Amelia looked around, and her cheeks went from colorless to vibrant, their flush accentuating the blue of her eyes. She smiled, and the gloom of the chamber became bright as sunlight. "Good morning," she replied.

"Do you enjoy books, Sister?"

"Oh, yes. Very much. They're tremendous companions. They were my greatest friends as I was growing up."

Lycaon crossed the room, falling in beside Amelia as she continued to move along the rows of books. "You have a very unusual collection of titles, my lord: *Discours de la Lycanthropie, A Treatise Against Witchcraft, Dialogi und Gesprache von der Lycanthropia.*" She glanced up at him, the smile yet flowing from her eyes. "You obviously hold a great deal of interest on the topic of werewolves."

"Does that appall you?"

"Not at all. I believe that curiosity is one of man's greatest attributes."

He laughed softly. "No wonder you found yourself in such disfavor with Father Marriott."

Amelia reached for *The Chronicles of Giraldus Cambrensis.* "I've seen this title before. In Father Marriott's office."

"A gift from my father."

"What is it about?"

"Are you certain you want to know?"

She looked at him again, and though her smile was not as bright, it was just as kind. Too kind. Its shadow of compassion flowed over him, and through him, like warm wind. The empathy of it stabbed him and he experienced a sharp sadness that she belonged to God instead of humankind. A strange ache roused in his chest, as if suddenly he realized that he had lost a most cherished object and would never get it back.

Moving to a window, Lycaon gazed out over the misty landscape. "Giraldus was an ecclesiastic who was elected to be bishop of St. David's in 1198. He chronicles accounts of werewolf sightings, particularly of a werewolf pair who requested last rites for the dying female. Giraldus was concerned with the ecclesiastical issues raised by this request: Since the divine nature took on human nature—that is, Christ became man—it is possible that God, not the Devil, would exercise his power in transforming a human being into a wolf. The question in his mind was: What is the nature of a werewolf? Be it human or animal? It is his opinion that the Devil cannot change the human form, although he can alter perceptions of it. The transubstantiation of the bread and wine into the body and blood of Christ in the Communion rite is an alteration not of appearance but of substance. Giraldus emphasizes how important it is to exercise compassion in the presence of human metamorphosis, and how vital it is to distinguish between the works of the Devil and of the Creator.''

''That would depend, I suppose, on whether the werewolf be good or evil,'' came her gentle reply. ''If his heart be kind and full of God, though he be cursed to transform into a beast, would not his goodness ultimately dictate his destiny? Even in life man must wage war against the evil that would lead him astray. Though he may beat his breast and feel savage toward others, his innate goodness will stop him from destroying another.''

''Spoken like a dedicated disciple of God.'' He looked at Amelia where she remained near the bookcase, her expression one of grave concern. Though the light had not gone from her eyes, an intensity had settled softly as shadows among her features' contours.

''How many wars have you waged here, Amelia?'' He placed his hand over his heart. ''You haven't an evil or unkind inkling in your body. I suspect you never have—not yet. You're much too young. You've been far too sheltered. You've not yet experienced the proverbial apple—the temptation, the one burning desire that would make you question everything you once considered important; the tiny, solitary seed of confusion and discontent that once it germinates, flourishes like grass in spring.''

Amelia made no perceptible movement, but he became aware of an indefinable change in her. She remained silent for so long that he wondered if perhaps she had no intention of responding. Quite suddenly he was conscious of a strange, overwhelming impulse to cross the room and take her in his arms, to tear the unflattering little cap from her head and fling it to the floor. To show her that evil was not easily definable or recognizable, that it could so easily mask itself in congeniality, polite conversation, and nobility.

"I'm sorry we're tardy," came Thomas's voice from the door. "Master Robert was a bit late in rising. But we're here now, and famished. Aren't we, lad?"

A heartbeat passed before Amelia managed to drag her gaze away from Lycaon and turn toward Thomas and Robert, who, standing side by side and hand in hand, waited just inside the library threshold. She appeared to collect herself before moving somewhat woodenly toward the pair, her habit making a shushing noise in the quiet.

The low buzz of conversation swirled around Lycaon as he turned back to the window and focused on the horizon and the flocks of razorbills and puffins that swirled in dark eddies above the whitecapped water. He could just make out the shadowy high peaks of the Treshnish Isles, a silent, lonely gathering of islands inhabited only by birds and seals.

"But I don't want to have breakfast with him," came his son's voice. "I want to go to my room."

"You're being very unkind, Master Robert, and most disrespectful," Amelia said. "Your father loves you very much, I'm certain. Your cruelty must make him very sad."

"I don't care if he's sad. He's a monster. My mother told me so."

"He seems very kind to me."

"Because you don't know him, do you?"

"Has he done something to hurt you? Hmm?"

"No."

"Did you ever witness his being unkind to your mother?"

". . . No."

"Then you're being very unfair, aren't you?"

Silence.

"Will you do something for me, Master Robert? Will

you sit with us during breakfast? I would very much like for you to tell me about the island's bird life, and perhaps later we can search out a nest or two along the cliffs. I do so enjoy hunting for eggs on such a lovely morning.''

"I have a collection of eggs," the boy offered with new enthusiasm. "I'll show them to you if you like."

"I'd like that very much. . . . My lord, will you be joining us?"

Lycaon turned. Amelia stood in the doorway, his son at her side as she held his small hand in hers. Again with her smile, radiating from her eyes and every exquisite facet of her face. *Trust me,* those eyes said. *I am here to give you strength and hope and courage.*

"Yes," he replied softly, and followed her from the room.

Two

Over the next days Amelia grew very fond of Robert, and enjoyed the hours she spent with him poring over books, traipsing along the blustery Ulva cliffs in search of black- or brown-speckled guillemots and the black-legged pearl gray kittiwakes that laid their eggs amid the craggy rocks along the loch shore.

But it was the time that she tucked him into bed that she appreciated most. Weary from their afternoon outings in the fresh air, he lay with his eyes closed as she read aloud from the Bible. With the passing of each day, he had become more serene and far less angry at his father. She suspected that she had in some way helped to alleviate the terrible hole in his life that had come from the tragic death of his mother—his loneliness exacerbating his turbulent emotions over the last year. Still, though not as obvious, the fierce anger was there, tottering on the cusp of his frangible temperament.

For that reason alone she had requested of Lycaon that he absent himself from the boy for a few days—if only to allow her and the child time to become better acquainted in an atmosphere of harmony. Lycaon had complied—to a point. More than once, however, she had sensed his presence, while reading aloud to Robert in the library, while singing from the old hymnals she had discovered in the ruins of the chapel, and as she and the boy wandered hand and hand amid the glorious landscape surrounding the castle.

It was a week after her arrival on Ulva that she sat at Robert's bedside, watching the gentle rise and fall of his chest as he slept. Upon closing the Bible, she bent and pressed a light kiss to his forehead. His long eyelashes fluttered and he looked up, lifted one hand, and lightly placed it against her cheek.

"You're very pretty," he said. "If I were older I might marry you."

Amelia smiled. "Nuns can't marry, Robert."

"Why?"

"Because we dedicate our lives to God."

"Because you love God more than you love children?" She raised both eyebrows and sat back in her chair.

"Don't you like children?" he pressed.

"I like them very much."

"Wouldn't you like a child of your own?"

"What do I need with a child of my own when I have you?"

His lips curved in pleasure.

"Go to sleep," she told him. "You'll need all the rest you can get if we intend to search out puffin eggs tomorrow." As she moved toward the door, he said:

"I have a secret, Amelia."

"Do you?" She smiled.

"A very big secret. Would you like to know what it is?"

"Once you tell me it won't be a secret any longer, will it?"

"It's about my father."

Her step slowed. Reaching the doorway, she reluctantly turned. Propped up on one elbow, Robert regarded her with an intensity that seemed to vibrate the air between them.

"He . . ." He looked down.

"Robert, I'm sure your father wouldn't appreciate your confiding his personal matters—"

"He sheltered Charles Stuart here for nearly three months. Thomas said that I was never to breathe a word about it. If the English were to find out they might kill my father." Robert fell back on the bed, crossing his arms behind his head. "My father supplied Prince Charles with enough ships and provisions so that he could sail to France."

"That's an astonishing secret, Robert, and one you should definitely keep to yourself."

He shrugged, his expression becoming something less than childlike, almost . . . cunning. "Maybe I will. And maybe I won't. I haven't made up my mind yet." Turning his head, he gave her a thin smile. "I wouldn't advise your walking the grounds this evening."

She frowned. "How do you know that I walk in the evening?"

"I watch you. From my window. You walk along the shore and feed the birds from your hand. Sometimes you remove your cap and allow your hair to fly in the wind."

"You see a great deal from your window, Master Robert."

He nodded.

"Why shouldn't I walk this evening?" Amelia asked.

"Because the moon is full. Everyone on Ulva knows it's not safe to be out when the moon is full."

"Why?"

"There are reasons. My father will become very, very angry if you go out tonight."

"What if I promise to come in before the moon rises?"

He shrugged again and closed his eyes. "I suppose that would be all right." As Amelia turned to go, Robert said, "Do you know what Ulva means? It's the Norse word for 'Wolf Island.' Lycaon is 'wolf' too." Turning his green eyes up to hers, he asked in an angry tone, "Don't you think it all very odd?"

Amelia did walk, far along the Loch Tuath shore, to a finger of sand that pointed directly toward the Treshnish Isles on the misty horizon. She came here every evening to watch the sun set beyond the distant isles. The serenity brought her peace—something that had been hard to grasp since her arrival on Ulva, particularly during the long hours she spent inside Lycaon Castle. Perhaps it was the intense solitude that pressed in on her. Aside from Robert's company she rarely saw or spoke to another person. Servants were scarce, and removed themselves from the premises long before dark, not returning until the sun was well risen. She had not spoken to Lycaon since the day after her arrival to the castle, and had only spoken to Thomas briefly. That alone had burdened her with a feeling of . . . disappointment—if only because she had found Lycaon's conversation fascinating and stimulating after the many months of monotonous discourses at St. Mary's.

But she was forced to acknowledge, if only to herself, that it was more than loneliness that had begun to bother her. Some feeling had crept into her being—some strange unrest that she had not experienced since arriving at St. Mary's months ago. It was a sensation that was, at the same time, mystifying, frightening, and exhilarating—and it mounted each time she saw Lycaon watching her from a distance. It roused her from sleep with a thumping heart and made her thoughts drift from scriptures and prayer to . . . what?

It was a feeling so alien to her normal state of well-being and contentment that she suddenly felt as if her entire existence was slightly out of kilter, like trying to look at the world through the distortion of bad glass. Her thoughts and emotions, which, until arriving on Ulva, had been so firmly entrenched—or so she had believed—now seemed as unbalanced and turbulent as the waves crashing against Bac Mor Point.

With her eyes closed, Amelia allowed the loch spray to cover her face, and when the wind rose, snapping at her clothes, she removed her cap and allowed her hair to fly like a silken banner behind her, its color as richly crimson as the fiery sun dipping below the western water. A smile turned up her lips as she thought of Robert's sitting in his window and watching when he was supposed to be sleeping, and with thoughts of the confused and lonely little boy came thoughts of his mother.

How could a mother, no matter how unhappy, purposefully choose to die and thereby destroy her family emotionally? What could have driven her to such madness?

The sun sank and the last of its light drained with it. Amelia hardly noticed. She was far too engrossed in the waves sluicing around the rock on which she was perched like a basking seal. She studied the way the hissing, thrusting water scalloped deep hollows in the sand and undercut the weeds that crowded the shoal. The dim thought occurred to her that back at St. Mary's she would be knelt before the altar in reverent prayer, her knees having long since grown numb, her shoulders aching, her neck stiff.

It wasn't until the moonlight began to reflect off the wet stones that she realized just how late it had become. She stretched and stood, tottered momentarily before dancing back to shore along the disappearing strut of rock. There, she paused at the sight of the full moon balanced atop Lycaon Castle's highest turret, and the memory of young Robert's warning rushed at her as suddenly as a north wind. She shivered—not because of the boy's fanciful warning, but because of the unexpected memory of the dead seal, its huge dead bulk tapping her in the back.

Carefully, she made her way along the vaguely rutted path that had been swallowed by night shadows, avoiding the outcropping of yew, making respectable time until rounding an elbow bend and finding a wide, deepening span of tide between her and the castle. She was forced to cut through the trees. Blindly, she felt her way through the wild undergrowth, the dark exaggerating the unpleasant smell of rotting vegetation.

Her breath burning her throat, Amelia stopped and leaned against a tree, willing back the sense of disquietude that seem to grow with each thud of her heart. She sensed, rather than felt, the shroud of night fog unfold over the forest. It had a smell about it: old, musty, salty, like rotting seaweed and the very bowels of the loch floor. The unsettling realization swept over her that she was lost. Very lost.

Earl Lycaon was going to be very angry.

Again, the memory: the seal, swinging in and out of the shadows, puppylike eyes wide and teeth bared in agony— or terror. With a rising feeling of panic, she swung her arms out before her and stumbled along, knocking against tree trunks, fighting with shrubs that ripped at her skirt with twigs and thorns.

Amelia was not certain when, exactly, she got the absolute feeling that she was being watched. Only that the sensation crept up on her as she leaned against a tree and rubbed her stinging face where a branch had clawed her cheek. She had often experienced the same sensation at St. Mary's. Sister Elizabeth had never cared for Amelia's presence at the convent, feeling that Amelia's dedication to God had primarily to do with escaping the rigors of an arranged marriage—arrangements that had apparently caused much grief to her older sisters—than it had to do with some deep spiritual desire to devote her life to God. Subsequently, Amelia had found herself being constantly watched for any transgression that might justify sending her packing back to her parents' estate.

It was that same feeling that wormed around in her stomach now, causing the hair to rouse on the back of her neck and her arms to develop gooseflesh. Slowly raising her head, she focused on the singular clearing in front of her—a space without shadow or trees, lit by a shaft of moonlight that flickered like a flame fanned by a child's breath while all around became utter blackness, and stillness, the quiet so brittle she heard a leaf drop as gently as a snowflake against the earth.

A being stared back at her, its eyes like twin lamps, burning red and then green, then yellow. Long black hair, with streaks of gray, framed a snouted face that had the teeth of a lion—sharp and white. Its hands, which were poised before it, were like reaping hooks, the nails were claws. Yet . . .

It had the body of a man.

"Amelia?" came the soft voice. "Amelia!"

The thing showed its teeth. A growl crawled from its throat and its eyes became fierce, its expression diabolically malignant as it fixed her with a savage exultation that made her legs become water. It crouched—

From the darkness, Robert moved up behind her, slid his hand into Amelia's, and said, "Come. Quickly! He shan't hurt you as long as you're with me."

She could not move.

Robert tugged on her hand. "Amelia. Quickly!"

Some rationale spurred her to follow. The child, wearing only his nightdress and barefoot, led her through a part in the trees, down along a ravine and through the ankle-deep water, where her feet sank slightly in mud and sucked at her shoes. Out they stumbled onto the rocky shoal, then ran along its foam-kissed surface until arriving back at the castle. Amelia followed Robert up staircase after staircase and down the dark gallery to his bedroom—afraid to look behind her, afraid not to. It was back there, following. She did not need to see the thing to know it was there; she felt it.

Robert sat her on the edge of his bed, then hurried back to lock the door, leaned against it, and took a deep breath.

"That was close," he said. "Perhaps now you'll listen to me when I tell you something."

She tried to speak. Impossible. Her teeth were chattering too furiously. The dampness of her feet and legs sent chills through her, causing her to shake. But it was the fear that immobilized her most. A scream had lodged in her throat those moments in the woods, and even now it would not subside. It swelled inside her like a bubble that would explode without warning at any moment.

Robert crossed the room and dropped to his knees at her feet. Carefully, he removed each muddy shoe and tossed it aside. He then rubbed her feet, first the right, then the left, his small hands as gentle and kind as her own might have been.

Finally, Amelia found the strength to ask, "What was it, Robert?"

"A wolf. Nothing more."

"*That was no wolf.*"

He looked at her, his sharp young features very somber and far too mature for his age. " 'Twas a wolf. There are a great many wolves on Ulva." Smiling, he stood and moved to the window, where he climbed upon the sill and rested against the wide embrasure. Amelia could no longer see him clearly, his face being curtained by shadows. At last, his head turned and he regarded her where she still sat on the bed edge, her fingers twisted around the tiny silver cross hanging from her neck.

His eyes narrowing and his lips turning under, he said, "That won't help you here, you know. God turned his back on Ulva a very long time ago."

*   *   *

As he had every morning since her arrival, Lycaon
watched from the turret as Amelia and his son walked the
hedge maze that skirted the enclosed gardens on the east
side of the castle. Over the last week the image of her with
Robert had brought him immense pleasure. For the first
time in years, his son's face had glowed with its old light
of happiness and enthusiasm. Holding hands, they had
danced along the paved paths skirting the beds of brilliantly blooming flowers. They had chased butterflies.
They had sat upon the carved stone benches and read aloud
from books. From his seclusion, Lycaon had done his best
to quell the nearly overwhelming hunger to join them, to
feast in the companionship of woman and child. To float
on the waves of her melodious voice, and his son's laughter. He had ached to somehow freeze in time the delicious
days so he could relive them at night.

But all of that had changed over the last twenty-four
hours. Today was different. The young woman was without her usual buoyancy. Her step was slow and she constantly looked behind her. Robert was constantly forced to
take her hand and encourage her onward. She did not sing,
nor did she dance. As the morning progressed and they sat
together on the bench, the books stacked and forgotten at
Amelia's side, she stared out at the trees, hardly acknowledging Robert at all.

Thomas joined Lycaon at the window. Silently, they
watched the pair below before Thomas said, "She asked
a great many questions this morning. She's understandably
upset, and frightened."

"Is she going to leave us?"

"No. I don't think so."

Lycaon raised one eyebrow and realized only then that
he had held his breath in anticipation of Thomas's reply.
"What sort of questions did she ask?"

"What is the beast in the woods?"

"And what did you say?" Lycaon turned his gaze on

Thomas, his lip curling. "Well? Did you explain away the beast as some freak of nature? Or perhaps try to convince her that she had allowed her imagination to get the better of her? Or perhaps you simply suggested that what she *thought* she saw was nothing more than a trick of light and shadow."

"I told her it was a wolf."

"And what did she say?"

"Only that it was a very unusual wolf."

Lycaon watched as Robert and Amelia returned to the castle. He turned for the door, paused, and, without looking again at Thomas, said, "Make certain she doesn't leave her room tonight. Or tomorrow night. Or any night, for that matter. We simply cannot risk losing her. She's come to mean far too much to Robert."

"Only to Robert?" Thomas asked in a gentle voice.

"Of course," he replied in a monotone that sounded strangely flat to his own ears. Then he left the room and made his way down the winding flights of stairs, his stride determined as he quit the house through the front door and made his way down the footpath to the highest precipice overlooking the loch. With his face tipped up to the dazzling sun and the biting winds gnashing at his clothes, he listened to the roar of the water below, the scream of the birds overhead, and did his best to rid his memory of the sound of his own words moments before trying lamely to assure Thomas that his concern over losing Amelia had nothing whatsoever to do with his own feelings, but only for his son's.

Robert desperately needed her compassion.

Robert craved her goodness.

Robert exalted in her kindness.

Her charity would uplift *Robert's* heart and soul and breathe sunlight into this dreary chasm of darkness and woe in which he had resided since long before his mother's death.

Finally, his hair windblown and damp from sea spray, along with his fine clothes, Lycaon returned to the castle.

The last place he suspected to happen upon Amelia was the little room off the old conservatory where he often came to immerse himself in introspection. The sight of her sitting in his chair surrounded by sprigs of plants, the sun splashing in prisms through the overhead panes, stopped him in his tracks. Sweet and still, her head bowed over the book in her lap, Amelia reflected the September light like silvered glass. She read silently, yet her lips moved upon each word as if they were something to be worshiped. Her soft profile, delicate and womanly, rendered him powerless to move, or speak, and his soul stirred inside him—a shift so powerful he felt as if he were suddenly weightless.

Amelia looked up.

She did not speak. The flush of color that normally radiated from her face like rosy sunlight was conspicuously absent as she regarded him with an intensity that closed off his throat.

"My lord," she finally said, and started to stand.

"No! You needn't bother to get up. I wouldn't think of intruding upon your privacy." He began to turn away.

"I would very much like you to join me," she said, motioning toward another chair. "Please."

Slowly, he moved to the chair and eased into it. Amelia took note of his disheveled hair and clothes. She regarded his muddy boots and the remnants of seaweed clinging to his pants legs. When her gaze returned to his, her eyes were full of intense concern.

"Something very strange happened to me last evening, my lord."

"So Thomas tells me. I'm sorry you were so frightened. I assure you, the . . . wolves on this island would never hurt you, despite what the villagers might say. The folk here are a superstitious lot. Too many outrageous tales passed on through generations of ignorance."

She laced her fingers together on the open book in her lap. "I hope you don't mind, but I borrowed one of the volumes from your library."

"What? No Bible?" He smiled thinly and glanced at the book under her hands. "I can't imagine that you would find dissertations on lycanthropy particularly stimulating."

"Why do you?"

He crossed his legs and plucked drying seaweed from his boot.

Sitting back in her chair, Amelia closed the book and placed it aside. "I should like to understand all facets of good and evil, and determine for myself the sources of both. Often, lack of understanding is the prejudice for perceived evil. People are frightened of what they don't understand. Their lack of understanding is, in itself, threatening to their existence. Therefore, is it not our duty as human beings to do our best to understand others' foibles before judging them fit or unfit for heaven?"

"It's my understanding that such judgment is to be left up to God."

Her lips curled slightly, and she lowered her eyes. A shadow crossed over her countenance, which showed that, as he suspected, she experienced a plethora of thoughts and emotions of which she would not dare admit—perhaps even to herself. The frock she wore, the cap that sat somewhat askew on her head like some crooked halo would demand that she refrain from showing too much of those feelings that would humanize her.

At last, she rallied her sensibilities and replied. "You're absolutely correct, my lord. I only wish life were that simple. Then perhaps we wouldn't be so inclined to destroy one another. Would we?"

He smiled and was suddenly aware of an immense restlessness inside himself that was neither pain nor anger. It was then that he noticed the thin scratches on Amelia's cheek. Leaning toward her, he touched the slight injuries with his fingertip, aware, even as he did so, that such an unthinkable lapse of judgment might well send her fleeing, but driven to do it anyway . . . willing to risk her disapproval for this fleeting contact.

Her eyes widened. Her lips parted. A soft gasp rushed from her, yet . . . she did *not* flee. Her hand came up and closed around his, pressing his flesh against hers in a manner that was less reverent than it was worshipful. A quiver passed through her, and her mien changed, however briefly—a slight contracting of her fine brows showing that his touch had affected her somehow.

"Your face," he whispered.

" 'Tis nothing, my lord. A scratch from a twig. I should have taken better care where I was walking."

"Don't walk in the woods again. Promise me. If anything happened to you . . ."

"What, my lord?"

"Robert would be heartbroken," he said softly. "He's come to care for you very much. Very much indeed."

Her lip began to tremble, and there came a faint dew to her blue eyes. With a great effort she unloosed her hand from his, slowly, gently, reluctantly, and returned it to her lap.

Thomas appeared at the door, and Lycaon sat back. The old man's face looked agitated as he announced, "You have a visitor, my lord. A woman from the village. She's desperate to speak with you."

"They are always desperate to speak with me," he sneered, "when they want something. Very well. Bring her here."

"She'll not step foot in this house."

Heat roused in his chest and face as Lycaon hesitated briefly, his gaze going back to Amelia's, who watched him with a mix of concern and curiosity. Had he imagined, those seconds before, that the look in her eyes had reflected a sort of affection—no, no, surely not. No more affection than she showed his son. 'Twas not affection, but kindness. Nothing more!

Standing, he followed Thomas from the room.

Three

"M' children are starvin, milord, as y' can well see. M' husband cannot fish. And since he cannot fish, we cannot eat. The tiny an' pitiful lads here are mere waifs, and—"

"*Why* can your husband not fish, Mrs. Wheeler?"

"The fishin' net got wrappin' round his arm and snap it in two as if it were a stick, milord."

"You lie, Mrs. Wheeler. I happen to know that your worthless husband broke his arm in falling out of a whore's window. I also happen to recognize your waifs— all of whom threw stones at my son and insulted his heritage not a fortnight ago."

Mrs. Wheeler narrowed her eyes and she jigged the crying baby in her arms more fiercely up and down. She glanced at Amelia, who stood at Thomas's side, then toward her own dirty and gaunt-faced children, who squirmed like little mice around her legs. "So what are y' tellin' me?" she finally said. "That y' intend to allow me chil'ren to starve?"

A moment of silence passed as Amelia, holding her breath, watched Lycaon's profile for any sign of compassion. At last it came, in the relaxing of his jaw, the almost sleepy blink of his eyes.

"Your children won't starve, Mrs. Wheeler. I'll make certain they have food for their supper. I'll have someone deliver you a basket by nightfall."

"I don't want yer foul food, milord. I'll buy me own food with what money you'll give me."

"Ah. I see. You want money." The anger returned; Lycaon's face grew dark and his eyes snapped. "And what will you do with your money, Mrs. Wheeler? Hand it over to your husband so he can spend it on more ale and whores?"

The woman's eyes grew round and her face red. The baby wailed louder and the child hanging on her skirt tail began to tug on her violently, causing her to totter before kneeing the lad so fiercely he fell hard on his bottom and began to scream.

"Take your brats and get out of my sight. You can tell your husband, who no doubt sent you here, that he should try spending his coins on his children instead of lice-infested wenches, then perhaps he wouldn't have the need to send his wife begging."

"Heartless bastard. Bloody monster. I'm not surprised y'd send me away—what with me bairn wailin' an' all. 'Sno wonder yer cursed—you an' all yer fathers. An' you!" She pointed at Amelia. "A disgrace to yer cloth. 'Tis no place for a Christian lass. No place for aught but divils an' dogs."

Tucking the babe more securely under her arm, Mrs. Wheeler turned on her heels and made for the road, yapping orders and insults to the pack of scrawny, sneering boys following her. Lycaon turned away, stopping abruptly upon finding Robert partially hidden behind the door, his young face expressionless as he watched the departure of the woman and children. Finally, the boy shifted his gaze up to his father's.

"Will you let them starve?" Robert said to his father. "Even the bairn?"

"Of course he won't," Amelia declared. "Your father would never allow children to go hungry. I was about to propose that I deliver the Wheelers a basket of food. I'm certain your father will agree that such an act of generosity will do much to lessen their extreme animosity toward this family."

"It'll take a great deal more than a basket of food to win the folk over," Robert said, never taking his gaze from his father.

"Mrs. Wheeler's visit isn't unusual," Lycaon explained, looking off at the horizon, where a bank of dark clouds were gathering. The cool, constant breeze kissed his face, giving it color and causing his black hair to tumble freely over his brow. "They are often pounding on my door and begging. It's our lot, isn't it? To make certain the people are properly taken care of? My wife was very good at that—for a while. I think the villagers almost came to respect us while Celia was living."

"Your wife sounds like a kind and generous woman," Amelia said. "You must miss her very much. Her death must have come as a great shock to you."

They walked in silence, side by side, their gazes following Robert, who ran along the shoal, hopping from one boulder to another, racing the whitecapped waves, pausing occasionally to glance back, his expression dark. Finally, Lycaon said wearily, as if to himself:

"I wonder what will become of him."

"Whatever he chooses, my lord."

"Naive child. Don't you realize that our lives are dictated by our birthright? My title, and its burdens, will all pass to him, whether he wants it or not."

"Why would he not want it, my lord?"

"For all the reasons he hates me."

"He doesn't hate you. I'm certain of it. Whatever anger he's held on to the last year wants desperately to mellow.

You mustn't be afraid of loving him. The ability to love
is, after all, God's greatest gift to mankind, as is compassion. All He asks for in return is faith in Him, and in His
miracles.'' Lightly placing her hand on his arm, she added,
''He never burdens us with more than we can endure.
While we may stagger under the weight of pain or sorrow
or disillusionment, these things will not crush us. Nothing
crushes the human spirit but doubt.''

His gaze still fixed on his son, Lycaon's countenance
grew intense and brooding. He did not respond.

As Amelia watched, Lycaon moved down the path and
joined Robert. They stood side by side, their faces to the
wind. Finally, Lycaon lay his hand on his son's shoulder.

Amelia smiled.

They built castles in the sand, Lycaon and his son. They
wandered the cliffs in search of nests. They counted kittiwakes and tossed bits of bread high in the air and laughed
as the birds caught them.

They hardly noticed as the clouds covered the sun and
the wind brought with it a cold cloak of mist that covered
their hair and faces like fine silver webs. With their pants
legs rolled to their knees, they waded into the water and
taunted the sea, all while Amelia watched from her precipice, her hair flying free and her pleasure like a fluttering
moth inside her.

Dusk fell softly over the land and sea. Sitting in the cool
grass, her legs folded under her, Amelia watched the light
fade and felt the first kiss of night brush her cheeks with
a chill that made her throat grow tight and her heartbeat
quicken. At last, with his coat tossed over one shoulder
and his legs dusted with sand, Lycaon made his way up
the faint footpath toward her. His eyes smiled, as did his
lips, as he stopped before her and caught his breath. With
no warning, he grabbed her up in his arms and swung her
around, hugging her so fiercely she lost her breath.

"It's a miracle, Amelia. I don't know what you said, or did, but I have my son back. What can I ever do to thank you?"

It seemed quite natural, and necessary, to hug him back, caught as she was against him. With her arms around his neck, his damp hair a spray across her face, she laughed and held him more tightly . . . until the heat of his body warmed her. Until the strength in his arms overwhelmed her. Until her soul became buoyant, and her heart a wild thing that resonated as vibrantly as the waves crashing in the distance.

"Amelia," he whispered, and continued to hold her. "Sweet Amelia."

How long they stood there embraced, she could not be certain. A moment. An eternity. She knew only that as she at last opened her eyes, nightfall had slipped in around them and the moon was peeking through a break in the scattering clouds overhead. Despairingly, refusing to let him go, she whispered, "Look, my lord. Where has time flown? Night has fallen so suddenly, and the moon has commenced."

He drew back with some effort, finally managing to peel her arms from around his shoulders. The wash of white light hollowed his eyes and cheeks, and the joy he had experienced moments before became a mask of such agony Amelia was struck speechless.

"Cursed moon," he whispered, lightly drawing his finger down her cheek, allowing his hand to caress her face before he backed away.

"Stay with us," Amelia cried, holding out her hand to him. "We'll have dinner together. We'll spend the evening in idle conversation and I shan't leave you for a moment, my lord, if you'll simply allow me to—"

"No! I can't." He shook his head. "I can't."

"Why can't you, my lord?"

"Cursed life. Cursed destiny. I have . . . obligations.

Previous plans. Please understand. I would if I could. I want to. I *dare* not. I . . . can't.''

He turned, and allowing his coat to fall to the ground, he walked swiftly toward the castle and was soon swallowed up by the darkness. She thought she saw him once, briefly, as the clouds parted and the moonlight flooded the landscape. Only then did Robert join her. He slipped his hand into Amelia's and turned his gaze up to hers. His eyes were large and luminous, his tears reflecting the moonlight like mirrors.

''We'd better go in now'' was all he said.

For a long while after Amelia put Robert to bed and read him to sleep, she sat alone in her room, listening to a clock tick off the minutes and hours, occasionally rousing from her odd stupor long enough to pray—sometimes silently, sometimes aloud. She prayed for Robert. She prayed for Lycaon. She prayed for herself, and her confused soul. She prayed that God forgive her for her weakness and hoped He understood that she was, after all, more human than she'd once cared to admit. Perhaps Father Marriott and Sister Elizabeth had been right all along. A woman who was serious about dedicating her life to God would never have experienced, much less acknowledged—if only to herself—the all too human sensations she'd felt while holding Lycaon in her arms.

As the night wore on the walls pressed in on her, and at last she quit the room, wandered down the dark gallery, passed closed doors, listening for any sound that might alert her to Lycaon's presence. She wanted to see him again. She *needed* to see him again. His nearness had suddenly become as necessary to her survival as the air she breathed—or the Bible she kept tucked under her pillow.

Amelia happened upon Thomas by accident. He appeared at the far end of a lower gallery, his arms wrapped around multitudes of dusty books as he shuffled from one room to another, muttering to himself. On tiptoe, she followed, keeping to the shadows, ducking around corners if he gave any sign at all that he might look back and discover her. She followed him to a room lined with shelves of crumbling, musty tomes, their pages as brittle and brown as old leaves. In the halo of a solitary candle, the old man bent over an open book, his finger following along as he read aloud.

"And the man is a born werewolf, compelled to pass three nights of every week, and especially during the fullest moon, in his animal shape. But though his nature be not menacing on those eves of full moon, he is, in nature, a beast and all who meet him are to be forewarned and cautious, for in his divine misery he is a lethal and loathsome creature, desirous of mayhem."

Amelia moved away, continued along the gallery, beyond the scattering of ill-lit rooms that were, she surmised, Thomas's quarters, coming finally to the end of the corridor. A narrow stairwell wound down into the dark, and though her mind compelled her to turn away, some strange and dreadful compulsion drew her forward, down the black hole, her hands inching along the damp walls and her feet sliding perilously on the slippery stone steps.

A gray light crept up the stairwell as she neared the bottom and discovered a vast, comfortable room with sprawling carpets and colorful tapestries. There were no windows, only stone walls and the rich, overpowering smell of earth that reminded her of a fresh-dug grave.

A sound—a moan, a murmur—drew her eyes to Lycaon where he sat in a chair, his head fallen back and his eyes closed, hands gripping the chair arms fiercely. His teeth showing, his face sweating profusely, he rolled his head from side to side as if in excruciating pain.

"My lord," she gasped, and his eyes flew open, but as she thought to approach, he rose from his chair with so wild and frightening a look she could not move.

"Little idiot. What the hell are you doing here? Get out. Now. If you value your pretty neck at all you'll leave here this instant!"

Someone grabbed her from behind. She turned and came face-to-face with Thomas. "He's in pain," she managed. "Dreadful pain. Please, help him."

"Get her out!" Lycaon roared, and kicked over a table, sending glass crashing to the floor.

Thomas ushered her up the stairs, his fingers digging into her arm. "Don't look back, lass. He'll not hurt ya, I swear it. I don't care what the lot of hypocritic morons say about him, he's not injured a solitary man or woman or child *ever,* nor did his poor father, God rest his troubled soul." He said nothing more until reaching her room, then he pointed one finger at her and admitted in a trembling voice, "To be truthful, I did not want y' here. I warned him against it, but he would not listen—he never does when it comes to the boy. I told him there would be naught but trouble if we brought an outsider here. Now do as I say for once and lock this bloody door."

Stepping from the room, he slammed the door closed between them.

A light rain fell, causing the tall grass along the path to bow low and the leaves overhead to rattle. Amelia moved silently along the rutted way, looking neither right nor left, focusing instead on the shadows that shifted like living beings around her. There was no point in asking herself what had driven her here—what perverse curiosity had taunted her to leave her room, despite Thomas's warning, and wander the rain-drenched path in the dark. Perhaps it wasn't curiosity at all, but desperation. An overwhelming hunger to acknowledge what she had come to suspect these last days, but had tried so fiercely to deny.

The sound came to her gradually at first, muffled by the dense copse of trees and canopy of mist. She moved si-

lently through the wild growth, visually straining to make
out any movement in the dark, allowing herself to be
drawn by the disturbing noises that both mystified and ter-
rified her. At last, she came to a clearing, and there focused
on a large dark shape in the distance.

Just when the recognition wormed into her consciousness she could not be certain. The memory of the dead
seal rushed before her mind's eye; her heart seemed in that
instant to cease its beating as her brain acknowledged the
immense bulk as that of a seal hanging by a rope from a
tree—and beside it a wolf, standing on its oddly formed
back legs, its jaws effortlessly ripping flesh from the dead
seal.

Perhaps she gasped. Or whimpered. The beast slowly
turned its head, and as it had the previous night, stared at
her with burning green eyes and its teeth showing in a
snarl.

It growled softly and turned, balancing on its back feet
as easily as a man as it moved toward her, clawed hands
opening and closing, its dark, gray-streaked hair bristling
around its powerful shoulders. Although every instinct in
her being screamed at her to flee, Amelia refused. Instead,
she closed her fingers around the little crucifix hanging
from her neck and began to silently pray and shiver violently as the beast began to circle her, each dragging step
bringing him closer, until she could feel the coarse fur of
his arms brush her, and the heat of his breath tickle her
face.

With her last fragment of courage, she looked into its
dreadful, burning eyes—so near her own. "Be thou not
afraid of evil, but confront it," she intoned, "and master
it with compassion and faith. No soul is lost that He cannot
save. No burden is so heavy that He cannot lighten, if you
trust Him."

The wolf snarled and wagged its head from side to side.
It slashed the air between them with its claws and raised

up to its full, horrible height. She stumbled back, and though filled with the overwhelming desire to scream, she could but stare into its hypnotic face like one in a trance, as mesmerized by its strange, unearthly beauty as she was horrified at its ghastliness. It threw back its head and howled—a long, mournful cry that wrought in Amelia a tremendous pain that gripped her heart and flooded her with incredible sorrow. Yet, it was the expression in the thing's eyes that shook her most: the intense sadness, the immeasurable grief and helplessness—a soul as incapable of saving itself as a butterfly caught in a spider's web.

Tears came, flowing down her cheeks. She did her best to stifle them, to no avail. The more fiercely she tried to hold them back, the harder they fell, until her body felt as if it would disintegrate into a thousand shards.

A moment passed before she realized that the only sound in the dark forest was the sound of her own weeping. She wiped her eyes and took a shaky breath. The beast watched, eyes narrowed, head cocked, mouth silently panting as it sat on its haunches amid the damp, rotting leaves.

Finally, the beast stood again, slowly, burdened, all fury wiped from its eyes and no-longer-snarling snout. Its body swayed from side to side and it held its head between its gnarled hands as it moved toward her, footsteps dragging and shoulders bent.

She could run now, and it would not follow her; Amelia felt certain of it. She could flee for the safety of the castle and her bedroom and lock the door and she would be safe for the remainder of the night—just as Thomas and Lycaon had promised her.

But she did not run. She would not. Not from *him*.

The beast gently laid a hand against her face and trailed one curled claw lightly down her cheek. It made a sound. Not a whimper, nor a snarl, but a quiet muffled whisper so tenderly uttered it seemed her entire world became a pinpoint of pain and swirling blackness.

"Amelia," the beast murmured. "Sweet Amelia."

Four

A cloud of black smoke hung like crepe along the church spires, making the air difficult to breathe as Amelia hurried along the oddly uninhabited road to the convent. The ferry ride across the loch had been rough—the water driven by storms somewhere over the Atlantic—leaving her light-headed and queasy. Or perhaps her nausea had more to do with the fact that she had not slept a wink all night. How could she? The very idea of closing her eyes had seemed absurd, after her experience in the woods.

Her uneasiness mounted as she reached the convent gates. Normally at the present hour the chapel doors would have been thrown open, beckoning the villagers to come pray. There would have been nuns scurrying about, each headed for her respective task. Sister Elizabeth would have been standing on the chapel steps like God's sentinel sent to search out any evil that might infest her flock.

She hurried to Father Marriott's office.

He sat at his desk, his head in his hands. "Father?" she called softly.

Raising his head slowly, he stared at her blankly before recognition set in. His mouth became a grim line as he sat back in his chair. "I wondered how long it would be before you returned."

"Then you know. You know and you sent me there anyway."

Father Marriott lowered his eyes. "Has he . . . harmed you in any way?"

Amelia crossed the floor and leaned on the desk. "Would it matter, Father? The purpose of a sacrifice is to protect the one who sacrifices, isn't it? What did you hope to gain? That you would rid the convent of a less than desirable novice without being forced to insult her father?"

His face drawn and white, Father Marriott remained silent.

"I want the truth, Father. All of it. How and why was this horrible curse cast on that family? And how can they be saved?"

"Two hundred years ago, Gawin Guaire was known for his cruelty and vengeance, sparing no one in his war to take and control the land. No one could stop him, save a single gypsy who cursed his soul for taking the life of her only son. From that night to this, every male child born of a Guaire would know the curse of the wolf upon his twenty-first birthday."

She thought of Robert, and her heart contracted. "There must be some way to end this horrible curse."

"Only one kissed by the grace of God, and who is willing to sacrifice all that he holds sacred, can save Lycaon and his son from their fate."

"Lycaon's father came to you for help, and you locked him away. He existed for years in that dank little cell like an animal, hoping that you would save him."

"He was an animal! The Devil incarnate. A beast to be feared and loathed. How can you think that I or my predecessors would sacrifice ourselves for a family that shakes its fist in the face of God—indeed curses God's very existence?''

Amelia walked to the window and looked out on the Lycaon mausoleum, erected outside the convent's hallowed grounds. The tomb shimmered under the morning light.

Father Marriott moved up behind her. "Even now they mock us. They lay in their coffins and bask in the shadow of this holy place of God. There isn't a night that I don't hear them cursing me as I lie in my bed."

"Are you certain it is they, Father? Perhaps the voice you hear is nothing more than your own conscience."

She moved to the door.

"Where are you going?" he called.

"Back to Lycaon."

"But you mustn't. It isn't safe.

"I'm not afraid of Lycaon. He would never harm me. I know that as surely as I know that my destiny—and my reason for coming to St. Mary's—has, at long last, revealed itself."

"It isn't Lycaon who concerns me now. There were English soldiers here last evening, looking for Charles Stuart."

"What are you telling me, Father? That they suspect Lycaon of harboring Charles? Did you do nothing to dissuade them?" She shook her head and backed away. "Merciful God, you sent them to Ulva, didn't you?"

"I had no choice. They would have burned this convent to the ground—destroyed the village and people—"

"And what better way to rid yourself of Lycaon. Did you think that by destroying him you would somehow cleanse your conscience? Out of sight, out of mind, Father?"

The priest's face became a white emotionless mask.

Amelia moved to the door. With her fingers tightened about the doorknob, gripping it desperately as she fought the rise of shame and fury in her breast, she stared into Father Marriott's tortured eyes. "You have just judged and possibly executed a family, Father. If you believed your conscience unbearably pained the last many years, I fear that will seem trivial compared to what you'll experience if English soldiers murder Lycaon and his son."

In light of the English threat, returning to Ulva proved no easy task. Amelia's frustration mounted as the day wore on, her requests for assistance falling on deaf ears as the ferrymen refused her time and again, finally relenting only on the condition that they wait until dark. The hours dragged, and her fear grew, as did her realization that all the prayers she could mutter for Lycaon's safety would prove fruitless against English soldiers if they discovered that he had sheltered Charles Stuart.

At last, as the sun sank into the burning sea and the coolness of the evening washed over her in a bone-chilling rush, she boarded the ferry for Ulva, her gaze rising constantly to the clear sky and the moon creeping up over the treetops. "Hurry," she pled to the ferryman, and he stared at her with wide, curious eyes as dark as the churning water beneath them.

"You're a nun, but you act more like a woman in a hurry to meet her lover," he said, causing her to stare at him fiercely without replying. Moments later, she walked to the rail, and removing the cap from her head, she tossed it into Loch Tuath.

When they docked at last, Amelia hurried up the same path she had taken on her first arrival in Ulva. The village sprawled along the craggy shoal, its roofs bathed in moonlight, its windows shuttered. Yet . . . something was amiss, and her step slowed as she searched the dim outlines of the houses and the scattering of shops. Finally, her senses acknowledged the smell of smoke, and focusing harder she detected the houses' scorched walls and kicked-in doors.

Voices came to her then. Hurrying around a bend in the road, she discovered the village population crowded around a bonfire, their faces contorted with anger.

"Lycaon has brought this on us. If it weren't for him them soldiers would never have come here."

"It weren't enough that we've had to put up with Guaire's cursed existence—our being forced to live in fear for our lives all these many years—but now he's brought the wrath of the crown on our heads. You heard what the soldiers said: If they learn that Lycaon has sheltered Charles Stuart they'll bloody burn us alive! I say, if the English don't kill him then we do. We rid ourselves of Lycaon once and for all!"

Amelia ran along the road, panting for breath, only vaguely feeling the bite of the wind, deaf to the roar of the water below. A multitude of images flashed before her mind's eye. She had witnessed the destruction of war before—the English laying waste to farms and villages, entire families wiped from the face of the earth. Shamefully, she acknowledged to herself that those deaths, while tragic, had never stabbed her so painfully as the prospect of finding Lycaon and his son slaughtered.

Winded, her body cramping and her lungs burning, Amelia fell to her knees and sought the strength to pray. Suddenly, the wind brought the pealing of the convent church bells spiraling over the cliffs, and the clear and melodious sound lifted her up and carried her forward like some great, powerful hand sent to help.

Lycaon Castle was ablaze with light. Flames of torches danced in the wind, as did great campfires dotting the landscape. Soldiers with swords and rifles searched the grounds. The beautiful gardens where she had played with Robert were trampled.

An hour passed, then two before she could enter the castle without being detected. She kept to the shadows, her senses attuned to the noise of furious voices merging into an indeterminate hum. She skirted gallery after gallery, each one as decimated as the other, paintings slashed, furnishings toppled and splintered; she caught glimpses of soldiers and was horrified by their gaunt, intense, and hate-filled features as they went about their destruction as easily as they might stroll their own homelands on a Sunday morning. It was their expressions, so immovably resolute, that frightened her most, because she knew they were beyond reason, and care. They were fixed on their quest to conquer and destroy.

Her fear grew and her body shook as she ducked into an unoccupied chamber that was illuminated only by the full moon spilling through the window. Standing in the pool of pale light, listening to her heart pound in her ears, Amelia covered her face with her hands and prayed:

"Heavenly Father, do not desert him in his hour of despair and fear and anger. Allow me the strength to lift him up and—"

A hand slammed hard on her shoulder and spun her around. The soldier grinned and dragged her close. "Gotcha," he sneered.

Beaten and bloody, Thomas lay on the floor, unconscious. Lycaon—his arms wrapped protectively around his son, his gaze taking in the destruction of his home, his body feeling none of the abuse the soldiers had inflicted on him over the last hours—listened to his old friend's rattling breaths and tried desperately to think of something, anything, to divert the overwhelming fury building in his chest. An odd numbness permeated his soul, and had since he'd awakened in the morning to discover Amelia gone. The English soldiers' unexpected arrival on his doorstep had only aggravated an already open, bleeding wound.

Therefore, when the doors flew open and Amelia appeared, dragged by a soldier into the room, he could only stare, at first, the image at length wrestling its way into his

consciousness, burning itself into his blurred realization.
For a long moment his mind refused to comprehend the
meaning of what he saw. Oh!—she was back. Oh!—to
jump up and grab her, to hold her as he had the day before
and bask in the pleasure of another human's compassion
and closeness. But not here. Not like this. Not when his
already cursed world was now splintering as assuredly as
the moon was climbing higher over Lycaon Castle.

Robert roused and struggled. He tore away from his father's arms and sprinted across the room toward Amelia,
only to fall hard to the floor as a soldier stuck out his leg
and tripped him.

Lycaon leapt to his feet and sprang for the soldier. The
man thrust the butt of his rifle hard into Lycaon's rib, then
up-cut into his jaw, sending him spiraling backward into
the wall. A fountain of red pain sprang through his mind
and body; it shivered along the raw nerves of his bleeding
injuries. An abyss opened before him and beckoned, yet
. . . he fought against the lure of black peaceful emptiness—even as the other, more familiar pain awoke and
scratched like razors inside his skin.

Soft hands touched his face, their coolness like winter
water washing over him. He opened his eyes, and Amelia
smiled. "Amelia. You came back," he whispered. "Foolish girl. Now look what you've got yourself into."

"Have faith, my lord. This, too, shall pass."

The soldier dragged her away. As Lycaon struggled to
his knees, the whoops and raucous cries of the soldiers
grew to a crescendo, followed by breaking glass and shattering wood. Blinking sweat and blood from his eyes, Lycaon watched the soldiers line Amelia, Robert, and
groaning Thomas against the wall.

"There now," the captain said. "I'll give the lot of you
one last chance. If you tell us where you've hid Charles
Stuart, I'll let you live."

Silence; then Robert slowly struggled to his feet. Amelia

attempted to grab him. He shook her off and turned his green eyes on Lycaon. It seemed a thousand emotions crossed his young face—all the hatred he had cast upon his father over the last year; the shattering grief he had experienced upon losing his mother; the immense bitterness of knowing that his life, like his father's, was cursed. The realization that his own son would now stand up and declare his father a traitor to the crown made Lycaon sink to the floor.

Drawing back his shoulders, Robert lifted his chin and declared, "Charles Stuart . . . has never stepped upon these floors."

"Impertinent little liar," the soldier smirked, then struck the boy hard enough to send his small body crashing against the wall.

As if muted by dense fog, Amelia's cry of despair touched Lycaon's ear but lightly, for the insensibility of white-hot rage rushed through his consciousness in so terrible a flood he felt separated from his soul. He moved. He struck wildly at his son's abuser, watching the man's face appear to disintegrate beneath his fists.

Like a swarm of angry hornets, the soldiers descended, driving their fists and weapons into Lycaon's body until the pain robbed him of all but the ability to curl into a fetal ball and attempt to shield himself from the blows. Reality ebbed and flowed, one moment shrieking with the cacophony of noise and voices, the next receding into a delicious silence that was as deep and spiraling as a galaxy. When he roused at last, it was to look into Amelia's eyes, which were blue as robins' eggs and full of tears.

"Robert," he called, and did his best to push Amelia aside.

"He's fine, my lord, and is sleeping. He'll boast a bruise to show for his bravery, but nothing more. Surely you know now how much he loves you."

He struggled to sit up, then looked at his hands; he

touched his cut and bleeding face, which was also sweating profusely. "Thomas?" he asked softly.

"They have Thomas. I fear they intend to do what they may to make him confess."

"Thomas will never confess. His loyalty would never allow it." He took a deep, weary breath, and leaning back against the wall focused on the distant window and the reflection of moonlight on the panes. "When I discovered you gone this morning, I was mad with anger and anguish. Robert has come to care for you very much. You've filled up his days with a brightness he hasn't experienced in years. You gave him a reason to look forward to each sunrise, and to tolerate the nights with far less loathing and pain. The idea of never hearing your laughter again . . . filled him with despair.

"I wanted to die," he confessed softly. "I wanted to end this cursed existence once and for all—not just for myself, but for my son as well. I have often thought of mercifully killing him, Amelia. Of ending his life now, before it becomes the nightmare of manhood. Before he must exist night after night with the awful fear that *this* night could be *the* night he might turn on another human being . . . and lose his soul forever. I've taken him to the highest precipice above Loch Tuath with every intention of throwing ourselves to the rocks below, and yet . . . how could I kill him when I love him so? On the other hand, if I love him so, how can I condemn him to this loveless life of hopeless horror?"

Amelia moved close and slid her arm around him. His head rested on her breast and she held him gently, as if he were a child. She nestled her cheek upon his hair and thought that it felt as soft as she had imagined it. How easy it would be, she mused, to turn her lips into his hair and press them into his warm skin. "I shan't leave you again," she assured him quietly.

A clock chimed midnight.

Somewhere in the silence, Thomas cried out, the terrible sound rattling of death.

There came a sudden pause in her thinking, as if for an infinitesimal moment she lost all human capacity to mentally experience anything other than fear. Reality honed to a blade edge, cutting off her breath. Then, with a rushing revival of soul, she closed her eyes and began to pray, only vaguely acknowledging to herself that Lycaon had moved.

Only after whispering "Amen" did she look up to find Lycaon huddled in the shadows, his back to her, his shoulders shaking and his fingers curled into the wall, his nails leaving little trenches grooved into the wood. A tumultuous impulse surged through her heart, and snapping the crucifix from her neck, she rushed to Lycaon and forced it into his hand.

He shoved her aside and turned away. "Get away. Stay . . . away. I'm too damned angry. And weak. Too tired of the fight. I don't think I can control the hunger of the beast. Its ferocity . . . overwhelms me at times."

A door opened. A pair of soldiers dragged Thomas's body into the room and flung it on the floor. Grinning, they said, "We'll give you a little time to reflect on what happens to traitors. Then we'll be back for the boy."

They quit the room and Amelia ran to Thomas's side, falling to her knees, taking his big rough hand in hers and pressing a kiss onto it. "We must find a way to protect Robert. If the English are so wicked as to murder an old man, they'll think nothing of using a child to—"

A sound. Familiar. Immobilizing. Her heart stricken into an unnatural stillness, she slowly, reluctantly, fearfully turned her head.

Lycaon was gone.

In his place stood the beast.

He crossed the room, his stride unsteady, his body quivering with something like pain as he moved. Dropping to all fours, he moved around Thomas's still body, nudging it, sniffing it, his intensely green eyes lifting occasionally to regard Amelia, who was shrinking away, less out of fear than reflex. Lycaon, the beast, responded with a low growl and a flash of his sharp white teeth. Although Amelia knew he would not harm her, her heart quickened to a point of pain. Blood rushed to her head in such a flood she felt like one trying desperately to breathe underwater. Her brain burned, as did her throat and eyes and the caverns of her skull. Fingers of weakness sluiced through her strangely inert body, and as if she had died and given up her soul, she seemed to rise out of her body and look down upon the shocking image of woman and fearsome beast. She watched the wolf's long, black tongue slide through its lips and cup around the droplets of blood staining the floor under Thomas's head.

The door was flung open in that moment. A pair of smirking soldiers crossed the threshold, their eyes glinting with eager mischief and malice. They stared down on the odd image a moment, their countenances shifting from cruelty to confusion as they tried to make sense of what they saw.

Lycaon raised onto his back legs and swung around to face them. Lips drawn back, exposing his blood-tinged teeth, he sprang.

Amelia awakened to darkness and the sound of voices. There was some vague memory of mayhem, of blood, of screams, then . . . nothing. Rousing, she looked around. Thomas still lay on the floor, as did two soldiers, their faces frozen in terror and their throats . . .

She looked away and managed to climb to her feet. Cautiously, she left the room, only to be brought up short at the sight of more death—the English fallen like ravaged lambs. A movement caught her eye.

The beast crouched in the shadows, its head buried in

its clawed hands as it rocked back and forth and groaned. Amelia hurried forth. Dropping to her knees beside him, she reached out her hand to comfort.

He cringed and moved away, wagged his head in denial. With his fist, he beat the floor, then his chest, his anguish and remorse so powerful it seemed to Amelia that his being would shatter at any moment.

"My lord . . . you were only protecting us. They would have murdered us all—"

He leapt to his feet and staggered to the window. Following, Amelia looked out on the villagers she had witnessed earlier that night, torches in hand as they stepped over the soldiers' bodies.

"I told y' it was only a matter of time before he killed a human being," someone yelled. "Now he's tasted blood and there won't be a safe man, woman, or child in all of Scotland."

"I say we kill 'im here and now. We've got no choice."

"The boy, too!" another shouted. "It's the only way to insure we end it once and for all."

Amelia looked into Lycaon's eyes. There was no anger there. No fear. Only sad resignation. "My lord, there's time yet. You can run—"

He shook his head and turned away, kicking a rifle toward her. He nudged it again, and his meaning sunk in.

"I won't do it," she told him firmly, shaking her head. "I won't destroy you."

She quivered at every nerve as the villagers began to break down the door. Lycaon snarled. He thrashed the air with his fists, and still she refused. "I will not destroy you," she repeated, more loudly and firmly as his anger mounted and the door began to shatter under the impact of the villagers' cudgels. "I implore you to flee," she cried. "For our sake. For those of us who love you. I swear I'll do everything in my power to help you—to heal you. To see that this dreadful curse is broken. You shan't suffer another night of this terrible torment, my lord. Please; have faith, if not in God, then in me.''

His eyes softened and, gently, he raised one hand and lightly brushed her cheek.

The door splintered and fell from its hinges. Shoulder to shoulder, their rifles raised, the villagers swept over the threshold with the force of floodwaters. Rising to his full height, his teeth showing, not in a snarl but in a taunting grin, Lycaon stepped around Amelia and opened his arms.

"Only one kissed by the grace of God, and who is willing to sacrifice all that he holds sacred, can save Lycaon and his son from their fate."

"No!" she cried, first at Lycaon, then at the men who raised their weapons and prepared to fire. Drawing herself up, she flung herself between Lycaon and his assassins just as the bullets were fired.

She did not feel them enter her body. There was no pain, only the swift impact of power that lifted her from her feet and dropped her gently into Lycaon's arms. For an instant they stood as they had the previous night, their arms locked around one another, each oblivious to anything but the vibrant ecstasy of their hearts beating together. Then, slowly, so slowly, as the strength evaporated from her legs, they sank to the floor.

He gripped her fiercely to his chest and rocked in inconsolable grief. Tears flowed from his eyes and he groaned like one dying.

"Christopher," she whispered, smiling. " 'Tis over. I give you my heart. My life. My soul. For it is my destiny to do so. Quickly! Let me kiss you." Weakly, she lifted her face and pressed her lips to his cheek.

A cold wind roused, springing forth through every window and door, lashing at the men huddled inside the threshold, their rifles still clutched in their hands as they gaped upon the fallen pair and steeled themselves against the storm. The torch flames grew, their light so blindingly bright it seemed as if a hundred bolts of lightning had converged in the room, all swirling around Amelia and the beast.

Then the wind died. As did the light.

The beast was gone.

Christopher Guaire, Earl Lycaon, lowered his head and lightly kissed Amelia's lips. "Sweet Amelia," he pled softly. "Please . . . don't leave me. Don't ever leave me."

"I shall never leave you," she vowed, smiling and curling her fingers around the little silver crucifix he pressed into her hand.

*Here is a preview of Maggie Shayne's
exciting new novel,*
Eternity
coming in December from Jove Books!

When dawn came, it brought with it the magistrate, and beside him his wife, looking red in the eyes and distressed. Behind them walked a man who wore the robes of a priest. He had an aged face, thin and harsh, with a hooked nose that made me think of a hawk, or of some other hungering bird of prey. He was pale, as if he were ill or weak.

"Lily St. James," the magistrate said, "you and your daughter are charged with the crime of Witchcraft. Will you confess to your crimes?"

My mother's voice was weaker now, and I could hear the pain in it. "I will confess only if you release my daughter. She is guilty of nothing."

"No," his wife said. "You must execute them now, Hiram. Both of them!"

"But the law—" he began.

"The law! What care do you have for the law when our own child has become ill overnight? What more proof do you need?"

At her words my heart fell. She blamed us for her child's illness, just as my aunt had done. No one could save us now.

I heard footsteps then, and sensed the magistrate had gone closer to my mother. Leaning over her, he said, "Lift this curse, woman. Lift it now, I beg of you."

"I have brought no curse upon you, nor your family, sir," my mother told him. "Were it in my power to help your child, I would gladly do so. As I would have for my own husband and for my nephew. But I cannot."

"Execute them!" the woman shouted. "Michael was fine until you arrested these two! They brought this curse on him, made him ill out of pure vengeance, I tell you, and if they live long enough to kill him they will! Execute them, husband. 'Tis the only way to save our son!"

The priest stepped forward then, his black robes hanging heavily about his feet and dragging through the wet snow. His steps were slow, as if they cost him a great effort. He went first to my mother, saying nothing, and I could not see what he did. But seconds later he came to me, and closed his hand briefly around mine.

A surge of something, a crackling, shocking sensation jolted my hand and sizzled into my forearm, startling me so that I cried out.

"Do not harm my daughter!" my mother shouted.

The priest took his hand away, and the odd sensation vanished with his touch, leaving me shaken and confused.

"I fear you are right," the priest said to the magistrate's wife. "They must die, or your son surely will. And I fear there is no time for a trial. But God will forgive you that."

Pacing away, his back to us, the magistrate muttered, "Then I have little choice." And the three of them left us alone again. But only for a few brief moments.

"Mother," I whispered. "I'm so afraid."

"You've nothing to fear from them, Raven."

But I *did* fear. I'd never *felt* such fear grip me as I was marched up the steps to stand beside her on the gallows, beneath a dangling noose. Someone lowered the rough rope around my neck, and pulled it tight, and I struggled to be brave and strong as my mother had so often told me I was. But I know I was trembling visibly, despite the warmth of the morning sun, and I could not stop my tears.

That priest whose touch had so jolted me stood on the platform as well, old and stern-faced, his eyes all but gleaming beneath their film of ill health as he stared at me . . . as if in anticipation. Beside him stood another man who wore the robes of clergy. This one was very young, my age, or perhaps a few years my elder. In his eyes there was no eagerness, no joy. Only horror, pure and undisguised. They were brown, his eyes, and they met mine and held them. I stared back at him, and he didn't look away, searching my eyes while his own registered surprise, confusion. I felt something pass between us. Something that had no place here, amid this violence and hatred. It was as if we touched, but did so without touching. A feeling of warmth moved between him and I, one so real it was palpable. And I knew he felt it too by the slight widening of his eyes.

Then his gaze broke away as he turned and said, "Nathanial, surely this is no way to serve the Lord."

"You are young, Brother Duncan," the older man said. "And this no doubt seems harsh to you."

"What it seems like to me, Father, is murder."

" 'Thou shalt not suffer a Witch to live,' " the priest quoted.

" 'Thou shalt not kill,' " the young Scot—Duncan— replied. He looked at me again. "They've not even been tried."

"They were tried in the square by the magistrate himself."

"It canna' be legal."

"His Honor's own child is ill with the plague. Would you have us wait for the wee one to die?"

"I would have us show mercy," he said softly. "We've no proof these women have brought the plague."

"And no proof they haven't. Why take the risk? They are only Witches."

The beautiful man looked at the older one sharply. "They are human creatures just as we are, Nathanial." And he shook his head sadly. "What are their names?"

"Their names are unfit for a man of the cloth to utter. If you so pity them, Duncan, ease your conscience by praying for their souls. For what good it might do."

" 'Tis wrong," Duncan said. "I'm sorry, Father, but I canna' be party to this."

"Then leave!" The priest thrust out a gnarled finger, pointing to the steps.

Duncan hurried toward them, but he paused as he passed close to me. He turned to face me, as if drawn by some unseen force. His hand rose, hesitated, then touched my hair, smoothing it away from my forehead. "Could I help you, mistress, believe me I would."

"Should you try they would only kill you, as well." My voice trembled as I spoke. "I beg you . . . Duncan . . ." His eyes shot to mine when I spoke his name, and I think he caught his breath. "Don't surrender your life in vain."

He looked at me so intently, it was as if he searched my very soul, and I thought I glimpsed a shimmer of tears in his eyes.

"I willna' forget you . . ." he whispered, then shook himself, blinked, and went on, ". . . in my prayers." Suddenly he leaned close, and pressed his lips to my forehead. Then he moved on, his black robes rustling as he hurried down the steps.

"Do you wish to confess your sins and beg the Lord's forgiveness?" the old priest asked my mother.

I saw her lift her chin. " 'Tis you who ought to be begging your God's forgiveness, sir. Not I."

The priest glared at her, then turned to me. "And you?"

"I have done nothing wrong," I said loudly. "My soul is far less stained than the soul of one who would hang an innocent and claim to do so in the name of God." Then I looked down at the crowd below us. "And far less stained than the souls of those who would turn out to watch murder being done!"

The crowd of spectators went silent, and I saw Duncan stop in his tracks there on the ground below us. He turned slowly, looking up and straight into my eyes. "Nay," he said, his voice firm. " 'Tis wrong, and I willna' allow it!" Then suddenly he lunged forward, toward the steps again. But the guard at the bottom caught him in burly arms, and flung him to the ground. A crowd closed around him as he tried to get up, and he was blocked from my view. I prayed they would not harm him.

"Be damned, then," the old priest said, and he turned away.

The hangman came to place a hood over my mother's head, but she flinched away from it. "Look upon my face as you kill me, if you have the courage."

Snarling, the man tossed the hood to the floor, and never offered one to me. He took his spot by the lever that would end our lives. I looked below again to see Duncan there, struggling while three large men held him fast. I had no idea what he thought he could do to prevent our deaths, but 'twas obvious he'd tried. Was still trying.

" 'Tis wrong! Donna' do this thing, Nathanial!" he shouted over and over, but his words fell on deaf ears.

"Take heart," my mother whispered. "You will see him again. And know this, my darling: I love you."

I turned to meet her loving eyes. And then the floor fell away from beneath my feet, and I plunged through it. I heard Duncan's anguished cry. Then the rope reached its end, and there was a sudden painful snap in my neck that made my head explode and my vision turn red. And then no more. Only darkness.